Unforeseen

Lauren Grimley

Malachite Quills
PUBLISHING

UNFORSEEN

Copyright © 2012 by Lauren Grimley
Edited by James Bassett
Cover Copyright © 2012 by Marquis DeVille
ISBN-13: 978-1623750213

ALL RIGHTS RESERVED: No part of this book may be reproduced, stored in a retrieval system, or transmitted, in any form or by any means, without the prior permission in writing of the publisher, nor be otherwise circulated in any form of binding or cover other than that in which it is published and without a similar condition including this condition being imposed on the subsequent purchaser. Your non-refundable purchase allows you to one legal copy of this work for your own personal use. You do not have resell or distribution rights without the prior written permission of both the publisher and copyright owner of this book. This book cannot be copied in any format, sold, or otherwise transferred from your computer to another through upload, or for a fee.

Warning: The unauthorized reproduction or distribution of this work is illegal. Criminal copyright infringement is investigated by the FBI and is punishable by up to 5 years in federal prison and a fine of $250,000.

Publisher's Note: This is a work of fiction. All characters, places, businesses, and incidents are from the author's imagination. Any resemblance to actual places, people, or events is purely coincidental. Any trademarks mentioned herein are not authorized by the trademark owners and do not in any way mean the work is sponsored by or associated with the trademark owners. Any trademarks used are specifically in a descriptive capacity.

First Edition

Visit our website: www.mquills.com

GRIMLEY

To all the ladies in my life whose feedback, advice, and support kept me writing. To those first readers: Christine, Lindsey, and Heather who plodded through those early drafts with keen eyes and kindly worded criticisms, and most especially to my first ever reader, editor, and fan: my mom. Thank you for believing in me always and for giving me the guts to believe in myself.

GRIMLEY

Chapter 1

She knew he was out there. She hadn't heard him approach over the music she'd been playing. And she couldn't see clearly through the windows of the two double doors due to the reflection cast by the soft yellow light of the small desk lamp. But Alex would have bet her summer paycheck he was right outside, standing silently in the dark corridor.

That afternoon she had been out the door of the middle school where she taught before the dismissal bell had ceased ringing. The heat and charged end-of-year atmosphere had left her spent and desperate for escape. Unfortunately there was no escaping her uncompleted work. So as soon as she was sure the final after-school activity had ended, she had returned and retreated to the comfort and quiet of the air-conditioned library with her stack of ungraded essays. It had seemed like a pretty smart plan at the time.

As she tapped her front teeth together repeatedly, she was second-guessing her wisdom. She supposed it was too late to flick off the light, mute the music, and hide under the librarian's desk. He knew she was in there, alone.

But why should she be the one hiding anyway? She had dumped him.

"Come on in, Peter." Alex stood up and gave a quick tug to the bottoms of her skimpy running shorts. They were probably not appropriate attire to be wearing in the workplace, even after the students had all gone home. She supposed she had little to worry about, though. Peter, as vice-principal, was her boss, and he had seen pretty much all of her. That was more than three years ago, when she had been fresh out of college and easily won over. She'd grown past that stage. Peter had missed the memo.

"Sorry. I, ah, didn't want to startle you." He flashed her a guilty grin as he entered the room rubbing his hand over what remained of his buzzed hair.

"Skulking in the hallway was a good idea, then," Alex said with just a shadow of a smile.

Peter chuckled. "Do you use that kind of sarcasm in your classroom, *Ms.* Crocker?"

She groaned at his form of address. Ms. rang of wizened old spinsters who reeked of chalk dust and sour coffee breath. At twenty-five, *Miss* Crocker was more of a laptop-and-sports-drink kind of gal.

"Are you here to kick me out, Peter?" She caught a glimpse of the clock over his shoulder. It was quarter of ten. She knew asking the night custodians to stay sixty seconds past their contracted hours could potentially lead to a union riot.

"Sorry, I know your place is a sauna on nights like this," he answered, as if she needed reminding he had spent more than a few hot—make that lukewarm—nights at her small one-bedroom apartment.

Alex took a deep breath. He was a good guy, a good friend. But the puppy-who-refused-to-give-up-his-favorite-chew-toy routine was getting old. Not that the chew toy had found a new dog, unfortunately.

Ugh, she thought. Did he really have her equating herself with something plastic and squeaky?

She must not have been successful at hiding her aggravation, though Peter misread the reason for her mood. "You know, if you needed some money to buy an air conditioner—"

"I don't need money." Alex knew she snapped a little too fiercely at his generosity. One of her many flaws was a proud independent streak that often bordered on pigheadedness. She had her father to thank for that. Alex sighed and continued in what she hoped was a softer tone. "Thank you, though, for offering."

"Right. Well, how about a ride home? At least allow me one act of chivalry." He looked down at her with his deep brown eyes. For a fleeting instant, as she met them, his emotions waxed into hers. She had a bad habit of falling for guys simply because they fell for her. She knew it was how they had become a couple to begin with, but she just couldn't help it. Some days everyone's emotions felt as contagious as the flu germs her students passed around each January. She mentally pinched herself, hard.

"Thanks, Prince Charming, but you'll need to find another damsel in distress. If I don't run, I'll never sleep."

Peter furrowed his brows. "You and your late-night runs."

"Yes, I'm such a wild child," Alex laughed. She hadn't been up past midnight more than twice in the last year. In fact, the most exciting thing she'd done since college had been with Peter—here at school, in a janitor's closet. She blushed remembering. She peeked up to see he was rosy, as well. "I've gone cold-turkey on the *Grey's Anatomy* marathons," she assured him. Though it still seemed unfair that young doctors had all the fun. "Perhaps you should lay off the *Law & Order* reruns—I'll be fine." Alex slung her school bag over her shoulder, scooped her beat-up iPod from the desk and started to the door, patting her pocket to double check she had her key to her apartment.

After dropping her bag in her classroom, she walked with Peter as far as the faculty parking lot. He stopped before crossing the dimly lit pavement to his car. Jingling his keys in his hand, he turned to her one last time.

"Are you—"

"Yes. I'm sure." Alex held up her right hand so he could see the bracelets that covered her wrist. She pointed to her runner's ID tag and flashed him a grin. "Don't worry, if some idiot kills me at a crosswalk, you'll be the first to know."

"Not funny, Alex."

She was already heading to the sidewalk, slipping the headphones blasting her alternative rock mix into each ear. She raised a hand to him to say goodnight.

Once on the main road, Alex's route home was practically a straight shot through the center of Bristol. The former mill city in Eastern Mass had its shabby sections, and it lacked the culture and sophistication of a bigger city like Boston, but it was her home and always had been. She had never felt afraid running the familiar four-and-a-half-mile trek between school and her place. Besides, what she told Peter was true: she needed to run. Handling her students' hormone-enhanced emotions could be draining. She needed an outlet. Since she could no longer afford karate in addition to her student loans and grad classes, she'd turned to running.

As she closed in on the final street before she'd be on her own block, she watched her shadow grow and shrink in the peaks and valleys of light cast by the evenly spaced streetlamps. She turned around, jogging backwards a few paces. The street behind her, like that ahead of her, was empty. The usual light traffic and occasional dog walker had been kept home by the oppressive humidity and the evening's earlier thunderstorms. It normally wouldn't have unnerved her. As a city girl, Alex usually relished the rare opportunity to be truly alone, especially on a night when the rain-washed pavement left the city streets smelling clean for once. So, feeling the unmistakable nervous twinge that turned her stomach and tightened her chest, she cursed the power of suggestion.

"Damn you, Peter."

Hoping to shake the ridiculous feeling of being followed and not wanting to squander the adrenaline, she took off at full speed. Her sneakers tore into the wet pavement, sending spray up her muscled calves. Halfway to the corner her lungs were burning. At just over five feet short, as her brothers used to say, speed had never been her thing.

Just to the next alley, she promised her aching chest. As soon as she reached the gap between the two commercial buildings, she let up. Her feet slapped the sidewalk as she tried to slow her momentum. She would walk the last block and a half home. It would allow her time to catch her breath, cool off, and calm down. She tried to focus on something mundane.

As she wiped the sweat from her brow, she thought about what Peter had offered. She'd never accept the charity, but she really could use a small air conditioner for her bedroom. She was sick of fighting with the landlord over the ancient hunk of metal that was supposed to cool her whole apartment. Midway through cursing the useless beer-gutted moron under her breath, she was overwhelmed with what might have felt like a wave of nausea to anyone else.

Alex was not anyone else. Part of being sensitive to others' emotions was having a killer sense of intuition, and hers was suddenly on high alert. This was not the vague undefined fear of moments before—this was real and immediate.

Before she had a chance to react, she found herself being dragged back towards the alleyway she had just passed.

Her every nightmare came true. She was being attacked and was too shocked and scared to scream. And she was being pulled along too fast to react, despite her years of karate. Christ, she taught self-defense to the girls at her school. And here she was: defenseless. What would they think when they heard she had been found beaten or . . . hell, no; she was not going to let this happen. Her voice caught up with her brain: she began to scream.

The man pulling her along was immense, easily dwarfing her petite frame. He had one thick arm around her neck, his hard bicep choking her. The other arm was tugging at her waist. As he tried to adjust his hand over her mouth to quiet her, she attempted to drop her weight, so her feet could find purchase on the slippery pavement. Alex thought she had succeeded when for a split second his hand left her side. As she fought to spin free of his grip, she felt the knife tip against her skin.

"Shut up, woman!" The gravelly command sounded more like a growl than a human voice. It silenced her instantly. A shiver shot up Alex's spine, her intuition flaring. This man was dangerous, deadly, yet she sensed he was ecstatic. He was enjoying her fear, or his power, or both. With the knife pressing into her, she was certain there was no escaping without injury. He would kill her before letting her get away. Her training taught her not to fight an armed attacker. It was dangerous, stupid. She repeated to her girls, "Be smart, wait for an opening, if needed, give them what they want. Staying alive is what's important."

As he pulled her, struggling, into the darkness of the alley, she regretted ever teaching that. And in the back of her mind she vowed that if she lived she would begin the first lesson next year with the message screaming through her body now: "Fight like hell!"

With a surge of adrenaline spurred on by a mixture of terror and anger, Alex again dropped her weight, this time pushing back against her attacker, whose rock solid torso she slammed into as she attempted to knock him against the brick wall lining the alley. She gasped as the blade tip pierced the soft flesh on her side, but she continued to struggle. She jammed her heel up between her attacker's legs with a mighty wrench and knew she aimed true when he involuntarily lurched forward.

"You fucking bi—" but the curse was cut short when Alex jabbed her free elbow into his nose and jerked away from the blade that dug deeper into her skin. Stumbling, she tried desperately to dart back to the street. She was able to grab hold of something to keep her on her feet. Something that hadn't been there just moments before. Something that grabbed back at her.

"Sweet. It's like they rolled up the sidewalks; there isn't anyone in sight. We'll be bored out of our skulls and back to the house by one, two tops." Rocky continued to ramble, not necessarily wanting, and certainly not expecting, a response from Sage.

The two males had parked their Jeep on the street near McNally's, the Irish pub where they often began and ended their nights. Outside the pub, which was always humming, though somewhat quieter tonight, Sage had chosen a route that led them away from the restaurant- and bar-lined streets where they patrolled most evenings. He'd read the police reports posted online. There had been an increase in muggings and assaults in the more residential neighborhoods surrounding the recently revived business district. He figured the heavy storms from earlier would make it a good night to scout the area without alerting some overzealous Neighborhood Watch member. The irony was, despite appearances, he and Rocky were a type of watch group. Granted, they were better trained, a hell of a lot stronger, and much more heavily armed than the soccer mom with her cell phone and flashlight, but those were minor details, really.

They rounded the corner onto a more middle-class street, leaving the brownstones behind. Sage, working hard to drown out his partner's incessant chatter, thought this was a neighborhood where the two could blend in. The multi-storied apartment buildings were maintained, but the furnishings that could be seen through the lit windows screamed of Ikea. The cars on the street were a mixture of inexpensive small sedans or hatchbacks. The residents were likely a similar mixture of grad students and single young professionals. No one here would be affronted by their boots, worn jeans, or the dark hoodies they wore to conceal a weapon or two. Though the weapons themselves might not be welcome in the candle-scented living rooms.

Sage grabbed Rocky's arm. "Shut up." He pointed up the street to where a young woman had just stopped her all-out sprint. Sage wondered whether she had heard them and whether she would be bothered by their presence.

"She's just slowing down. Chill out," Rocky started in. He toned down the attitude after reading the glare Sage returned. "She's got headphones on, probably can't hear a damn thing."

"Stupid," Sage muttered.

"Why am I stupid just because—"

"Not, you, idiot, her." Sage was about to add they weren't the only things she couldn't hear with headphones on, when movement ahead of them rendered the statement unnecessary. A few feet behind the girl another figure had stalked out of a small alleyway between buildings.

"Is that—" Rocky began.

"Yup," Sage answered with a bit more enthusiasm than was appropriate. They both knew what was going to happen before it did. Being a bit green, Rocky was about to yell, hoping to forewarn the girl. Sage silenced him, pulling him into a doorway and out of sight.

"No, if he knows we're here, she'll be dead before we can get to her." Sage had the patience that came with age and experience. He tried to hear and sense what was happening, waiting for the right moment to move. Rocky was having none of it.

"Screw that! She may be worse than dead if we wait." He slipped past Sage, who made an attempt to grab him, and sprinted down the street. Watching his partner run, Sage began cursing heavily. He vowed to ring the rookie's neck if the female got hurt because of his impulsiveness. Hoping to keep them both alive, he followed in a blur.

Alex looked up into the face of the man holding her upper arms. The accomplice wasn't as tall as her original attacker, but he was built. His broad shoulders filled the oversized hooded sweatshirt he wore, and she could see his thick quads were defined even though the jeans he wore were loose and low slung. She tried to read his face, looking into his dark eyes. But confusion swept her as his look of immense anger dissipated. He pulled her up almost gently and tried to steady her. She doubted what she saw, except her intuition was telling her the same thing: he was concerned. Just as a trickle of hope flared within her, she felt a searing pain shoot through her calf. She glimpsed a blur of movement in her peripheral vision and turned to see what had caused both.

In an instant, she comprehended her mistake. Her captor's look of concern had not been for her, but for his partner, who, knife in hand, had been knocked to the ground by a third fierce man, a tall blond. Unfortunately for Alex, the original attacker had managed to stab her leg as he hit the ground. Before she could think to kick away the knife, which now lay at her feet, the blond snatched it. He sliced the first attacker's throat so deeply the six-inch blade nearly disappeared as it tore through the mess of muscle, bone, and tissue.

The blood and violence she witnessed sent Alex into a frenzy. She began shrieking so wildly she didn't even recognize her own voice. And she began to fight with every scrap of her surviving energy. Returning her focus to the shorter, olive-skinned man still holding her arms, she kicked hard into his groin. He released her, but remained blocking her escape. Panicking, she spun around to the man she had just seen murder another and released a punch that split his lip and surely broke her knuckles.

"Damn it, Rocky, hold her still! She'll have half the Bristol police force here before I can wipe her." Though he spoke through a swelling bloody mess, Alex could make out the words over her screams. She tried to move before having her arms pinned from behind. She thrashed violently as the murderer, with a solid build, cold blue-grey eyes, and a scarred eyebrow, reached out and attempted to hold her face.

"Calm down, woman." His deep voice was less terrifying than expected, but neither his words nor his tone could do anything to soothe Alex. "We're trying to help." He was staring intensely in her eyes, like he was trying to penetrate them. After a few seconds, he shook his head, as if trying to clear his mind. He glanced uncertainly at his partner before trying again. Alex had no idea what he was after, but she could sense his growing frustration and had no intention of being cooperative. She averted her eyes and tried again to lash out at him or the man behind her.

"Can you work your mojo a bit quicker, Sage, I don't have much skin left on my shins." Rocky had to shout to be heard over the girl's shrieking. His partner's shins were the least of Sage's worries.

"It's not working." Sage pinched his dark brows together in frustration and disbelief.

"What do you mean? It always works. It can't just not work," Rocky said.

"I don't know, but we've got to shut her up, now." To confirm his statement, sirens could be heard growing closer to their location. "Shit," Sage hissed, his upper lip curling back from his top teeth, revealing partially elongated fangs on either side. He dropped his hold on her face. Before Rocky or the girl realized his intention, he threw a hard punch to the side of her head. Her eyes widened for a split second. Then she was silent.

"Creator's sake, Sage, you just killed her—an innocent woman! What the hell?" Rocky, still holding her body, was starting to panic. Sage slapped him hard to focus him.

"Get a grip. She's unconscious, not dead. We're taking her back to the house. I'll wipe her memory when she's calmer. Right now, throw her over your shoulder and take her out the back way to the car—and try to move fast enough not to be seen. You're a vampire, not a track star," Sage said with obvious contempt. Rocky had run to the woman's aid like a bumbling human. "I'll go play with some cops' brains so we have a cover story when we dump her later."

"You mean when we return her safely?" Rocky suggested. Sage didn't bother to respond as he headed back past the now disintegrated remains of the Other to greet the two cops entering the alleyway. He looked back to be sure he was obeyed. Rocky became a blur as he headed to the Jeep with the woman, beaten and bleeding, cradled in his arms.

When Sage returned to the car a few minutes later, he stopped to watch Rocky and the girl. His partner had laid her across the back seat, positioning her so her injured body wouldn't be jostled during the drive back. Rocky sat in the front passenger's seat, turned to face her. Sage couldn't be sure, because Rocky's back was to the window, but he was almost positive Rocky was chewing his nails again. Sage knew it was a childhood habit Rocky never managed to break, despite his father's best effort to shame and humiliate him into stopping. Not that Rocky had admitted to the habit. And he certainly hadn't had a heart-to-heart with Sage about the bastard his father had been and still was, for that matter.

But knowing his closest friends' every thought, no matter how personal or private, was one *luxury* of Sage's gift. Sage had volunteered a little over a year ago to work with the young vamp who was serving the coven's Regan as restitution. He hadn't yet told Rocky he was beginning to hear him. He supposed he should; it was only fair. Then again, the Regan didn't keep him around because his gift was fair.

Rocky watched the young woman's chest rise and fall. Her breathing was steady, strong, despite her recent trauma. With his enhanced vision, he felt he could almost perceive the bruises blossoming under her skin. She'd look a mess by morning. Not that she looked great now. As he mentally catalogued her injuries, Rocky felt infuriated. Though the human was probably a few years older, he couldn't help but be reminded of his younger sister. He couldn't be sure if the protectiveness he felt was truly for this woman lying across the back seat or an echo of what he once felt for Maria. Either way, as he clenched his teeth and steadied his breath, he was glad to have an outlet to seek revenge against bastards who hurt females. Though it had altered the course of his life drastically, he didn't regret defending his sister. It had led to a boatload of trouble, but it also had landed him here, working alongside the warriors.

Rocky looked again at the blood and bruises on her body. Alex, the name on her bracelet read. The name was short, and Rocky thought it sounded strong. With her spiky brown hair and killer front kick, it seemed to suit her. He grinned; this was a female worth saving. Though from the looks of her injuries, saving her would require medical treatment—and the sooner the better.

As he began to wonder where the hell Sage was, the older vamp opened the driver's door. He shot Rocky a glance that he couldn't read. Sage was far from what one might call a warm-fuzzy, but he almost looked concerned. Rocky refocused; he wouldn't waste time on what was obviously a delusion.

"She needs a doctor, Sage. In a real hospital."

"She'll be fine. Call Markus. Have him get Briant to meet us back at the house." After a second he added, "And don't say it's for a human, just that we need a medic." Rocky raised a brow at Sage who was flying around the city corners as fast as the nine year old Jeep could take them. Sage seemed aggravated by the need to explain. "Darian will blow a gasket. Better if he sees for himself when he gets home."

"You mean it's better if we blindside him in front of witnesses?" Rocky didn't think surprising the Regan with an unexpected human visitor was wise.

"Just call."

"Okie dokie, but if you piss him off in addition to killing her—" Rocky mumbled under his breath, though he knew Sage heard.

"Did you just 'okie dokie' me, asshole? What did I do to deserve getting stuck with you?"

"Well, you annoy Darian on a daily basis, and—"

"Do you need to be reminded what a rhetorical question is?" Sage snarled. Rocky rubbed his arm with a slight wince remembering their last unpleasant and painful discussion about this. But after glancing back at Alex, who still showed no signs of gaining consciousness, he pressed the previous issue.

"It's a lot of blood, and your love tap didn't seem to help her any. She's still out cold. Human chicks don't heal like we do."

"You into human chicks now, Sly?" Sage taunted him by calling him the shortened form of his birth name, Sylvester. "She smell too tempting?"

"Not my thing." But there was something off about Alex's scent. It didn't make him want to feed from her, but it didn't smell weak or diluted like most humans' blood. There was something different about this woman—and it wasn't just that she knew how to throw a killer left hook. He probed Sage, "Now you mention it, she doesn't smell bad. Her essence is unusually strong, isn't it?"

Sage made an exaggerated effort to roll his eyes so Rocky could see it. If truth were told, though, he had noticed it earlier. In the alley, when his first attempt to manipulate her memories hadn't worked, he tried to make sense of her. No one had ever been immune to his gift. And Sage was used to dealing with cops, thugs, and vampires. That a tiny female had somehow resisted him was beyond curious. It was maddening. Something about her was off, way off. And he had a feeling he ought to recognize what it was.

"I suppose if every female in a five-coven radius wouldn't feed me with a six-foot straw, anything's blood might smell good. I think it's a sign you need some quality essence." Sage knew it was a low blow to bring up the coven's unspoken agreement not to talk with, let alone feed, Rocky, but he was hoping it would shut him up long enough for Sage to figure out what he was going to say to Darian when the Regan saw the extent of the human's injuries.

No such luck.

"I get fed well enough. Some females dig the 'forbidden fruit,' if you catch my drift." Rocky wagged his eyebrows.

Sage couldn't blame him for trying to salvage a sliver of his male pride, but he couldn't let the comment go either, in case there was any truth to it.

"The only whiff I'm catching is from the shit you're full of." Sage threw out the bait, hoping Rocky's words or thoughts would reveal from whom he was feeding. Rocky only shrugged. His thoughts weren't clear enough for Sage to make anything of them. Yet. It wouldn't be long before Sage knew Rocky's thoughts as well as he knew his own.

"Whatever. But Creator help you if one of their fathers or brothers finds out. Darian held off the mob for you once; he won't be able to do it again—even if he wanted to." Sage tacked on the end because fear was a healthy deterrent for stupidity. And young vampires, especially young, cocky, male vampires, had a knack for stupidity.

Rocky tried to appear unconcerned as he turned from Sage to look out the window, but from the corner of his eye, Sage could tell Rocky was back to gnawing at his stubby nails.

"Hey, festering fruit for brains, you forgetting something?" Sage kept his tone light as he pointed to the cell still in Rocky's hand.

Rocky cracked a smile and dialed Markus.

When Sage pulled the Jeep off the dirt drive and stepped out of the driver's door, Markus appeared at his side. The large farmhouse was glowing behind him, light pouring out from too many of the windows. Sage looked next to the barn. Parked beside Markus's pick up was the sedan Darian and his mate, Sarah, had left in earlier that evening, when she dragged him from the testosterone-filled house to enjoy more civilized company. Their early return was undesired. Though after Rocky had caved during the phone conversation with Markus, spilling the beans about whom they were bringing home to be treated, it was not entirely unexpected. Sage wasn't sure who to be the most irritated with, his gutless partner or his pompous pal.

"You better have a solid reason for bringing her here, Sage. Darian's furious." Markus was right up in his grill. He was at least three inches shorter than Sage, who was easily six-five, but he held himself with an air of authority that bristled nearly everyone but the Knower.

"Well, if you hadn't felt it your *duty*" —he pronounced the word like it was something highly unpleasant— "to inform the Regan while he was out with Sarah, he'd have no reason to want my head. We clearly requested Briant meet us here—not you, and certainly not Darian."

"Darian is the Regan of your coven, and I am the lead warrior, and therefore your boss. You'd do well to remember both," Markus snapped. Despite Sage, Markus, and Darian having been friends for longer than any human had ever lived, Markus and Darian both took their leadership positions seriously—at times, a little too seriously. Neither had qualms about demanding respect from anyone, even old friends, and especially Sage. Then again, he enjoyed rocking the boat. "If you mouth off or try to screw with him tonight, he'll have you by the balls," Markus finished.

Sage, having never mastered being a "yes" man, was about to snap back with some sarcastic response, when his protégé unwisely stepped in for him.

"Is it that time of the month again already?" Rocky quipped as he came along side them carrying Alex.

Markus's jaw dropped with incredulity before responding in a voice tight with tension. "Sage is given allowances, because he has worked and fought alongside Darian and me since long before Darian became Regan and long, long before you were even born." He paused here to imply his opinion on that matter. Sage braced himself for what was certain to be a long portentous reprimand about respect, but Markus had stopped mid-sentence. He was examining the human in Rocky's arms. Sage heard his concern.

"They're not deep. Just the leg maybe. She'll be fine. Trust me, she's a fighter," Sage said licking the dried blood off his swollen lip. He hoped to ease both Markus's worry and his temper.

"I can see." Markus lifted her swelling left hand and grazed his thumb tenderly over her bruised knuckles. Sage fumbled the car keys as Markus's thoughts continued to linger on the girl. Incredible.

Sage's expression must have reflected his shock and disapproval, because, upon seeing it, Markus spun around and swept up the porch stairs and into the house. But not before Sage saw the blush that had crept up Markus's cheeks when he realized Sage was in his head. Sage smiled; this was going to provide weeks of ammunition.

"Does he ever take that stick out of his—" Rocky was silenced when Sage slapped him upside the head.

"Do you think he can't hear you? He's right: you don't have the status to shoot your mouth off. Just take the girl inside and keep your mouth shut. And let me explain to Darian, got it?" Sage looked at

Alex, then shot Rocky a glance to be sure he understood exactly what not to say.

"Yeah, sure," Rocky said, then muttered under his breath, "good luck with that."

"Hey, moron, I'm nearly as old as Markus, and even if I didn't manage to hear you say that aloud, I can hear it in your head." Sage waited for a reaction, but keeping in stride, Rocky recovered his wise-ass expression almost instantly. Apparently he didn't think Sage's earlier advice applied to interactions with his partner.

"I'm touched. You're starting to hear me. Does this mean I'm officially part of the family?"

Sage held the front door open for Rocky, letting the light pour out onto the wrap-around porch. "It means either I'm days away from going insane, or your days are numbered."

When they entered the foyer they found quite a welcoming committee. Markus was leaning against the stair banister, his arms crossed over his chest, his strong jaw set. Briant, the coven's medic, stood in his blue hospital scrubs beside the doorway to the large kitchen and dining area. He looked as if he were trying to blend into the country décor. Sage thought it was a good idea considering the Regan's apparent mood. Rocky inched back, recognizing Darian's expression as one he usually wore right before he read someone the riot act.

Darian ceased his pacing to run his hands through his tousled hair, stopping midway to tug at the wavy strands. He was starting across the floor, fists at his side, when his mate entered from the hall carrying an armful of clean folded towels. She looked around at him and his males, and then to the young woman in Rocky's arms, who was dripping blood onto her pristine tile.

"Well?" Her voice was a soft but clear reprimand. "Sage, put these on the back counter. Rocky, Briant and I have prepared the island as a makeshift examination table. Markus, help him lay her out gently on the sheet. Briant, get started cleaning those wounds before any infection sets in." As if they had been scolded by their own mothers, the males began to move at once. All except Darian, who relaxed his fists and rested his hands on Sarah's shoulders. Her purposeful but calm demeanor seemed out of place, but he knew her focus was where his should be. As usual, Sarah knew just what he needed.

"No orders for me?" Darian whispered lasciviously. He loved seeing her effect on his males, knowing that without her quiet strength and gentle manner situations like this would come to blows on a more regular basis. He ran one hand over her head, twirling her ponytail around his fingers.

"If I ordered you not beat either of them senseless tonight, would you listen?"

"Is it the senseless part or the tonight part you're having trouble with?" Darian asked, dropping his hands to his sides. Despite being honored to serve his race, the Regan liked his position of power as much as any decent leader did—which was to say, most nights, very little. "Could you at least wait until I'm sure Briant and I won't need either of them to assist?" She smiled at him, reaching to smooth the creases in his forehead.

"Deal."

Sarah gave him a quick peck on the cheek and walked into the kitchen, leaving him alone. He paused a moment, watching her long, lean legs sweep through the doorway. With a sigh, he called for the two males.

Before Sage could start what was sure to be a much-edited bullshit version of events, Darian faced Rocky. "Tell me what happened tonight, kid."

Rocky gritted his teeth, probably taking issue with Darian's choice of address, but recovered quickly and launched into the account. For once, he stuck to the basic facts, keeping the superfluous details and commentary to himself. Though he probably felt he was doing a great job of covering for his mentor, this precise report left Darian even more suspicious than before. When Rocky reached the end, he very confidently finished with, "Sage realized he couldn't wipe her, and she was badly injured, so he ordered me to the car with her, so he could straighten things out with the cops who were arriving on the scene."

Well done, Darian thought. The young vamp hadn't implicated his partner, and he seemed to have carefully avoided outright lying to his Regan.

"And you were able to take care of the officers, despite not being able to use your gift on the female?" Darian asked finally turning to Sage. It seemed doubtful; his gift had never failed before.

"Yup, I was just the nosy neighbor coming to see what the screams were all about. I told them they had stopped, and the alley was empty by the time I arrived. They were conveniently easy to convince and left without examining anything too carefully." Sage smirked, no doubt amused by whatever weird-ass memory he had inserted into the officers' minds in place of what they had really witnessed.

Darian was not convinced he had heard all there was to the story, but as far as dealing with the human cops, he had to admit having Sage around was useful. He shot Sage a look that made it clear his questioning was not likely to end there, then headed into the kitchen.

Nearing the island where the woman was being treated, Darian paused. He sniffed the air. Something was off. As he put together the pieces of Rocky and Sage's unusual story and the girl's strange scent, an idea crossed his mind. But it was impossible. There had to be another explanation. He heard the other two behind him and continued across the room.

With the bloody towels, bowls of stained gauze pads, hypodermic needles, and both Sarah and Briant gloved and working on the patient, Sarah's usually warm, inviting kitchen looked like a cross between an ER and a set for a horror film.

"What's the damage, Briant?"

"The puncture wound on her side needed stitches, but wasn't deep enough to do any internal damage. The stab wound to her calf is deep, penetrating some muscle. We've cleaned it and injected a local anesthesia; as soon as that has a chance to work, I'll stitch it up. It's going to take awhile. She probably should have had a general anesthesia with the extent of her wounds, but Sarah and I aren't fully trained or equipped to do that here. If she wakes, she'll be in tremendous pain."

"Lucky for her S—uh, somebody knocked her out so hard." Rocky had blurted the first few words and made a fumbling attempt to cover his mistake by finishing the sentence. He stole a glance at Sage who was shooting him an exasperated glare. Darian caught the exchange and fumed. He turned to Sage, but the Knower was looking at the young woman to avoid the accusatory stare.

Briant sensed the tension and paused a moment before continuing. "She really ought to have a CT scan to assure there's no internal bleeding, but neither Sarah nor I could feel any bone damage on her skull, and her vitals are strong. Hopefully her prolonged loss of consciousness is just due to the combination of blood loss, shock, and a mild concussion. She should be coming to soon, which is why we could use some help holding her still while we fix up that leg," he finished, addressing Darian.

"Markus and Rocky can assist. As soon as she's treated, try to rouse her, and bring her to my office." Sarah was about to protest, but Darian held his ground. "There are some questions that need to be answered before we can send her home, Sarah. The sooner we get answers, the sooner we can bring her back. I wouldn't cause her further distress if it wasn't necessary." The human was a mystery, and even without knowing why, Darian was quite certain the answers he sought were important.

"I know you wouldn't." To the others, Sarah's quiet response may have sounded like a vote of confidence, but Darian had been mated to her long enough to read both her tone and her intense gaze as a hint of a threat as well. He gave her the smallest nod of acknowledgment before averting his eyes.

"Sage, with me, now." Darian left the room with perfect assurance he would be obeyed.

Chapter 2

The door to Darian's office was ajar. As Sage entered the room he found the Regan already leaning against the front of the dark cherry desk, his arms crossed over his massive chest. Sarah had arranged the Regan's office to have the appearance of a room suited for easy but civilized conversation. It often contrasted sharply with the reality of what occurred here. As Sage caught glimpses of Darian's thoughts, he felt this was going to be one of those nights. Sage walked to the center of the room between the couch and the two armchairs in the sitting area. He didn't feel the need to be within arms' reach of the other imposing vampire.

"Explain how this happened."

Sage knew exactly what Darian wanted explained, but wasn't about to directly answer the question. For one, he still hoped he could skirt the issue of him using the girl's head as a piñata on which he could take out his frustration. Secondly, Darian demanded Sage stay out of his head as much as possible. Sage obliged, when it was convenient. At other times he at least tried to hide it.

"Rocky's recounting didn't leave much out."

"I'm wondering about the 'much' part, Sage. According to Rocky, you couldn't use your gift because she was hysterical, not because she was already out cold. So when exactly did her head injury happen?"

Despite Rocky's best attempt at obscuring the finer points of the evening, Darian had deduced what went down. Fine, Sage thought, he was willing to cop to that one if needed, willing even to accept whatever reprimand the Regan dished out for unnecessarily striking a human. What he was not okay with was Darian leveling his added anger at him because of some crackpot theory about the girl. A theory he wouldn't even admit to.

"I know what you're thinking, and yes, I know you hate that, but we both know what you're wondering about her isn't possible. And even if it were, I certainly didn't know it at the time, so it wouldn't have made a difference."

"So you admit you struck her, an innocent woman? You could easily have killed her, Sage," Darian snapped, still unwilling to address his real concern.

"Please, I might have hit her a bit harder than needed, but I wouldn't have killed her. She was screaming loud enough to wake the dead; knocking her out was our only option."

"Hitting a female, of any race, is never a valid option."

"So you'd rather I waited until she had the entire Bristol PD arriving and then attempt to use my malfunctioning 'gift' on them?" Sage returned.

"But it worked on the two cops who came, didn't it? So I'd rather you had kept your cool and thought of another way. Running, calling for back up, gagging her even, but not losing control and nearly bashing her skull in. There are consequences when we aren't careful, Sage." Darian's controlled anger was boiling into something more intense.

Sage perceived this in time to catch himself from replying with 'whatever' or another equally disrespectful retort.

"Can you honestly tell me you hit her because you believed it was your only option? And not because you were pissed your powers didn't work on a small human female?"

Sage didn't respond. He'd skirt the truth to save his ass any day. But he would never lie to Darian. Not because an experienced vampire like Darian could tell, which he could, but because he was the warrior's Regan and friend.

Looking into the Regan's eyes, he knew what was coming, not that it stopped the searing pain of the blow to his right eye. But at least it allowed him the split second to brace himself, which was probably the only reason he was still standing. It also allowed him to know Darian didn't take pleasure in this part of his job. The Regan knew some of the codes the vampires lived by could be seen as barbaric, but paradoxically he understood his ability to enforce the rules and uphold the traditions was what maintained civility within his coven.

"Yeah, I get it, D," Sage answered as if Darian had spoken these thoughts aloud. "But if the purpose was to make a point, it seems useless to do it up here without witnesses."

Darian flashed him the quickest of grins as he motioned behind Sage toward the doorway. There, Rocky and Briant stood awkwardly awaiting to announce themselves. Rocky was once again holding Alex, who was bandaged and braced and seemed to be drifting in and out of consciousness.

Recovering his stern expression, Darian turned to them to address Briant. "Thank you for helping tonight, as always. I see she's coming to."

"Yes, Regan, but she vomited when she first regained consciousness," he began.

"Yeah, Markus is having a rough night, too," Rocky muttered to Sage, who just glared.

"It could be just shock, but it's also a symptom of a more serious concussion. She'll need to be watched closely for a day or two. I can stay over for the daylight hours if you need me to," Briant offered Darian. But the reply came not from the Regan, but from the hall.

"I can do that, Briant, no need for you to be away from your family," Sarah said as she entered the office after cleaning up down stairs.

"Well, you heard the lady, but I may need you to fabricate some records at the clinic to corroborate whatever memory Sage gives her when we return her home," Darian said. Sage raised his eyebrows, but when he felt the pain in his quickly swelling eye, he wished he hadn't.

Briant, who was training at a human college to become a doctor, worked nights at an urgent care clinic just outside the city. His medical expertise, which transferred well to vampires, as well as his access to medical records of humans whom the coven 'interacted' with, made him valuable, but not unique. There were other, older members of the coven who had much more medical training and field experience. What put Briant at the top of Darian's list was his knack for knowing when not to ask questions. He averted his gaze from the woman, and Sage wondered if the medic had as many doubts as he did about whether this human was ever going home.

"No problem, Regan. Sarah, goodnight." He bowed to them both and headed out the door as Markus was heading in.

With Briant gone and Markus returned, Darian seemed ready to get to work.

"Rocky, put her on the couch. I'd like to see if we can get some information out of her before Sage tries to play with her memory again."

Sarah began to protest, arguing to give the injured female more time before questioning her, but Rocky was already starting towards the sofa. A few yards into the room, nearly in the center of the sitting area, Rocky yelped and dropped the girl, who landed hard on the wood floor.

"Rocky!" nearly every voice yelled at once.

More in shock than pain, Rocky held out his arm to them. "She bit me!" he said, watching a small amount of blood bead up from circular cut on his bicep.

Sarah was the first to react, rushing to Alex who was now sprawled on the floor. Sarah must have seen the flash of fear in her eyes when she got too close. She was not surprised or upset when the young woman defensively shoved her away.

Darian, however, protective of his mate, was ready to spring at her. He closed the gap between his mate and Alex before anyone could register his movement.

"No, Darian," Sarah said, tugging at his wrist, pulling him away from the woman, who had fallen back to the floor and seemed once again to be fighting to remain conscious. "I'm fine; she's the one who's scared and hurt. She's doing what any of us would in her situation."

Sarah's words brought Darian out of his protective stance. He backed off, but kept his eyes locked on Alex. And so he missed the smug grin Sage wore, watching as the human had much the same effect on the Regan she had had on him.

Back on her feet, Sarah offered Rocky a tissue to wipe the blood from his arm.

"She's got spunk," he remarked, accepting the offer. "You've got to admire her effort." Hearing Darian's grunt of disapproval and Sarah's chuckle, he added to his Regan's mate, "I don't mean her trying to hurt you, just her will."

"I knew what you meant, Rocky, and I too admire it," she said looking back down to the girl. "But you need to rest, Alex. No more harm will come to you here." Though trying to comfort Alex, the look Sarah shot Darian seemed to imply her words also served as a reminder to her mate. "I'll go set up the guest room. Don't keep her long, Darian."

Surely she was going mad. The last thing Alex remembered before the murderous blond with the messed up eyebrow had knocked her senseless was catching a flash of what could only be described as his fangs. It wasn't even Fourth of July, never mind Halloween. And Bristol was much too boring to open some new Goth club. Her brain must have been muddled prior to that final blow. People didn't have fangs.

She vaguely remembered regaining consciousness while being stitched up. The pain had been severe. She was almost positive she had thrown up all over one of the men holding her. She hoped that memory was accurate. She looked around the room and, sure enough, spotted a vaguely familiar face on a guy who seemed to be sporting a freshly laundered t-shirt and jeans. His feet were bare. He obviously hadn't had time to clean his boots. The thought pleased her.

Nothing else was clear until she had found herself in this room in the arms of one of her attackers. If that realization hadn't jolted her fully conscious, the jolt of dropping the five feet to the floor after turning her head and biting her captor's arm had done the trick. As the pain in nearly every inch of her body sent her swooning again, she had begun to think attempting to escape was futile. Until she could manage to walk on her own, she would be at the mercy of the five figures in front of her.

But as one had made a sudden movement toward her, her body reacted instinctively by shoving the woman away. There had been another sudden movement as one of the men had rushed to the blonde's defense. Alex didn't pay much attention; she was trying to make sense of her surroundings. A woman?

It wasn't the only surprise. She would have expected to find herself in another dark alley, an abandoned warehouse, or even a slum apartment being used as a meth lab. But as she absorbed what she was seeing around her, she was confused by the pine floorboards under her and the modern country furnishings. She would have ventured to guess she was in a man's office, by the heavy wooden desk and lack of personal items, but it was obvious from the soft blue Oriental rug and coordinating curtains the room had been given a woman's touch.

Finally, she examined her body. Her right calf had been bandaged from ankle to knee, her left hand was in a brace, and she could feel under her tank that her torso had been wrapped tightly. She felt the tug of stitches there, too. All of the dressings were clean and neat. They had tended to her wounds with a degree of expertise before carrying her to this room. But why?

Adding to Alex's confusion, though she hadn't been listening to the conversation, the tall, lean woman who had just calmed her partner was addressing her gently. Alex could hardly make sense of her words as the pains in her body, especially her head, left her fighting to remain conscious again. But she was aware when the woman suddenly left the room, and the men shifted closer to her. She wanted to call her back but couldn't find her voice. She heard her name again, but was finding it difficult to focus.

"Alex?" Darian asked turning to Markus.

On the small side for a vampire, Markus might have been perceived as less menacing than the others. But Creator help the vampire who picked a fight with the lead warrior. Darian hadn't chosen Markus to be his right hand man solely for his intellect and self-control. He could also skewer two Vengatti twice his size with the flick of one knife and with his other hand throw another at a moving target with more accuracy than most warriors could shoot a gun. Though, Darian hoped these skills wouldn't be necessary with this diminutive female.

"Alex Crocker. Rocky found this on her. We removed it with her other bracelets so Sarah could clean her up." Markus pulled a strip of nylon from his back pocket and handed it to Darian, pointing to the name, address, and emergency contact number engraved on a small metal plate attached to it. "I've seen them in commercials on ESPN. They're meant to help identify runners in situations like this where they've become ill or injured." While Darian examined the tag, thinking it could be handy, Rocky spoke up.

"Actually, I'm pretty sure the ad doesn't mention getting attacked by a member of a rogue coven of vampires and then kidnapped by—"

"Enough!" Darian silenced him.

"Smooth, moron," Sage muttered.

"What?" Rocky apparently didn't understand the fuss. Darian took a deep breath and tried to remember Rocky was still adjusting to his place in the household and deserved more patience than he had to give at the moment.

Thankfully, Markus answered. "She's semi-conscious," he said with little more tolerance than Darian would have shown, pointing to Alex whose eyes had fluttered open at the word vampire.

"Sorry, but wasn't the whole point of bringing her here to wipe her memory?"

Markus ground his teeth. They all knew Rocky was well-intentioned, but his impulsivity when it came to his mouth and his actions was a bone of contention. It especially bothered Markus, who rarely acted or spoke without careful forethought.

"Let's not make that any harder than it needs to be, especially considering how well it went earlier in the evening," Darian said, stepping in before his lead warrior felt the need to intervene. "If you want to stay while I question her, Rocky, you will keep quiet." Darian waited until Rocky acknowledged the command before turning back to Alex.

Markus followed his gaze, looking from Sage to her. "Any thoughts on that, yet?"

"Plenty, which is why I need her awake." Darian stood over Alex who was stirring on the floor. When she had managed to push herself into a sitting position, he spoke. "I'd like you to be more comfortable while I ask you a few questions. Will you allow us to move you to the couch without drawing blood from anyone else?"

"Do I have a choice?" The message was stronger than her shaking voice.

Darian scoffed. Was this fragile human female, surrounded by four male vampires, really going to be difficult? "Certainly—you can remain on the floor," he said.

"I could remain silent, too," she replied.

Darian sighed. That answered that question.

Alex could sense their curiosity and knew it would irk them to not get answers. She hoped it would gain her some leverage. But as her brain cleared and her focus returned, something shook her. She had an overwhelming sense of someone's emotions somewhere in the room. She glanced around, disturbed by this sudden increase in her intuition. As she met the blond's stare, his shocked expression matched her own emotions. Alex knew, for the first time in her life, what she sensed from him was more than intuition: she could sense his feelings as clearly as she could her own. It was unexpected, inexplicable, and uncomfortable. But it was also a bit empowering.

She looked at him feeling somewhat triumphant. She was surprised and confused by his changing expression. A moment ago she had been sure he somehow knew what she was doing. But his look of shock was replaced with a sneer. And the anger and surprise he had been feeling faded. What she sensed now was amusement. It left her ill at ease.

She became aware that the longer-haired brunette, whom the woman had called Darian, stood over her, addressing her again. She tried to concentrate on the words he was speaking aloud, rather than what she was feeling inside.

"Yes, you could remain silent," he said, "but it will only prolong your stay, and I get the feeling you're a reluctant guest. Let's not play games."

The blond cut in. "Actually, there's no need for her to speak, so let the games begin."

There was a moment of quiet. Alex saw the confused looks of his partners and was glad she wasn't the only one who didn't understand.

"You're not saying you can—? Without eye contact or touch?" asked the handsome one on whom she had vomited. "Why would that part of your power be so strong with her, Sage, but the other not work at all?"

Power? Alex felt more and more like she had entered the twilight zone. What the hell were they talking about? And why was everyone staring at her that way?

"I don't know," Sage said looking between the others. "But it means, as long as you can ask her the right questions, we should be able to get answers."

Like hell, Alex thought. *Not unless you plan on plucking them from my head.*

Sage, the man who had attacked her earlier and whose emotions she could now sense clearly, laughed. She felt his satisfaction.

Crap. The blow to her head was putting her brain on slow-mo. Hearing the thoughts in her mind was exactly what he planned to do. Actually, it seemed to be what he was already doing. He hadn't been bothered by what she could feel. He had been surprised by his own ability. Once that wore off, he began to enjoy it. Alex squirmed just thinking about the insight this intrusion gave him. Trying to convince herself such things were impossible was futile. She looked at him again, wondering what to make of it all. She shook her head as if jostling it about a bit more tonight would make this all seem more real—or better yet, might wake her up from a very strange dream. Watching him, she saw his smile grow. He was starting to piss her off.

"You seem to be enjoying this more than usual, Sage," the smaller of them remarked. Alex couldn't be sure, but he almost seemed as leery of his comrade's intentions as she was. She wondered how she previously had missed the concern he seemed to feel for her.

"I never knew humans could be so amusing. Does it bother you, Markus?" Sage asked. Markus ground his teeth, but remained silent. "Fire away, D," Sage continued, addressing Darian. He seemed to be the leader of this group and didn't seem to appreciate the informality of being addressed by a nickname. His glare lingered a minute on Sage, who was feeling defiant. Alex wondered if the mind reader knew his leader's thoughts as well.

Darian turned to her again, "Last time I'll offer." He gestured to the couch and extended his hand to her. Alex hated giving in, but she was throbbing all over and the soft cushions looked inviting. Her mind was in turmoil; her body, at least, needed some comfort. Gritting her teeth, she tried to take his hand. But as her left was injured and she needed a way to steady herself so she could balance on her uninjured leg, she ended up falling back on her rear.

Darian grinned at her. "I'll carry you, if you let me, but you'll want to behave—payback's a bitch." He flashed his fangs at her and had her easily in his arms before she had time to react. She gasped from both fear and the pain of being suddenly moved.

As he laid her out on the sofa, she heard the others laughing. She pursed her lips and bit back the thank you she had considered saying. They were playing with her. Despite any care or consideration they may pretend to display, she was well aware it would end as soon as they got out of her what they wanted. Having clearly seen for the second time evidence of what these creatures were, she tried not to think how it would end. She focused instead on what they seemed to want: answers. *Well,* she thought, *good luck with that*. If denying them meant staying alive a little longer, she could play games too.

"That's better, right?" Darian didn't wait for an answer before he began his real questioning. "Now, who were you with before you went for your run tonight?"

She tried not to think about school or Peter. Instead she pictured her empty apartment, which had seemed extra empty the last month, since Brady had disappeared. Her thoughts jumped between his favorite spot on her worn couch to the way he liked to curl up next to her in bed.

When it became obvious she wasn't planning to answer, Darian looked to Sage.

"Who's Brady?" Sage asked with a smirk.

Alex had to think of a better plan. She would not let them use her this way, pulling personal information from her, reminding her of painful memories. Brady had been her cat. An all-black stray she had adopted shortly after moving to her apartment. For the last four years Brady had been her only steady companion, as none of her boyfriends ever lasted long. She had been heartbroken when one night she arrived back at her apartment to find he had somehow escaped. She had stayed up searching for him the whole night and looked for him whenever she ran the streets near her apartment ever since. And now these goons would surely mock her for caring so deeply about a damn pet she couldn't keep out of her thoughts and memories.

"Missing cat," Sage informed the others who were waiting to be filled in. Surprisingly, he made no other comment.

Seeing her expression, the fourth male who had remained mostly silent to that point, spoke up. "That sucks. I had a dog that ran away when I was a kid. Although, knowing my dad, I wouldn't be surprised if he ran it over. It liked to chew his shoes. I loved that mutt."

Markus shook his head. Sage rolled his eyes. And Darian snapped at him.

"Not helping, Rocky. Keep quiet."

But Alex had chuckled a bit, and the knot at the back of her throat eased.

"Who was the last male you were with?" Darian continued. Alex blinked in shock. Was he asking about her love life? Hell, no, she was not discussing that with a group of strangers. She didn't care who or what they were. Her strong internal 'no' reminded her of something, which gave her an idea of how she could otherwise occupy her mind. In her head, she began reciting a favorite poem of the first graders she had worked with at camp last summer, aptly entitled, "No."

It wasn't the most sophisticated poem for an English teacher who had just completed her Master's degree to recite, but nothing of Dickenson, Hughes, or Frost seemed to work quite as well for the occasion.

She stopped reciting when laughter roared from behind her. Sage, who had been leaning against the wall near the door, had thrown back his head in amusement. The others looked at him oddly. When he realized he was being watched, he gained control and explained.

"She's reciting poetry to keep me out. Highly intellectual stuff, too. She thought you were asking her to share her sexual history."

Markus blushed on her behalf; she couldn't help but feel gratitude. But Sage, Rocky, and Darian chuckled.

"As fascinating as I'm sure that would be," Darian said, trying to keep a straight face, "I just wanted to know who you have been near in the last day or two. Males, including lovers, but also friends, coworkers, family—anyone you may have brushed up against, sat with, hugged. Maybe you were just wearing a borrowed sweatshirt from a brother?"

Alex, annoyed at being further embarrassed, was trying to remember the second stanza when the last question about a brother made her lose focus. Undesired, but unavoidably, the images of her own brothers flashed in her mind, and the aching tightness in her throat returned.

"She has two brothers, I think, they're probably in their late teens. It's not clear though, too many emotions in the way."

"No!" Alex shouted, her voice cracking. "Enough. You will not speak for me, not about them." She turned to look at Darian.

"By all means, I'll get him to shut up, if you're willing to cooperate."

"Can you stop it, then?" she asked Sage. She hated to give in, but hated more to let him hear this, of all things, in her head. Her brothers were off limits. If he had heard even one of her painful memories, she would have expected even a murderous bastard like him to feel some sympathy. But what she sensed instead was anger.

"Have you had any luck stopping your little parlor trick?" Sage retorted.

So that was it. He did know what she was doing, and he enjoyed it about as much as she enjoyed him plucking her thoughts from her head. But there was more to it, too. She sensed his insecurity. What she was doing, or what he had been unable to do, made him question his ability. It left Alex with questions, too.

"What are you two talking about, Sage?" Darian was obviously unaware of their connection and seemed irritated Sage hadn't mentioned anything earlier.

"It's not just that I can hear her thoughts," Sage answered reluctantly. "It seems I have no choice. I can't drown them out, the way I do with you. It's like she's shouting them at me." He turned from Darian to glare at Alex like she had physically assaulted him, instead of the other way around.

"The only two words I want to shout at you are probably best kept in my head."

Sage snarled at her tone and the accompanying curse she hadn't tried to keep out of her thoughts.

"Simmer down." Darian looked at Sage, and then turned to Alex. "That means you, too."

A fresh set of swears meant for Darian was forming on her lips, when he stepped closer and held up a hand to her formidably.

"If you haven't noticed, I struck him, my warrior and friend, for hitting you when he lost control. I ask, in return, for some respect and a bit of control on your part."

Alex glanced to Sage's swollen eye, an injury she had assumed he suffered during the fight in the alley. She turned back to Darian with a new perspective. Alex sensed he wasn't asking for, so much as demanding, her deference and control, but despite herself, she understood. Her experience in the classroom taught her sometimes being an authority figure required taking away others' ability to choose. If he had been honorable enough to hold his own friends to his expectations and values, then he deserved her respect—for now.

"Thank you," she managed, gesturing to Sage's shiner when Darian looked confused.

"My pleasure," Darian whispered. Though she wondered from their expressions if the others in the room could hear him. "I probably ought to do it more often. He can be an insolent S.O.B., in addition to his gift being a real pain in the ass sometimes. Which reminds me, he seems to be aggravated by something you can do. Mind explaining it?"

Darian sat across from her on the edge of the cream colored upholstered wing back. His temper was calm, and as he leaned over, resting his elbows on the knees of his khaki pants, Alex struggled to remember who, or what, she was having this conversation with. The only reason she answered him was because her own curiosity couldn't be quelled.

"I don't know how, really. It's never happened before. Not like this, not so strong. And it's like he said, I can't seem to stop it or block it out," Alex was as much working through her own thoughts, as answering Darian's question.

"But what is it you can do, exactly?"

"I—this is going to seem nuts—"

"You're in a room full of vampires, one of whom has been reading your thoughts for the last half hour. That in itself would seem nuts to most humans," Rocky pointed out.

"Can I gag him?" Markus asked Darian.

"What? He's the one flashing his fangs at her. You think she passed that off as a dental anomaly?"

Darian began to run his hands through his hair again. The moment Rocky saw it he blanched and quickly backpedaled.

"Sorry, Regan, I just—sorry." He looked at his feet. Seeing the reaction, Alex wondered how often Darian doled out shiners, but for the meantime, he maintained his cool.

"Please, continue, Alex."

Alex looked at Sage who looked away. She had never put words to what she could do before. Ever since she was a teen she had fought an over-active mind. That wasn't right, either. It wasn't her mind—it was her emotions, or her other sense, as she thought of it. She was hypersensitive to others' feelings, and not just guys crushing on her. She had often found herself caught up in the emotions of her family, friends, even her students. A school counselor once labeled her extremely empathetic, though when others' moods distracted or upset her, she had just felt pathetic. And that was when what she felt was merely vague glimpses.

"I can sense his emotions. I can sense them as strongly as if they were my own. It's disconcerting."

"Tell me about it," Sage muttered.

"Is Sage the only one you can sense?"

"Yes. Well, the only one I can feel with such consistency and clarity. I . . . I think I may have been doing it to a lesser degree since I was a kid, though. I've just got really good intuition, I guess." Alex wasn't sure whether she tacked on the last sentence to sound less insane to them or to herself. Because if she were going to be honest with herself, she had always wondered if it was more than that. In fact, until tonight, she had worried a bit about her sanity. After all, in the real world extra senses and mind reading didn't exist. But, tonight, in this alternate reality she found herself in, she was almost able to accept she was something more than just freakishly oversensitive. Maybe there was another explanation. She was beginning to think she wanted answers as much as they did.

"And your brothers, are either of them also . . . intuitive, as you call it?" Darian asked Alex, but his eyes flickered to Sage. She tried to feel what Sage's reaction to this was, but her own emotions about this topic were too intense.

"My brothers are both dead." Alex's voice hung heavy in the air.

"How did they die?" Darian asked sitting erect. She watched him and Sage exchange another glance and began to wonder why they were asking these questions.

"A car crash. Dave was nineteen, Levi was seventeen, and I was fifteen. Why does it matter?"

"Were you with them?" Darian asked leaning forward again. He ignored her question.

"No, they were alone. Well, the cops think they may have been drag racing another car, but no one ever came forward." Alex knew her voice had the mechanical sound of someone who had told this tragic story enough times to be able to maintain a limited amount of control over her emotions.

"How old are you now, Alex?" Darian asked.

"Is that important?" Alex wasn't going to relay her life story without a reason.

"I'm sorry," Darian said misjudging her tone, "I know it's rude to ask a lady her age, but—"

"It's not that. I just get the sense there's a reason you're asking me. Actually, I'm wondering why you brought me here to begin with?"

When she began to think about it, Alex had an infinite number of questions. Why did they attack her? Clearly, they didn't want to mug her; from the looks of this office, they didn't need the money—not that a jogger without a purse would have any on her anyway. If they had wanted to hurt her or rape her, they wouldn't have bothered to bring her back here and treat her wounds, never mind waste time inundating her with all these questions. And then there was the third attacker. Was he one of them? Were they angry he hurt her or jealous he found her first? She got a shiver down her spine as she remembered Sage slitting his throat from ear to ear, the blood spilling out in a rush.

Chapter 3

Blood. Was that it? Did they save her so they could use her as a living blood bank? But, then, why all the questions about males? Maybe they needed a male, also, to feed the female vampire who had seemed so gentle. Her heart began to race, her breath catching in her tightening chest. Why had she spoken to them, begun to trust them, even? The minute she had realized what they were, she should have run from the house shrieking. She shifted on the couch and then, pain reigniting, remembered the reason she hadn't tried to escape earlier. Would they let her heal before they began to feed from her? Maybe she could bolt when the sun came up. She'd only have to make it to the door. Then maybe she could scream for help.

Sage was laughing at her again. Darian, who seemed to be reluctant to answer her, sat up and looked at him.

"I think you're going to have to tell her, Darian. She's got quite the imagination and is about to hyperventilate. For your information, human, your kind isn't really all that appetizing to us. Don't believe everything you see on TV."

"She's not the only one who is curious about your questions, Regan, if I may say," Markus said. Alex noticed his tone was polite and respectful, very different from how Sage interacted with their leader.

"I'll explain—to all of you. But I do have a few more questions. Starting with your age," Darian turned back to Alex whose breathing was slowly returning to normal.

She didn't seem to be in any immediate danger, and her curiosity was still piqued, so she answered. "I'll be twenty-six in August."

"Another eighties baby, nice," Rocky said giving her a nod of approval, before Darian's annoyed glance shut him up.

"And you started noticing your po—" Darian adjusted his word choice mid-sentence, "increased intuition around the time you began. . . ." he paused and blushed a little.

Alex's confusion lasted only a moment before she knew what he was getting at.

"Menstruating, puberty? What personal, none-of-your-business word would you prefer? Because really, I'd hate to make you uncomfortable or embarrassed," Alex snapped. She was angry he was asking this but also a bit surprised he knew to ask. His question reminded her that before she had gone on the pill, her senses had increased noticeably during the week of her period. She had used to cry and beg her mother to let her stay home, because being in a high school with so many emos and drama queens had been torture. It was the reason her mother had agreed to secretly take her to the doctor, against her father's wishes, and allow her to go on birth control. Alex had always thought she was a wimp who couldn't handle her own hormone swings. Now she wondered if there was something else to it.

"Tell him that," Sage said.

Alex realized he had heard her thoughts and gave him a glacial stare. "I really dislike being around you."

"Now who's embarrassed about her womanly functions? He's got a mate, he can handle it."

"If you're so comfortable listening to and commenting on my personal experiences, you tell him." Alex crossed her arms, set her jaw, and stared at her own knees, hoping it would look like she was being stubborn, when really she was mortified. She had grown up with two brothers, a strict, traditional father, and a mother whose idea of explaining such things involved a trip to the linen closet, where she had silently pointed to a neatly hidden box of tampons, before bustling out of the room to return to her safe world of vacuuming.

Sage stammered a bit as he began. And the only way Alex made it through his recounting of her thoughts was to focus on the embarrassment and anger he felt over his own gift blowing up in his face. By the end, he was beet red, and she was grinning.

"Huh," was all Darian had to say when Sage finished. Despite Sage's assurance the Regan could handle it, he didn't seem to want to discuss it further. "And your parents? Your father? Is he still alive?" Darian resumed, changing the topic.

Alex looked up at him and sighed. He had a knack for asking all the questions she'd rather not answer.

"Yeah, they're both still alive, last I knew."

"Which means?" Darian asked, not understanding her answer or her anger.

"Which means I'm daughter of the year. I send my mother a check every month, because the disability they get since my father's stroke isn't really enough to live on. If it doesn't get returned, I assume nothing's changed. Beyond that I don't interact with them much." Guessing what Darian was about to ask, she added, "And if my father was able to sense others' emotions, then he was more of a bastard than I thought." *Because he sure didn't give a shit about mine or my mother's,* she added internally, but didn't care to share that with a room full of strangers.

"I'm sorry, Alex, that so much of this was painful for you." Darian spoke in a tone Alex might have read as comforting if she hadn't considered the source. "And I'm not sure what I can tell you, because I'm not sure what I really know." Alex looked at him accusingly. "I'm not saying I won't try, just that I don't have much definitive information right now. And I'd like to try something first, if you'll allow it?"

"What?" Alex rubbed the sweaty palm of her uninjured hand on the couch as she eyed Darian.

"You know already Sage can hear your thoughts. And most of ours, too, for that matter. Usually his gift requires eye contact or physical touch, but with those he becomes close to, he gains the ability to 'hear them,' as he calls it, simply by being near them. You, however, seem to be an exception, for some reason," Darian explained.

"Lucky me."

"Well, that power isn't the only reason Sage is marked as a Knower."

"Marked?" she asked, her curiosity overriding her annoyance.

"The two lines across his eyebrow. They allow other vampires to know what he can do. I guess the Creator felt it was only fair to forewarn us," Darian said smirking at Sage. The Knower furrowed his thick brows, which were a much darker shade of brown than his dirty blond overgrown crew cut. The contrast to his light hair as well as to his piercing pale blue-grey eyes made them a defining facial feature.

"Huh. I thought he was just a fan of Vanilla Ice." Alex kept a straight face, waiting for the others to get the jibe. But the confused looks on Sage, Markus and Darian's faces told her she had missed her mark. Until she noticed Rocky, hand over his mouth, shaking with silent laughter. Alex admitted to herself that if the two had met under different circumstances, she might have liked him.

Sage, who was quick enough to realize he was being ridiculed, was becoming annoyed. That being her intention, his mood only egged her on. She turned to Rocky.

"Were these three living under a rock during the nineties? Really, boys, Google it sometime."

Darian silenced Rocky's continued chuckles with a single look. "There's a second part to his gift," he said to Alex. The forced control was evident in his tone.

She considered asking if he could rock a mic like a vandal, but caught herself. Darian had stood up. He was nearly as tall as Sage and twice as broad. With him towering over her, it was easier to remember how precarious her situation was. She swallowed her comment with her returning fear.

Darian continued. "One of the reasons Sage and Rocky brought you here was because that gift didn't work on you, Alex."

She remembered how intensely Sage had stared at her in the alley. "What was it? What was he trying to do?"

"He was trying to manipulate your memories. To get you to remember a different set of circumstances. One that would be less traumatic and more believable," Darian said.

"And you want me to let him try again?" She wasn't opposed to not remembering some of the more graphic images from the evening, but the idea of willingly allowing someone to screw with her head was incomprehensible. Almost as incomprehensible as the fact she believed he could do it.

"Please, I just want to be sure," Darian asked Alex.

"You really hate asking him for help, huh?" Sage cut in. He knew he was crossing the line with Darian, but he was having a hard time with the fact his gifts seemed tainted when Alex was in proximity to him. He was already pissed that the tables had been turned on him, leaving him equally exposed for once. To add to that, Darian wanted to have him fail at what had always worked, in front of all of them.

"What I hate is you using my own thoughts to question my authority. And, yes, I also hate looking like an inexperienced fool in front of my father. Which is exactly how I'll look if I drag him down here only to discover your inability to enter her mind was a one time fluke surrounded by a series of coincidences." Darian's volume had continued to rise, so he was nearly shouting by the time he finished.

"You really believe in coincidences, D?"

"That's twice tonight, warrior. I believe in double-checking. So, with Alex's consent, you will try again."

Sage was almost positive he would fail. The girl didn't fit with what Darian was thinking, but she wasn't right either. He had been reading Darian's thoughts all night and knew he didn't want to have to go to his father unless there was no other way to confirm his suspicions about her. Neither Sage nor Darian could remember ever studying anything about Knowers' gifts interacting oddly with the gifts of others, but if there were something in any of the coven's histories, the Elder Regan would know.

"It won't work," Sage said rubbing his eyebrow.

Rocky, seeing him rub above his eye, which had swollen to a mere slit, turned to Darian. "Aim for the nose next time, Regan. It's messier, but hurts like hell and won't screw with his vision or his gift."

"Maybe I should practice on you, first," Darian spat.

Sage cut in, shaking his head. "It's not that. It's her mind and her essence. It's all odd."

They're sporting fangs and 'marked' brows, and I'm the one being called odd, Alex thought, scoffing at Sage's remark. Sage grinned as he heard it, acknowledging the irony.

Darian wouldn't let it rest. "Humor me."

Sage sighed. He crossed the room to stand next to Alex, knowing she sensed his reluctance and hint of nervousness. Knowing it and hating it. She tried to return the smug grin he had given her earlier when he first realized he could hear her. His jaw was clenched, and his hand twitched, eager to wipe the grin off her face much the same way he had gotten her to shut up in the alley. The only thing that kept him calm was hearing her increasing fear as he approached. He tried to remind himself that she had more to worry about and more to lose than he did. Darian would never hurt an innocent human, but he would also never risk exposing the secret his kind had kept for ages.

Without consciously registering it, Alex adjusted her body, freeing her uninjured arm from where it had been pressed between her body and the back of the couch. Sage noticed the shift and almost laughed. Rocky was right, she was a tough one.

"If this works, you'll get the hell out of here, which will make us both happy. How 'bout we aim to send you home with one hand intact?" He spoke softly to her, hoping to put her at ease. "It doesn't hurt, and besides, do you really want to remember all this tomorrow?"

"Will I believe it even if I do?" Alex asked.

"Probably not. At least this way you won't think you're losing your mind."

"Humph." Sage knew from the sound and her thoughts, Alex worried it was too late for that. "Fine," she said taking a deep breath. "What do I have to do?" She watched as Sage looked at her bare arm, started to reach out to it, then pulled back.

"Am I contagious?" Sage didn't answer except to narrow his eyes at her. Forgetting he could hear her reason for asking, Alex clarified. "You don't want to touch me; you're nervous."

Sage sneered at the suggestion for the benefit of the others in the room. "It's unnecessary. The connection seems strong enough. Just maintain eye contact and try not to fight it."

They each took a deep breath. Sage knew what to expect, but doubted it would happen; Alex braced for the unknown. They looked into each other's eyes for a long, awkward moment.

Sage looked away first, cursing. He glanced at Darian and knew the Regan wasn't going to be satisfied until he tried to use his gift the conventional way. He had a bad feeling the physical contact wouldn't help. In fact, he had a really bad feeling it would make everything worse.

"Hold still," he told Alex, who seemed to know what was coming. He was surprised when she didn't flinch or pull back.

They locked gazes again as Sage held her chin as he had done in the alley.

There was a rush of energy. The onslaught of emotions that flowed between them was overwhelming Alex. It was a hundred times stronger than before. As Sage's emotions became her own, she struggled to breathe, never mind stay still or maintain eye contact. Unable to separate out her own feelings from his, she began to lose sense of herself. Her instinct kicking in, she swiped at Sage. She missed only because he had pulled away just as quickly.

"Not happening," Sage said as he backed away from Alex, stopping when he had returned to his position along the wall.

"Thank you, both of you, for trying," Darian said. He had stood up when Sage had approached Alex and now began pacing in front of his desk.

"So, I'm not going home?" Alex asked watching him. She wasn't sure whether she should be scared, angry, or perhaps a bit relieved. She wanted answers. She just wasn't sure what she was willing to sacrifice to get them.

"Not tonight. You'll stay here and recover some, and in a night or two when we've sorted things out we'll. . . ." He paused, running his hands through his hair. "We'll decide what's best."

Alex wasn't fooled by the use of the royal 'we.' She should have argued he had no right to keep her. She should have protested she had to go to work the next day, or at least call in, because otherwise her colleagues, Peter especially, would worry and search for her. But what concerned her most was he seemed to be dismissing her for the night.

"And the answers you promised?"

"You'll get, but not until I'm more sure of them myself. We're going to do some research while you rest. We'll talk again tomorrow night," Darian said. "Markus, can you carry her to the guest room? Sarah's probably in there waiting, fussing."

Markus nodded and approached Alex. She was turning to Darian ready to argue when Markus held out his hands and asked, "May I?" Alex looked up at him and saw him clearly for the first time. He was tall and lean. Still big, but unlike the others, whose sizes only added to their superhuman-like qualities, Markus didn't seem unreal or frightening. His hair was cut short and kept neat. As he stood in the light from the lamp behind him, she could make out auburn highlights mixed in his dark brown strands. And she found she was a bit breathless as she took in his jade green eyes. She nodded. He picked her up easily and carried her carefully into the hall.

Alone with him in the long hallway dotted with three other identical dark wooden doors, warmly lit by the simple brass sconces between each, the silence began to feel awkward. So she spoke, blurting the first thing that came to her mind.

"I'm sorry I puked on you earlier." The minute the words left her mouth Alex cringed at the hideous conversation starter. Markus chuckled.

"I didn't think you would remember that. But don't worry, I've been around enough fights; I've built up a tolerance for body fluids." His speech was even and thoughtful. Alex doubted he ever shot off his mouth like his two peers did—like she did, for that matter. It made her feel a bit insecure.

"I ruined your shoes, though, I take it?"

"Well, Sarah's usually kind enough to do the laundry, but that would have been above and beyond. I stripped in the foyer, so I didn't track anything through the house and threw the whole lot into a garbage bag, boots included."

Alex thought she would have liked to see that, had she been conscious at the time. Catching herself, she flushed scarlet, hoping Sage was too far away to hear her thoughts and Markus was too busy trying to open the door to the room they had stopped in front of to notice her sudden change in coloration.

Just then, the door opened, and the female, Sarah, appeared in the entrance.

"A few questions?" Sarah accused Markus as she motioned him in and pulled the covers down so Alex could be propped against the mountain of pillows. "I was ready to barge down his door and carry her in here myself." She turned to Alex, "You must be exhausted. I'm Sarah, Darian's mate. Did they even bother to introduce themselves?" When Alex just smiled, Sarah turned on Markus, who was looking at the floor. "Were you all raised by humans?" She realized her faux pas immediately and looked mortified. "I'm so sorry. It's just an expression we use—and really shouldn't."

Alex thought Sarah was putting this on the top of her list of things to scold her husband about. She laughed, but wished she hadn't; the painkillers seemed to have worn off.

"It's okay. Human guys are just as bad," Alex tried to assure Sarah, while holding her side.

"Yes, but they haven't had three hundred years to learn some manners," Sarah said, looking disdainfully at Markus, who was edging toward the door.

"Right, my apologies. I'm Markus. Nice to . . . officially . . . meet you. Do you need anything? I think Darian wanted me to help him with his research, but—"

"Go," Sarah said. "I've got it, but tell him not to stay up half the day again." Markus nodded and shut the door on his way out.

"Are you okay?" she asked, once they were alone.

"I'm fine," Alex said, "but I could use some aspirin."

"Of course, well, non-aspirin only, due to the concussion. Aspirin thins the blood. But that's not what I meant. I meant are you handling this okay? You suffered a traumatic attack and woke up to all this. And I know Darian has asked—or required, if we're being honest—you to stay here. You must be reeling."

When reminded of it all, Alex discovered she was. The calm she had maintained in front of the males in the office was fading. Her stomach was churning and her limbs felt shaky. Afraid the growing lump in her throat would win over if she spoke, Alex nodded.

"I want you to know, despite their gruff appearances, they really are a good group of males." The way she said 'good' gave Alex the impression Sarah wasn't simply giving a vague compliment about their characters, but rather making a sincere remark about what she believed to be true of their very essences. Though her survival instinct told her to question everything, Alex's sense and her heart were confirming Sarah's assertion.

"It might be the blow to the head, but I think I believe that," she admitted. Sarah smiled so warmly Alex didn't even jolt at seeing the tips of her exposed fangs.

After an hour of tending to Alex's every possible need, Sarah had Alex back in bed, fed, drugged, cleaned as best she could around the bandages, and in fresh clothes. Alex's short athletic figure was the exact opposite of Sarah's tall, straight build, so the t-shirt and sweats Sarah leant her were ill-fitting. But Alex had never appreciated a change of clothes more. Just having Sarah's calming presence and woman's touch had been a welcome relief. With her nerves somewhat soothed, Alex knew sleep would come quickly. She felt how much her body needed it to begin the healing process. Still, she was reluctant when Sarah started to leave. Sarah seemed to notice this and turned at the door.

"I can stay until you fall asleep," she offered.

"No, it's okay," Alex said. But as she watched Sarah hesitate at the door, she was reminded of Darian's hesitation before he dismissed her. Something about it had bothered her. Her exhausted mind was just starting to comprehend why. "Can I ask you something, though?"

"Sure," Sarah replied with just a hint of reluctance.

"Do you ever interact with humans? Do you let humans know you exist?"

"Well, you know about us now," Sarah said. Her lips spread into a soft smile that never reached her eyes.

Alex didn't need any more of an answer than Sarah's expression. She hid her shaking hands under the covers.

"Right," she said with her own forced smile, trying to match Sarah's tone. "Well, goodnight, or good morning, I guess."

"Are you sure you don't want me to stay with you?"

"No, thank you, though, for everything."

Sarah examined Alex for a moment, then nodded. Before she left, however, she turned back to address Alex one last time.

"You're at the end of the hall. If you go right, you'll walk past Markus's room, then the office you were in earlier. The last door before the stairs is Darian and my bedroom. Sage and Rocky have rooms in the basement. They may try to work through the morning, but by noon or so everyone will probably be asleep. We're sound sleepers during the midday, so it's not easy to wake us," Sarah paused. "I thought that might be helpful . . . in case you need anything." With that, Sarah shut the door behind her. Alex's heartbeat eventually slowed and exhaustion overcame her.

Alex awoke after a bad dream. She knew she had been sad and maybe scared, but she couldn't remember why. As she began to open her eyes and take in the room Sarah had settled her in last night, it occurred to her she had awoken from one bad dream into another. Only, though she didn't want to, she was beginning to accept that this current situation was actually her new reality.

Had it been less than twenty-four hours since she had left behind her work responsibilities and headed out for a run? It seemed like in those few short hours her whole life had turned upside down. And something was tugging at her brain. There was a crucial piece of information she was supposed to remember regarding her circumstances, and it had nothing to do with escaping her schoolwork.

Escaping. Alex cursed. What time was it? Sarah had informed her, quite discretely, exactly how and when to get away. Alex believed Darian and the others didn't want to hurt her. But she was also positive, especially after her brief conversation with Sarah, that she would not be allowed to leave knowing what she knew: vampires existed and were living in her city. The best she could hope was they'd figure out a way to use her 'gift,' as they seemed to think it was. Then she would be kept alive, but used against her will to serve them. She had been too independent for too long to be okay with that, even if it meant understanding her sense better. If they wanted to figure her out, that was fine, but they'd have to do it on her terms, in her world.

As she tried to sit up, the pain in both her head and side was excruciating.

Suck it up, she told herself. She would just have to make it outside. She could see the bright sunlight trying to peek out from behind the thick, lined, burgundy curtains and knew she could find the strength to make it to the front door. Convincing herself of that, she attempted to stand. She staggered a bit, using the nightstand to steady herself. Her calf throbbed, but she tried to pretend it wasn't much worse than the time in college she ran the last mile of a 10K with a killer charley horse because the heat and previous night's partying had left her dehydrated. As she stumbled to the door, she tried to remember how she had felt crossing the finish line.

Before leaving she scanned the room for her sneakers, but they were nowhere to be seen. Thinking it was probably better, bare feet being quieter on the floor, she crept into the hall.

The upstairs was laid out as Sarah had said. Her room was at the end of a hall that, at the far side, led to the wide staircase leading down to the foyer. The first door, Markus's, was closed, so she could softly tread farther, remaining on the center runner rather than risking the potentially squeaky hardwood floor closer to the wall. The next door was the office she had been in earlier that evening. She began to panic when she realized the door was slightly ajar and a light still shone from behind the desk. But as she moved closer, she couldn't see or otherwise detect anyone, so she hurried past, as fast as her injuries allowed.

At the final door, she paused. The heavy wooden door was closed tight, leaving a clear path to the top of the stairs, a clear path to escape. But she stopped a moment to say a silent thank you to Sarah. Alex hoped Sage wouldn't read the kind vampire's thoughts after she left and discover Sarah had helped her. She sensed only kindness and pure intentions from the female, and wished her well as she started her painful descent down the stairs.

There were a few creaky steps. Every old farmhouse, as Alex realized this was, had those few treacherous stairs that made it impossible for sneaky teens to get past lightly sleeping fathers. But Sarah had said they were heavy sleepers, at least at midday. Alex prayed it was still early afternoon, but as every window was heavily curtained, it was impossible to tell. The foyer, into which she had just stepped, had no windows in or around the door, making it almost completely dark.

Alex examined the door; it had a dead bolt in addition to the regular lock. Searching the walls around it, she saw no signs of an alarm. Well, they were vampires. She supposed an alarm in addition to fangs, mind-reading, and whatever else they were capable of was probably overkill.

She crept the last few feet, feeling her spirits soar as she closed in on freedom and safety. As she stepped out onto the wrap-around porch and shut the door quietly behind her, she half expected someone to jump up and snatch her. No one did.

She stumbled, quicker now, not caring how loud her footsteps were. Finally she hobbled down the three wooden steps that put her onto the sunny lawn. Her elation was short-lived.

Two things caught her off guard and sent her heart racing again. First, she was nowhere near the city anymore. In fact, scanning her surroundings, she couldn't see the nearest house. The farmhouse style was apparently genuine; Alex found herself on an old farm. There was a barn to the left of the house. It had been repaired, possibly completely rebuilt; the fresh boards showed no signs of rot, and the grey and white paint job was pristine. To either side of the two buildings were large grassy fields, fenced-in naturally on all three sides by woods made up of pines and oaks. There were a few trees along the long winding gravel drive as well, which obscured the view to the road—a road she was sure had no public busses or taxis. She was completely out of her element here.

The second shock was the approximate time of day. Though it was plenty bright, she knew from the sun's position in the sky and the soft orange tint of the light that it was well past midday. She guessed it was closer to early evening. Since it was mid-June, she hoped it would still give her a few hours to get away. But the long winding exit and lack of nearby neighbors had her trying desperately to run over the sharp rocks of the driveway.

Rocky heard the click, followed by the beep, whose pitch had been purposely set too high for a human to hear, and dropped the spoon that was halfway to his mouth.

"No freakin' way."

He had been in the kitchen starting in on his first bowl of Trix when he guessed he had half fallen asleep. As a young vamp who required less daytime rest, he was almost always up before the others, but today Darian had kept them up most of the morning researching Seers, whatever the hell those were. Rocky wasn't well versed in his own species' history, thanks to having had a father who would rather have conversed with humans than his own son. He had spent the morning mostly getting in the way again. Some days he wondered why Darian and the others bothered with him. And he had the feeling they wondered it even more frequently.

But as he flashed into the foyer, knocking aside the picture that partially hid the alarm, he felt he might have a shot at proving his usefulness today. The others had the strength and knowledge that came with having been around a few centuries, but being twenty-four had one advantage. He wouldn't be a prisoner to the sun for another six or seven decades. He slammed the panic button to alert the others as he bolted out the front door.

He spotted her halfway down the driveway. If he hadn't been a bit irritated, a bit sympathetic, and entirely determined to recapture her, he would have stopped to laugh. She was attempting to run, he guessed one would call it. But between her injured leg, bare feet, and the effect the head injury was still having on her balance, she looked like a drunken firewalker. And the look she wore when she heard the alarm and turned to see him stride off the porch and across the sunny lawn was priceless. There was no need for him to move at full speed. She was going nowhere fast.

"Sage did warn you not to believe everything you read about us," he called out, deciding he would have a little fun with her. Alex stammered and continued to try retreating.

"Look, Ma, no flames!" Rocky held out his bare arms and laughed at his own lame joke.

"Please, just let me go," she implored. Alex seemed broken by the realization that her plan had been foiled. Rocky frowned sympathetically. He knew her fear was unwarranted, but understood not wanting to be held against her will.

"Sorry, Alex, but even if I wanted to, I couldn't." Rocky nodded toward the house where three other vampires stood watching from inside the doorway.

"They can't come out here, can they?" Alex asked.

Rocky raised an eyebrow. Did she really think he needed the others to help him? He was young, and sometimes stupid, but he wasn't completely incompetent.

"Any day now, Rocky," Sage called out. Alex squinted back at him.

"There are perks to being young," Rocky answered Alex's question, bringing her attention back to him. "Not that it would kill them, not instantly, but it would do some serious damage, which is what they'll do to me if you don't come back in the house. I can carry you if you want. You look like you're struggling," he said with a smile.

"Fine," Alex sighed, letting him approach.

Probably plucking her plan from her head, Sage called out a warning. "Rocky, watch—"

Too late. Alex kicked Rocky in the groin for the second time in less than two days. Lucky for him, but unfortunate for her, not having a strong leg to brace herself with meant she couldn't strike too hard. She managed to knock herself on her ass on the small sharp stones. They both let out a grunt of pain, but Rocky recovered first.

"You have got to stop doing that!" he snarled at her and with a rough jerk had her on her feet and off them again in an instant. But he was not cradling her gently as he had the night before. He had thrown her over his shoulder, facing her forward so he could use his free hand to hold her wrists, keeping her from thrashing at him.

"Put me down! You're hurting me!"

"Yeah, tell it to my nuts," Rocky growled cruising across the lawn.

"I hate you!" Alex spit at him.

"You know, until about thirty seconds ago, I was actually starting to like you, despite the fact you bit me and kicked me once before. If you would be patient enough to let us explain why we've kept you here," he said crossing the porch already, "you would realize we are probably doing you a favor." He meant it, too, all of it. He had admired her strength from the beginning, and found her funny the previous night. But the fact she either didn't realize they had saved her, or didn't appreciate it, was aggravating.

As they entered the foyer, Markus, Darian, and Sage backed into the semi-darkness, blinking like a flash had gone off in their eyes.

"Did he just lecture someone on patience?" Sage muttered to Markus.

"Incredible, huh?" Markus said. Rocky tried not to sneer at the leader of the warriors, but found it trying.

Darian was not in the mood for the light banter. "Upstairs, now," he ordered.

"Your office?" Rocky clarified. He doubted Darian would put her back in her room without a friendly chat, but figured he should ask.

"Put me down first. I can walk," Alex demanded, though her voice was breathy. Rocky dropped her on her feet, not bothering to take into account her injuries or her size.

"You're in no position to be giving orders," Darian shouted too late. At the Regan's words Rocky adjusted his hold on her hands, so he was holding them behind her back. He looked up at Darian to see if this would suffice. Darian was already starting up the stairs, stomping despite his bare feet.

"Move." Rocky pushed Alex from behind, but she didn't respond. Her face had gone white. She staggered, Rocky's grasp possibly the only thing keeping her upright.

Markus approached, sniffing the air. "Regan, she's bleeding again. Probably popped a stitch."

Darian stopped halfway to the landing and spun around. He was starting to comment on how little he cared, when Sarah came out of the bedroom, pulling her hair back in an elastic band.

"Let me look at it," she said. In a soothing gesture she brushed her hand along her mate's arm as she passed.

Hoping not to give anything away, Alex averted her eyes. If she had the opportunity later, she would apologize for messing up, oversleeping, not asking where her shoes were. It was a good try, and Sarah's information was almost enough to make it work.

"Rocky, hold her—gently. Alex, can you lift your shirt up, please?" Sarah was all business, also avoiding eye contact with Alex.

Suddenly a sense of disbelief broke through Alex's pain. She looked up to see Sage glance at Sarah and then her, in a move the others couldn't miss. He must have realized he had given them away. He dropped his gaze to the tile floor as Alex's heart dropped to her stomach.

"What?" Darian demanded, looking protectively to his mate.

"Nothing. Not that, for sure," Sage answered.

"Tell me, Sage, now."

Alex was careful not to look at him, but in her head she was screaming, *Please, no, Sage. She was just trying to help me. She didn't really know I'd try it. Please don't tell him. She's been good to me.*

"Alex was just thinking how kind Sarah had been. She feels safe around her. She seems to know Sarah keeps us calmer at times."

Well, that was true. Alex was glad he hadn't had to lie.

"I try," Sarah said, glancing up at Alex, from where she knelt examining her stitches.

"I know," Alex whispered back. Then she added a dozen silent thank-yous to Sage.

Darian seemed drowsy enough to buy it, and Sage's comment, as well as Sarah and Alex's exchange, seemed to abate his fury.

"The stitches are all intact, the wound was just too fresh to withstand being jostled. I can put on a fresh bandage and rewrap it tightly, and she should be fine," Sarah told him.

"Does it need to be done now?"

"It should be," Sarah said standing up and facing him with one hand on her hip. Despite the kindness she had shown, Alex was beginning to appreciate that Sarah could be a formidable female.

"Does it need to be?" Darian asked again, undaunted by her.

"No," Sarah said curtly, replacing the original bandage and letting Alex know she could drop the shirt. She started back up the stairs, stopping one step above Darian. She leaned over with such speed and intensity he staggered. "But before you take out your anger on her," Sarah said, "remember who made the decision to send her off to bed with more questions than answers, and who, vastly underestimating the woman's strength and will power, decided not to have anyone guard her. And finally, think about what you would want your own mate to do. What if *I* were being held against *my* will?" Sarah didn't wait for an answer as she stormed up the last few stairs and slammed the bedroom door shut behind her.

With Markus and Rocky on either side and Sage behind, just in case, they made a slow but steady procession up the stairs and into the office. Markus led Alex to the couch, where she sat, her injured leg up on the cushion, the other on the floor. She ran her fingers over the plaid pattern, not meeting anyone's gaze.

"You may leave," Darian addressed the others. "Go have breakfast. I'll call if I want you." Not one of them spoke as they exited, though Markus paused by the door like wanted to say something. Sage shut it in front of him. Darian walked behind the desk, stopping to lean over and grip the lacquered top so hard Alex half expected the wood to crack. When he spoke his voice was strained from trying to keep it controlled.

"I don't say this often, but Rocky was right. He and Sage stopped you from being abducted or killed last night. My mate and coven member tended to your wounds. I kept my warriors up half the day researching, trying to find answers to your questions. I trusted you enough to treat you as a guest. And you sneak out hoping to burn us, pun intended, and attack the male trying to bring you back to safety." Darian's voice showed little control as he continued, his volume rising with his anger. "You're an ungrateful, impatient, deceitful little twerp. And until you prove otherwise, you'll be treated as such. If you can't act like a guest, you can be treated like a prisoner."

Alex's own anger flared. She hated being treated like a child by others who thought their greater size and strength made them superior. Moreover, she hated hypocrisy.

"Too bad you're not human; you'd make a great politician. You can spin anything to make yourself look rosy, can't you?" she started. "Rocky got in my way of escaping that alley, causing me to get stabbed in the leg. Sage nearly bashed in my skull. My wounds were tended to so you could question me, because, really, you're more interested in figuring me out than I am. Probably because I can be of some twisted use to you and your band of bloodsucking fiends. If we're into name-calling, *Regan*, you're a cocky, conniving, bullying son of a bitch."

Darian let out a snarl that had Alex's hair standing up, but she would be damned if she would back down. Her own anger, mixed with what she sensed of his, surged through her.

She somehow managed to get to her feet and spit at him, "Flash your fangs at someone who cares!"

Darian grabbed a solid glass paperweight the size of a baseball off his desk with such speed that Alex hardly had time to register the blur of movement, never mind react. She flinched, bracing herself for impact. Instead of pain, a loud colorful series of curses came from behind her. In another blur, Markus was suddenly standing in front of the Regan, while Sage, still shaking out his left hand, sauntered across the room holding the glass ball in his right. He stopped beside Alex.

"I know you don't want to die, woman, so you really don't want to continue this argument." He pushed her shoulders, just enough to knock her back onto the couch. "And you don't actually want to kill her, Regan," Sage said as he approached the desk and replaced the paperweight. "I don't even think you meant to break my hand."

Darian glowered at him. "I was aiming for the door. Had you obeyed my order to stay downstairs—"

"We'd be replacing the door, best case scenario," Markus said calmly. "Instead, I thought we could volunteer to take the first shift of watching her."

Darian took a deep breath, and stared Markus down. The warrior held his ground. So Darian replied, addressing Markus and Sage, ignoring Alex's presence. "Fine, but let me lay down the ground rules. She is not to be allowed near a phone or computer. She is not to leave the guest room unless physically escorted, and she is not to leave your sight."

"What am I, thirteen again?" Alex snapped.

"If you were thirteen, I'd—" Darian began, his jaw set. With a sneer, he finished, "Well, I'd likely be having this conversation with your older brothers, which I'm sure would be much more pleasant."

Alex's breath caught in her chest. It was hard to say whose face portrayed more shock, as Alex, Markus, and even Sage, all looked at the Regan in disbelief at the cruelty of his reply. He spun from their accusing glares, and with his back to them added his final blow.

"And she's not to be alone with Sarah."

"You bastard!" Alex shouted in frustration, her voice on the verge of cracking. "You know I wouldn't hurt or betray Sarah. You're trying to punish me, when really you're just pissed at your own poor decisions."

He turned back to face her. "As humans of your generation love to say: Your point?"

"Fu—" A hand clamped over her mouth. She should have realized from the connection between them it was Sage, but she was too wrapped up in her own emotions to register his.

"You're right. He's just angry," Sage whispered, pulling her to the door. "Let it go for now. We'll talk to him when he calms down."

Alex let Sage pull her from the room as Markus followed and closed the door behind them. Once in the hall, Sage removed his hand and let Markus step in. Markus cupped her elbow, to help her stay on her feet. She welcomed the gentle touch but was too upset to enjoy it.

"Would you like something to eat before we take you back?" Markus asked.

Alex shook her head. "Just bed," she said, unable to form a complete sentence without breaking into sobs. At least there, even with them watching, she could have the privacy of muffling her crying with the pillows and covering her tears with the sheets.

Markus and Sage said nothing as they slowly walked her back down the hall that had so recently served as an escape route. But the compassion she sensed—she knew—they felt was comforting, so much so that Alex, without looking at him, reached out her arm to Sage. Hearing what she wanted, he touched her forearm allowing his emotions to drown out her own.

In bed, away from Sage and Markus's touch, Alex's emotions rushed back at her like a quickly rising tide, threatening to drown her with their strength and depth. The tears came, as she knew they would, but the reasons for them changed with each sob she worked to keep silent. She was angry with Darian, both for his cruelty and his lack of understanding. Had he really expected she would stay willingly? She was angry with herself for failing, but also for ever thinking she could succeed. And she was scared, not just because it seemed her life was in danger, but also because her survival and future seemed to hinge on her having some kind of power or ability that she had forced herself to deny for years.

Accepting that what she did was out of the ordinary meant accepting that what she thought she knew of the world was wrong. This was hard to grasp, but as she had been surviving the last eighteen hours under the new knowledge that vampires existed, it somehow seemed feasible—assuming, of course, she wasn't suffering a psychotic break. What was harder to grasp was how her knowledge of herself could have been so limited for so long. Alex had worked through some difficult times during her adolescence. Even more than most teens, perhaps, she had struggled with her sense of self, but she had come into her own eventually and never thought she would return to a time when she would once again feel so unsure, so tormented by her own identity.

As her sobs subsided, she began to realize she was angry with herself for one more reason. Despite logically knowing it was a stupid, dangerous desire, she wanted to know the truth more than she wanted to leave.

Chapter 4

It seemed like hours before Alex managed to cry herself into an exhaustion so deep sleep finally overtook her. She had tried admirably to hide her crying from them, biting at the pillow and covering her face with the sheet. Neither Markus nor Sage had informed her they could discern even her most muffled sobs with their enhanced hearing. With a bit of bewilderment Markus became conscious of his breathing slowing in time with hers. He hadn't realized how anxious he felt watching her suffer. As a warrior, Markus had witnessed the pain of too many victims, vampire and human. Like any soldier, he had learned to rein in his sympathies to focus on the job at hand. But this human was testing that control. He was drawn to her. And unlike the others, Markus was in awe of her due to the inner strength she exuded, not because of her unusually strong essence. And he was intrigued not by any ability, or gift, she may or may not possess, but by her ability to make him feel emotions he thought he had permanently repressed.

It dawned on him that Sage was watching him curiously. He sighed. His friend liked to delude himself and the others in the house into believing he actually tried to stay out of their private thoughts, but Markus knew Sage was as nosy as an old biddy. Sage scowled at this thought and turned away. Markus attempted to redirect his attention to someone other than Alex. After a moment he turned to Sage, who quietly answered the unspoken question.

"Yes, he's feeling like a prick, but he really ought to be feeling worse, so by all means, go remind him of it."

Markus smiled. "That's what friends are for."

He didn't bother to knock, but rather entered the room silently and sat in one of the chairs across from Darian's desk. Darian was seated behind it, his head in both hands so that his chin-length hair curtained his face. Markus would have liked to feel sympathy for him, but after listening to Alex cry herself to sleep, none came.

"Can I talk to you, as a friend?"

Darian looked up and sighed. "You mean, will I not rip your fangs out for telling me I'm everything Alex accused me of and worse? That I clearly don't have the essence worthy of an amoeba, never mind a Regan? Yeah, go for it."

Markus sat waiting for Darian to continue. It was clear from his tortured face he didn't need Markus to confirm any of this. Markus had known Darian long enough to know that underneath the pompous façade the Regan was aware of his shortcomings. Markus and Sage, being the only two members of the coven Darian thought of as friends and not just subjects, might have gotten away with reminding him of those shortcomings now and again, but it was better, safer, to let him get there on his own.

"I was so frustrated when she realized I was either going to use her or . . . I don't know what I'll do if she's not a Seer."

Markus sucked in a sharp breath. He knew as well as Darian what their only option would be. *Darian's* option—he'd take no part in it. He wasn't even sure he could stand by and allow the Regan to do it. Though interfering would lose him his position, possibly his freedom. He hoped to hell it didn't come to that.

"And I'm not even pissed she knew. It's clear she's smart enough to have figured it out sooner or later. I'm angry because I don't want to force her either way. But I'm in as much of a corner as she is." Darian paused and looked up. Markus knew he wanted the comfort that came with confirmation. He nodded so Darian knew he understood.

"I don't mind giving orders to you guys, because if even you don't like the particular order, you chose to serve me and your coven," Darian continued. "But Alex doesn't have a choice. Either she serves us and we protect her, or she leaves and is killed, or worse, by the Others."

"You really think she could be a Seer? And you think the Vengatti already know?"

"Yes, to both. But I don't want to tell her more than I have to until I know for sure," Darian replied.

Markus disagreed with not telling Alex everything up front, but he kept that opinion quiet for now. "But you do have to apologize," he said instead, knowing it was an equally unpopular suggestion. "If we want her to willingly serve us, or at least to realize we're protecting her so she'll stop attempting to run, *you* need to earn back *her* trust and respect."

Darian sighed. Markus was throwing back his own words at him, which he may not have liked, but seemed to agree with.

"I know apologies aren't taught in the Regan line," Markus added with just the hint of a smile, "but you dealt some low blows, so now you've got to suck it up. I found groveling worked well with Alia," Markus finished, shooting him a knowing glance.

"You're telling me to apologize and grovel to two females in one night?" Darian asked.

"Well, it sounded like you were a bit out of your league earlier," Markus said referring to the fight he and Sage had heard between Darian and Sarah shortly after bringing Alex to bed.

"You heard that, huh? Being mated in a house full of other vampires really robs a male of his dignity."

Markus raised an eyebrow at Darian. "Buddy, you didn't have much dignity to begin with this afternoon. Besides, who needs enhanced hearing when sitting next to Sage?"

"Do I need to remind him he doesn't get paid extra for play-by-play commentary?" Darian asked, in slightly better spirits.

"Why bother, he hears, but he doesn't listen."

"But you obviously forget I *can* do both from anywhere in the house," Sage spoke from down the hall. He didn't need to speak loudly; they could all clearly hear each other.

"We didn't forget; we just don't care," Markus called back.

"And bring Alex back when she's awake and has had a chance to eat and clean up," Darian said.

"On it. She's awake, though she's pretending she's not."

Markus and Darian exchanged a look and both shook their heads. For someone who could read thoughts, Sage could be extra oblivious to the needs of others.

"For Creator's sake, Sage, let her pretend in peace," Markus whispered, so Sage could hear, but hoping Alex could not. "Don't remind her she'll never have privacy again."

"Too late," Alex's groggy voice could be heard followed by a soft thud. Markus grinned as Sage complained from the other room.

"What is it with people throwing things at me today?"

"At least Alex only throws pillows," Markus said, but, as he finished, a louder thud was heard. "I retract that. Sounds like she found her sneakers."

"Hey, Little Miss Transferred Aggression, save the other shoe—the male you really want is two doors down," Sage could be heard telling her.

Darian rolled his eyes, but as he heard Alex attempting to make her way down the hall, Markus crossed his arms over his chest and glared at him. It seemed Darian needed a reminder of Markus's earlier advice.

Not until she stood in the doorway, seeing Darian and Markus both looking at her, did it occur to Alex that she ought to be embarrassed to be seen. The t-shirt and sweats Sarah had lent her were rumpled from the various fits of sleeping she had done in them. The seat of her pants she could only guess was dirty from falling in the driveway, and her shirt had a stain on it from where her reopened wound had bled through the bandage. With her bed-head hair and puffy red eyes, she imagined she was the picture of splendor. This sudden awareness left her fumbling with her second sneaker, which she guessed Sarah had left by her bed while she slept.

"I'd give you a free shot," Darian said, unsuccessfully stifling a laugh, "but I'm guessing, by which hand you broke punching Sage, you're a lefty. If you tried lobbing that at me, you're likely to hit Markus, who is probably the only one of us who doesn't deserve it. He brought you your shoes. He also called your work so they wouldn't worry or think you played hooky."

Alex peeked at Markus again and involuntarily blushed.

"Is it customary for humans to use their boss as an emergency contact?" Sage asked coming up behind her and gesturing for her to enter the office.

Alex looked away from Markus and began comprehending what Darian had said. As she did, her annoyance with Darian's continued inability to be honest about his motivations returned. As if having Markus call wasn't intended to keep her friends and coworkers from looking for her.

Her tone was tense again as she answered Sage. "He's a friend, too." As she addressed Markus, though, she dialed down her anger. "It was the last day of school; I'd never call in. What did you tell him?"

"That you had met up with friends from college late last night, and as you were driving home, you were in a car accident. You were treated at the community hospital and were going to be released into a friend's care this evening," Markus replied, having the decency to have a twinge of guilt in his voice.

"How did you know I went to a nearby college?" Alex asked, but then remembered the outfit she had had on when she had been attacked. "My running shorts?" The black mesh shorts had her Alma mater's insignia on the right thigh.

"Yes," Markus answered.

Alex thought about Peter whose protectiveness she had rebuffed the night before. He had been clingy and possessive even after they broke up, but she knew it stemmed from genuine feelings for her. Despite how he aggravated her some days, he had become a good friend. Actually, he was one of Alex's only friends.

After her brothers died and her family fell apart, Alex found she had little tolerance for the petty squabbles and superficiality of girls her own age. Besides, teenage girls are teeming with emotion, and as Alex's sense first developed, it was hard to be around too many of them at once. If she had to be around people, she found comfort in the more muted emotions of males. So she had spent her evenings and weekends at the karate dojo, where she was usually the only female in a room full of focused, disciplined adult men.

In college, when she decided to become an education major, she knew she'd have to immerse herself in classes dominated by young women. But, as a whole, she found teachers to be compassionate and dedicated, without being overly dramatic, so they were relatively easy to be around. Still, she stuck to single dorm rooms and often gravitated toward the guys in her classes, not to flirt, but to be able to have open straightforward conversations.

She wondered how her vice principal and friend would take the news she had been in a car accident. Would it occur to him, who knew her family's past, how exceptionally hard it would be for her to recover from the emotional trauma of that? She hoped he wouldn't worry too much over the concocted story, as he was supposed to be heading off to enjoy the first days of his vacation.

"Wait—" something clicked in Alex's brain. "You told Peter I was driving home when I had the accident?" Even if he believed she had gone out after her run, he'd never buy this fact.

"Yes," Markus replied, confused by her sudden change in expression.

Alex laughed triumphantly. She was no longer determined to escape, but was defiant enough to enjoy this mistake. "Perfect. I didn't need to attempt to leave after all."

"Shit." Sage turned to Markus and Darian who still looked confused. "She doesn't drive. Never even got a license. He knows that because they dated. And he left work with her last night." Alex could tell he was pissed she had been able to hide that from him. She smirked.

Darian asked with annoyance, "What woman your age doesn't drive?"

Alex's fury returned tenfold at the Regan's thoughtless remark. "One whose two brothers died in a car crash, asshole."

"Smooth, Darian. What happened to apologizing and groveling?" Sage asked. Markus shook his head incredulously.

Darian squeezed his eyes and scrunched his face. Alex wondered for a moment if he'd have the audacity to get angry with them. But as his chin dropped to his chest, she felt his wave of guilt.

"I'm truly sorry, Alex. I forgot."

"That must be nice," she said softly.

The three males were silent for a moment. Alex refused to speak and end their discomfort. Darian realized Sage and Markus were looking for him to continue.

"If you'd like, after you've eaten and cleaned up, you can call him and allay his concerns."

"You mean I can lie to him, so he'll think all is well, so you can hold me here without anyone knowing enough to come looking for me?" Alex snarled. He was doing it again, dealing in half-truths to make himself feel better about his actions.

He surprised her when he answered, "That's part of it, yes."

"Finally, an honest answer."

"But I did also think it might make you feel better knowing he wouldn't call and scare your parents with the news you'd been hurt in a crash when he didn't hear from you. I am sorry. Had I thought more about it, I would have had Markus tell him something different," Darian added.

Alex made her way to the couch and sat down. She hadn't thought of this, but now it worried her to think of how her mother would handle such news. She wasn't particularly close to her parents, but she loved them and didn't want them to suffer unnecessarily. Her mother, especially, had suffered enough for one lifetime. Alex eventually looked up at Darian and scowled.

"I'll call. And I'll lie—for their sake, not yours. But in return I want answers, tonight."

Darian's jaw was tense. Apparently he wasn't used to receiving demands, but eventually he nodded. "Deal."

There was quiet for another minute, before Markus cleared his throat.

"Right, ah, I also wanted to apologize for some of what I said earlier," Darian began.

"Some?" Alex questioned. Markus and Sage smiled; she couldn't tell whether it was at her pluck or his inability to fully apologize. She really hoped it was the latter.

"Yes, some, because, though you were right about me not being totally honest about our motivations, some of what I said was true. Rocky and Sage did want to save you, despite the roughness of their actions."

Alex looked to Sage who lost the grin and shrugged. It was Darian's turn to clear his throat.

"Oh, yeah," Sage began after catching on or reading Darian's thoughts, "I'm sorry, too, I guess, about the whole knocking you unconscious thing."

Alex had to laugh a little at both males' incompetence when it came to admitting their faults. It seemed the human and vampire species had more in common than people might imagine.

"I was also being honest when I said we are keeping you here to—well, partly to keep you safe," Darian continued.

Alex didn't exactly understand what he meant, and from the grave tone his voice had suddenly taken, she wasn't sure she wanted to, but she sensed he genuinely believed what he said.

"Thank you, for finally being honest and for being man enough to apologize in front of your friends." Alex knew, from her own experience with men, positive reinforcement worked as well with them as it did with children, meaning minimally, but she figured it couldn't hurt.

"Well, the term 'man enough' is only a loose translation," Sage started, "and he's still got one more of these to go tonight. We'll see how he fares with that one."

Markus and Sage chuckled, while Darian glowered. When he noticed Alex's confusion though, he explained.

"It seems my mate has taken a great liking to you. So much so she's refusing to speak to me until I 'get my head out of my—' Well, she only swears every half century or so, which tells you how furious she was. So, yes, I'll need to repeat this pleasant experience when she returns."

"If she returns," Sage mumbled with a grin.

"She left?" Alex had been enraged by Darian, but even then would not have wanted anything to upset Sarah so much. She felt even greater loyalty to the female after hearing this.

"No, no," Darian corrected. He glared at Sage, before continuing. "She just went to get my father, the Elder Regan. He's going to help us tonight. They should be here by ten or so. Why don't you have breakfast and freshen up."

Alex was beginning to feel better after clearing the air and knowing she would get more answers soon. As she got up to leave she turned to Darian and said sincerely, "Thank you."

He nodded and turned to Markus, "Have her back here by 9:30, please."

"I still need an escort?" Alex asked in disbelief, her calm evaporating as quickly as it had come. She didn't know where to go in the house on her own, and she certainly didn't object to the particular escort Darian assigned her, but the implication that she required one aggravated her.

"Sorry, but that decision I am not revoking."

Alex let out a huff and attempted to storm, rather than hobble, out of the room.

Darian was circling the office for the countless time since Markus had escorted Alex back. Rocky and Sage stood together near the door watching the procession. Sage seemed to find humor in it, but as Alex watched Rocky try to surreptitiously bite his nails, she guessed he was uncomfortable, either with Darian's mood or with the idea of the soon-to-arrive guest. Sitting in one of the chairs in front of the desk, Markus looked calm and alert as usual. He had been a charming guard over the last two hours, ignoring a few of Darian's initial mandates to allow Alex some privacy as she washed and changed. She'd never admit it to Darian, but Alex was almost glad he had ordered the supervision. Like Sarah, Markus had a calm demeanor, which had provided Alex a short spell of solace. Solace that had evaporated instantly when she walked into the thick tension of Darian's office.

Alex was once again experiencing a torrent of emotions ranging from annoyance at still being treated like Darian's prisoner, or at least a scolded puppy, to intense curiosity about what she might learn about herself in the next few hours. As this emotion began to drown out the rest, she wished she, too, had the strength to pace the room, as her impatience needed a form of relief.

"He's late, as usual," Darian complained as he turned at the door, heading back across the carpet towards his desk.

Markus had been looking in that general direction but seemed to be focused on something else. "Actually, Regan, I think—" he began, trying to alert Darian to what he and the others, even Alex, heard. Darian cut him off.

"I call on him maybe twice a year. You'd think he could come when I asked," he huffed.

"Just as one might think a father and Elder Regan of the coven might be shown a smidge of respect from his only son?" Ardellus spoke as he entered the room. His tone wasn't angry, but never the less it demanded respect. Alex watched as the older gentleman crossed the room with perfect confidence and an air of dignity that seemed out of place in the world she knew. His tweed suit jacket was perfectly tailored, and there wasn't a crease in his khaki pants, despite the long car ride. Alex recognized the brown wavy hair he shared with his son, though Ardellus's was shorter and speckled with grey. As Markus stood and he, Rocky, and Sage bowed to the Elder Regan, she felt for a moment, as if she had been transferred to some royal society in which she didn't belong. Before her nerves kicked in too much, though, Sarah entered the room behind him and flashed Alex a warm smile.

Darian swore under his breath. "Sorry, Father, it's been a long night already. I was just venting." Alex smiled back at Sarah. She knew they shared the same enjoyment watching Darian squirm in his father's presence. Sarah returned a quick wink.

"No need to make excuses for your lack of control. I raised you and trained you, after all. I am as aware of your faults as I am my own," Ardellus said sitting next to Alex without invitation. He motioned to Markus and Darian to sit as well. Darian paused for a moment. The internal struggle over whether to comment was evident on his face. Ardellus didn't wait for him to sit or speak before continuing. "If you called on me more often, perhaps I would leave a bag packed, so when you sent *Sarah* to pick me up, I'd be ready."

"A bag?" Darian said with no pretense of politeness. He turned to Sarah.

"Yes. I invited the Elder Regan to stay with us a few days. You won't likely have everything sorted out right away, and he shouldn't be shuttled back and forth so much. Besides, he hasn't visited overnight since the winter holidays." Sarah smiled at him. Alex had the notion this was one way Sarah was exacting revenge after their earlier fight. She rubbed her nose to hide her smile. Darian grimaced, then tried to recover a straight face before addressing his father.

"Of course, I mean, you're always welcome. It's just that the guest room is already occupied and—"

"Markus was gracious enough to give up his room for a few nights. I asked him before I left," Sarah said. "I'm going to go get things set up now." Flashing Darian a final smile that seemed a bit like a sneer, she turned on her heels and left the office, closing the door behind her.

Darian shot a look at Markus. It was clear to Alex, who sensed his annoyance, that Darian was unhappy with his warrior's act of omission by forgetting to relay this information to him. But Markus seemed to misread the reason for the look, so instead of apologizing, he confirmed.

"I'll crash on the couch in the basement office."

"No," Darian corrected, "Rocky can take the couch. You can take Rocky's room." Alex glanced to Rocky to see what his reaction to this would be. He was scuffing his left boot on the hardwood and didn't look up.

"There's no sense in moving us both, Darian," Markus said.

Darian glanced at Ardellus. "I've made my decision," he said leaning over his desk to get in Markus's face. Markus raised an eyebrow but remained silent. Alex could sense the growing tension from all of them.

"Let's all tone down the testosterone, shall we?" she cut in, impatient and annoyed with the masculine face-off. "I'll move down to the basement. If I'm here as your prisoner still, then we can drop the pretenses. Add some deadbolts and bars down there and make it official."

"Actually—" Rocky started, but stopped when Sage elbowed him hard in the ribs. Her words had achieved the desired effect, however. All eyes turned to her. Ardellus seemed to study her as he looked at her directly for the first time. After an awkward moment of quiet, during which Alex did her best to maintain eye contact with her examiner, Ardellus turned back to Darian, seemingly upset.

"Prisoner?"

"We had an incident this afternoon. She's being watched for her own safety," Darian explained. Alex didn't try to hide her exaggerated eye roll.

"Then you will be her guardian, not her warden," Ardellus said. He waited as though he expected a response, and when he got none, he pushed the issue. "Darian," he said in a tone Alex recognized as one a teacher or parent used when demanding agreement from a child. She wanted to laugh as Darian's face flushed with anger and humiliation, but sensing his emotions unwillingly sent a wave of sympathy through her.

"Am I—" Darian began. He obviously wanted to remind his father who was in charge, but something made him stop. Alex couldn't quite sense whether it was intimidation, or respect, or perhaps a bit of each. "Sometimes they come to one and the same, Elder," Darian finished firmly.

Focusing again on his words, rather than his emotions, Alex bristled at this statement. Ardellus saw her indignation and frowned slightly.

"In actions, I suppose," he conceded, "but not in intent. For a coven to imprison its Seer would be disgraceful, especially when she is so close to maturity."

Everyone in the room started in with questions and comments. Alex tried to make it clear she did not belong to any coven and had reached maturity years ago, but was cut off by Ardellus, who with a mere hand gesture silenced the rest of them instantly. The abrupt silence took Alex off guard, so she too stopped to listen when the Elder spoke.

"My job is to advise the Regan," he began addressing the rest of them, all of whom started for the door except Alex, who remained seated, with her arms folded over her chest. There was no way she was going anywhere without answers.

"No, it's okay," Darian said to them, before turning to his father. "This has already affected our patrols, so Markus needs to be fully informed. And Sage might have some insight that will help."

"Your ward?" Ardellus said gesturing towards Rocky with obvious disdain.

"Will sit at the bottom of the stairs and listen in anyways," Darian returned, giving Rocky a small grin. Rocky shrugged and nodded guiltily.

"Glad to see he is controlling his strength and senses these days," Ardellus commented. Darian frowned. Alex was starting to see why Rocky had been anxious about the Elder's visit. She didn't know either of them or their history, but she was bothered by the contempt the older male so publicly displayed. She was pleased to see Darian trying to give Rocky an apologetic glance and sorry he didn't see it. He stood staring at the floor clenching his fists.

"As for the young woman, we will certainly want her close by to answer questions, but I think—" Ardellus began.

"She answered my questions last night. I promised her answers today," Darian said cutting him off.

"Certainly, but perhaps—"

"She stays, father, at least for awhile."

Alex nodded to Darian to show her appreciation. If he kept this up, she might end up liking him.

"As you wish, Regan." Ardellus said *Regan* with the same intonation Darian had used the title *Elder* to address his father. Neither had shown the respect Alex assumed each position usually commanded.

"But all of you will listen only, unless asked a question, or you will leave," Darian added looking first to Sage then Rocky. Finally, he turned to Alex, whom he must have felt needed specific instructions. "If you want answers, you will cooperate without the charades and without commentary. This information may be about you, but it is also about my coven, and I don't screw around where they're concerned, understood?"

"Yes," Alex answered, again feeling that reluctant respect for Darian as a leader. However, this didn't keep her from almost instantly interrupting. "Just one question before you start, though."

Darian looked annoyed, Ardellus amused.

"One," Darian agreed.

"Last night when everyone was saying coven, I was thinking it meant family or small group of . . . you know. But, I can sense your protectiveness and concern, and it seems like it involves more than the five, or six, of you," she corrected herself to include Ardellus.

"You can 'sense' it?" Darian asked sitting forward in his chair behind the desk.

Alex, realizing her word choice had set him off, corrected him. "No, not like Sage, just a vague sense. Like I said, just strong intuition." Darian looked doubtful. She felt he was becoming more intrigued by her by the moment. It worried her. Ardellus nodded, as if he expected such answers. This annoyed her.

"I don't want to go into all the details now, but, yes, it's a much larger group," Darian said answering her initial question, hoping to move on.

"And 'Regan,' that's a title. You're like the president of the vamps?" Alex asked, and then stopped. She was a little surprised by her own use of the word.

Darian smiled. Across the room Sage cursed. Ardellus and Alex both looked at him curiously as he pulled a twenty out of his pocket and handed it to Rocky, who grinned and winked at Alex. Darian shook his head, but turned to explain to his father and her.

"They took a bet on how long it would take you to say 'vampire.' Sage thought it would be at least twenty-fours hours."

Alex matched Rocky's grin, which seemed to annoy Sage more. She wasn't bothered by this, but tried to be fair. "Well, technically I only said vamp. Does that count?" she asked Darian. Sage was already trying to snatch back the bill, but Darian ruled.

"Close enough. And since you're suddenly so interested in learning about our world, you should know the term 'vamp' is considered crude."

Alex laughed aloud; the idea of being corrected on vampire etiquette was too much. "Good to know my knack for being crass transfers to your world so well," she told him. Darian scowled, apparently not appreciating her humor.

"And another thing," he began standing up, "Vampires don't believe in democracy. In my coven, which you are now a part of, I'm king."

Alex began to protest, informing him again she was not a part of anyone's coven. Darian probably would have continued the argument had Ardellus not spoken up.

"Alexandra." Alex stopped talking and turned to face him, her brows furrowed in confusion. "That is your full name, is it not?" Ardellus asked.

"Ah . . . yes, it is, but no one ever calls me that, and no one ever pronounces it correctly," Alex answered, referring to the fact he had pronounced the middle syllable as *ahn*, not *an*, as most Bay Staters did. She had spent her childhood being embarrassed by her father's need to correct everybody from teachers to strangers in the grocery store.

"Is that why you adopted the nickname?" Ardellus asked with genuine curiosity.

"No, I just prefer Alex." She wasn't in the mood to go into the power struggle she and her father had over what name she went by with another father who seemed to love control almost as much as her own had.

"As you wish, Alex." Ardellus seemed to know there was more to the story, but let it rest. "I know you must be very curious about us and our world, but there will be time to get those answers later. What I thought you would most want to know tonight is who you are."

"Yes, I do." Alex felt it cost her to admit this, as she was already struggling internally with this issue. Admitting that this stranger in front of her, a being who was not even human, could possibly know more about her than she did herself was difficult.

"Then let us start with everyone's first question," Ardellus said turning to Darian. "Yes, she is a Seer, Darian." The Regan began to protest, but his father stopped him. "You worry about them interrupting. You need to listen as well." He turned to Alex who was eager for an explanation. "Alex, Darian and the others are having a hard time accepting what their senses are telling them, because you are not the typical Seer. And because we are taught to rely on our histories, sometimes to the point it keeps us from accepting things that are new or unique." Ardellus could tell she was eager to interrupt and allowed her to ask her questions.

"What do you mean by Seer? What I can do isn't like the Seers from ancient mythology who could supposedly predict the future or whatever," Alex said with skepticism.

The others exchanged grins as Ardellus answered. "Vampires and our histories predate your 'ancient mythology,' Alex. And though some of those stories are based on actual vampires and Seers, they are just that: stories, which were embellished or altered to suit the humans and, more importantly, to protect the covens of the time."

Again Alex interrupted, this time without waiting for anybody's permission. "But those stories are about gods and goddesses, heroes, and magical creatures, not vampires and freakishly intuitive humans," she argued.

"They are about beings with preternatural strength, unbelievable speed, and senses beyond what humans could comprehend. Certainly you can see some similarities," Ardellus said with an understanding smile.

Alex's brain whirled. "Well, that's sure to put an interesting spin on my unit about Greek and Roman myths next year. My students might actually listen to that lecture."

Rocky laughed, but Darian was getting frustrated with the pace of the conversation. "Focus, Alex," he chastised.

"Right," she said trying to clear her head. "So what's a Seer, then, in your world?" She couldn't bring herself to say 'in the real world,' because somehow this world still didn't seem real.

"The short answer is a Seer is a human who can 'see' or feel others' emotions," Darian answered.

"Which means there's a long answer," Alex started, and waited for someone to continue. No one said anything. "Which obviously I'm not going to hear right now. Super." She glared accusingly at Darian.

"It's not that easy. Every Seer in our histories has been slightly different. The power to sense others' feelings is the only thing that has been perfectly consistent. You're sure to be unique, and it's too early to speculate how," Darian answered with a tone of finality.

Alex was feeling resentful, but she also still had many questions. She knew she would get nowhere butting heads with Darian, so she tried another course. "You mentioned they could all 'sense' me. Does that mean all vampires can do what I do?" she asked turning to Ardellus.

"No, Alex, you are the only Seer among us. Perhaps the only full-blooded Seer on earth, certainly the only one in this country." Darian and the others took in sharp breaths at Ardellus's comments. "Yes," he continued, "I did a little research myself during the daylight hours. I could not be entirely certain from what I found until I met her, but the strength of her essence confirms it. Surely, Sage, you must have felt it too?"

Sage shifted his weight and shrugged. "I didn't know what it meant," he admitted. "I've never met a Seer before."

Ardellus nodded. "Nor had I until today, but my father protected the last known Seer, and what he and the histories said are true. Your essence is strong and pure," he said to Alex. She wondered if this was some form of compliment that she was supposed to thank him for, but her confusion overrode her concern about being polite.

"What does that mean, exactly?"

Ardellus didn't seem offended by her question, so she supposed it was a legitimate one to ask. "It means you have a strong sense of self; you know who you are," he answered.

Alex scoffed. Clearly he was mistaken, since they were having this conversation.

"Not labels you give yourself, or even your own gifts, but who you really are, at your core. You have a deep knowledge of what is right and wrong, good and bad, and always you know when you stray from it."

Alex was shaken by the serious turn the conversation had taken. She was uncomfortable discussing her morality with anyone, never mind a group of vampires. She tried to change the tone. "Actually, my mother had a run-in with Catholicism for a few years when I was growing up. My dad eventually rescued my brothers and me from Sunday school, but the guilt was pretty ingrained by then," she quipped.

The others laughed, but Ardellus maintained a grim expression, not fooled by her tactic.

"It is not guilt, child, it is your anchor. When your powers mature you will be inundated with the emotions of others. You will soon sense others' pure, positive emotions: love, compassion, trust. But you will also sense others' less admirable sides—their lust, jealousy, greed, and hatred. If you cannot use that anchor to find yourself and separate out your feelings from those of others around you, others who may not be as good or pure as you, you will live a tortured life."

Chapter 5

The room was silent. Alex was shell-shocked. What Ardellus described was not the vague sense she often had of others' emotions. A sense that sometimes bothered her, but never to the degree she would describe it as torture. What he was describing implied her sense would soon intensify dramatically. She was jolted after a minute when she realized she had involuntarily been holding her breath. She tried rubbing her wrists, nervously twisting her usual array of cuff bracelets, as she often did when she was upset, but with her left arm braced it proved too difficult; she had no outlet. Instead her hands shook on her lap.

"He's not trying to frighten you, Alex," Darian said, his voice soft. He turned and looked daggers at his father.

"No, I am not," Ardellus answered the accusing glare. "But she needs to know the truth. All of it. If a healthy dose of fear will keep her focused in the next few weeks, so she can learn to control her powers before they mature, I am not opposed to scaring her. Besides, from what Sarah told me on the way over, she is quite a fighter. You will need that strength, Alex."

Alex continued to stare at her lap. She knew the strength he referred to was not the kind of which Sarah had spoken. Neither her defense skills nor her stubbornness would help her prepare for what Ardellus had described.

"What if I'm not that strong? What if I'm not that good or that pure?" she whispered. As he shook his head, she knew he didn't understand. Awkwardly, she used her injured hand to push back the bracelets she wore to cover her right wrist. The dozen thin white lines had faded and softened over the years, but she knew they would be as obvious to a vampire's enhanced vision as they were to the one who put them there.

Ardellus reached forward, closing the gap between them. He covered her wrist with his hands.

"You made those a long time ago." It was a statement, not a question, but Alex answered him anyway.

"After my brothers died, and my sense started getting stronger, and my father was falling apart. The pain helped to block it all out." Alex wanted to add that she had been too weak to handle her own emotions at the time, never mind those of others, but she couldn't voice what seemed so disgraceful to her. She didn't have to, though; Ardellus seemed to know what was left unsaid.

"But you stopped. And not because your sense dulled or the loss of your brothers was any less intense."

"My father was working and drinking himself to death. He didn't have the compassion to see it was hurting my mother and me more. Or he didn't have the strength to stop. It disgusted me. I stopped because I realized I was doing the same thing, just by different means." She was speaking to Ardellus, but was intensely aware the others were listening. Her humiliation was tempered only by the fact she could sense their sympathy and compassion.

"You stopped because you had the strength to stop," Ardellus corrected.

"But I left. Even after his stroke. I left them to live my own life. How can that make me good or pure?" she asked herself more than anyone else. It had been easy to rationalize her decisions when no one was putting her on a pedestal. Under this spotlight, she was beginning to question her own character.

"Your goodness is more than the sum of all your actions or even your mistakes," Ardellus said as if he had heard her thoughts. "It is also your intentions, your compassion; it is your very essence. And anyone in this room right now can tell you, without even having to taste your blood, your essence is strong. Stronger than many vampires'."

Alex flinched at the mention of her blood being tasted. Sage had allayed this fear the night before, or so she thought. She looked to him for clarification, but it was Darian who answered.

"Vampires feed off each other, not for the blood itself, but for what's in our blood: our essence. We draw energy from it." He paused, but continued when Alex's puzzled expression remained. "It's what it sounds like. It's a sense of the donor. The stronger the other vampire's sense of self and the more good he or she possesses, the stronger and purer the essence. As a species, humans' blood is weaker because it has less essence. Not that it's diluted with vice, any more than ours is, just that your life energy is usually weaker."

"Usually?" Alex asked.

"Yours smells quite strong. That's one of the reasons I wondered if you were a Seer. No normal human's essence is ever that strong."

Alex tried not to be bothered by the implication that she was somehow abnormal. "And the other reason?" she asked. "Was it that Sage couldn't mess with my memories?"

"Yes," Darian answered, but turned to Ardellus. "But is that always the case? We couldn't find anything mention of it in the histories."

"Nor could I," Ardellus answered. "But it makes sense. Sage manipulates a human or vampire's sense of himself. If he couldn't find a weakness in that sense, he wouldn't be able to modify what they knew to be true: their own memories. A Seer has to have an abnormally strong sense of self to survive. So it would follow that that part of a Knower's gift would not work on a Seer."

Sage nodded in understanding, but still spoke up. "Why can she sense me so strongly, though, when she hasn't matured? And why could I read her instantly, without eye contact?""And is there any way to stop it?" Alex added in all seriousness, though everyone except she and Sage laughed at the question. They waited for Ardellus to answer with matching grimaces.

"Sage, you read Darian, Sarah, and Markus, and even me without eye contact. Why should your ability to read Alex surprise you?" Ardellus finally asked.

"I just met her," Sage answered, not fully able to suppress the attitude in his tone. "I've been working with Rocky every damn day for over a year and didn't start hearing him until a month or so ago."

Rocky's head jerked up. "A month? You just told me—" He saw both Sage and Darian glaring at him and stopped. He mumbled an apology, but crossed his arms over his chest, as he slouched back against the wall.

"Yes, but what is it that allows you to hear others without contact?" Ardellus asked, rather than providing Sage with an answer. Alex was reminded of her own teaching style, but found she was still lost in the current conversation.

"I know them well. Oh," Sage said seeming to comprehend. Luckily for Alex, who still didn't, Ardellus continued to explain.

"Yes, you have a strong sense of them. A Seer's sense is so strong you would not need to get to know her. Alex knows herself enough for both of you. As for why she can sense you already, I can only guess. Both of your gifts involve reading and/or manipulating another's sense. That similarity may allow Alex to make a connection to you easier than she can with others."

"Can we break that connection somehow?" Alex asked, not caring if the others were amused.

"When you learn to control your power and block out others' emotions, the connection may be less intrusive for both of you, but it may always be hardest with Sage," Ardellus answered.

Alex shared an exasperated look with Sage, who then grinned. She knew he could hear her contemplating spending a lifetime feeling his emotions and having him hear her thoughts. Though she sensed he felt the same revulsion, he also enjoyed her discomfort. It intensified her frustration—and her desperation to be able to do something about it. The word *tortured* still echoed in her thoughts. She turned to Darian and Ardellus hoping for more answers.

"Is there a book on this? How can I start learning to control it?"

"We'll get there, Alex, but not tonight," Darian answered as he stood up and walked from behind his desk. Alex had a strong feeling he was trying to bring the conversation to an end, and she was not having it.

"I still have a hundred questions, and you promised me answers," she reminded him before he could even breach the subject.

"Like you, I just found out for sure you are a full-blooded Seer. I have questions of my own, but I need more time to figure things out. Sage and the Elder and I will work out what we can, and we will tell you. Later," he added to be clear.

"Can I at least ask about that? You," she said turning to Ardellus, "I'm sorry, what should I call you? 'Elder' just seems rude. You're clearly not that old." She would have continued, but all the others, including Ardellus himself, were laughing heartily. Alex wondered, as she watched their reaction to her statement, how old vampires lived to be. Sarah had implied Darian and Markus were around three hundred, which seemed absurd, considering neither looked a day over thirty-five. If that math held true, this vampire, whom she would have guessed was a gentleman in his late sixties could be. . . . Her mind couldn't comprehend it.

"Looks can be deceiving, Alex," he said, still smiling, "but you may call me Ardellus, if you prefer."

"Thank you. Ardellus, you mentioned they didn't believe I could be a Seer, because I was unusual. What does that mean?" How much more unusual could she be, she wondered. "And what do you all still have to figure out?"

"That's two questions," Darian said leaning against the front of his desk, hooking his thumbs into the belt loops of his khakis. "The first of which I'll answer now. Seers are . . . well, have always been human males who have inherited the power from the small line of original Seers. Because many of them don't reach maturity, they are very rare."

When he saw the others looking at him, Alex thought Darian cringed. She sensed Sage's dread and uncertainty, and knew there was something in Darian's words she had initially misinterpreted. She looked from Sage to Darian, slowly understanding where she went wrong.

"When you say 'don't reach maturity' you're not just talking about their gift, as you call it, not achieving full strength, are you, Regan?" She strained to keep her voice steady.

Darian looked to his father with uncertainty. But it was Sage who spoke first.

"Tell her, Darian. She has a right to know."

Darian nodded and turned to her. "No, Alex, you're right. Many die during their maturity. Others have historically been hunted and killed."

Alex swooned; a million questions and fears flooded her head making it ache. Once she acknowledged the pain in her head, it seemed to flare through the rest of her body as well. The adrenaline and curiosity that had kept her mind focused and her aches in check had drained from her with this last bit of information. She suddenly felt shaky, weak, and nauseated. She was unsure whether she needed sugar, more pain meds, fresh air—or maybe she could try again to wake from this nightmare.

Sage, who had obviously been hearing her thoughts, and Markus, who had been watching closely enough to see the color leave her face, both flashed to her side just as she nearly toppled off the couch. As soon as he was sure of Markus's hold, Sage released her and went back across the room.

"Are you okay?" Markus asked, as she fought off the fainting spell.

Sage beat her to a response. "No, she needs food and more medicine for the pain. And seeing as we all know how much she actually slept today, a few hours of real recovery time wouldn't hurt." At the moment Alex was too weak to argue and too appreciative of the concern he felt to bother sending him a dirty look.

"Agreed," Darian said. "Rocky, could you bring her back to her room and take the first watch? She's done for tonight." Alex revived at this statement.

"Like hell!" She shocked even herself by finding the strength to stand. Though it was only with Markus's support she was able to stay upright. "You can't drop that on me and then dismiss me with no further explanation."

Darian approached her calmly, but sternly replied, "Actually, I can. I'm the Regan, remember? You have enough to digest for one night. Go rest."

Markus tugged gently on her arm, guiding her to the door where Rocky stood waiting. Embarrassed, she could feel the tears streaming down her face. She hadn't cried openly in front of anyone in years, and now she had broken down in front of them twice in one day. Her mind was still racing, though; she had to know more. She had to understand this if she was going to come to grips with it. As her emotions engulfed her, she turned to Sage.

If he was reading her thoughts, he had to feel some sympathy. As she thought the word in her mind, she realized she had been sensing it; he'd been feeling it all along. She almost paused to wonder why it was so strong, when clearly he didn't like her, but there wasn't time. Markus was insistently leading her away from Darian, who seemed intent on her obedience. *Please,* she thought, asking for Sage's help in this strange manner for the second time that day, hoping it was not one time too many.

Sage sighed, amazed at his willingness to risk getting the matching set of shiners to help this half-sized human, because, Seer or not, the little chick was annoying. But it was equally disturbing to hear the girl's fear echo in his head.

"Wait," he called to Markus, who just shook his head. Sage turned to Darian, and even without listening carefully, he was pretty sure the Regan was contemplating the most painful way to rip him a new one. Hating to stoop to it, but knowing it might save him a beating later, he decided to pull a page from Markus's book and use a little ass kissing.

"Regan, I went through something similar when my gifts matured. I went through it alone, and it—" was terrifying, mind-blowing insanity? He didn't want to admit that, so, convincing himself that he was downplaying it for Alex's sake, stuck with, "It sucked, royally. At least until you and Markus found me and brought me to your father, who explained everything and helped me control it. Knowing what to expect ahead of time would have made it—" he paused again searching for the right words.

"Suck less," Alex offered wiping her cheeks. "That's all I want," she pleaded with Darian. The Regan sighed. Sage was amazed by the effect females could have on an otherwise headstrong male.

"And you'll get it—but not now," Darian began. He noticed her immediate intent to argue, and continued to explain, "You'll need your strength soon, and if you get sick or your wounds don't heal before you mature, it could make it even more dangerous. Explaining everything and answering your questions could take all night and day, and there is other related business to attend to." He looked to his father who nodded to confirm.

Sage was curious about this and wanted to listen in, but knew Alex would continue to plead. Instead he spoke on her behalf.

"Then why not let her read the histories—at least the parts that pertain to her kind, and perhaps maybe a little about the Others as well," he suggested, knowing he was rocking the boat.

"Humans, even Seers, never read any part of the histories," Ardellus addressed Sage with incredulity. Sage had about had it with the Elder's condescending tone.

"Yeah, well, until twenty-four hours ago females were never Seers. Times change," he snapped, finding just enough self-control not to add *old man* at the end.

"Watch your tone," Darian warned, but as Sage had listened to the Regan's own thoughts about his father all night, he took the reprimand with a grain of salt.

Ardellus paused, but surprised everyone with his reply. "Perhaps he is correct, though, Son. If we had all been more willing to accept that, we might have been looking for Alex and found her before the Vengatti did."

Sage heard Alex trying to make sense of this. "The third vampire—he was a vampire, right? The one you killed," she said, turning to Sage, then back to Darian. "You said Seers were hunted. Was he after me? Why? What do they want?" Alex was shaken; this idea had heightened not only her fear, but also her desire to know more.

Sage laughed. "She really has no intention of giving up and lying down anytime soon, Darian."

Darian ignored him and turned instead to the Elder Regan. "But it would be dangerous for us and for her to allow her to read all the histories. If she were to be found—"

"I'll go through them and mark the sections for her to read. I know them almost as well as you. Ardellus had me study all the gifts when I was learning about Knowers," Sage said.

"I did, and that may work fine, but—" Ardellus shot Sage a look that was inviting him to hear the rest of his sentence so as not to say aloud in front of Alex what he was concerned about. *The girl is curious, which is admirable, but what is to keep her from reading more than what is good for her?* He waited for Sage to reply to be sure he understood.

"Someone can sit with her if they have to. We're guarding her anyways," Sage said getting exasperated, but he almost instantly regretted it when he heard Darian's thought before he voiced it.

"Nice of you to volunteer. Rocky can take first watch while you mark passages. As soon as you're done, the Elder and I will approve them, and then you can help Alex make sense of them," Darian said with a smirk, knowing this was not working out how Sage had planned. He began to protest, but Darian cut in, "No, no, you're absolutely right. You are the best one by far to help her understand this."

Though Sage admitted Darian was probably right, he wasn't happy about it. Alex shot him an apologetic glance. She knew she was getting what she wanted at his expense and at least felt somewhat guilty about it, especially as she sensed his anger. What she didn't know, and he didn't plan to tell her, was that most of it was aimed at himself.

"And until then," Darian added, speaking to Alex again, "you will do as I've asked, now that you've gotten your way, and rest."

Alex managed to smile at him before he continued. "And even when Sage brings you the books, if he tells you to take a break, you will."

"I'll try," Alex answered.

"It's not a request, Alex," Darian snapped.

"I meant I'll try to rest," she said, though Sage knew from her thoughts she had fully intended the double meaning. "It's been twenty-four hours—any chance I can get some real pain killers now?"

"That's up to Sarah," Darian answered her, narrowing his eyes. It didn't escape him or anyone else she hadn't agreed to the second stipulation. When she wasn't annoying him, Sage had to admit she was entertaining to have around. Though he imagined that working with her could be the ultimate test of his patience.

"Fair enough," she said, turning to the door, but before leaving she turned back. "Thank you, all of you."

Sage listened for the sarcastic or snide remark he was sure would follow. None came, spoken aloud or in her head. She was truly appreciative. And trusting. Perhaps Ardellus was right; beneath the rough edges, her essence was pure.

Sage almost felt guilty as he listened in to the conversation between her and Rocky.

"Do you want me to carry her?" Markus had offered at the door, a little too eagerly.

"I got it," Rocky said sweeping her off the floor and heading out into the hall.

"You could have let him," Alex told Rocky. "Or I could have walked," she added quickly.

"Yeah, Sage said you enjoyed Markus's company."

"He—what? Who did he say that to?"

Rocky informed her that the whole house had been made aware of her attraction to Markus. What Sage's mentee left out was that Sage had also spilled that Alex's feelings were reciprocated. The lead warrior had made one too many condescending comments to Rocky that morning, the last of which coincided with Sage's Google search of Vanilla Ice.

With one little 'slip,' Sage had gotten revenge for both himself and his partner. He smirked now as both Markus and Alex sent a silent but vivid string of curses his way.

Alex lay in bed trying to make sense of what she had discovered about herself and this other world. She wasn't ready to digest the frightening facts she had learned about her ability and the dangers it posed. Facing her mortality in her current state of exhaustion didn't seem like a good idea. Successfully repressing that, she focused instead on what she had learned about her captors. The first thing she knew was that there was still so much to know. These vampires had a long history, traditions, and beliefs unique to them. Understanding who she was would require understanding their world and her place in it.

That was the second thing Alex knew, though it was harder for her to accept. She had realized sometime over the last few hours that she belonged in this world. All her life she had wondered why she never quite fit in, never felt a strong attachment to the people and places she had encountered. Now she felt like everything had been leading up to this. Though the puzzle pieces didn't all make sense to her yet, she knew this would be the place she learned to fit them together. The idea of leaving behind what remained of her other life didn't bother her as much as she thought maybe it should.

She glanced at Rocky, who lounged in a chair in the doorway, his foot propped on the jamb like he was blocking access into or out of the room. Incredibly, this was no longer necessary. She wasn't going anywhere. Not just because she wanted answers, and not because she no longer feared for her safety, at least from the six vampires in the house, but also because she was beginning to feel a connection with these vampires, this coven, who had taken her in. Not a connection like she shared with Sage, which was unavoidable and undesirable. This connection was a choice, and one she was okay with making.

As she watched Rocky's foot tap incessantly, she realized she was as restless as he was. Or her mind was anyway; her body was happy to be fed, medicated, and resting, all of which Sarah had once again seen to with her gentle manner. Though she knew she might benefit from a few hours of deep sleep, she wouldn't admit it if it meant postponing learning more. She wondered what she could wheedle out of Rocky while she waited for sleep to overcome her or for Sage to finish, whichever came first.

"So, Rocky," she said catching him off guard. The front legs of the chair hit the floor with a thud as he turned to her.

"You still awake?" he asked despite the obvious answer.

"Can't sleep—too much on my mind. Care to entertain me until I can crash?" she asked as innocently as possible.

He eyed her suspiciously before answering. "I'm not good with bedtime stories. I'm pretty sure the stories I'd tell you wouldn't help you sleep," he said with a devilish grin. She was tempted to ask him to try her, but remembering what species he belonged to, decided against it.

"I was actually referring to answering some of my questions." She hoped her honesty might buy her a few answers.

"Well, that would be an even bigger no," he said turning around and pushing back the chair again.

"Why?" Alex asked, though she could guess the answer, and it had little to do with her crushing his manhood earlier in the day. From the remarks Ardellus had made earlier, she guessed Rocky was low man on the totem pole, which meant he was probably afraid of being put in a precarious situation by sharing more than Darian wanted. She hoped she could work around this, a little bit, at least, without getting him in trouble.

"First of all, I like being able to see out of both my eyes. And my nose can't take being broken again. Second, I don't know much. If you haven't figured it out, I'm new to this. And though as the oldest son of an original family, I could have read the histories, my father didn't think much of me growing up, so I was never allowed," he answered with more honesty and openness than Alex expected or thought she deserved. Rocky seemed to realize he had shared too much and began to blush as he picked at a hole in the leg of his jeans.

"Sorry, Rocky, that sucks," Alex tried to comfort, "but if you're working for the Regan now, why not just ask him to let you read them?"

Rocky shifted uncomfortably, switching the leg he used to lean the chair back. "I'm serving a sentence with the Regan, it's not quite the same thing. And since I'm no longer the son of an original family, he couldn't let me anyway. And, no," he said, watching her shift in bed as he piqued her curiosity, "I don't feel like explaining all that to you." Alex was disappointed, but understood. Rocky, however, seemed to feel bad and added, "Not now, anyway."

"You don't need to explain," Alex answered, "but you could certainly tell me the basics of being a vampire. They can't get angry with that. After all, Darian himself let that out of the bag first. And if I'm going to be part of a coven, I ought to know who and what I'm dealing with. Besides," she added, hoping to soften him up, "being the youngest, you probably know more about my world, so you'd know what to clarify and de-myth."

"Yeah, I guess." Rocky grinned. "But only the basics," he added. Alex was pleased and nodded for him to begin. "Well, we're not dead, for one. That's got to be the craziest misconception. Mummies are dead, but we eat, sleep, breath, mate, and even age, though once we mature that slows considerably."

Alex stopped him. "The mummy thing was a joke, right?" She knew it sounded stupid and blushed as he laughed, but after everything she had learned in the last twenty-four hours, she had to be sure.

"Yes, gullible, it was a joke," he answered when he managed to catch his breath.

"Thanks," she sneered, but continued to question him. "So how old can you get?"

"Personally, Sage and Darian have both told me I'll be lucky to make it to my next birthday, but for your average vampire, well, I guess we could live indefinitely, if we kept getting essence, but most choose to return to the Creator sometime after ten or twelve centuries."

Alex wasn't sure what part of Rocky's answer she wanted to address first. She couldn't fathom a life span over a century, never mind a millennium, but his last fact intrigued her more. "Return to the Creator?" she asked, realizing it wasn't really a question.

"I don't know, Alex." Rocky hesitated. "That's in the histories, though everyone knows about it, so I guess it's not technically protected information."

Alex sensed his reluctance and stopped him. "It's okay. I won't ask. What else?"

Rocky gave her an appreciative nod before resuming. "Well, we mature around twenty, which means we begin getting stronger, faster, our senses become enhanced. And of course, our fangs come in and we need to feed, which as Darian said earlier is how we maintain our life energy, our strength."

"How often do you feed?" Alex asked.

"Once every week or two is enough. Mates might feed more, because sex often leads to feeding and vice versa. The strongest blood comes from someone you love or care for. Mates are the strongest, but parents and even siblings feed each other too. Young vampires often feed off of close friends until they mate. Actually, it often leads to mating, because we try to feed from the opposite sex. The essence of the other gender is more completing. And since taking one's blood, one's essence, can be so intimate, feeding from one another often leads to stronger relationships."

Alex was sitting up, enthralled. There was such disparity between the image Rocky created and the horror movie depictions Alex had associated with vampires.

"So there are no loners in the vamp world, huh? I mean, how long can you go without blood?"

Rocky was quiet for minute. He was looking at threads he had pulled loose from his pants, but Alex sensed he was lost in a memory, an unpleasant memory. She was becoming even more curious about Rocky's history.

"It depends," he finally answered, sucking in a steadying breath, "Older vampires can go longer if needed, and really old vamps—and yes, we all use that word when Ardellus isn't around—probably only a feed once a month. But for a younger vamp, four or five weeks is torture; longer could probably kill us, and that's not easily done. That's why a coven is so close-knit. We're actually downright inbred, but it's out of necessity, so you just learn to deal."

Alex chuckled at this last description, but then thought about her lack of connections with people, including her family. She was glad she was human.

She tried to change the topic to something less intense. "How about the whole dematerializing thing? Can you zap yourself through time and space?" she asked with a grin.

"Yeah, right after I turn myself into a bat. Please, Alex, get real." But he seemed glad to have the conversation return to more lighthearted questions.

"Oh, pardon me, because Sage's ability to hear people's thoughts or my emotion detector is so much more scientifically feasible?"

"I was home-schooled, which was a bit of a joke, but I'm pretty sure there's been more scientific studies on matter and its make up, than on exactly how thoughts and emotions work," Rocky argued. He had a point.

"Okay, so we're not at Hogwarts, I get it."

"Another reference those uncultured lug nuts wouldn't get. Well, maybe Sage; he's read everything printed since the Gutenberg. But I'm positive Darian hasn't seen a movie since he took over as Regan shortly after the silent film era. And Markus has every street and building in all of Bristol memorized, which is good, since he probably doesn't know GPS has been invented. Apparently, when you've been around a few centuries, being behind a decade or two doesn't seem like such a big deal." They both started laughing. Alex stopped short, but Rocky continued, "Darian doesn't even have a decent computer in his office. He acts like it's because he's so traditional, but, really, the dude's just a Luddite."

By the time Rocky realized what Alex was gesturing with her uninjured hand, Darian had him out of the chair in a chokehold. Alex grimaced in sympathy.

"The Luddite would like to remind you he can hear you anywhere in the house without the use of technology." Darian gave a squeeze. Rocky's face started to change from red to purple. "So unless you want to test your earlier theory about how long you could go again without being fed, you will show some respect."

Rocky dropped onto the chair coughing and gasping, trying to regain the use of his voice. As soon as it returned, he apologized profusely. Alex remained silent but gave Darian an accusing stare for his excessive use of force. When he seemed to tire of both her look and Rocky's mumbling, he continued.

"Enough," he said to Rocky. "I'm not here to listen to you grovel. If you're sorry, learn to shut up," Darian leaned in to whisper, "especially when the Elder Regan is right down the hall."

Rocky nodded. He seemed relieved he hadn't actually offended the Regan. Alex shook her head, unsure whether she was more bothered by Darian's act for the benefit of his father or Rocky's apparent acceptance of it.

"I'm really here to remind our guest, again, she'll have the opportunity to ask questions after she has rested." Darian whispered again, "You're killing me, Alex. Between the Elder and Sarah, I'll never get a moment's peace until you are resting and healing. I understand if you're still upset with me from earlier, but for everybody's sake, will you please get some sleep? Rocky's been here long enough to know if Sarah isn't happy, nobody's really happy."

Rocky confirmed. "I nearly lost an ear for leaving my socks in the living room last time they fought."

Alex laughed, but remembering something that had been bothering her, stopped short and looked at Darian. "I'd sympathize, but as I have no socks, or clean underwear, or clothes that fit me, you'll have to do better than our earlier arrangement, Regan. Will you promise me if I rest, you'll have someone take me to my apartment to pack up some of my things as soon as I can make it up and down the stairs on my own?"

Darian sighed. "I promise if you rest, we will get your things."

Alex narrowed her eyes. "I work with teenagers. Don't think I didn't notice you amended my request."

Darian smiled. "Good night, Alex." Just before he turned off the light, though, he turned back to her. "I'm glad you've decided to stay, willingly."

Chapter 6

The glass shattered as it hit the interior bricks of the fireplace. The remaining swig of whiskey it had held caused the flames to flare briefly. Leonce sighed and crossed his arms. It wasn't that he didn't share his lead warrior's frustration. He just didn't see the need to resort to such behavior.

"Are you through, Ty?" he asked when the cussing ceased.

The large warrior spun around, flashing his dark eyes at the Vengatti Regan. "I'll be through when every last member of that human family is dead."

Leonce nodded. He had been listening to Ty's thoughts. He knew it was not the loss of one of his best warriors, but the memory of another loss that was bothering Ty. Theran had died at the hands of two Rectinatti warriors while trying to capture the girl. It was an honorable death. His remains had already been collected from the alley and would be sent back to the Creator in a returning ceremony attended by his family, fellow warriors, and Leonce himself. The Vengatti Regan attended nearly all such ceremonies of fallen warriors.

It was the memory of one of the few exceptions that had Ty fuming this night. His brother had died at the hands of the oldest Crocker child—a mere boy at the time. His cockiness and carelessness had cost him his life. Ty's need for revenge had cost the coven the chance to have two Seers at their disposal. So Leonce had denied his brother a true returning ceremony, sending the message to his warriors that those too weak or foolish to survive a fight with a human were unworthy of an honorable send-off. Ty had been indignant at the time, but knew better than to direct his anger openly at his Regan. He had channeled his fury at the surviving human male instead. Ty had been more than willing to help Leonce train the boy—feeding from him frequently enough to keep him subservient, beating him regularly just to assure his misery. The prospect of catching another sibling to torture had made Ty as elated as the grave warrior ever became. Having the plan foiled had resurfaced his hatred.

Leonce grinned. He never wasted such passion.

"Death is peaceful, Ty. Surely, you want the girl alive—at least for awhile."

Ty looked at the Regan with narrowed eyes. "You made it clear you didn't care—I do. I want her dead."

Leonce knew he would have added, 'and the boy, too,' had he not already had and lost this argument dozens of times.

"I didn't care, when I still believed the Rectinatti were unaware of her. But as I was apparently misinformed—"

"They didn't know about her," Ty growled, further infuriated by the accusation he and his males had missed something.

"I don't believe in coincidences, Ty. They were there. They knew. Perhaps she wasn't in contact with them, perhaps she wasn't even aware of them—but they were aware of her. If she's important enough to be protected so carefully by her family and the Rectinatti, I want to know why. And somehow I doubt Darian is going to tell me over tea. If the girl's truly like her brother, she'll have no choice. My orders have changed: I want her alive."

"How do we know your pet isn't playing us? How do we know he isn't bluffing to save his own ass?"

"The boy hasn't been able to play me in years," Leonce snarled. "The prophecy of which he speaks is in our histories as well. How the girl fits into it is yet to be seen, but I'm taking no chances. She cannot remain with the Rectinatti."

Ty paced the dark wood floors of the living room as he tried to control his desire to argue. Leonce sat back on the leather couch, willing to wait him out. He mindlessly picked a shard of glass from the cuff of his meticulously pressed trousers. He knew Ty eventually would seek another outlet for his rage. Leonce had one ready.

"How the hell do you suppose we find her now?" Ty asked, finally coming to a stop at the end of the couch. "They'll have brought her to their Regan's for sure."

"Yes. And it won't take long for her to realize we were hunting her last night, so she'll likely stay there, where she's safe. Unless, of course, we can give her a good enough reason to leave." Leonce paused just long enough to annoy Ty. "Go fetch the boy." He stood and began unbuttoning the cuffs of his white shirt.

One corner of Ty's mouth began to curl up. It fell just as fast. "Bait does us no good if we can't contact her."

Leonce shook his head. "I know you like to think of the boy as little more than an easy meal, but he does know a few tricks. Though like any animal he may need a little prodding. I can do it myself, of course, if you prefer to keep your hands clean."

Ty examined the Regan, who was rolling his sleeves neatly to the elbow. Leonce was wearing his usual starched dress shirt with the collar unbuttoned, tucked into tailored designer pants. His leather belt alone likely cost more than Ty's entire rumpled wardrobe. Leonce returned the look. He never apologized for his expensive taste in fine clothing. He was the Regan—he never apologized, period.

Ty knew him as well as anyone, which was the only reason he was excused for the obvious eye roll and the thought he didn't bother to keep in his head.

"I don't ever mind getting a little blood on my hands—or my shirt, for that matter," Ty muttered as he headed down the hall.

Leonce actually chuckled at the comment. It was the truth—and the very reason Ty was second in command.

Alex woke up on the plaid couch in the basement family room—the basement family room of her parents' house. She was curled on her side with the old brown afghan pulled up to her ears. Peeking out at the room, she saw two figures at the far end standing on either side of the foosball table.

The one called Rocky spun a handle and shouted in victory.

"Take that sucker. I crushed you. Admit it, I am the foosball king!"

"Good to see you made something of your life, bro." The bigger one, Sage, leaned over and pushed the visor of his partner's ball cap over the smaller male's brows. Then he was gone. Alex rubbed her eyes and searched the room for him.

"He never sticks around," the other said, turning to Alex and pulling off his East Bristol Bobcat's cap and running his hands through his blond waves. Blond? Rocky's hair was straight and black. Alex sat up so fast her head spun. Levi's electric blue eyes looked up at her from under long dark lashes. She had been too young and uninterested in her appearance before he had passed away to know enough to be jealous of her brother's gorgeous features. She mussed her short, pin straight, nothing-special-brown hair and sighed.

"Ah, don't sweat it, kiddo. You didn't turn out half as ugly as Dave and I thought you would. Although we did drop you a lot as a baby, so maybe your misshapen head is partly our fault," Levi said with a grin as he made his way across the room to her.

Even in her dream Alex realized something was wrong. Levi wasn't the strong but stringy athletic teenager he had been when he had died. He appeared to her now as he would if he were still alive. Still alive, but having led a hard life. His gaunt cheeks hadn't been shaven and his once soft skin appeared weathered and scarred in places. When he turned to face her, expecting a response, she thought she could make out the discoloration of bruises in various stages of healing.

"You always were the wise ass," she finally answered.

"'Were', 'passed away'—you're killing me, sis. And you couldn't do that if I were already dead."

Alex tried to smile at him, but the tears were coursing down her cheeks. She rubbed her right wrist remembering the pain of losing them. Levi watched her hand rub the scarred flesh.

"We'll discuss that later," he said with a frown. "But for now, how about a game of hide and seek for old times' sake?"

"I'm too old to fall for that one, Levi. You and Dave would leave me hiding for hours and never come looking for me," Alex laughed remembering.

"You've left me hiding for eleven years, Alexandra. It's time to find me." Levi's eyes were suddenly cold; the sense he was sending to Alex lacked all of the warmth she always associated with her middle brother. A chill shot down her spine making her shiver.

She woke with a start, overwhelmed with a sense of urgency, but also despair. She couldn't help but wonder if what she was sensing were her own emotions or those of the grown Levi from her dream.

She flailed around in the pitch-black room, grasping for the lamp she remembered being on the nightstand next to her. As she knocked over the glass of water Sarah had left for her earlier, the lights came on.

Rocky was sitting by the door, his hand on the switch next to him. He was chuckling and about to tease her when he saw her tortured expression.

"You okay? Are you hurt again?" He was on the edge of his chair, about to call for help.

Alex shook her head and blinked against the bright light. "I'm fine. I just had a weird dream."

"Good weird or bad weird?" Rocky asked perceptively reading her expression.

"Bad weird. Kind of." As painful as it was to see her brother, especially in the state Levi was in, it was nice to imagine he was all grown up somewhere, watching over her.

Rocky was starting to ask if she wanted to talk about it, when there was a soft knock on the door. The Regan didn't wait for a reply before opening it.

"My father heard you were awake and insisted I ask you to dinner," he said. "We were just sitting down."

"Oh, um. . . ." Alex was still waking up and was a little surprised by the sudden hospitality. "I'm not really dressed for dinner." This was true. Though Sarah had given her a fresh outfit, it was casual and ill-fitting like the last, aside from the fact she had slept in it. "Of course, we could remedy that now that I've fulfilled my part of the bargain and slept," Alex said smiling at him, while simultaneously trying to fix her bed head with her uninjured hand.

"Tomorrow, it's nearly dawn. Have dinner with us now to satisfy the Elder Regan. Sarah's a good cook, they'll be too busy eating to worry about your clothes—or your hair for that matter," he said with a grin, watching her make an even greater mess of hers.

"Is she talking to you again, then?" Alex dropped her hand, not wanting to seem vain.

"You're making them wait," Darian said, ignoring the question.

"Good," Alex said, slowly getting out of bed, "a woman should never forgive after only the first apology."

Darian pursed his lips. Alex sensed he was annoyed, and she intensified this by continuing as they headed into the hall. "And it needs to be tomorrow. My grades are due by Monday, and I need to finish correcting."

Alex saw his raised eyebrows and partial eye roll as she walked slowly next to him. She wondered if this was because he knew, as she did, she was unlikely to return to her job. Fighting the fear that accompanied this thought, she explained. "I know it seems crazy to you, but whether I go back or not, I owe them. My students become like my own little coven during the year, and I have a responsibility to them. I honor my responsibilities. It's something you should relate to, even if you can't fully understand it."

Darian looked at her quizzically, but nodded. "Okay," he said, offering her his hand, which she took so she could carefully maneuver the stairs. "I get it, Alex," he continued. "I guess I have as much to learn about you and your world as you do about ours."

Alex wasn't sure her world was as complicated or as unnerving as this world she had stumbled into, but she grinned, glad to be reaching an understanding with him. "I kind of got the impression your world was going to be my world, now."

Darian seemed to hear the hesitation in her voice. "Despite what you've seen thus far, it's not such a bad world to be in," he said leading her into the kitchen, "especially when you have such a loving, forgiving mate, who also happens to make a mean roast."

Alex laughed at his attempt to get in Sarah's good graces.

Sarah held out a chair for her. Markus and Ardellus, who were already at the table with Sage and Sarah, both stood politely until she was seated. Sage didn't bother and managed to ignore both Ardellus's and Sarah's looks.

"Forgiving, huh? So now you have another mate?" Sarah said putting the last dish on the table. She glowered at Darian, but gave a quick wink to Alex as she handed her a loaded plate.

The small talk resumed. Alex was relieved they didn't make her the center of attention, but rather let her settle in and just observe. Markus seemed to be informing Darian about ongoing patrols. Sarah began asking Ardellus what he had been busy with during the spring. Sage was quiet; he seemed to be half listening to both conversations.

Alex was somewhat surprised by the normalcy of it all. Then she realized someone was missing. She looked around the table. There wasn't an extra place set for him. She caught Sage, who sat across from her, looking at her and knew he had been listening to her thoughts.

"He eats in his room," he said confirming it.

"Why?" Alex asked. Rocky seemed like the most social of the group; she couldn't imagine him wanting to eat alone.

"Because he is told to. And because it would be improper for him to be given any more allowances than he already is," Ardellus answered after hearing her question and guessing whom she and Sage were talking about.

Alex turned to Ardellus, shocked by this reply. Sage attempted to catch her attention again and mouthed "later" hoping she would drop it. Darian, who had heard where the conversation was headed, tried to quiet the Elder Regan with a single plea of "Father." But Alex couldn't let it rest.

"I don't know what Rocky supposedly did, but I've been here just over twenty-four hours and already I can tell he's a good person—or vampire. And from what I can sense, he cares for you all and wants to please you," she turned to Darian, "not because he's told to, but because he respects you. Doesn't that deserve a little respect and leniency in return?"

A bit shocked by her own outburst, Alex felt the blush creep up her cheeks. She would never normally have been so rude as a dinner guest in someone's home. But her dream had left her rattled. As was clear from it, Rocky reminded her of her middle brother, Levi. Both could be mouthy and rambunctious, but they were full of life, full of spirit. She wanted nothing to do with crushing that by shunning Rocky.

"As you said, child, you have been here just over twenty-four hours, and you have much to learn. We have rules and traditions that must be followed," Ardellus said. He remained calm, but his tone made it clear he was annoyed by her boldness.

Alex turned to Darian again. "But you're the Regan. You make the rules, right? What would it hurt to let him have dinner with everyone?"

"I've changed things I believed to be wrong when I could, Alex," he said, "But vampires have long memories and don't make changes easily. Rocky understands."

"I'm glad, because I don't." Alex debated leaving the table and even started to push her chair back.

"You will," Sage cut in. "I've gone through enough of the histories. We can start reading a little after dinner, if you're not too tired."

She knew he was trying to appease her with this carrot. But she could sense Sage's apprehension and wondered whether her leaving would cause more trouble than she anticipated. "I'm not," Alex answered, still riled. She scooted her chair back in as Sage continued.

"Fine, then, as soon as I finish another plate of Sarah's fine cooking, we'll start." Sage winked at Sarah, as he took another heaping scoop of everything. Sarah smiled at him and Alex, soothing the tense atmosphere.

Alex offered to help with the dishes after they had finished, but Sarah wouldn't hear of it.

"Do you want me to save your plate?" she offered. "I noticed you didn't eat much. If you don't eat meat, I can—"

"No, no." Alex felt horrible she had noticed. "I'm a carnivore, trust me. It's just kind of early. This is around the time I wake up to get ready for work. I'm lucky if I can stomach a banana and a cup of coffee, usually."

"Of course," Sarah said. "Then I'll definitely wrap it. You'll be hungry later in the day. And it won't matter who's with you—none of them can cook."

Alex laughed. "That'd be great, thanks."

As she started to leave, Sarah spoke up. "And, Alex, you'll get used to it."

"Oh, I know. But I slept half the night, so—"

"I meant about Rocky and all our other antiquated ways," Sarah explained. "Darian does try, but he fought the coven on Rocky's behalf and lost some ground demanding an agreement the other original families weren't happy with. For now, at least, he needs to uphold his side of that agreement."

Alex didn't know what all of that meant, and she knew she didn't have the full story, but she still felt the situation was unfair. "I guess, but in the house? Who would know?"

"Darian would know. He's a vampire of honor, and I respect that, Alex," Rocky said, coming into the room with his dirty plate. "Not that the rules don't suck sometimes, but I get why he follows them." Rocky turned away from her to wash his plate in the sink. He left it in the drying rack and walked back to where she stood. He put his hand gently on her shoulder. "But thanks for—"

He didn't finish because Alex staggered back into the counter suddenly.

"Alex, what is it?" Sarah asked. Rocky had dropped his hand, afraid he'd hurt her.

"I'm f-fine," she said, trying to regain her composure. "You're welcome, Rocky. Where did Sage go?" Alex started to the door, trying to comprehend what had happened.

Sage appeared in the doorway. "What's the matter?" he asked, looking from Alex to Rocky.

"I just touched her shoulder to say thanks," Rocky assured him. "It wasn't hard. I don't think." He seemed unsure as he observed Alex's pale face.

Despite appearances, Alex was quickly recovering. To prove it, she snorted at Rocky's comment. "We humans aren't that fragile." She turned to Sage and explained. "When he touched me, I could sense him, strongly. Like last night, when you touched me. It just startled me." Because it had drowned out every other one of her senses like she was ten feet under water. But she didn't want to admit that. She turned to Rocky with a forced smile, "But it was nice you were so grateful—and that you were concerned about me."

"Great," Rocky blushed. "Her gift is going to be just as annoying as yours," he said to Sage.

Sage ignored the jibe. He was looking at Alex curiously. He knew what she hadn't said, yet asked anyways.

"Try it again."

Alex and Rocky both looked at him like he was nuts.

"I'm all set with being the guinea pig, actually," Rocky said, unconsciously backing away from Alex.

"I wasn't giving you a choice, Rocky."

Alex would have protested on Rocky's behalf, but Sarah stepped forward.

"You can try with me," she said offering her hand.

Alex looked to Sage, not for permission, but to see if he would insist she try with somebody.

"That'll work," he answered. He ignored the curses she silently sent him.

Alex smiled nervously as she reached for Sarah's long, perfectly manicured hand. She flinched as they made contact, thinking she'd be overwhelmed with emotions again. But as she held Sarah's cool fingers, nothing came. She looked up at Sage, puzzled.

"Normal—it comes in waves as you near maturity. If Ardellus was close when he predicted the timeline, the periods when your sense is stronger will become longer and more frequent," Sage explained to her.

"Great," she muttered. Alex wondered about something else, though. "Rocky said vampires mature around twenty. And last night Darian wanted to know my age. When do Seers usually mature?"

"It's all in the histories. Let's go read." Sage started to head out. But Sarah stopped him.

"That is not in the histories, Sage." She continued as he started to interrupt. "Yes, the age of a typical Seer's maturity is mentioned, but Alex isn't typical. And Ardellus and I have a theory about that," she finished.

"Yeah, I heard," Sage said, apparently not keen on discussing it.

Sarah continued, turning to Alex. "Male Seers mature the same age as male vampires, which is why Darian wanted to know your age. He knew you seemed a little too old to be just maturing."

"Wow, I'm feeling a bit insecure. Do I need to invest in under-eye cream?"

"No," Sarah laughed, "You don't look old. He could just tell you were too mature to be a teen."

Alex wondered if Sarah tried to twist it to make her feel better. She decided she was okay with that. "So what's your theory? I seem to be five or six years late."

"Not at all," Sarah began. "Males mature when they are reaching a physical peak. When they've hit their final growth spurt, their muscle tone is developed, and they've lost all semblance of boyishness."

Alex thought briefly of the Levi from her dream, the Levi whose body had undergone the changes of which Sarah spoke. She shook her head to remind herself it was only a dream.

"But a woman's body could be considered at its peak when it is best able to carry a baby and give birth. We weren't sure exactly when that was for humans, so we did a little research," Sarah continued. "If I may ask, Alex, when did you first start menstruating?"

They really loved embarrassing topics Alex thought as she blushed. At least this time she was being asked by another female, although one of a different species.

"It was later than my friends, about fifteen, I guess. And I was really into sports, karate and running, so all the exercise messed with it. I wasn't regular until after college, even with the pill." She addressed Sarah, trying to pretend Rocky and Sage weren't still in the room.

"Then it makes sense you'd just be maturing now. Your body is at its peak. So now your gift can reach its peak, too," Sarah said.

"I guess that seems reasonable." Alex turned to Sage who wore an uncomfortable expression.

"Can we go read what the histories say, instead of speculating? That was T.M.I.."

"I'm very impressed with your use of the vernacular, Vanilla," Alex laughed, turning to Rocky. "Have you been tutoring him?"

Sage scowled and lunged at Rocky who was laughing uncontrollably. As he tried to grapple him to the floor, Sarah called out sharply.

"Boys, either take it to the barn or break it up and go about your business. But do *not* destroy my kitchen." She pointed to the door as Sage and Rocky disengaged. Rocky mysteriously landed on the floor before Sage stepped away.

"Fine," Sage said turning to Alex, "just don't believe everything this one tells you," Sage said gesturing to Rocky who was getting to his feet rubbing the back of his head. "We know enough about your world to operate in it undetected—keep in mind the skills that requires."

Alex knew the last line was meant to be a threat. "I'm sorry," she said trying to sound contrite for about a second before adding, "I can call you Ice, if you prefer. I just thought seeing you already had the herb thing going on with your real name, a spicy nickname might be nice."

Sage remained eerily calm, as he glared at her. Towering over her, he reminded Alex of how he appeared in the alley when she first encountered him: menacing.

"I get even, midget."

She tried not to wince and held his gaze. "In addition to being socially insensitive, that nickname has been so overused on me, I'm immune to it. You're going to have to try again."

"Oh, I will," Sage said sweeping out of the room, leaving behind a wave of determination and deviousness that didn't require contact to stagger Alex.

Twelve leather-bound volumes were stacked neatly on the coffee table in the living room. They were each close to three inches thick and had the same two letters engraved on the front and spine, a capital R and capital H, in the kind of overly ornate font Alex forbade her students from using on their essays as it was hard to read after awhile. She hoped the whole book wasn't written in the same.

"Are the others joining us?" Alex asked as she crossed the room to the off-white couch next to where Sage sat. "I'm just wondering about all the copies," she clarified when she saw his look of confusion.

"Those aren't copies. Those are the histories. All of them," Sage explained with a chuckle.

"Right. I forgot you guys have been around awhile." Sage raised a brow at the understatement. "I'm guessing 'H' is for histories; what's the 'R' stand for?" she asked.

"Rectinatti. It's the formal name of the coven," he answered. It hadn't occurred to Alex the coven would have a name, but then again, she knew there was at least one other coven, so it made sense they would have a way of referring to themselves.

"Italian?"

"Old Latin, originally, from rectitudo or rectus. But, yeah, when our coven was in Italy during the Renaissance they decided to go a little nuts with the spellings and names. Their translations of documents have been questioned for centuries since, because they were more concerned with the flowery language than accuracy," Sage vented. Alex tried to wrap her head around both the name and the apparent age of the books before her.

"In English it would mean right. Like righteousness or rectitude?" she asked eventually.

Sage smiled. "You take Latin in high school?"

"A little. I'm a word geek—English teacher, remember. So what's behind the name?" Alex didn't want to comment that to most humans it would seem a bit ridiculous, never mind a little pompous, for a group of creatures most would consider monsters to choose such a noble name. Sage plucked the thought from her head anyway.

"Most humans never get to know we exist outside of bad movies, never mind what we stand for. You will, if you can be patient and polite," he answered. She rolled her eyes. The mind-reader lecturing her on the impoliteness of her private thoughts seemed a bit unfair, not to mention irritating.

"It's in there, why the name was chosen," Sage said pointing the stack. "Although I didn't mark it. I don't think Darian would mind, though; it's important to know who you're serving. I didn't think it would be the first thing you'd want to know, though," he finished.

"I want to know everything," Alex said, but she knew what he was getting at. Earlier this evening she had learned this gift she had been given could kill her. And if she survived, but couldn't control it, it would likely drive her insane. One might think the passages concerning those topics would be the first she asked to read. But Alex wasn't sure she was ready for that yet. She thought if she was going through all this because of some connection she had to these vampires, it might be better and less frightening to learn about them first.

"You can't know everything. In fact, it's a miracle you're being allowed to read anything," Sage said leaning back in the upholstered chair in which he sat.

"Yeah, Rocky implied only certain vampires could read them. If it's your history and traditions, why wouldn't all vampires have access to them?"

"Well, these are just the histories of our coven, not all vampires. As Darian mentioned earlier, though, our coven's actually quite large—about two hundred families, twice the size of most. The books include our traditions, ceremonies, laws, as well as the personal histories of all the Regans, the original families, and all gifted members of the coven. Some of that information is general knowledge, passed on within families. But some of the information could be dangerous in the wrong hands, which is why only a couple dozen or so members at one time have read them. Markus hasn't even read them," Sage finished. He knew Alex would be interested in this. She sensed his amusement and tried hard not to acknowledge the reason he was right.

She curled her uninjured leg under her on the couch. "But why? He's the Regan's right-hand man, right?"

"Doesn't matter. He's not from an original family, and he's not gifted," Sage said.

"So are you actually in there?" Alex said grinning, pointing towards the stack.

"Yes," Sage answered shortly.

"Can I read that part?" she asked, knowing it was bothering him.

"Nope. Only what's necessary, and that's not." He picked up the top book and handed it to her. She could see the sticky notes peeking out from both the top and bottom.

"The top marks the places to start, the bottom where you need to stop. And you will stop, because I'll know if you don't." He tapped his brow over his black eye. She noticed with curiosity and aggravation how quickly it seemed to be healing, compared to the side of her head, which was still swollen and sore. Another vampire trait, she guessed.

"Should you really put stickies in these? How old are they?" They couldn't be from the Renaissance; they had to have been translated into English sometime after the coven moved here, but even two-hundred-year-old books shouldn't be touched with bare hands.

Sage read her thoughts and chuckled.

"I can get you gloves if you want, but these aren't that old. The Regan only copied them at the turn of the last century, and they're made out of heavy vellum, so they're pretty durable."

"Wait, did you say he copied them?" She opened the book he had handed her to discover the pages were filled with neat, slanted cursive.

"Every Regan must make a copy of the histories as part of his training, and maintain a copy until he becomes the Elder Regan. So you are right about wanting to be careful with these. They're usually secured in a climate-controlled cabinet in the office. If Darian has to make another copy anytime soon, he'll have a long stretch of grumpy. I was around the first time, and his father was relentless—keeping him up two or three days at a time to copy over pages he deemed unfit. It was his favorite punishment, I think, because Darian was so damn restless back then. It nearly killed him to sit still and focus. He wasn't fun to be around after. We don't want a repeat."

"I'll be careful," Alex said, gingerly turning the book in her hands to examine it. She eyed the stack on the table and marveled at the idea of hand-writing every word. They obviously took their training and their histories very seriously. She found the first bookmark in the book she was holding and carefully opened to the page.

It was at this time, the first Seer, Timian, was born unto the coven. Born to Theos, a great Knower, and the human woman Cassandra, known for her strange dreams and premonitions, it was to the surprise of the elders, the boy was fully human and developed normally for the first fourteen years of his youth.

Alex looked up at Sage, who was on the chair at the opposite end of the sitting area with one foot up on the coffee table. He was flipping through another book, one of the later volumes of the histories, with a square of yellow notes resting on the upholstered arm of the chair.

"How can you read and listen at the same time?"

"Oh, sorry, were you speaking?" he asked, purposely misinterpreting her meaning. Alex sighed, annoyed. "That passage is pretty straightforward. What is it you don't understand?" he asked, giving in.

"Vampires and humans can . . . have children?"

"Yeah," he answered with a shrug. "Not sure why a vamp would want to mate a human, but it's not impossible. Why? Anyone in particular you thinking about?" he goaded.

Alex tried hard to stay focused on her next question and not let a particular pair of stunning green eyes enter her thoughts.

"They were surprised he was human, why? And how would they know when he was just a baby?"

"Being a superior species, our genes are usually dominant. And we can tell our young apart from yours because they have a stronger essence—not to mention they are much better looking," he said cocking an eyebrow.

"Lovely, but if he was a Seer, wouldn't his essence be strong like a vampire. Darian said—"

"Yes, like a vampire, but not a vampire. It's hard to explain, but we can smell the difference, sense the difference," Sage said.

"And his father was a Knower," Alex said smiling.

"You teach your young to read?"

"We could be distant cousins. You want me to add you to the invite list for the next family reunion?" she teased.

"This is going to be a very long few nights." Sage turned back to his volume. Alex got the hint and was returning to hers when another question came to her. Sage sighed and looked up, realizing she was going to ask it despite his aggravation.

"Why are Knowers marked, but not Seers?" Not that she wanted some visible sign that she was odd, but it did seem unfair.

"I don't really have a direct connection to the Creator to ask her why we were made the way we were," he mocked, but continued anyway. "My guess is, though, it's because you won't need anything to make you stand out more; once you mature and your essence reaches full strength, any vampire within a mile of you will be able to smell you and know you're not a normal human. That will make you vulnerable enough, no matter how strong your powers develop."

Alex wasn't exactly comforted by this contradiction. What was the point of having 'power' if it made her a walking target?

"Power is dangerous, both to those wielding it and to those having it wielded upon them. The Creator knew that; our whole world is about balance. A Seer's gift is more hidden and, as you'll see—if you ever get back to reading—potentially more dangerous to others. To balance that it was given to the weaker species, which makes it more dangerous to you, too."

Sensing Sage's emotions as he explained this, Alex realized the Knower felt much the same way she did about having won the 'gifted' lottery. Actually, he seemed to like it even less. Considering he'd been living with it for centuries, his emotions didn't soothe Alex's anxiety.

She read on, attempting to suppress her trepidation, as the passage described the senses Timian began to develop. Though the writers of the histories had difficulties clearly conveying what Timian had felt, Alex understood completely. She sympathized with this young teen, born thousands of years before her, who had gone through these odd changes without anyone knowing what he would become.

As the young man neared his nineteenth birthday, the intensity and duration of these periods of increased sensibility grew. Theos had thought the boy, whose essence was unusually strong for a human, might develop a few vampire qualities after all, but Cassandra knew her child would become a gifted male, but remain human in most other ways.

Alex wanted to ask about the 'most' part but decided to keep reading in case it was explained in the next paragraph.

Finally, a week into the nineteenth year of his birth, Timian's powers reached maturity. After a brief spell, he awoke to the horror, pleasure, and power that mark the life of a Seer.

Alex reread the last line again and again. It was hard not to miss the word the author had chosen to list first: horror. She supposed she had been foolish to expect to hear anything more comforting than what Darian and Ardellus had told her earlier. But she had still hoped they were being dramatic, because until an hour ago, she couldn't really envision why it would be so difficult. Obviously, sensing others' emotions wasn't always going to be pleasant, but one's own emotions weren't always pleasant. She had thought it would be easier to sense others' pain or anger, knowing it was not her own. But from Ardellus's warning about not being able to separate her own feelings from those of others and her episode with Rocky when she experienced just such a feeling, something clicked. If she could suddenly sense everyone as strongly as when she touched Sage or Rocky, it would be impossible to separate out her own emotions. And even if she only sensed others the way she could normally sense Sage, without contact, it would be maddening. She wouldn't just be feeling one other's emotions, but those of everyone near her. Being in a crowded place or walking the halls of the school where she taught would be unfathomable. It would be horrific.

She couldn't understand where pleasure or power played into this situation. She wouldn't find pleasure in invading the privacy of anyone in the vicinity of her. And power was never something she sought and not something she felt she would be entirely comfortable possessing, even if it didn't bring with it the added dangers Sage had just explained.

Reluctantly Alex read on, wondering how much the histories would explain each of these aspects of being a Seer. But they didn't seem to be much help explaining any of them. The passage glossed over Timian's first years as a Seer, stating lamely, *Through much determination, the Seer gained control over his gift and, much like our kind, his powers grew over the years.* Alex hoped some of the other pages Sage had marked went into a little more detail than this, because as far as owner manuals went, so far, this one sucked.

Sage laughed softly as he heard the thought. Alex kept quiet, but cast him a weary look before returning to the last paragraphs of this section. She could see the purple sticky tab denoting where she was to stop.

Alex was thinking she could have entirely skipped these paragraphs. They described Timian's mating to a female vampire and then read like a genealogy chart of their children. Nine were human male Seers, though only three lived past maturity, a statistic Alex tried not to dwell on. The tenth was a female vampire. But at the end of the passage, Alex read, *After two and a half centuries together, Timian perished an early death at the hands of his mate who, unable to control her thirst after the birth of her last child, overfed from the Seer's strong, pure essence.*

"Um, Sage, I hate to tell Darian, but he made a mistake copying. This says centuries, but it must mean decades," Alex said speaking up.

Sage shook his head. "Nope. That's right."

"Timian was human, Sage. We've never lived two hundred and fifty years, especially back before modern medicine."

"Timian was a Seer. The rules are different for Seers."

Alex's jaw dropped. She didn't know why she could believe in centuries-old vampires and mystical powers but not wrap her head around a human living that long, but she couldn't. It was what every human secretly longed for, and yet the idea of it terrified her. What state would one's body and mind be in after that long?

Seeing she needed further explanation or confirmation, Sage explained. "You won't age as quickly once you mature. Actually, it seems to slow about as much as for vampires." Noting her look of shock, he added, "Hey, there have to be some perks to these things."

She wasn't sure perks was the right word. "So, how long could he have lived?" Alex was much more comfortable talking about this in terms of Timian rather than herself.

"I'd guess as long as a vampire, but no one knows for sure—" Sage seemed to stop short, and Alex could sense his hesitation.

"Why?"

Sage sighed. "Because no Seer has ever died a natural death."

Chapter 7

"What?" From what Alex could tell, Seers had been around since shortly after vampires and humans, meaning thousands and thousands of years. In all that time, surely one of these men had lived to grow old.

Sage sighed, realizing he'd have to explain. "You've got three strikes against you as a group," he started. "One, you're humans who hang around vampires. Two, your essence makes your blood tempting, to some vamps, anyway. Three, your gift gives you power other vampires and their covens envy or want destroyed."

Sage watched her as he finished. She knew he was waiting for her to fall apart, something she wasn't about to do in front of him. This wasn't exactly the information Alex wanted to hear, but it reminded her of another question, one Darian had skirted. One she was equally interested in and only slightly less terrified of.

"Powers beyond just sensing others' emotions, you mean? Because I don't see how that in itself is of any use." She was beginning to accept she had been hunted, but couldn't see why. Her gift had to be more valuable or threatening than she perceived it. Sage had even used the word *dangerous* earlier.

"For some Seers there are other powers. But don't underestimate just sensing others. The right knowledge in the wrong hands *can* be dangerous," he answered both her spoken question and her thoughts. "Knowing your enemies and your allies, without having to get too close, can be a great advantage, especially in battle," Sage answered.

Alex started to ask about the other parts of her gift, as well as what types of battles modern day vampires got into, but Sage leaned over and took the book from her lap.

"Tomorrow night. Somebody had the audacity to wake me from a sound sleep two hours early today, so I'm not staying up all morning again."

Alex turned behind them and could see the light coming in from around the curtains. It was past sunrise. Sage had scooped up the volumes and was starting to beckon for her to follow him when Rocky appeared. He looked tired.

"You here to take the daytime shift?" Sage asked him.

"Yeah," Rocky responded with a frown. "It seems I pissed off the Regan more than I thought earlier. I was just told I'm on permanent daylight duty."

Sage laughed. "Someday you'll learn to shut up, or at least learn Darian has a real knack for turning up just as you're about to shoot your mouth off."

"Did he learn that from his father?" Rocky asked quietly wearing a grin. Remembering Ardellus's earlier entrance and Darian's floundering apparently made Rocky feel a bit better about his own indiscretions. Alex smiled too.

"He learned a lot from the Elder Regan, but don't try to get him to admit it," Sage warned the younger vampire.

"Noted," Rocky said.

Sage left the room with the volumes that made up the histories. Evidently there'd be no reading without Sage or Darian present. Alex was still on the couch, but turned to face Rocky, who waited by the door. She enjoyed the juxtaposition of this dark-haired, olive-skinned, bulky vampire in destroyed jeans and a black sleeveless t-shirt standing next to the white bead boarding that fell below the chair rail and the navy and white toile wallpaper that was above. Though the others were equally menacing and as informal in their appearances, they all seemed like they could blend into this proper, tame decor if necessary. Rocky, however, came across uncomfortable. She wondered if it was his lack of experience, his age, or just who he was.

"So, you going to bed?" he asked breaking the silence.

"Are you asking or was that a polite way of telling me I have no choice?"

"It's a choice. I just thought you'd be tired," Rocky answered, still in the doorway.

"Well, my schedule is completely messed up, but I'm not really tired yet." As she watched him stifle a yawn though, she wondered if she'd be keeping him up. "But if you're tired, I can try falling back asleep for awhile. And I'll wake you when I get up."

Rocky grinned at her offer. "I have to stay up anyway, so honestly, having you awake is easier." Alex nodded. They both seemed a little unsure of what to do next.

Alex searched for a distraction. She knew there were bookshelves filled with reading material in Darian's office, but she had a feeling she wouldn't find too many *New York Times* bestsellers among those tomes. She was also almost certain she and Rocky would be about as welcome to browse through them as they'd be to take a stroll outside. She'd have to work on both these areas next time she caught Darian in a good mood. If they wanted her sane, books and fresh air were necessities.

Looking around the living room with the pristine light-colored upholstery, dark wood, and heavy drapes, she saw nothing that would make the next eight hours of daylight fly by. There were hardly any knick-knacks or photographs on the coffee and end tables, and only candles in solid silver candle sticks on the mantle over the fireplace.

"Do vampires not believe in entertainment? No TV? No magazines? No Monopoly, even?" she asked breaking the awkward silence.

Rocky laughed glancing around the room as well. "This isn't where we hang out really. This is where Sarah and Darian entertain guests, mostly. Sage sometimes likes to read in here. But it's a bit too. . . ."

"Formal? Stuffy?" Alex offered.

"Well, yeah," he answered. "You want to watch TV, though, I can take you downstairs. The office Markus uses, which is also where I'm sleeping now, has a sweet flat screen."

Alex could tell this idea appealed to him. "Lead the way." She was never a big TV watcher herself, but thought the type of mental distraction it could offer her was what she needed after the last thirty-six hours.

Following Rocky down a well-lit stairway to the basement, Alex was pleasantly surprised. Somehow when she tried to picture the basement of an old farmhouse currently being occupied by five vampires, this was not the image she conjured. The stairs and hallway were hardwood, though newer than the wide knotted pine of the floors above. The walls and trim were all off-white, and the lighting in the ceiling gave off a soft but bright glow.

Rocky quietly pointed out doors, as they passed. His bedroom, which Markus temporarily occupied, was between Sage's and the office. He also pointed out the laundry room, a storage space, and finally a door that led to the barn. Not lingering on this last door, he started into the office.

"There's a tunnel between the house and the barn?" Alex asked intrigued.

"Yeah, the barn is a gym now, though. The tunnel is just in case we need to move and it's light out," he explained.

"Is it just a tunnel or are there rooms or a basement under there too?" Alex was curious and hoped maybe to get the grand tour despite the fact her leg was already aching.

Rocky was reluctant to answer, and Alex sensed quite strongly, though not as strongly as when he touched her earlier that day, what Rocky was feeling. Whatever else was through that doorway was painful for Rocky to think about.

"Never mind. I can be annoyingly curious about new things. Let's go watch some mindless daytime television," Alex said, not wanting to bother him further.

She walked through the door he had been holding open and headed to a large black leather couch that was on one end of the room, with two matching leather recliners flanking it. They were positioned, of course, in front of a wall-mounted flat-screen that Alex was sure would not have fit on any wall in her apartment. It was evident this was where the males of the house could be themselves. There were men's sports and fitness magazines scattering the table, which was marked with rings from numerous drinks having been placed on it without coasters. The floor was scattered with various pairs of sneakers and boots, and she was pretty sure what was a pair of boxers Rocky was kicking under a chair. The sports posters on the walls ranged from basketball to boxing. While some were dated, others were more modern.

"I take it sports is an area they stay up-to-date on?"

Rocky nodded. "Sage likes to bet on anything, and he's good with numbers and stats, so you'd be dumb to bet against him—most of the time." He flashed her the twenty he had won earlier. "Thanks for that, by the way."

"Any time. And Markus?" Alex couldn't help but ask. She turned to look at the posters to avoid Rocky's knowing grin.

"His job keeps him almost as busy as Darian, but he watches occasionally—especially boxing and martial arts tournaments. He likes to study how humans fight. I'd guess he chose that one," he said pointing to the poster Alex had been looking at.

"He has Ali, but no Rocky? Has he got something against Stallone?"

"No fictional athletes allowed," he laughed. "But as I share his horrible name, I should ask them to make an exception."

"Are you referring to Rocky or Sylvester?" Alex asked, handing him the remote. Not only was it too complicated-looking for her to want to mess with, but she also guessed Rocky didn't often have the chance to be in charge. He looked pleased and was willing to answer her question.

"Both, actually. My given name was Sylvester. I tried to go by Sly, but even that sucked as nicknames go. And then when. . ." he paused momentarily, but finally continued, "when my family disowned me, I could no longer be recognized by my father's name or my given name. Sage thought it would be funny to call me Rocky, considering how I got here. He also knew it would irritate my father, which it did. That was all the convincing it took to get me to adopt it permanently." He seemed leery as he waited for Alex's reaction. She wasn't sure if he was nervous she would ask for details or worried she would judge him on what little she knew.

"Rocky, I know last night I said I wouldn't ask, but will you tell me about what happened, why you're here?" Alex hoped she wasn't pushing him to do something he wasn't ready to do.

"Yeah," he said nodding, "but it's kind of a long story, if you want all of it."

"Well, no offense to ESPN, but I think I'd rather hear your story, than sit through an entire day of Sports Center," Alex said motioning to the television.

"You know why guys like sports so much?" he asked, the tenor of his voice changing, "Because it's always cut and dry. At the end of the day, someone wins, and someone loses. There's no politics, no personal complications, none of the bullshit real life entails."

As he said this and began telling his story, Alex thought Rocky, who was as young as she, had lived through a lot in his life. He may not always say the right things or know when to hold his tongue, but he was not the young, naïve vampire the others seemed to treat him as.

Every year the original families hosted a ball in honor of Creator's Day, a winter holiday much like the humans' Christmas. It was the highlight of the year for many of the coven. The original families gloated over the opportunity to show off their wealth and power with an ostentatious display of formal attire, designer or vintage gowns, and more bling than the Oscars, Emmys, and Grammys combined. The other members of the coven enjoyed the opportunity to rub elbows with the upper echelon, or at least have the opportunity to badmouth them from a lesser distance. And of course, all members of the coven delighted in the presentation of that year's newly matured vampires, as it proved the strength and stability of the coven and the generosity of the Creator.

Sly himself had been presented just three years prior. Though his father, he was sure, had taken little joy in it, his mother had secretly sought out her son the night before to give him a presentation gift. He remembered her tears of joy as he opened the black velvet box that held a silver pocket watch that had belonged to her father. As she had been her parents' only child, the heirloom was his by right, but still she had asked he keep it from his father's view. He knew this meant his father did not yet think his son ready to accept such an important symbol of his change to adulthood and his position as an eldest son in an original family.

He had kept the watch on him always after that. Whenever his father was criticizing him, he would dig his hands deep into his pocket and rub over the ornate cursive R that marked all the coven's heirlooms. He had been clenching it in his pocket that afternoon a year and a half ago as his father, Antonio, had called the family into his study. From behind his mother, Sly watched, leaning against the wall nearest the door, as his father presented his younger sister with her grandmother's sapphire necklace. Maria had begun her maturation, but was not fully through it yet. Her sore gums and loose incisors meant she was probably only a week or two away from the final transformation. She was excited to reach maturity; the youngest in the family, she was always eager to prove her dignity and sophistication. Though Sly loved her dearly and protected her fiercely, both from her father's often harsh criticism and from anyone outside the family who would dare give her a hard time, he couldn't help but feel bitter as he watched their father secure the clasp with his eyes glistening.

Sly knew his father's protection of her was overbearing, but still he almost longed for it. He was free to mingle and brawl in the human world, something he did often to seek his father's attention, as negative as it was. But Maria was rarely allowed out. Their father treated her like the black-haired porcelain doll she resembled. Her experience outside the house was limited, and interactions outside the coven strictly forbidden. Which was why she was so obviously elated by her father's presentation.

"Does this mean I can go?" Maria looked from her father to her mother quickly. Though Antonio didn't know it, the two females had been conspiratorially planning for the ball since late August.

"Maria, we've spoken of this enough," her father answered, his words saying she had received his final answer, his tone implying he had all but given in. Sly looked at the ground so his father wouldn't catch his eye roll. Maria, seeing the opportunity, pressed on.

"But, Father, I'm days away. My essence is plenty strong now, and if I don't go, I'll have to wait a whole other year to be presented," she pleaded.

"Maria, the Regan and the Elder will be there, and you haven't even gotten your fangs yet. It's too great a risk; we can't be seen as breaking tradition, not as—"

"An original family," Maria mimicked his deep voice in a manner that would have gotten Sly slapped upside the head for impunity, but Maria went on, unadmonished. "I doubt the Regan will stoop to conversing with any of the younger vampires, Father, and I really doubt members spend the evening flashing their fangs at one another."

At this, Sly snorted. The ball was notorious among the younger vamps for providing an opportunity to broaden one's feeding horizons. It was the only reason he was willing to don the monkey suit every December, and, though he'd been too timid to make a move in the previous years, he was determined to find a suitable feeding partner this year. In fact, he knew exactly what young female he hoped to bite.

"Sylvester," his father took a step toward him and waited. Sly contemplated trying to stare him down, but when his father's large frame became another step closer, he caved.

"Sorry, Father," he mumbled in shame, not at the improper reaction to his sister's comment, but at his inability to stand up to his father.

"Very well, Maria," Antonio said, turning to face his daughter, "but you will leave without argument after the first hour of dancing, *before things get a little looser."* He stopped to shoot his son a look, perhaps thinking, though he'd never admit it, that Sly had a point. *"And you will escort her home and remain here with her until your mother and I return,"* he finished directing Sly.

"What? The girls spend the first hour dancing with their fathers, brothers, and the elders. Like hell I'm leaving then," Sly snapped before really thinking about his words or checking his attitude.

His father had flashed across the room and had him by the shirt collar before he could blink. *"Excuse me?"* Antonio's voice was deadly quiet, his dark brown eyes narrowed to slits.

"It's not fair," Sly said softly, but clearly. He was surely going to be struck anyway; he might as well argue his case.

"When you are head of this family, and Creator help us if that day happens soon, you can decide what is fair. Until then you will do as you are told without complaint."

Sly braced himself for the blow, but it never came. Maria, using her newfound speed, tried as best she could to step in front of her father.

"Father, wait, please. Sylvester is right. We're both nearing mating age. It would not only be unfair, but perhaps improper," she used the magic word, *"for us to leave without at least a little time to mingle with the other young unmated. It might appear condescending to the other families, especially the two other original families who have young being presented this year, if we swept from the room without even giving them one dance."*

Sly marveled at his sister's ability to work their father. She was meek and timid at times growing up, but lately she had learned to use her keen intellect and her father's deep sense of family honor to bend him to her will.

Antonio released Sly's shirt and lowered his raised hand slowly, never dropping his son's gaze. Sly worked hard to hide his relief.

"Perhaps. But two hours only—and if you still have her there a minute longer, there will be consequences, understood?"

"Yes, sir."

Two nights later Sly stood at the bottom of the grand staircase of their grandiose house just outside the city. He tried not to fidget or tug at his collar as he waited for the females to be ready. He was also trying not to think about his thirst. He knew he should have fed sooner, but with the ball so close he'd be damned if he was going to *rely on his mother's essence any longer. He would find a feeding partner tonight, despite having to baby-sit Maria.*

"You have cab fare?" his father was asking as the two females started down the stairs. Sylvester was astounded that this gorgeous young female in the low-cut sapphire gown and high silver stilettos was his baby sister.

"Isn't that dress a little—" he started to protest.

"Stunning," his father cut him off. "You are both absolutely stunning," he finished, taking his wife on one arm and his daughter on the other as they headed to the limo. Though Sly didn't disagree, he had a feeling his sister had just made his job of watching out for her a whole lot harder.

And Sly wasn't wrong. As all the young females who had matured in the last year were presented after dinner, it was obvious which one the other unmated young males were all staring at. Sly huffed, already in over-protective-brother mode, as he wondered how many of them would feel that way if they knew she hadn't really even reached maturity. But as she gave a modest smile, careful not to show her teeth, and perfectly curtsied to the table where the Regan, his wife, and the Elder sat, he was starting to realize most wouldn't care.

Antonio returned to the table with Maria after the first dance. As he handed her off to Sly, who was traditionally supposed to take the next dance, he glanced at his watch.

"Midnight," he whispered to his son. Sly nodded in return, then swept his sister onto the floor. Though he had earned a reputation for being loud-mouthed and quick-tempered as a teen and newly matured male vamp, his mother hadn't failed him when it came to teaching him the finer parts of being a vampire of status. And though all the rules of etiquette and propriety sometimes eluded him, he excelled at dancing. As the two moved across the floor with grace, heads turned.

"You're getting quite the fan club. I don't like it much," Sly informed his little sister.

"I'm pretty sure Melanie isn't checking out my *rear end, actually, Sly," she teased back. Sly glanced around the room trying to find the beautiful redhead he had fallen for the first year he had been dragged to the ball. He found her standing with another single friend on the side of the dance floor. She was as gorgeous as he*

remembered. This was the year he had decided he wasn't leaving without approaching her.

"We've only got two hours until one of us turns into a pumpkin. You really want to spend it dancing with your sister?" Maria asked as the song ended and another began.

"As I'm the one who will be pumpkin puree and I have . . . things to do before we leave, I think not." Sly winked, gave her a slight bow, then handed her off to the young male who had approached them hoping to cut in.

A little after midnight, Sly left the upstairs room Melanie had dragged him to after just one dance and entered the hall in a daze. He was simultaneously physically satisfied in all ways possible and mentally disgusted. Feeding from Melanie had satiated his thirst, but knowing how easily she gave herself to him made the experience feel cheap. And when she had dismissed him from the room so she could freshen up before returning to the ball, it was with a definite sense that their time together was at an end.

He shoved his bow tie into his jacket pocket and felt his grandfather's watch. He hoped for his sake his sister had had the sense to stay out of their father's sight. He was hurrying down the stairs to find her when he heard her voice. It wasn't coming from the hotel lobby, as he would have expected. It was coming from down the hall he had just been in. She sounded scared and hurt.

"Stop it, please. I said no!" Sly heard the protests through her sobs. In an instant he had flashed down the hall and broken through the door. In horror, he registered what he was seeing. Maria was pinned on the bed with the skirt of her dress pushed up. The male vampire over her was one Sly recognized as a member of another original family. He had matured five or six years before Sly.

"Get away from her, now!" Sly spoke shaking with rage, his fangs fully elongated.

"Or what, Sly, you think you can bust my face like you do in your little squabbles with humans? Your sister asked for this, didn't you, Maria? Now run along to that slut you were banging down the hall."

Sly's vision blurred as he struggled to maintain control. Maria didn't speak up, but the tears were streaming down her face. Not wanting to scare her further was the only thing that had so far kept him from tearing this cretin's throat out.

"The Regan and his warriors are right downstairs, Lucas," Sly managed, remembering the attacker's name.

"And they've got better things to worry about than a thug and his tramp sister who wanted a little of my essence. Face it, Sly, when you smear your own rep, you can't blame others for taking advantage. No one will believe you, and as for her, it would be a shame if the whole coven discovered she lost her virginity before her fangs even came in."

Sly didn't need to wait for the sob that escaped Maria's throat before deciding to act. In a blur of power and fury, he had tackled the bastard away from his sister and was pummeling his face. When Lucas finally reacted, he was hardly able to shake Sly off long enough to get to his feet. He backed up, fear replacing his smug expression as he saw the wild look in Sly's eyes as he came at him again. This time Sly grabbed Lucas by the hair and, spinning him around, smashed his face into the stone mantle of the fireplace. The crunching sound that accompanied both Lucas's and Maria's screams should have alerted Sly to the egregious act of violence he had just committed against another vampire, but he had long since lost control. When the others arrived in the doorway, it was to find him back on the floor on top of Lucas pounding relentlessly at the injured vampire's kidneys.

He was still swinging as one of the Regan's warriors, Sage, pulled him off and pinned his arms. The Regan himself stood in the doorway assessing the scene.

"Get Briant up here, now," he told his other warrior, Markus.

"The injured male's father, is Christo, the surgeon, Regan," Markus whispered.

"Shit. Fine, get him, too, then." Turning to Sly, whose bloody fists were held in Sage's firm grasp, he asked, "Why were you attacking this male?"

"He was—" Sly began, but as Maria whimpered and faced him, he could almost hear her silent pleas. He stopped, unwilling to ruin her reputation, but unable to defend himself.

The Regan noticed this exchange and stepped over to Maria, who had sat up on the bed and covered her knees sometime during the fight. She wouldn't meet his eyes as he contemplated her rumpled gown and tear-streaked face.

"This is your brother, is it not? Was he protecting you?" the Regan demanded. Maria took a moment to find her voice.

"Yes. I mean, he thought he was. Nothing happened though," she sobbed into her hands as Sly's look of shock caught her eye.

Before the Regan could continue his questioning, both Lucas's and Sly and Maria's fathers entered the room, followed by Markus and the medic, Briant. Antonio stopped only for an instant to scowl at his son, before rushing to Maria's side. Christo was kneeling over Lucas who was moaning on the floor. He stood suddenly and rushed at Sylvester who, being held, was unable to defend himself.

"You little bastard, you've ruined him!" Christo shouted, but before he could get in a second punch, Darian himself stepped in.

"Enough. What do you mean?" He turned to Briant who was examining the injured vampire. Briant looked up, startled. His face confirmed Christo's accusation before he spoke.

"He crushed one of his fangs."

There was silence in the room as this sunk in. In the vampire world damaging or removing a vampire's fang, especially one of a prominent male, was the equivalent to castration. The injured male would not just suffer the loss of one of two teeth needed for feeding, but in turn would loose much of his stature, as strength traditionally equated to power. The punishment for inflicting such an injury was always severe—and often, death.

Sly's knees gave out and only Sage's firm grip on him kept him on his feet.

"Regan, our family and my son are due justice. He should be turned over to us immediately," Christo spoke, the rage in his voice clear. The Regan was beginning to reply when Antonio spoke up.

"He's right, Regan. My son has dishonored his family and his coven. He needs to pay the consequences."

Sly couldn't suppress the shudder that shook his whole body. His own father had just given up his right to a trial. He looked one last time at Maria, hoping she would have the courage to speak up. She just sat silently rocking herself, her arms wrapped tightly over her chest.

Both Markus and Darian witnessed this and exchanged looks of suspicion.

"Though I agree this matter is serious," the Regan began, "It would be rash—and improper of me—to make a hasty decision in such a case. We'll take him back and hold him in custody until we have time to talk to all involved."

Both Christo and Antonio began to speak up, but the Regan cut them off.

"Tonight you both need to tend to your other family members," he said with finality, and motioned to Sage and Markus to head to the door. But Antonio stopped them and spoke anyway.

"Maria and my wife are now my only family members. I will not recognize that male as my own from here on out and wish the coven will do the same, Regan, if you please."

Darian turned to the vampire who stood by his daughter's side and gave him a look that was certainly one of disbelief and possibly disgust.

"As you wish. He will choose a new name for himself, as tradition demands, and be recognized by that name from this night on. All ties to your family are severed."

Sly was glad he was then ushered from the room. He didn't want to give his father the satisfaction of seeing the tears that rolled down his cheeks.

The room he was kept in was windowless, and no light shone from under the heavy metal door. He had no notion of time passing, counting the days only by the meals he was given. He knew he had been there longer than a week, but how much longer he was unsure. Being denied essence, he was beginning to lose strength. As a younger vampire he needed feeding more frequently than those further from maturity. He was actually glad he had fed from Melanie that night, considering his situation.

Despite his weakness, though, his senses were still keen enough to make out the conversation being held outside his door. Looking back on it, he was pretty sure that was what Darian and the others had intended.

"There's not much we can do for him if he won't defend himself," Markus said.

"His sister still won't say anymore?" Darian asked.

"No," Sage replied, "and her father is refusing to let me hear her."

"That's his right," Darian said.

"Doesn't make it suck any less," Sage answered.

"And if we turn him over?" Markus asked.

Darian answered grimly, "There are fifteen members of the coven pledging to exact justice on Lucas's behalf."

"The coward won't do it himself?"

"Briant told me he should be fully recovered, other than the fang, of course, but his father claims otherwise. I think he's too ashamed to show his fangless face," Darian said.

"Technically it was only one fang little Rocky in there knocked out," Sage said. "It hardly deserves the type of brutality those fifteen males will serve up. A young vampire like him would be lucky to survive. Especially since he hasn't fed."

"I can't help that. It's coven law. But let's give him one more chance to save his sorry ass."

When the three finally turned on the light, which was off unless someone from outside turned it on, they were not surprised to find the young male sitting on the floor right by the door.

Darian walked to the center of the room and waited for Sly to get up and meet him there. He obeyed, but had to work to keep his knees still.

"Rocky, the coven needs my decision, and you're leaving me little choice. I am offering you one last chance—" Sly began to shake his head, but Darian stopped him. "Let me finish, because I will not offer again. You can let Sage read your memories of that night, which only entails you thinking of them while he maintains eye contact. You don't need to speak, therefore you break no confidence with your sister—"

"Which is more than she deserves, in my opinion," Sage cut in.

"Sage." Darian glared at him before turning back to Rocky. "I don't think I need to explain the alternative. What will it be?"

He hoped for more time to consider, but the Regan's expression made it clear time was up.

"No one will know?" he asked quietly.

"I can't promise that," Darian said. "They need answers in order to understand."

"It'll ruin her, more than any busted fang. No male will want her. My mother will be crushed. I need to know it won't get out," he pleaded, trying to keep his voice from cracking. He knew he was pushing it, questioning the Regan when he was being offered a chance to save himself, but it was important to him.

Darian sighed. "It may mean you'll face lesser charges. And the consequences of those could also be rather unpleasant."

"I lost it on him. I'll accept responsibility for that if it saves her reputation," Sly agreed.

"I don't know if you're naïve, stupid, or brave as hell. But you're honest and honorable, and I like that, Rocky. It's a deal."

"Is that my new name?" he asked Darian, but it was Sage who answered.

"I thought it was fitting—in so many ways," he said with a smirk.

"But you're the one who gets to pick," Darian added.

"No, I like it," Rocky said.

"You ready?" Sage had asked stepping in front of him, so he'd be able to make eye contact and hear his thoughts.

"As I'll ever be," Rocky had replied.

"And that's about it," Rocky finished, "Well, no, there were almost three more weeks of me practically dying of thirst while Darian forced Lucas's family to agree to a deal. But having them all know I was mostly justified made it bearable." Rocky looked at Alex a bit nervously. She had not said anything while he had told her the story, and now he wondered if it had been a good idea.

"But why? You were totally justified, Rocky," Alex said passionately, allaying any of his concerns.

"Because unlike your legal system, coven law follows a guilty until proven innocent model. I couldn't be allowed to feed until everything was decided. Even though he was following tradition, I think Darian felt bad about it; he fed me himself when I was freed. It's not too often a Regan shares his essence with a subject, especially one who had just been stripped of all his status." It was one of the many reasons he didn't argue over the other terms of his sentence. Sarah was right; for whatever reason, Darian had come to Rocky's defense more willingly than any member of his own family.

"But that still doesn't explain why you're here instead of that bastard Lucas."

Rocky sighed. "Because my sister wouldn't confirm or deny my defense for the coven. So no charges could be brought against Lucas." Rocky bit back his anger toward his baby sister. Even more than their father's hubris, it was Maria's inability to stand up for herself or the brother who loved her more than his own life which had led to Rocky's current situation. He wanted to believe she was paralyzed by fear, but wasn't totally convinced selfishness hadn't played into it. She was daddy's little girl, after all. "If my father hadn't thrown me out of the family, I could have pressed charges on Maria's behalf as her older brother. As a coven lawyer, my father certainly knew that. He also knew by disowning me, any restitution owed to Lucas's family would be solely mine to pay off, and not my family's." Rocky clenched and unclenched his fists, trying not to relive the anger he experienced when he first made these realizations.

"But why would you have any punishment to begin with?" Alex asked confused.

"Because, justified or not, I lost control and permanently injured him. It's not so different in the human courts, is it?"

Alex shrugged. "I guess. So Darian gave you a job so you can pay off Lucas?"

Rocky grimaced; he knew Alex would have a harder time understanding his next answer.

"Sort of. I'm serving a sentence, under which I'm required to work as Darian sees fit until I've paid back my debt. So I don't really ever get to see my paycheck, as almost the entire sum goes to that S.O.B."

"For how long?" Alex asked, indignant on his behalf.

Rocky laughed dryly. "Vampire time is a bit slower. You wouldn't understand."

"So something ridiculous like fifty or sixty years?"

"Something ridiculous like that." He wished more vampires thought like Alex did.

"How long?"

Rocky sighed at her persistence. "Two hundred years or until he and his family release me from my debt. Which will happen when hell freezes over, so I guess just two hundred years."

"You've got to be kidding!" Alex shouted, outraged. Rocky motioned to the door while shushing her.

"It is what it is," Rocky said. "Besides, I would have chosen to do this. Like you said last night, I don't do this just because I have to."

"But the fact you do have to is hard to swallow at first," Alex said.

Rocky knew what she was getting at. "Our cases are a little different. First, you didn't try to kill someone—"

"True, actually, I think the other vampire was trying to kill me," Alex failed to repress her shudder. "But it comes down to the same. We were both faced with the choice of serving Darian and the coven or likely being hunted and killed, which means we didn't really have a choice."

Rocky could tell this bothered her, but the fierce anger of the previous afternoon had abated. "But you made the same decision I did, didn't you, Alex, and for the same reason." Rocky was making a statement, not asking a question. Alex's change of attitude since learning about what she was made it obvious she had accepted her role. Though he could tell she was struggling to let go of her independence and control, two things individuals in the vampire world had little of.

"I don't quite know why yet," Alex said. "It's not like he's winning awards for charm since I've been here." She smiled at Rocky, but the look he returned was serious. He had spent enough time mingling in the human world to know it operated very differently. There were certain things Alex would have to be told and some major adjustments she'd have to make.

"Darian's not used to dealing with humans, especially strong-willed female ones. But that doesn't mean he doesn't like you, and he'll do all he can to protect you, whether you choose to use your gift to help us or not."

"What makes you think he likes me?"

"Because otherwise when Markus and Sage broke up your argument earlier, he would have been aiming for your head," Rocky said seriously, but then they shared a laugh.

Rocky leaned back in the recliner and Alex settled more comfortably into the couch. He flipped through the channels, finally stopping on a random chick flick he assumed she would enjoy. She lifted her head off the pillow and raised an eyebrow in his direction.

"You really want to be discovered by any of them watching this? I get enough female drama at work. How about a comedy?"

Rocky chuckled, but he was relieved. He continued to surf. Finally discovering an Adam Sandler marathon on one of the comedy channels, they both settled in to watch in silence. Before long they both were sound asleep.

Chapter 8

"Will somebody get the kid a happy meal?" The voice from the television jolted Alex to consciousness. Disconcerted at first, she finally realized she was in the basement room Rocky had brought her to the morning before. She had the feeling someone had been trying to get her attention, but couldn't tell if it was in her dream or on TV. Suddenly she bolted upright, about to yell. Someone else was in the room.

"Shh," Darian said with a wicked smile. He leaned over Rocky as his fangs snapped to full length. Alex gasped. Before she made the decision to scream and warn Rocky, Darian spoke in his ear.

"Evening, Sunshine." With a quick nip he woke him from a sound sleep.

"What the hell, Sage?" Rocky awoke blaming and cursing his partner. "You broke the skin, asswipe." He spun instead to see Darian who wore a serious expression of authority. Rocky's jaw dropped as he backed away while finding the words to apologize. Not until he tripped and fell over the coffee table did Darian let them know it had been a joke by laughing freely at both Alex and Rocky's expressions.

"Don't do that," they both said. Alex clutched her chest as if that could calm her rapidly beating heart. Rocky wiped the small trickle of blood off his neck. The cut had already stopped bleeding.

Darian chuckled. "There are benefits to being me." He winked at Alex.

"You're in a good mood today. Or is it night already?"

"It's night, yes. And I'm usually in a good mood when I'm well rested and not arguing with half the house," Darian said.

Alex decided to take advantage of this. "So does your good mood mean I'll be going to get my stuff, as promised?" She noticed his quiet sigh, but also a shadow of a grin. She hoped he was learning that even half asleep she was going to be persistent.

"Sage is already upstairs ready to go. Rocky, grab your gear and join him," Darian said to him.

Rocky headed to the other end of the room and began rifling through a duffle bag of what Alex assumed was some of his clothes. She turned back to Darian as he addressed her.

"I thought while they're gone Ardellus and I could show you something."

"Wait, while *they* are gone? No," Alex said getting off the couch to argue. "I'm going with them, Darian."

"No, you're not, and this is non-negotiable, Alex, so please don't spoil my mood by getting into a useless battle of wills with me. It's aggravating this early in the night, and as I told you yesterday, in my coven, I always win."

Alex somehow doubted Sarah would confirm this statement, but she guessed there were exceptions to every rule. Having had the wind taken out of her sails, she could only scowl. But out of the corner of her eye she caught Rocky sticking something into the back of his waistband, and she turned back to Darian.

"Is this just a convenient way for you to flex your authoritative muscle, or is there a reason for not letting me go?" She knew he saw her glance again in Rocky's direction as he started down the hall, and wondered whether he would start the day playing games or being straight.

"Are humans all smarter than they look, or is it just you?" Darian didn't wait for the quip she was prepared to offer as answer to the rhetorical question. "Yes, there is another reason. We need to make sure it's safe." His expression was all business again.

"You think they know where I live?" Alex tried to keep her voice steady as she contemplated this.

"They knew your running route," Darian replied. "I wouldn't be surprised if they've been tracking you for awhile."

Alex had desired honesty, but was overwhelmed with the truth. Her right hand shook by her side.

"But why?" she asked again. She was desperate to understand. "Who are they?"

"They are another coven of vampires, though we use the word loosely when referring to them." Darian spoke of them with obvious disdain. "We sometimes refer to them as the Others, though, like our own coven, they have a traditional name they call themselves: the Vengatti. It means—"

"Vengeance?" Alex cut in. "Against your coven?" Alex watched as Darian ran his hand through his hair. Whoever these vampires were, they caused the Regan a significant amount of stress.

"Maybe in recent history," he answered. "But not originally. At first it was just against humans."

"Humans? What did we ever do? What could we do?" Alex thought it seemed crazy that such a powerful group of creatures could ever be put in a position where they would feel the need to seek vengeance against a significantly weaker species.

"Vampires believe the Creator created both humans and vampires, each species with their own strengths and weaknesses," Darian started. "Vampires' strengths should have allowed them to be the more powerful species, and for a while we were. But the human race grew and developed quickly and were able to spread all over the globe, while vampires, who can usually reproduce only enough to keep the population steady, had to stay together to feed within their covens. Most vampires never minded this. Our ancestors enjoyed living apart from humans. But as the world became more populated and total isolation became impossible, some vampires became bitter over the weaker species forcing us to live in secret. A group of these vampires broke off from one of the original covens, and, as they saw it, began to exact justice on the human race."

Darian paused and seemed to examine how Alex was absorbing all this. She had been intrigued hearing him explain more about this world, but guessing what was coming next, trembled slightly. Noticing this, he might have left it there, but Alex urged him to finish.

"They began feeding from humans instead of just each other. In order to stay strong feeding off weaker essences, they developed a way of feeding from the strongest part of humans' essence. Because humans don't feed in return, all that's left behind is the weaker, undesirable parts. In other words, they feed off people's goodness, leaving them. . . ." Darian shrugged and shook his head. He was unable to put words to this horror.

Conscienceless? Evil? Alex finished in her mind, too shocked to speak. When Darian and then Rocky had first described how their breed of vampires fed by sharing their essence with the ones they loved, she had begun to think of feeding as an intimate and almost romantic notion. But as she imagined the monsters that survived by draining the good from people, she was horrified.

"Does it kill them?" she asked in little more than a whisper.

"Not always. If they are not drained, people with strong essence sometimes recover. Other times, they don't. In those cases, if we find them, we usually have to destroy them."

"You kill humans?" Alex backed away in shock and fear, nearly following Rocky's tumble over the coffee table. Darian reached out to catch her, but she shook his arm away as soon as she steadied herself.

"We prefer to kill the Vengatti, but, yes, if a victim of theirs is seen as a danger to others, we kill him. We take no pleasure in it, Alex. It may seem hard to believe, but our coven is trying to protect humans. We believe the Creator meant for there to be a balance of power between her creations. As the humans don't know we exist, and we prefer to keep it that way, we work on their behalf to maintain that balance. And because of that, the Vengatti take any opportunity they find to feed from our coven as well."

"Feed from, not kill?" Alex couldn't imagine the creatures Darian described showing mercy.

"Well, vampire essence is stronger, which benefits them. But if enough of it is taken forcefully, the effects can be much the same as those on humans. The Vengatti know we thrive off the love and compassion for those in our coven. It strengthens the very essence we feed from. They know the way they can hurt us most is to leave us the decision of having to destroy one of our own, or let them loose with no more sense of right or good, to possibly hurt another coven member or the humans around us. Just to be cruel, the bastards almost always try to attack mated females or the newly matured." Darian finished, his voice laden with a heavy sadness, all the playfulness of earlier evaporated. Alex regretted her earlier accusation and fear. This was not the leader of a group who enjoyed violence.

"Have you had to. . . ." She couldn't finish the gruesome thought.

"Two in the last two years. Both times the families elected to have me do it, rather than do it themselves."

Alex saw him clench and unclench his fists by his side. She wanted to offer help, but didn't see how she could.

"What good can I be to you?" she asked first. But remembering how this morbid conversation had started, asked with more urgency, "And what use would I be to them?"

"It depends how your gift develops, but at the very least you could be used to sense those with essences that are strong and pure and filled with the positive emotions they feed from.""They'd use me to find their next meal? Their next victim?" Alex shook her head sharply. "They'd have a hell of a time getting me to agree to that."

"If you became too bothersome, they'd think nothing of using *you* for their next meal. Either way, we wouldn't have you, so they'd feel like they had won."

When Darian finished, he continued to watch Alex. She figured he was waiting for her to faint again. Alex herself wondered why her heart hadn't raced faster during his explanation. She had come to realize Sage and Rocky had rescued her from something worse than rape or death. She was beginning to understand she would never again be safe running alone at night. She even had thought about the fact she might not live long enough to miss those freedoms. Yet the fear that truly shook her was still the one Ardellus had provoked—the thought of losing her sense of self, her inner sanctuary. Darian and his warriors could protect her from the Vengatti. And she could learn to live with a reasonable set of protective precautions. If her maturity killed her, she at least hoped it would be quick. Worrying about it was natural, but foolish, since nothing could be done to prevent it. But if she survived all that and matured, who would be able to protect her from her own power? This was the thought that rattled her most. She'd rather die than live trapped in her own body.

Her expression must have given away some of this fear, though not the reason behind it.

"What the Elder and I wanted to show you can wait, Alex, if it's too much," Darian said.

"No. It can't, so let's go hear it." With as much sense of purpose as she could manage, Alex headed down the hallway. As Darian helped her climb both sets of stairs to his office, she knew she was right. Fear wouldn't stop what was or what would be. And time was short.

Ardellus sat on one end of the couch with a book spread open on the coffee table. At first Alex thought it was one of the volumes of the histories, but as she crossed the room and was able to examine it more closely she realized it was not. This book was also leather-bound, but truly did look like it could have been around for half a millennium. The leather was darkened on the spine and edges of the covers from handling; the pages were frayed and yellow.

After he stood to greet her and gestured for her to join him, Ardellus spoke. "Alex, Darian and I shared with you a few of the reasons you are unusual for a Seer. Tonight I would like to share with you the reason I believe you are truly special and perhaps can be a savior both to our kind and yours."

Alex fidgeted on the couch wondering if it was too late to take Darian up on his offer of postponing this discussion. Surely the old vamp was being a bit melodramatic.

Darian saw her reaction and spoke up. "Slow down, Father. Let's start from the beginning. We're not even sure if any of this applies to Alex." He turned to her to explain. "We'd like you to read a prophecy that was made about a Seer and see if some of the wording might make any sense in relation to you."

"A prophecy, like, about the future?" Alex wondered when her suspension of disbelief would find the end of its rope. She predicted it could be soon.

"Yes. I know it's hard to swallow," Darian said. "I'm not sure how much stake to put in any of these either, Alex, but traditionally both Seers and Knowers have occasionally claimed to be able to prophesize about important matters concerning their covens. This one was made by a Knower over six hundred years ago, after the last known Seer died and just before the battles with the Others heated up and we started becoming targets."

Alex peered at the page open before her. It was handwritten like the histories, but this script was cramped and embellished. What it read she had no idea.

"Is that Latin?" she asked, hoping she was close.

"An old form of it, yes. Being slow to adapt to new things, our records didn't change to a more modern form of the language until it was nearly out of favor altogether," Ardellus answered.

Alex chuckled, needing to break the tension she felt. "Vampires using an old, dead language—figures."

"As we're not dead, and only some of us are truly old—" grinning, Darian pointed to his father behind his back—"it really doesn't 'figure,' but we can gladly translate for the human who only reads and speaks one language." He leaned forward with both hands on the back of the couch waiting for her reply.

"The *human* has only been alive twenty-five years, and already has a Masters degree in the language she speaks." Alex was annoyed by the insinuation she was less intelligent than he, just because she couldn't make sense of the words on the page.

Ardellus helped her mood when he spoke to Darian. "Oh, have you improved your Old Latin then, Son? I was under the impression Sarah and Sage were the only two in the house competent enough to translate."

"Just read it to her, please," Darian said as Alex giggled.

She thoroughly enjoyed watching him be put in his place. Her focus returned to the book, though, as Ardellus began. Darian settled behind his desk and was ready with pen and notebook to record pertinent information.

"The prophecy reads:
The last of three,
Where essence is strong, marred
And before the turn, battle-worn
From which will then be born to us
A unique warrior
Tis' he who Sees a way
To victory."

"That's it?" Alex asked seeing the eager look on Ardellus's face as he waited for her to explain the lines. It hardly made sense. It sounded like chunks of the lines were missing.

"It's okay, Alex. I didn't see how it fit, either. For one thing, it clearly refers to a male," Darian said. He dropped the pen, looking only a little disappointed.

"Only this version, son," Ardellus corrected. "The footnote states the spelling was changed from the original copy written by the Knower who prophesized it. The transcriber changed the pronoun to the masculine, because he believed the feminine form to be a transcription error."

"And why wouldn't he? It refers to the Seer as a warrior," Darian pointed out.

"So?" Alex asked sitting up straight.

"In vampire culture all males were traditionally called warriors and females protectors, because those were the roles they played in the coven," Darian explained.

"Well, the prophecy isn't about a vampire, it's about a Seer. And it refers to a 'unique warrior.' As the first female, I'd be unique," Alex argued, irked by the sexist stereotyping. She saw the corner of Ardellus's mouth twitch. She hadn't liked his earlier attitude towards Rocky, but he had potential.

"Unique as a Seer, yes, but females, especially human females, can't be warriors," Darian said.

"Just because we're smart enough not to look for a fight, doesn't mean we aren't capable of fighting. You call your females protectors. Have you ever seen a female protect her best friend, her child, or her lover for that matter? We can be fierce. Your Sarah seems calm and controlled, but I bet if anyone tried to harm you, she'd rip him limb from limb, right?" Alex asked Darian. She smirked when he didn't deny it. "You'd be a fool to underestimate or underutilize half a population based solely on gender. The Others seem to have come to that conclusion a few days ahead of you, or I wouldn't have been grabbed in that alley. Don't make the same mistake twice, Regan," Alex finished. Darian remained still at his desk, his brows raised and mouth open, while Ardellus clapped a few times, smiling.

"Well said, child. What do you make of the rest of it?"

Surprisingly, the argument with Darian had somehow diminished her doubt about the prophecy. She asked to hear it again, and listened this time with an open mind. Alex had Ardellus reread it so many times Darian got flustered and copied an English translation for her. Finally, as she held the piece of notebook paper he had written on, she explained her thoughts aloud.

"Well, I'm the youngest of three children and the last surviving child of my family," she said, attempting to hide the pain that surfaced with this topic. "And you told me my essence is stronger than most."

"But how is it marred? You don't seem like the type to have committed any great acts against humanity," Darian said, still intent on being a skeptic. "My father said it: you are pure."

Alex didn't care to return to the days of Sunday afternoon confession and run down a laundry list of her transgressions, so she tried a different tack.

"Maybe we're reading it too deeply," she suggested. "What if it's referring to the place my essence is strong. Essence is carried in the blood, right? My neck and wrists have the strongest pulse." She didn't want to remind them of the scars that marked her wrists. She saw them as a symbol of her weakness. She hadn't been mentally tough, so she used physical pain to numb her emotions. The cuff bracelets and extra long sleeves she often wore hid them from others, but she would never be without the reminder. "The skin is marred," Alex said simply before continuing.

Darian and Ardellus didn't ask to see them again. They evidently remembered, even if neither likely understood.

"And I was attacked, before having matured, and have the new scars to show for it. That could be battle-worn. And from that battle I was brought here. Born is just a form of bear, which can literally mean carry. And since I was unconscious, I'm guessing someone carried me. I don't think I need to explain the warrior line again." She paused to glare at Darian. "So that just leaves the end. I'm guessing that's pretty straightforward. But since I'm really not even sure what a Seer can do yet, and I haven't matured, whatever that entails, I have no idea how to beat those creeps."

Put in her own words, Alex found the prophecy less intimidating. Though as she watched Ardellus's elated expression, she wondered if she had done herself a disservice convincing them the prophecy referred to her. If they believed her to be this Seer, what expectations would they have that she might not be able to live up to? She hadn't heard of the Vengatti until an hour ago, and now she was supposed to figure out a way for the coven to defeat them. Something they hadn't been able to do for centuries.

"Of course, it's written like poetry—rather bad poetry, at that," she added, "It could mean a hundred different things. Any chance the Knower is still alive?"

"No, he returned to the Creator shortly after making the prophecy," Ardellus answered.

"Well, I guess we can't know for certain who it's about then." Alex looked to Darian to support this comment. Instead he gazed at her curiously.

"Do you really believe that?"

"Don't you?" She was looking for him to convince her that her gut was wrong.

"I did," was all he offered.

"Now?"

Ardellus spoke what they all now believed. "It seems, child, you were foreseen."

Just after ten, Sage drove the Jeep around the corner from the street where Alex had been attacked. He parked it a couple hundred yards past the alley.

"Her apartment's on the next block," Rocky said. Sage looked at him with a raised eyebrow. "Right," he said realizing his mistake, "which is why we're parking here."

As they stepped onto the street, Sage was still able to catch the Other's scent easily. He looked to Rocky and was pleased to see his young protégé seemed to have found it, too. Rocky seemed to be waiting for Sage to take point.

"No, you do it tonight," Sage said. Rocky tried to nod casually, but what his expression hid, Sage could hear in his head. Rocky was pleased and determined to prove himself.

Sage followed as Rocky headed down the street, following the scent Alex and the Other had left behind when they had first struggled out in the open. Rocky paused only for a second before finding that the Other's scent had come from the direction of Alex's street.

"He wasn't following her on her route," Rocky said, "which means he already knew she'd come home this way."

Sage nodded as they continued around the corner. Sure enough, the scent led them to the doorway of the apartment building next to Alex's. The five-story building conveniently had a broken bulb over the steps leading into the inside hallway. They stopped only for a moment before following the scent farther.

Rocky halted at the door to Alex's building. Sage watched and listened to see if Rocky would pick up the same thing he did.

"It's not the same scent. And it's old, weeks old. Damn, they'd been watching her awhile." This bothered Rocky, who already felt protective of the Seer. Sage silently agreed. "So why'd they wait?"

"Probably because it was as hard for them to believe as it was for us. Their early histories are the same as ours, remember. The better question is how did they find her to begin with?" Sage felt like they were missing something obvious. "Keep following the fresh trail. Let's see if it leads anywhere useful."

A block later the scent ended abruptly by the curb.

"Figures," Rocky said, "who else would drive a piece of shit mini-van."

Sage slapped him upside the back of his head. "That's not the Other's car, moron. Can't you smell human offspring all over this?" He looked in the window at the car seat covered in crushed orange fish-shaped crackers with an expression of curiosity mingled with disgust. "They must have realized their buddy wasn't coming back and came for the car."

Sage recognized Rocky's disappointment, but it was his job to train the kid, not boost his ego. Rocky nodded, biting his lip at his error.

"Whatever, no sweat. Ya' done good." Crap, he sounded like a female. "Let's go back to her apartment and see how far the other bastards got."

Darian was circling his office as he and Ardellus spoke. Alex guessed this wasn't unusual, as Ardellus didn't bother to try to follow his son's progression, but instead quite naturally spoke to the room at large. Alex, however, wished he would settle in one place. The dizzying movement was adding to her distractedness. Though she was sure the two males were talking about matters concerning her, she had stopped following the conversation moments earlier. She had heard all the information about herself and her fate she could handle in one night.

Just as she was debating whether or not it would be terribly rude to excuse herself and return to drowning out her thoughts in front of the television, she realized she sensed a wave of anger and indignation that was not her own. She had been so engrossed in her own emotions as Darian had first explained about the Vengatti and then the prophecy, she hadn't noticed the absence of Sage's emotions when he first left the house. But at their return, she regretted not enjoying the solitude of feeling just her own emotions.

"Sage and Rocky are back," she interrupted the Regan and the Elder. "And from the feel of it, something happened." She was standing up, ready to head to the foyer to meet them, when Darian and Ardellus's expressions made her freeze. They looked at her like she had spoken to them in a foreign tongue.

"You can sense Sage? Now?" Darian had stopped pacing and double-checked his watch.

"Yes," Alex answered, annoyed. This was nothing new. "I can sense him in the house and the yard, too, I guess. They must have just pulled in."

Darian shook his head. "We're forty minutes from the city, Alex."

"Then they forgot something." Alex refused to believe what he was implying.

"Alex, Darian and I can hear a car as soon as it enters the drive. No one has returned," Ardellus said.

"Then it must be someone else in the house. Markus, maybe, or Sarah."

"Do we all feel the same to you?" Ardellus asked.

Sometimes Alex wondered if the Elder was also a Knower. Because he was right. When Alex had sensed Rocky last night, and even as she got weak impressions from the others, she could distinguish them as different. It was as if each one's essence had slight nuances that set it apart. She knew it was Sage she was sensing, though her certainty provided little comfort.

Ardellus and Darian, both intrigued, started in with questions.

"Is it as strong as when he is in the house? Could it just be that he is upset?" Ardellus asked.

"Do they need back-up, Alex? Can you tell if they're in danger?" Darian added.

"Were you trying to sense him when it started?"

Feeling Darian's concern, Ardellus's intrigue, Sage's anger, and her own anxiety and shock, Alex couldn't breathe, let alone think. "Stop!" she shouted. "I don't know. I don't know how or why I'm doing it. I don't know why it only just started. And I don't know if they're okay or not. I can't do this. I can't help you."

Alex ran out of the room slamming the door behind her. Ignoring the pain in her leg and side, she hobbled down the stairs and dashed for the front door. Before she could reach the handle, Darian flashed in front of her.

"Alex, we're sorry. We know—"

"Get out of my way. I need some fresh air." Alex dodged beneath his arm and grabbed for the knob. Darian grabbed her arm, hard, and held her.

"Look, woman, you may—"

"Darian, let her go. She needs a break." Markus had come up from the basement and had his hand on the Regan's arm. Though he was respectful and mild with his tone, he also held Darian's glare with no sign of fear and no sign of backing down. Even through her anger and panic, Alex was grateful.

Darian released his grip on Alex, who rushed out the door, slamming it in his face.

"Ah . . . Sage?" Rocky called from the living room. His tone had Sage flashing to his side at full speed, his hand on the hilt of his knife. The young vamp shoved him from his position, so he no longer stood directly in front of the small desk where Alex kept her clunky old laptop. Rocky pointed to the small black square above the screen. "We're on candid camera."

"Turn it off—now."

Rocky nodded and pulled a cable from the back. He then sat at the desk, his fingers flying over the keyboard faster than Sage could follow. Finally, Rocky closed the screen and looked up at his mentor.

"It's safe to take. We can't be traced. But if anyone was watching that feed tonight. . . ."

Sage didn't need him to finish. They both knew the Vengatti wouldn't have gone through the trouble of bugging Alex's apartment without having someone at the other end to watch her every move. After one of their males failed to return from his assignment to capture the girl, they'd likely be watching extra carefully, hoping for another chance at her or the enemy who had killed their warrior. Rocky and Sage had walked right into their snare. By now they were likely surrounded—sitting ducks.

Sage threw the duffle bag at Rocky. "Bare minimum. I need to be able to fight with that on my back."

Rocky nodded and headed for Alex's bedroom. Sage went to survey the scene. Peering out of one of her front windows, he saw nothing at first. Just as he turned from the second, he heard the faint crunch of gravel below. His eyes scanned the scene again, honing in on the alley across the street from which the sound had emanated. Sage grinned. Among the amorphous shadows he discerned the silhouette of a large male.

Rocky returned from the bedroom and glanced over Sage's shoulder. "There's at least one in the back, too."

"It's a miracle she's alive," Sage said taking the bag from Rocky.

Their first inspection of Alex's cramped apartment had left them both bewildered. The flimsy lock on the front door was locked, but the deadbolt wasn't, and she hadn't had the sense to close and lock her bedroom window. The small egress emptied out onto the building's fire escape, which led to an alley much like the one she had been dragged into two nights ago. Sage knew she had been ignorant of the added danger she was in, but couldn't believe any half-intelligent female could lack the self-preservation to lock her windows and forgo late-night runs.

Rocky scanned the space again. It was clean and relatively neat, but every piece of furniture, every appliance, even the clothes they had packed were more than gently used. Sage had been impressed by her ingenuity—Alex had proved that duct tape really could fix just about anything. But Rocky had been shocked and sympathetic. Despite his condemnation of wealth since the split with his family, Rocky had grown up with every luxury imaginable. Sage thought it was healthy for him to see how the rest of the world lived.

"Maybe it was all she could afford?" It was definitely a question.

"Poverty is no excuse for stupidity."

Rocky pursed his lips in her defense. "She was naïve, not stupid. Obviously her family didn't know enough to warn her."

Sage wasn't so sure about that. Someone knew. Slipping information about her existence might have been accidental. But her being found wasn't coincidental. The Vengatti didn't just happen upon a strong-smelling human female and jump to the conclusion she was a Seer.

Lost in his thoughts, Sage hadn't seen Rocky remove his gun. But hearing the safety click, he intervened. He snapped at his mentee, who was leaning against the window frame.

Rocky sighed casually. "Have some faith. I can make this with my eyes closed."

The chance of an experienced warrior fatally wounding another matured vampire with one shot was near impossible. Only a clean shot to the head or heart would kill. No way one could be that accurate from this distance with a handgun. Then again, before his sentence, Rocky had spent hours each week with his father at the coven's shooting range. It was the only thing the two seemed to have in common. Antonio had won nearly every marksmanship competition in the last century—at least until Rocky was about fifteen, when he began beating his old man. That and the fact his son had the mettle and drive to put his skill to real use hadn't helped with father-son bonding.

"It's your call tonight," Sage said against his better judgment.

Rocky leveled the gun and fired at the shadowy figure before Sage could change his mind. He turned to smirk at his mentor as the corpse slumped to the sidewalk.

Sage growled and pointed to where two Others had flashed to the sound of the shot. "Of course, we just lost the element of surprise."

"Oh. Right. Hadn't thought of that. Go, I'll cover." Rocky got off two more quick shots, injuring another of the males, as Sage flashed to the street to procure an escape route. He soon heard Rocky not far behind fighting the third Vengatti male as they edged deeper into the alley, out of the way of prying human eyes.

Not having an alternative method of stress relief, Alex was attempting to run. She hadn't gone more than fifty feet before she was holding her stitched side and limping every other step. When Markus fell in beside her, she noticed he was following with just a brisk walk. She continued a few more mangled strides before he spoke up.

"Alex, please stop. You're hurting yourself. You're not ready to run yet. Let's just walk." He politely kept his distance, staying a pace behind her so she didn't feel crowded.

"I need to run," Alex said, though she had slowed to a lurching limp. Despite the contrast, Markus seemed to understand her meaning.

"And you will, but not until you're ready. Otherwise, you could do permanent damage," he said. "The wound to your calf was deep. You have several internal stitches in addition to those you can see. So if you need to walk, we'll walk, but let's stick to that until you heal and regain your strength."

Alex paused so they were side by side. She was struck by his patience and control. By comparison she felt immature and embarrassed by her outburst. But she also felt pleased, very pleased, when she realized he had said "we."

"I have a feeling I may be having more than my fair share of these fits in the next few weeks. Are you sure you want to sign on for this?" she asked, not able to meet his eyes.

"It would be my pleasure," Markus said. He gestured for her to lead the way. Alex led him over the dewy grass in silence. She caught him watching her as she clenched and unclenched her uninjured fist. She stopped immediately, leaving her hand still by her side.

"You shouldn't beat yourself up over not knowing what to make of your gift yet. You'll find a way to make sense of it."

Alex chuckled when she realized he knew more than she thought. "You all worry about what Sage can 'hear' and what I'll be able to sense, but you seem to have no privacy anyway."

"Yes, but what little privacy we had is about to end." He smiled, but Alex wondered if he was actually concerned.

"Are you worried about me knowing what you're feeling or worried I'll tell the others?" She wasn't too surprised to find her heart was racing, and knew it had nothing to do with their slow walking.

"Perhaps a little of each." He held her gaze for a brief moment before looking ahead.

"Oh," was all she could manage. As her head tried to make sense of his meaning, her foot had a misstep. She fell forward and instinctively reached out to maintain her balance. Quick to react, Markus grasped her wrist to steady her. Despite his cool hand, a flood of warmth shot up her arm. Her whole body tingled with a feeling so good in comparison to those she had felt lately, it left her breathless. Without his knowing it, their brief contact had given Alex a flash of those feelings he hoped to keep hidden from her.

"This is probably far enough tonight," he said dropping her hand. He seemed to misinterpret her stumble and staggered breath for over-exertion.

"Right," she sighed, looking back towards the house.

"We can sit on the porch if you're not ready to go in," Markus said as they strolled back. Alex knew she shouldn't, but was sorely tempted.

"I like apologizing about as much as Darian, but postponing it won't help."

"You realize you only call him Regan when you're angry or being sarcastic?" Markus asked. His tone seemed more curious than chiding, but Alex still felt embarrassed.

"I guess I also have issues with male authority figures. Growing up with an overbearing father, meek mother, and two bossy older brothers can do that to a girl." Alex cringed. She seemed to spew whatever was in her head whenever Markus was around. "I really shouldn't bore you with all my faults, though—it's a longer list than I thought. I have a knack for over-sharing sometimes, sorry."

"Don't apologize. You're just very open, honest. I find it endearing, actually." He smiled at her again and she blushed, her cheeks burning. Because after sensing him earlier, she knew he wasn't just soothing her. He truly did find her endearing. And she found that pretty amazing.

Markus stood up from the white wicker chair he had been sitting in before Alex could even see the headlights casting shadows from around the bend in the driveway. She leaned forward waiting to see or hear the car as it entered the yard.

"He's pissed about something still," she told Markus as the Jeep tore up the drive and skidded a few feet on the gravel as Sage threw it into park. Markus nodded as he watched Sage get out and slam the door. He headed to the porch holding only Alex's cell phone and laptop, leaving Rocky to carry the black duffle.

Sage paused for a moment to take in Markus's hand on the back of Alex's chair. He rolled his eyes and shook his head before passing them without a word. In the porch light Alex noticed his clothes were dirty. She was just about to ask about the dark stain on his torn pant leg, but by the time she had risen both Sage and Markus could be seen as a mere blur entering Darian's office.

"That's going to be annoying even when I can do more than hobble," she muttered. She turned to Rocky, who still stood in the shadows of the lawn. "Want me to carry something?"

"This is it," Rocky answered, "and I think I can probably handle it." He flung the bag over his shoulder like it was filled with packing peanuts. Alex eyed it with apprehension. Though it was long enough to hold a body—at least a short one like hers—the bag couldn't have held half of her clothes, not to mention any of her other belongings. Rocky caught her expression and explained.

"Sage was in a bit of a hurry to get back to report to Markus and Darian." As he stepped closer, Alex saw his swollen lip. Her clothes seemed a little less important as she tried to make sense of their disheveled appearances.

"I know. What happened? Are you both okay?" Rocky didn't understand how she could know, and Alex didn't want to get into it. She felt guilty enough knowing they'd been hurt again trying to help her. She didn't need them knowing she had sensed something was wrong and had been unable to do anything about it.

"We're fine. Better let them explain," he said. "I'll put this in your room." Before Alex could question him further, he, too, was in the house and up the stairs. *Definitely annoying*, she thought as she trudged along after him.

"I'll get Remalt to look at it first thing tomorrow night. If anyone can trace it, he can," Sage said to Darian as Alex entered the office. The computer was on the desk between them. As Alex moved closer she realized her phone was in pieces next to it.

"Is there a reason my cell phone resembles a jigsaw puzzle?" She casually positioned herself between Markus and Darian, as she leaned over to pick up her crushed SIM card.

"Do you carry this everywhere?" Sage asked.

"I keep it in my purse or school bag, so yeah. I don't have a landline. Why?" Alex was getting nervous as the pieces in her mind were beginning to clunk together. Seeing Markus and Sage turn to Darian for instruction or permission, her panic grew. "What did you find at my apartment?" she demanded. "And what happened to you and Rocky?"

"Rocky and I had a run-in with three of your secret admirers," Sage snarled.

Alex didn't understand. Sage's anger frightened her, so she turned to Darian.

"The vampire that attacked you the other night was definitely one of the Vengatti. They've been watching you, Alex, probably trying to determine if you really were a Seer and also likely wondering if you knew it and were in contact with anyone from our coven," he answered.

"What do you mean 'watching' me?" Alex had to force herself to breathe and remain calm.

Sage looked to Darian again before answering. The Regan nodded and sat back down as Sage explained. "It seems they were physically watching and following you outside your apartment. They had also gotten into your apartment and onto your computer. They probably found your cell phone number and billing info from there, too. From what we can tell they rigged the GPS feature of your phone to track you during the day."

Alex's stomach flipped. She had spent half of last Saturday morning on the phone with her provider arguing over the charge on her phone bill. They had insisted she had activated the GPS and were refusing to drop the extra charge.

"But that's impossible," Alex said trying to convince both them and herself. "My apartment has a deadbolt that I had added after I moved in. Not even maintenance has a key. And I haven't been broken into—"

She would have continued, but Sage cut her off. "The deadbolt only works if you lock it. Then again, with your bedroom window wide open to that charming back alley, why bother?"

Alex blushed deeply. She only locked the deadbolt when she was home; she'd never wanted to carry the extra key on her runs. And on hot nights she had slept with the back window open without a second thought. In hindsight it sounded foolish. Sage scowled. Okay, dangerous. She continued meekly, "But my computer has one password to log in and another to access my other accounts."

"Rocky got into your computer in about two minutes. No one ever told you not to use your pet's name as a password?"

Brady. She forgot she had told them about her missing cat the first night she was here. To be more precise, Sage had plucked it from her mind, but either way, they had remembered the information. But Alex had never met these other vampires, and though she loved her cat, she wasn't the type to talk about him with strangers at the bar. Assuming they broke in after he disappeared, they couldn't have even read his collar. Her heart ached a little thinking of the Patriots collar she had ordered online for him with his name and the number twelve engraved on the football shaped tag. It was supposed to be for a small dog, but as Brady was the size of a large panther cub, it had fit just fine.

With a wave of sudden comprehension, Alex's heart nearly burst. When her knees began to buckle, it was Markus's strong arms that caught her and moved her to the nearest chair. But she regained her footing and pounded her fist on the desk as she shouted what had dawned on her.

"Those fuckers killed my cat!"

The three males appeared shocked at the intensity of her outburst and the certainty with which she delivered it.

"The day he went missing maintenance called to say they were going to replace the old garbage disposal. Only when I got home, it had never been replaced, and Brady was gone, his collar on the floor. His name was on his collar. He didn't like strangers; he would have bitten them if they tried to take it off. When I called the landlord, he had no record of them scheduling a repair. I wasn't suspicious; I figured he was as good at recordkeeping as he was at maintaining his property."

When Alex had finished, she collapsed into the chair Markus had led her to. She was shaking, not from the sobs that should have come but from an intense anger that left her wanting to pound at something or someone. Attacking the two males who had killed one of their own seemed wrong to her, but natural to them, she supposed. Hunting her, who they believed could be of use to them, was horrible, but in some twisted way made sense. But slaughtering an innocent animal just because it was convenient was sickening.

"And your other password?" Sage asked after a moment's silence.

"I don't know how they got that. It's a nickname my brothers used to call me. I've never shared it. Besides, I added both their high school football numbers to the end to make it more secure."

"They could have gotten the second one from watching her type it once they activated the web cam," Rocky said entering the room. Markus and Darian shot him furious looks, but it was too late.

"The web cam? They've been watching me through my computer for over a month?" Now the tears came in a flood. She felt so violated. Strangers had not only rifled through her belongings, searched her emails and financial documents, and followed or tracked her movements, but they had been watching her every movement in the privacy of her own home. It was terrifying, humiliating, and infuriating.

No one acknowledged Rocky's numerous apologies, nor did anyone comment when Markus leaned over to squeeze Alex's shoulder.

With one final quake, she wiped her face on her sleeve. She was way past preserving her pride. She looked up at Darian and worked to steady her breathing.

"I'm sorry about earlier. I want to learn to use my sense, and I will be of use to this coven. Not just because you've asked me to, or because I owe you all my life, which I apparently do," she paused for a second to acknowledge Sage and Rocky, "but also because stopping these evil bastards is the right thing to do."

Rocky caught her attention and gave her a quick nod. They both knew she had found the reason she had been searching for to stay and fight.

Chapter 9

 Levi sat in the passenger's seat smacking the ball hard into his glove. He was annoyed with Dave, who gunned the 1990 Plymouth Acclaim, pushing the engine as if it were a Miata. Eight innings into a pick-up game of baseball with some high school friends and college guys home for the summer, his older brother had grabbed his glove, told the other guys he'd catch them next week, and headed to the car. Having to share the used piece of shit and not living that close to any of the others, Levi had been forced to follow. He reached over and turned down the radio, which was still playing a grunge band whose popularity had peaked five years ago when he was in middle school.

 "Those guys think they're hot shit 'cause they play college ball, but we totally would have schooled them if you hadn't bailed," Levi said. He turned to his brother who was cranking the A.C. a little high for this time of night even with the August humidity.

 "With or without your continued cheating?" Dave asked cranking down his window too.

 "It was one play," Levi shrugged off. "Besides, Dad'll be psyched I finally projected without contact."

 "You think he'll be psyched to hear you were testing your power in front of twenty people?" Dave asked.

 "Yeah, on second thought, maybe we shouldn't share that." Levi tried to seem nonchalant, but looked at Dave to see whether he could gauge his brother's mood. There were times Dave would have gladly arrived home and immediately thrown him under the bus by telling his father. He got overly righteous about their 'gift' sometimes. But Dave seemed distracted. He was wiping his sweaty face with his cap and checking the rearview mirror. It seemed like Levi's secret was safe.

 It had been one out into the last inning when Levi had hit a grounder straight at the second baseman's feet, setting up a potential double play. Somehow, though, Levi managed to send a wave of confusion at him causing him to hesitate—much longer than was necessary, actually—for both Levi and the runner who had been on first to make it safely to base.

As the second baseman's teammates had rolled their eyes and Levi's team razzed the guy from the bench, Dave had caught Levi's Cheshire grin and shook his head disapprovingly.

Levi wondered if it was one of the reasons Dave decided to make a sudden departure. They had left Keefe's field, the only lighted field in the Bristol suburbs open to pick-up games, and drove back to town avoiding the main roads. Levi wished he were driving as Dave took advantage of the curves and lack of cops that made the route as enticing to two teenage guys as an Indy race track.

The car swerved, crossing the double yellow line.

"Watch it!" Levi dropped the ball and reached over to jerk the wheel, grabbing Dave's wrist. "Somebody spike your Gatorade—" he began, but feeling his brother's clammy skin he stopped. "Christ, Dave, you're burning up. You're not . . . ?"

"I don't know," Dave answered. He glanced in the rearview mirror again. He pushed the gas harder making the nine-year-old engine whine.

"Pull over. Let me drive," Levi urged.

"Can't. We're being followed."

"What?" Levi spun around, the seatbelt cutting into his neck. There had been no headlights shining in the back window, but sure enough, even in the dark moonless night, he could make out the outline of a large SUV tailing them.

"How long?" Levi asked his older brother. He tried to hide the fear in his voice, but his hands shook in his lap.

"Last half mile," Dave said struggling to breathe.

"Dave your powers are maturing. We can't let them catch us. You know what Dad said." Levi was reaching panic state. What he hated most was being able to do nothing in the car. But they had no way of knowing who or what was in the vehicle behind them. Stopping to fight would be suicide.

The SUV sped up coming along side them. Dave seemed to expect it as the black vehicle swerved into their lane. He slammed on the brakes and spun the wheel hard, hoping to send the car into a one-eighty so they could head in the opposite direction to lose their pursuers. But this road wasn't like the open parking lots the brothers took their little sister to, trying to impress and terrify her by doing donuts after a December nor'easter. This was a tree-lined road with no houses and therefore no guardrails or curbs. The car spun the desired amount but continued to skid sideways as the two back tires hit gravel on the opposite side of the road. With a deafening crash the back end slammed into a tree.

Even with the seat belt, Levi's head hit the door's window, cracking the glass and knocking him out.

He came to being dragged from the car through the smashed passenger's window. As rough hands yanked him by the underarms over the rough edge of the remaining glass, cutting his bare calves, he knew it was no EMT moving him. He tried to find his footing so he could fight, but as soon as his captor tried standing him up, he felt the ground rushing up at him, smacking his face hard as skin and gravel met.

"Leave him, Ty. This one wants a fight." The second male who had apparently been in the SUV addressed his partner without turning his back to the car. Levi saw with a small amount of satisfaction the reason for this caution. Dave, who appeared uninjured from the crash, was up against the driver's door of the blue sedan, using the now totaled vehicle both as a shield from a sneak attack from the rear and as a prop; his body was struggling with the effects of the transition it was undergoing. In his left hand he held a knife, a small dagger the boys' father had tucked under the seat with the hope it would never be needed for a situation like this, but with the knowledge it was possible.

"I know what you are. I'll never go with you," Dave managed to say. Levi was proud of his brother's resolution, but afraid he meant it.

"If you know what we are, then you know you don't have a choice, Seer," the second male said closing in on Dave.

In height alone the two were equal, but Levi knew his older brother's strength was no match for the two male vampires that faced him. He struggled to pull himself off the ground, desperately wanting to help. He could see Dave's determination, but also the physical toll his maturation was having on him. There was no way Dave could use his power in the state he was in. And Levi's head was spinning too much to even know where to begin. He had managed to get to his hands and knees before being kicked back down with a blow to the side that cracked his ribs. His breath caught as the pain seared through his torso. The same large boot slammed *onto his back pinning him to the ground. Levi felt defeated, but cried out to his brother.*

"Dave—" He didn't want to be captured, taken in by a group of creatures he knew were inherently cruel and heartless. But he was seventeen. He didn't want to die either.

His older brother looked away from his attacker for just a moment to acknowledge Levi's plea. There was no need to speak. Dave had sensed Levi's fear and desperation, just as Levi had sensed Dave's resigned determination. He knew before the flash of movement what the outcome would be.

Dave lurched forward slashing the knife at the male in front of him who laughed as he easily deflected the blow and disarmed him. Levi struggled again to get up as the vampire held his brother with the knife against his throat.

"They always think they can fight, bro," the other vampire said to Ty with a grin. The grin morphed into a howl of pain and anger. The pressure on Levi's back was relieved as Ty flashed to his partner's side.

Finally able to sit up and discern what was happening, Levi saw Dave being stripped of a second knife, his hand covered in blood. Levi realized his brother had tucked another small switchblade into his waistband and managed to use it to gravely injure the vampire holding him.

A cry rang out echoing along the deserted road as Ty watched his partner crumble to the ground. Enraged, Ty sliced Dave's throat with a backward slash, the blood spattering mere feet from a frozen Levi.

"Dave, no!" Levi screamed, finally finding the strength to stumble forward. He caught his brother's body as it fell to the roadside. He cradled his big brother's larger frame, shrieking for help as the life drained from Dave's deep brown eyes as his blood, his essence, flowed from his wound.

Alex awoke shortly after sunset. She knew she had been having another nightmare, a regular occurrence over the last three weeks. She couldn't remember the details, but her heart was racing. Listening to the soft sounds of the household, she tried to calm herself. She could hear the nightly news playing softly next door, which told her Markus was up getting ready for his evening patrol.

Ardellus had returned to his home a few nights after her arrival. Though from what Darian said, he was calling nightly to check on her. She thought this was very kind of the Elder, but she also thought it nice to have Markus right next door. From down the hall she could make out Sarah's soft laughter and a deep voice that was likely Darian's. And though she couldn't hear it, she could guess with a degree of certainty she could walk into the kitchen to find Rocky finishing a second or third bowl of some children's cereal. Sage would be leaning against the counter ragging on him for it, while eating handfuls of the stuff right from the box.

Though it wasn't how she had planned her summer to be unfolding, she was surprisingly settled with this new routine, and not entirely unhappy with her situation. She had already become a night owl, reversing her days and nights, so she could be awake with the other members of the house. It had messed with her internal clock for days, leaving her unable to eat, sleep, and function properly, but she adjusted. She missed lying in the sun at the park reading her books, her biggest worry the damage she was doing to her skin. But despite her stress and fear, she found that now that she had other activities to distract her, and people, or vampires—one in particular—to comfort her, she was able to enjoy waking to the quiet nocturnal sounds of the fields outside her bedroom window.

Since her stitches had been removed and the wounds were healing well, Alex had been cleared to walk around more. Though always a fast healer, her rate of recovery had surprised them all. Not entirely sure what to make of it, the medic, Briant, had attributed it to her ever-strengthening essence. Alex thought it might have had something to do with her strong motivation: Markus's promise to keep her company. It was a promise he made good on each evening before he went to work, even after Darian had lifted the mandate that she be watched twenty-four-seven, which would have allowed her the freedom to walk unescorted—if she had wanted to. She hadn't. Markus was as calming as Sarah, but Alex's attraction to him always had her heart beating rapidly. She knew she was doing it again, falling for someone just because of the feelings she sensed from him in return. She even knew now that this bad habit was likely due to her gift. Reading the histories with Sage she had learned that some Seers could manipulate others' emotions. Too bad she wasn't having any luck curbing her own feelings.

Instead, she found her herself hoping each evening Markus would speak again of his, but despite the connection they had made and kept since that first walk, nothing more had developed. She had made it clear she reciprocated his attraction, but refused to go further. Not only would it be incredibly awkward if she confronted him only to find she had misread him that first night, but she was also a strong believer in the idea that a man, or male vampire in this case, should make the first move. If he was attracted to her, but was unwilling to act on it, she felt there might have been a reason for it. Either way, the rest of her life at the moment was too tense and fragile to push and potentially ruin the one good part of it.

Focusing on that good part, she hopped out of bed and hurried to get ready. She took considerably longer than necessary to get dressed to workout, chuckling at her vanity when she stopped to curl her lashes before heading downstairs.

She entered the kitchen to see Sage slam a bowl into the sink so hard it broke.

"Fine, but hurry up," he spat at Markus. Tossing the shards of white porcelain into the trash, he thundered out.

"Someone woke up on the wrong side of their coffin," Alex said as she heard the door to the basement slam.

"He's always pissy when he's thirsty," Rocky said. He washed his own bowl and spoon and put them in the drying rack. Markus shot him a look. "Right, ah, I think Darian's ready. I'll see you both later." He exited avoiding either of their looks.

"He's going out with Darian tonight?" From what Alex gathered, Darian rarely went on patrol, and Rocky almost always worked with Sage.

"They're finally going to see if Remalt found out anything from your computer. He's been working on it for three weeks with no luck, so far as we know." He continued after a pause, "Sage and I have the night off." He fumbled with the hard-boiled egg he was peeling.

Alex didn't ask, but tried without much luck to use her growing sense to read him. Frustrated, she finished her banana in silence.

"Ready?" she asked when she had thrown away the peel. "I'm thinking tonight's the night I finish a lap running." She had yet to make it once around the perimeter of the property, which they estimated to be only about a mile.

Markus smiled. "I'll try to keep up."

He kindly didn't comment, when half a lap in, she slowed from a run to a slow jog and by the three-quarter mark was once again walking beside him.

"Tomorrow," she said holding her side.

"Definitely," he agreed with only a hint of mockery.

"So what's your plan for your night off?" Alex knew he had avoided the subject earlier but couldn't help asking.

"Sage and I are heading out for a bit," he said, "but I'll drag him back as soon as possible," he added evidently seeing the disappointment she had tried to hide. As she was starting to perk up, he continued. "Maybe you two can have a bit more time to work on the histories that way."

Alex was annoyed. He had to know that wasn't why she asked.

"Actually, our standing after-dinner arrangement is working nicely. It's enough time to get through a few passages, but not so much time we want to rip each other limb from limb."

"So, it's going well, then?" He kept a straight face, but his green eyes were playful. She didn't want to, but found herself smiling.

"Yes, once he stopped questioning my intelligence each time I asked a question, and I stopped humming the chorus to 'Ice, Ice Baby' in return, we began to make progress. We're almost into periods of history I actually studied in school. But we haven't gotten to your birth announcement, so I guess we've still got a ways to go," Alex teased.

"Quite a ways, but you won't find my name in there anyway. My family have served as warriors for as far back as anyone can remember, which as you so kindly insinuated is quite some time," Markus said.

"Warriors are mentioned in the histories," Alex informed him.

"Not by name though, right?" Markus asked. Alex remembered he had never read them himself. She thought back to the mentions of warriors and realized he was right.

"Yes, and why is that?"

"Well, in the very early years all males served as warriors, so it was viewed simply as a duty, not a service worthy of any mention. But as vampires began to adapt to the humans' more modern ways and work beside them in other jobs outside the coven, a limited number of males still fulfilled that duty. Ardellus was the first Regan to have to mandate training and service. And when Darian took over and a few of the older warriors, like my father, could no longer serve full-time, he increased the number of nights each male was required to help. It was one of the early decisions he made that was questioned by the elders, who worried more about their sons being able to work and make money in the human world than performing their duty in their own world. They were furious when Darian came right out and told them the coven had become remiss, or at the very least, indifferent when it came to finding and destroying the Vengatti. He doesn't mince words."

"I'll bet they loved that." Alex would have liked to have been a fly on the wall when Darian made that declaration to a group of old vamps whom she couldn't help but picture being as uptight and presumptuous as Ardellus.

"They gave him hell for it, actually. A few refused to show up until Darian paid them a personal visit. It was a rough couple years." Markus wore a grim expression, and Alex could tell he respected his friend and believed in his purpose.

"But they understand now?" Alex asked.

"They should have understood then; it was the reason Darian took over at such an early age. The Vengatti moved here during the famine. They couldn't get enough strength from the sickly population, so rather than feed from one another, as our kind was meant to, they decided to come terrorize the humans here." It was clear to Alex the absolute revulsion Markus felt toward them. "Ardellus was a strong leader and well-respected, but he struggled to adapt to the new surroundings. Ireland was slower to develop than America, and we had always stayed outside the larger cities, where the Vengatti had been satisfied preying on nighttime travelers. Here they settled right in the heart of Bristol, which was booming with the money and people the mills brought in. Attacks on humans increased dramatically. Ardellus was outraged but a bit at a loss as to how to stop them in an urban setting while still protecting the secret of our existence. Many of the original families, and quite a few of the other coven families, were too busy trying to establish themselves to want to help. The rest were afraid the Vengatti would grow stronger with a bigger food supply. Darian agreed, and he convinced his father, and mine, who was still lead warrior at the time, to act on it. He came to me and a few of the other younger warriors, and together we overhauled how the patrols were run. His initiative saved a lot of lives. No one should have questioned him when Ardellus stepped down."

"But they did, so what finally convinced them?"

"The Vengatti choosing a new favorite target—us. Three vampires have been killed since Darian ascended, and four more have been left worse than dead. There were a few in the coven who would have had the audacity to blame the new Regan for that too, but he made it clear, until we all took the threat more seriously, the blame lay equally on all our shoulders," Markus said.

"So when did you start serving the Regan?" Alex asked as they reached the driveway for a second time. They both saw the curtain in the living room flutter like someone had just been looking out. Alex, sensing Sage's impatience, didn't need to wonder whom. Markus frowned, then turned back to answer Alex.

"It's a long story. You up for another lap?"

"You're keeping him waiting," Alex said.

"That bothers you?"

"Not at all," she said grinning, and when Markus held out his arm for her to take, her grin turned into a smile that stretched ear to ear. Her own elation didn't match the other strong emotions she felt. Emotions she knew weren't connected to the physical contact between her and Markus.

"He's annoyed," Alex said. "I hate it when we're feeling two different things. It's like I've got an internal tug-of-war going on." Alex wished her sense wouldn't interfere with these moments.

"Is he just annoyed?" Markus looked at his feet; he seemed a bit uncomfortable asking.

Alex wondered what exactly he wanted to know. "He's not jealous, if that's what you're wondering. That would make sense. I mean, not that . . . it's just a more typical guy emotion." *Great,* she cringed, *he must think I'm conceited—or deluded into thinking this is anything more than him being a gentleman.* "He seems to worry when we're together. Which doesn't make sense to me."

"You don't know who or what he's worrying about?"

"No clue. He's the one who can hear the thoughts, I just get the feelings behind 'em," she answered.

"Well, then, it remains a mystery, I guess," he said with a grin.

Alex returned the smile and happily continued walking with him. She wanted to simply enjoy the warmth of his touch. But as they walked, she couldn't help but think of Markus's wording. If the 'who' was Alex, Sage probably just worried she'd get hurt when Markus finally ended these nightly jaunts. Thinking of this possibility hurt, because it would mean Sage had been in Markus's head and knew he didn't feel as strongly about Alex as she felt for him. But Sage had just met Alex, and with the amount of time they spent bumping heads, she couldn't see him worrying that much over the possibility of her being let down. If the 'who' was Markus, which made more sense, since he and Sage had been friends and comrades for so long, then what was he worried about? Whether either of them liked it or not, Sage heard all of her thoughts. He had to know she was sincere about her feelings for Markus. And even if he missed some of this, she would be living here for the foreseeable future; he had to realize she wasn't about to lead on a member of the house, only to have to face him every day. Although who knew how many days that would be? Though she fought nightly not to think about it, her future was unforeseeable.

And that's when she knew. She might not be living here much longer. She might not live until the end of the summer. And no one, not even a male like Sage, who liked to appear blasé about everything, would want to see a friend fall for someone who had a possible expiration date of any day now.

Alex stopped abruptly and dropped Markus's arm. He examined her with concern. She wondered what her expression gave away.

"My leg's starting to hurt. Maybe you could tell me the story another time." She hoped the pain on her face would make the lie believable.

"Of course, no problem. We'll save it for tomorrow." Markus turned around with her and headed back to the porch. He had reached out his other hand after they changed directions, but Alex used her hand to hold her side, as if that hurt too.

"Right, or some other time," she said, looking straight ahead, not wanting to see the look she imagined he gave her.

They walked like this in silence until they reached the steps. Markus reached out and clutched her shoulder, turning her to face him. As he began to speak, the door opened. Markus growled at the interruption, or more likely, the interrupter. Alex used the distraction as a means to break his hold and head for the front door, which Sage held open for her.

"It took you long enough," he said directing the comment at Markus. But the quick glance he shot at Alex, accompanied by the relief she could sense, told her the real message was for her.

"If you had a particular *dead*line in mind, you could have just said so," she spat as she brushed past. Sage smiled at the play on words, though she caught the wash of sympathy and regret that he'd never outwardly display.

When she slammed the door, Markus spoke to Sage. "Did I do or say something I shouldn't have?"

"Nope. Human chicks are just weird. Let's go find our females and get fed from a species we understand," Sage said, jingling the car keys.

On the other side of the door, Alex sank to the floor, once again in tears. She didn't need vampire hearing or mind reading to realize where Sage and Markus had been planning to go all evening. And she didn't need any gift to know the heart she felt breaking was her own.

Alex didn't wait for the males to return. She excused herself from dinner before they arrived back, telling Sarah and then Rocky, who tried to bring her a tray, that she just wasn't feeling well. She asked Rocky to shut off her light and to pass along the message to Sage that she wouldn't be reading with him later, as she was going to bed.

She fell into a fitful sleep and returned to her nightmares. This time it was Markus's face that morphed into Levi's. He was freshly bruised as he looked up from the foosball table.

"What happened to you, Levi?" her dream-self asked.

"They don't like me talking to you this way," he answered. "They don't understand our connection."

Talk about projecting real life into dreams, Alex thought, but she spoke to comfort him, because really she was comforting herself. "Yeah, I know, Levi."

"Do you? Because you're still looking for answers in the wrong places, squirt." He turned his back to her and tossed a dart, which she didn't realize he had been holding, onto the dartboard across the room. It hit two rings from the center. "Hmm," he said examining his spot, "Not a bad place to start." Turning to her, his eyes had gone cold again. "You're turn, squirt. Put down the cat and come find me."

Alex looked on her lap to find Brady curled up. Only when she started to stand and reached to put him down, she realized why she hadn't heard him purring or felt his warmth on her legs. She was holding his lifeless body, his head hanging at an awkward angle to one side. Shrieking she dropped him and fell back onto the couch sobbing.

When Alex woke, it was to find she had fallen back onto her pillows. The sobbing had been real, but the rest, she told herself, was just a dream. She listened for movement in the house. If she had been screaming as loudly in reality, someone would have woken. When she was convinced she was the only one awake, she slid out of bed. There'd be no more sleep today.

She reached the foyer with her sneakers laced up and her headphones in. From the faint glow coming through the curtains in the kitchen, she knew it was partially light out. She was relieved. The still setting sun meant she would have a half hour or more of privacy. She grabbed a notepad and pen from the drawer in the kitchen.

Rocky—Just running, not away. Don't wake them. Be back by breakfast. A.

She tucked the paper behind the picture she now knew hid the alarm. If anyone were conscious enough to hear the door close when she left, it would be him.

The setting sun was still hot; it had been a scorching summer day she guessed. The heat rising from the browning grass felt good. And the female voice of the lead vocalist of her favorite alternative group sounded strong and empowering as the music pounded in her ear. Facing an open field as she rounded the first corner, Alex was resigned to feeling content with such solitude. She had lived alone and isolated herself outside of work for the last four years. Why had she decided now, when her fate, her future was so uncertain, to open herself up to new relationships? Sage was right. It was unfair, not just to Markus, but to the others as well. She couldn't continue building bonds that might very soon be broken in a sudden and permanent manner. Besides, she was trying to convince herself, it was better for her too. Facing the unknown would be easier if she didn't have to worry about people and commitments she was leaving behind.

She rounded the final corner just as the last light was fading behind the house. It had been closer to evening than she thought, but still there was no light coming from the kitchen, so either Rocky had slept through the sound of her leaving or had gotten her note and let her be.

She pulled up at the driveway, realizing with mild satisfaction she had made it a mile without walking.

"Feeling better, I see," Markus said, appearing in front of her in a blur of movement. He looked irritated, which frustrated Alex, who took out her earphones and answered.

"I left a note," she said stepping around him and continuing along her route, walking briskly.

"Yes. To Rocky. I didn't realize he was the one you've been walking with every evening." He didn't attempt to hide his sarcasm or the underlying anger. Both were unusual and caught Alex off guard, though she tried to hide it.

"I figured you were out late having fun with your female friend and might want to sleep in." She would have liked nothing more than for him to storm off.

"Actually, I came home early, as I promised. I hoped to apologize for whatever it was I said or did that upset you." He matched her quickening stride.

She stopped. Despite her real reason for backing away from their growing relationship, she couldn't let this go. It had hurt too much when he left with Sage last night.

"Whatever it was? Don't you mean whomever? Do you need me to hold a mirror up to your neck, Markus?" She reached up and tugged open his collar, revealing two healing marks on the left side.

Markus clenched his jaw and pursed his lips until they were white. Alex dropped his shirt, stepping back. She had never seen him not in perfect control, but he was struggling now.

"Cormelia has been my friend and feeding partner for nearly two centuries. She was my mate's best friend before the Others slaughtered Alia in our bed while I was out on a raid. We meet just as often as is necessary and ask of each other only to share our essence, essence that is strengthened by our mutual love for and remembrance of Alia."

Alex stood stunned. She couldn't have felt worse if Markus had struck her.

"It seems you have a nice arrangement," Alex said, struggling as much as Markus had to control her voice, though the emotions she hid were different. "All I could do is mess that up."

Alex turned back to the house, her eyes averted. Markus grabbed her by both shoulders, so she had to face him.

"Why are you doing this?"

"It's better, for both of us," Alex answered. She tried not to blink, afraid the welling tears would spill over, giving her away.

"Do you think I'm stupid? Just because you and Sage hold half your conversations in your head and the other half in some double-speak doesn't mean the rest of us can't figure out we've missed something. Sarah and Rocky told us how upset you were last night. It was then I understood your conversation before we left, and got him to admit it. Alex—"

"No, Markus, he's right."

"He's an idiot who only thinks he's right, Alex." He shook her shoulders. "I lost my first mate. I know how intense that pain is, but because of Alia I also know to appreciate every moment. It's not right to stop living because you might die, Alex."

As she watched his chest heaving up and down with the intensity of what he was trying to convey, Alex knew it didn't matter. Whether it was right or wrong, she had already fallen for him too hard to walk away. She looked up at him, letting her tears fall freely down her sweaty cheeks.

"Then why have you waited almost three weeks to kiss me?"

Markus was perplexed for a moment, frozen. Finally he let out a relieved laugh. "I thought that was customary."

"Get with the times, vampire." She stepped forward and grabbed his shirt again, this time pulling him down so they were face to face. She paused for a moment, breathing in his earthy scent and bracing herself before making contact. When their lips met, and a feeling so warm, so pure, so good rushed between them, Alex understood better than she had believed she could what the histories meant when they mentioned the pleasure of being a Seer.

It had been a very quiet half hour. After purposefully delaying their meeting by helping Sarah with the dinner dishes, Alex had entered the living room where Sage had been waiting. She silently picked up the fourth volume off the coffee table and began to read. Sage was content to let her avoid confronting him. He hardly looked up from the medical text he was reading and remained equally silent as he half-listened to her thoughts as she worked her way through the passages.

She had managed to avoid or ignore him up until dinner, obviously sensing his emotions. Not that he attempted to hide them. Sage was annoyed that Alex had surrendered to her feelings, strengthening rather than severing ties with Markus as he hoped she would. But his real indignation stemmed from the fact the rest of the house was pissed at him. The glacial looks that Sarah, especially, shot him throughout dinner rendered his gift unnecessary. Yes, he knew he could be a bastard. Sometimes he even took pleasure in it. But that hadn't been the case this time, and Sarah and Darian, at least, should have known that. He had just met Markus, Sarah, and Darian when Alia had been murdered. He had seen how long Markus was tortured by that loss. They all had. He didn't think any male could suffer like that twice and recover.

And whether the rest of them wanted to admit it or not, Alex's chances were slim. He had read the histories she read now. He knew family after family of Seers lost most of their sons to their maturity. And those were strong, healthy males, whose fathers and coven had trained them both physically and mentally for years prior. He looked over the top of the book at Alex, who sat cross-legged on one corner of the couch. Despite being fit, her short pixie hair and small frame made her look more like a child than a woman, and certainly she was no warrior.

She looked up to catch him staring at her.

"What?" she snapped.

"I just thought tonight's passages would have you asking more questions than normal," he lied.

"Why bother? I'm not likely to live long enough to use this, right? Will you be happy to have your evenings free again?"

Her words stung him. "Do you really think I'm that cold?" He was the one who had spent the last three weeks in her head. Ever since that second night, when she realized she could sense him from across town, he, too, found that if he focused he could hear her at any distance. He was the one who knew her greatest fears, deepest pain, and most intense worries. He was also the one who heard her compassionate thoughts about the others, the funny comments she kept to herself, the love for one of his best friends that she felt but hadn't even fully admitted to yet, and the loyalty and determination that drove her to want to survive so she could help the coven.

"Whether you like it or not, I know you better than any of them," he said. "And because of that, I will miss you more intensely. Whether I like it or not."

Alex shifted her position on the couch. She didn't know how to respond to this. Being uncomfortable with the idea of someone in her head all the time, she tried to think about Sage's gift as little as possible. She hadn't stopped to think what it was like for Sage to hear all of her thoughts, all of the thoughts of everyone to whom he was close. She remembered how uncomfortable it felt to sense his emotions when they didn't mesh with hers or to know when another member of the house was angry with her. She tried to imagine hearing all the reasoning behind those emotions. She wondered if the section of the histories about Knowers also employed the word horror. It seemed to fit as well as anything she could think of. Perhaps she had been quick to judge Sage. His thick skin wasn't for show; it was for survival.

She felt his discomfort and realized, of course, he was hearing this too. She stopped crumpling the sticky note in her hand and looked awkwardly back to her book, trying to focus. Reading another few lines reminded Alex of Sage's original comment. He had been right in guessing tonight's reading would interest her. It wasn't that the lives of the two Seers she read about stood out in many distinguishable ways from the others she had studied. The only thing remarkable about these two men was that they were twins who had both survived their maturities. It was the first time since Timian's children that more than one son of the same Seer lived to use his gift. What Sage knew would make these passages both fascinating and heartbreaking for Alex were the names of the two men: Leviathan and Davidian. These were also the full names of her two older brothers, though they had wisely gone by Levi and Dave in school.

"My brothers weren't twins though," she informed Sage, who had looked up when her thoughts had strayed to them.

"True, but it means your father or mother knew what their children could become. They knew about your family's gift and your kind's histories," Sage said.

A question formed in Alex's mind, but before she could ask it, Sage answered.

"Most likely. They both would have been close to maturity. They probably just kept it from you."

"No," Alex said, "If they thought they had some 'gift', they would have loved to brag about it."

"Would you tell your little sister something that would scare her, worry her, and possibly put her in danger?" Sage asked.

She knew he was right. "But then my parents . . . they had to have known about me, too. Otherwise my brothers would never have known to keep it from me." Sage nodded as Alex thought more about her parents, her father in particular. He had always been so overbearing, so strict, and not just with the boys but with her as well. He only allowed healthy food in the house, pushed them to exercise, encouraged their martial-arts training, and dictated strict curfews—hours earlier than any of their friends', especially as the boys aged. And then there were the odd things he asked them to do, like making them memorize long verses of poetry only to blare the television or radio when he asked them to recite it. Alex realized he had been trying to prepare them. Thinking of the dangers she had faced recently, the danger she still faced, she was furious he hadn't been more straightforward. But she also felt rueful. All the times they had argued with him, all the spiteful remarks she had made behind his back, and he was just trying to help them survive. No wonder he had gone mad when his two sons died the same night. He had worried his whole life about losing them to their maturity or to the Vengatti, only to lose them in a very normal human tragedy.

Alex was deep in thought when Sage let out a very obvious and dramatic yawn.

"Let me just finish this section. There are only a couple pages left." She threw the couch pillow at him when he started to complain.

She was trying to read quickly, but still not miss anything important or new. She was nearing the end, so she knew, after having read the life stories of half a dozen other Seers, these would no doubt end in a violent death. Sure enough, both Leviathan and

Davidian were captured during a large-scale battle between the Rectinatti and Vengatti covens. When the Rectinatti Regan refused to help the Others assassinate the human king in charge of the region they were living in, the two brothers were sentenced to be beheaded on opposite ends of the battlefield. *Lovely*, Alex was thinking as she skimmed over the last line ready to close the book.

"Wait. What does this mean?" she asked Sage, who had already dog-eared his own book and was standing to collect the histories.

"Beheading: to have one's body separated from one's head, usually by a bloody and violent means," Sage answered dryly.

"The next line, Jerk-o. It says, 'As a final show of defiance, the two said their goodbyes silently, using the trance-like form of communication only possible between two living Seers.'"

Sage shrugged. "Not sure, really. They were the last two Seer siblings, and the only two ever known to have been able to do it. But I think Ardellus told me there was another old account of the battle that mentioned they looked almost like they were asleep, like they could communicate in their dreams," he said. "Not to be harsh, but you don't have to worry about it, as you have no living siblings and are the only living Seer, as far as we know." Sage took the book Alex had let drop to her lap. He waited for her to get up, but her body was frozen. Her mind however raced through the information that was falling into place. Before Sage could make sense of her thoughts and respond, she jumped from the couch and sprinted by him. It wasn't Sage she needed.

She slammed into Markus who had been leaving Darian's office with a serious expression. Not stopping to make apologies, she burst into the room and didn't stop running until she nearly crashed into Darian's desk, throwing out her hands to stop herself.

"My brothers are alive. And they have them. We need to find them, now!" Alex knew she was yelling. She knew the pain in her left hand, which had mostly healed, was from her gripping Darian's desk with all her strength. She knew she sounded crazy. She knew, but she didn't care. She wanted immediate action. Darian just sat behind his desk, looking perplexed. She was becoming frantic. She watched as he looked up at Sage who had entered the room, followed by Markus who was asking him what he had done to upset her.

"Where did this come from?" Darian asked Sage.

Alex hated that Darian asked him to translate her outbursts. "Seers can communicate through dreams," she answered for herself.

"Oh," Darian said, a look of understanding dawning, "You're at Leviathan and Davidian's passages."

"Yes, and—"

"Alex, I know it must be upsetting thinking about your brothers, but—"

"What is upsetting is you not listening!" She pounded the Regan's desk right in front of where he sat. Darian sat up and scowled at her.

"Regan, perhaps—" Markus began, but Darian's stare stopped him.

"Alex, sit down and tell us what you believe," Darian said, in a tightly controlled voice. He gripped the arms of his desk chair waiting for her to obey, which she had no intention of doing. When Alex remained standing, he pointed to the chair opposite from him, next to where she stood. "Please."

She tried to catch her breath and remind herself that people listened better to logic. She sat, remaining on the very edge of the seat, still gripping his desk. She needed to convince him. She needed to find Levi. Which meant she needed to stay calm.

"I don't *believe* anything, Darian. I know my brothers . . . well, I know Levi is still alive. Dave, I guess, must really be dead." She stopped a moment, because saying this aloud hurt. She had believed, for a split second, that maybe they could both be alive, but thinking back to her dreams she knew there was a reason it was only ever Levi who spoke to her.

She explained her dreams to Darian. She told him what Levi kept telling her, that she had to find him, that she was looking for answers in the wrong place, that they had a connection the Others were unhappy about. She described the changes in his appearance: he was a grown man, but one who had been beaten repeatedly, both mentally and physically tortured. She described everything except the cold look he sometimes had in his eyes. She couldn't bring herself to linger on that change in her brother's demeanor.

"And last night he looked different, even more bruised than before. They had beaten him recently. He said they caught him trying to talk to me. I know this is hard to believe, Darian. I've been having these dreams for three weeks and didn't believe them. But now I'm sure. He's alive. He's a Seer. And he needs me, he needs us to save him." Alex had pleaded as calmly and politely as she could manage given the desperate situation.

"Alex, I know—" Darian began. He stopped when he noticed Alex gritting her teeth and clenching her fists again. She could tell by his tone he didn't believe her. "I listened," he said. "Now it's your turn to let me explain. When you told us your brothers died at the ages they did, in a car crash with no witnesses, we, too, were suspicious. Before it could have occurred to you that the Vengatti could have been involved, we wondered. And we investigated. Markus himself got the police and medical examiner's reports. There were two sets of remains in the burned out wreckage. They matched your brothers' physical descriptions, and what was left of the clothing matched as well. Your brother Levi's license was pulled from the wallet in his back pocket, and there were enough of Dave's remains to get a dental record ID. I'm sorry, Alex, but your brothers really did die in that car crash." Darian finished, and with a sympathetic gesture he reached out to Alex, whose fists were still resting on his desk. She pulled away. She didn't want his comfort; she wanted his trust.

"Then it was staged. They could have switched the clothes, used two other boys the same build, falsified the records. You can't tell me a coven like that doesn't have the means to cover their tracks."

"Alex, this isn't some crime novel," Darian said.

"Oh, I'm sorry, pardon me for confusing fiction with reality in a room full of vampires." She was on her feet again and furious.

"Alex." Markus came up beside her and laid his hand on her back to calm her.

She spun on him. "No, Markus. He wants me to trust him and his decisions and to help him and his coven, the people he cares for, but what do I get when I ask for the same in return?"

"They are just dreams, Alex," Darian said, also rising to his feet. "There's nothing I can do."

"You could believe me and at least go look," she implored.

"It's not that easy. It's not like we can simply look up Vengatti in the Yellow Pages and take a stroll by their headquarters," Darian said.

"I didn't realize being a good leader was supposed to be easy, Regan," she said, knowing the accusation would prick both his conscience and his pride. He shook his head, but refused to take her bait. She was beyond angry; she was crushed. "So that's it? You're going to let him die or be tortured another ten years and expect me to sit idle while he begs me every day to find him?"

"I'm sorry these dreams cause you so much pain, Alex, but they are just dreams."

"They are not just dreams! And you do not know pain!" But as Alex's whole body shook violently, they all knew her pain. Because as she screamed the last word, each of them felt the pain and anger she radiated out from her body. Markus and Darian staggered back with the shock and force of it. Sage, already against the wall, hit his head as it was jerked back. Alex caught a glimpse of their reactions and subsequent astonished expressions. She realized what she had managed to do without intending to. As the pain and anger she had projected rebounded back to her, she was overwhelmed with the force of it and the energy it had drained from her. She collapsed, hitting the carpet unconscious.

"I think you need to get Ardellus as soon as the sun sets, Darian." Sarah's tense voice was becoming clear to Alex. She could feel the soft pillows behind her and a light sheet over her and guessed she was in bed. She was vaguely aware that she had been stripped of her jeans and flip-flops, but was too groggy to care. A cool, damp cloth was pressed to her forehead. She wanted to thank whoever it was who was gently wiping her flushed cheeks.

"You said her fever broke," Darian answered from somewhere on the other side of the room. "Besides, unfortunately, I'm not sure what he can do for her."

"His father, your grandfather, knew the last Seer; maybe he knows what to expect. If she's maturing, there may be things she needs that I don't know about."

Alex tried to find the strength to open her eyes and sit up. Her whole body ached, like when she had the flu last January and missed three days of teaching.

"Right now she's thinking she just needs a glass of cold water," Sage spoke up. Alex's eyes fluttered open, and she tried to grin. For once, she was pleased to have Sage in her head.

"Oh, Alex," Sarah rushed to her other side, a wash of relief evident on her face. It hadn't been her applying the cool compress.

Alex turned her head to the side of the bed where she could feel someone sitting next to her. Markus's green eyes were looking down at her. She could see the dark circles under them and the worry lines in his furrowed brow. She smiled at him before looking around the rest of the room. Rocky and Sage stood by the door. Rocky extracted his gnawed fingernails from his mouth as she turned to them. Sage winked, looking cavalier as always. Darian was at the foot of the bed, with his hands on the footboard. From the state of his mussed waves, she imagined he had been pacing the carpet running his hands through his hair. All of them had the same dark under-eye circles as Markus, and she began to wonder how long she had been out and why they all looked so relieved to see her wake.

"Is that it? Are her powers mature? That wasn't so bad," Rocky said.

"She didn't mature, yet. Do you have any sense of smell? Her essence will be much stronger," Sage said, shaking his head at Rocky. He turned to answer Alex's unspoken questions. "You've been out all day. And you were running a fever. We were worried it was starting, but it seems it was just. . . ." He paused. Alex sensed his confusion.

"I projected," she said, hoping they could hear the raspy whisper.

"Alex, did you mean to do that?" Darian asked.

She shook her head. Sure, at the time she was glad to have them understand how much she hurt. But to say she intentionally forced her emotions on them would be an overstatement. She had no idea how it happened. She wondered if they were angry about the violation.

"I'm sorry."

"You have nothing to apologize for, Alex," Markus said. He ran his hands over her forehead, brushing aside her short damp bangs. He looked to the others as if daring them to disagree.

"He's right," Darian said. "Both your power and your passion are admirable. But right now, you need to rest. And the rest of you probably do, too. I can stay with her to make sure her fever doesn't return," he said to Markus, who held her shoulders so she could sip from the glass of ice water somebody had fetched.

"No," Markus said. "I'll stay. I'll come get Sarah if I need to."

"Fine." Darian eyed him warily before taking Sarah's hand and heading to the door.

"We're all very glad you're okay, Alex," Sarah said. "And you're in good hands," she added with a wink.

When the others had left the room, shutting the door behind them, Alex turned to Markus. "Is he still angry with me?" She wasn't at all remorseful about her outburst, but she needed Darian's help, which meant she needed his acceptance.

"No. Actually, he gave me permission to move a few patrols around to try to track some of the Others," Markus answered.

"To placate me so I stop shooting my emotions at him, or because he believes me?" Markus smiled at her. "He hates to be wrong, so he always double-checks," he said, not really answering. Alex smiled anyway. It came to the same: Darian would try to help. There was hope for Levi. "It's actually me he's miffed with. But that happened before you projected."

"Why?"

"He's not sure my courting you is a wise decision," Markus said.

Alex normally would have giggled at the word choice, but instead she reached out to take his hand. "For the same reason Sage doesn't like it; he's worried my days are numbered?" Markus winced, and Alex sensed his pain.

"No. He's quite convinced, as I am, you'll mature just fine. He's more concerned with what happens after. He worries we could become distractions to each other," Markus said.

Alex smirked. "He's seriously concerned about your job performance?"

"*Our* job performance." They shared a smile. "You should rest now."

"Will you sleep with me?" she asked. Markus's face flushed, and his mouth hung open as he tried to form a response. Alex, seeing his expression, blushed in return. "Oh, sure, *that* modern dating term you know," she said. "I just meant it literally, because you've apparently been awake all day caring for me."

If anything, she thought Markus's blush intensified after she explained.

"Of course, I wasn't assuming—I mean—Yes, I'd love to stay with you," he said. Alex tried not to laugh at him as he circled the bed so she didn't have to move. He dropped his heavy boots on the throw rug at the end of the footboard. Finally, he climbed onto the mattress, remaining above the blankets and taking care, despite his size, not to jostle her with his movements. When he had settled next to her, Alex reached over and took his hand again. She tried to project into him the feelings that permeated her but found herself unable. She settled for falling asleep seeing them reflected in Markus's eyes.

Chapter 10

Ty wiped the trickle of blood from his chin. He began to shut the door of the small cell, but just before locking it, he heard the whimper. He turned in disgust to the frail human boy who huddled along the back wall. Man, he corrected himself; he hadn't been a boy in years, though he often acted like one still. Ty wondered if such weakness was common among human males or if the prolonged captivity had somehow damaged his pride. A male from Ty's coven would be ridiculed or ostracized, at best, for such behavior. More likely his father and uncles would have beaten it out of him—long before he matured. Pain and self-pity were for pansies and over-emotional females. And perhaps Seers. Feeling and messing with emotions, after all, was what should have made the freak valuable. But the human's gift had come to nothing—not worth the life lost to acquire him.

At the memory of his brother, Ty flashed back across the cell. He lifted the human by his shaggy blonde hair and slapped him hard across the face. "Stop whining like a woman," he growled, "or I'll beat you like the little bitch you are." The boy kept quiet as Ty backhanded his other cheek and dropped him back onto the filthy floor.

Slamming the door, Ty realized the boy's essence left a rancid taste in his mouth. He stopped in the kitchen and grabbed two beers before heading into the living room. He uncapped them both. Downing his own, he dropped the second onto the dark coffee table in front of where the Regan sat, arms spread over the back of the leather couch. His head was reclined. He looked down his nose at Ty.

"Leave the training of the human to me, please, Ty." Leonce sat up and moved the beer bottle onto one of the coasters.

Ty tried to hide his eye roll. Leonce's insistence on etiquette and civility, at least in domestic areas, had never caught on with his lead warrior.

"Some days manners are all that separate us from the human scum we feed from," Leonce commented, hearing the thoughts in Ty's head.

It annoyed Ty, but he wouldn't say so. Especially not lately. Leonce had pounced, quite literally, on anyone stupid enough to cross his path since the girl disappeared, apparently with two Rectinatti warriors.

"The boy's useless, and frankly I've lost my patience and my appetite for him," Ty said. "What makes you think the female will be any better?"

Leonce said nothing as he drank, but his eyes never left Ty. The warrior knew he was pushing it, questioning his Regan about this issue again, but the woman was turning into Leonce's latest obsession. It had already cost Ty two of his warriors and left another injured. When the Regan became hyper-focused, he could become oblivious to the demands of the coven. Ty's job, his duty, was to redirect him, even, perhaps especially, when he didn't want to hear it. He was given his position because he was one of the few males in the coven fierce enough to face Leonce's wrath again and again.

"This is different, warrior, as I've already explained to you," Leonce said finally. "There was a reason her father and brothers worked so hard to keep her from either coven."

Ty shook his head. He'd heard this before. After years of silence about his sister, the human male had suddenly divulged the girl was also gifted. Moreover, he said their father claimed it was foretold she would be more powerful than any male Seer who had preceded her. Ty believed it was a crock, a last ditch ploy for the male to prolong his miserable existence. Leonce had been more willing to entertain the possibility he was telling the truth. He even found an old prophecy among his father's records that possibly referred to a female Seer. Only problem was the boy claimed it was incomplete—the second half he had conveniently never read, but thought existed in the histories of Seers his father once maintained.

"Even if it were true, Leonce, so what? She's still just a human—a small female human. I doubt her 'gift,' even if it is ten times stronger than her brother's, would level the playing field."

Leonce sneered. "Spend fewer hours sharpening your weapons and screwing your mate and more time reading the histories of your own kind, and you'd know what a stupid comment that was. Seers' powers vary, Ty, but the powerful ones have been known to incapacitate an enemy merely by overwhelming them with an emotion. Some are said to have been able to affect multiple vampires at once, without contact. If you were rendered unconscious, and she was armed and trained, do you suppose that would level the playing field? Fool."

Ty had both brows raised. He wasn't sure he believed the accuracy of all the stories that supposedly existed in the coven's histories, but admitted that if this were true it made the girl more desirable than he originally believed.

"Not to mention a Seer's more subtle use of his gifts," Leonce continued. "A Seer in control of his power can influence a person's decisions."

"Isn't that your area of expertise?" Ty scoffed.

"A Knower can only change the memory of what has happened. A Seer can change a person's attitude before they act." Leonce was standing, his hands in his back pockets. "Let's be honest, the humans are still running amuck, while the Rectinatti defend them. And some in our coven have become . . . disinterested in our mission to stop that."

Ty growled at the understatement. He'd have had all the traitorous cowards rounded up and beaten to death, but Leonce refused. He was convinced they could be made loyal again. He liked to pick them off one a time, choosing a scapegoat, whom the others respected, to be publicly tortured. But such psychological terror was only effective as long as the memories were fresh.

"Exactly," Leonce answered Ty's thoughts. "But what if we could permanently change their attitudes? What if we could once again oppose the humans and Rectinatti as a unified front?" Leonce smirked. Ty knew the smile hid grander schemes. The prophecy mentioned victory. Leonce believed whoever possessed the female would be the victor.

"You really think one human can do all that?" Ty asked.

Leonce scowled. "I don't know. But I'm sure as hell not about to let the Rectinatti find out first. The boy needs to lead his sister to the prophecy and then to us—sooner rather than later." Leonce moved to stand in front of the fire that burned in the tile fireplace despite the summer heat. He held the end of the poker in the flame until it glowed orange.

"The boy's been fed from?" the Regan asked in a mellifluous tone that contrasted sharply with his intentions.

"Yes, Regan," Ty answered with a growing grin.

"Bring him here. Perhaps with a weakened essence and the right ... motivation," he said, turning the hot metal tool in his hand, "we can speed things along."

Ty nodded and flashed from the room. At least they agreed on one thing tonight.

Shaken awake by another unsettling nightmare she couldn't clearly recall, Alex rolled over. Her heartbeat slowed and a smile spread across her face as she found Markus waking up beside her. Being the third day he'd shared her bed, she had thought perhaps she could convince him it would be perfectly acceptable for him to sleep under the covers with her, especially since he slept in sweats and a t-shirt, at least when he was with her. Markus had politely refused, claiming he didn't want to risk disturbing the sleep she so badly needed as she neared her maturity. Alex knew it was a crock, but liked him all the more for it.

It may have been her gift that initially drew her to him. It may have been the contrast to all the unpleasant emotions she was feeling that caused her attraction to become so intense, so fast. But the time they spent together during the last couple days convinced Alex that, whatever the reason, her feelings were genuine. Markus gave her balance. Where she spoke bluntly, often without forethought, Markus chose his words carefully and was sometimes guarded. Where Alex was impatient and wanted to rush, he waited for the right moment to do something well. Where she would have let passion lead to impropriety, Markus led with logic and dignity. And though these contrasts could have driven a woman nuts, the quiet confidence with which Markus went about his nights was constantly forcing Alex to recalibrate her own ways. And she knew she was better for it.

So despite having her early evening attempts at corrupting him gently rebuffed, she was feeling content as she entered the kitchen with Markus. Rocky looked at her oddly, though, as she headed to the cabinet where the bowls were kept. Her cheeks burned as she wondered how much of her thwarted sexual advances he and Sage had overheard. She was thrilled when his question was totally unrelated.

"Am I underfed, or is she rocking some hard core essence lately?" he asked Sage, who was standing behind him eating from the cereal box again. Sage cocked an eyebrow at him.

"Are you underfed?" he asked. "That might explain your stupidity."

"If you continue to make rude comments, there'll be an open vein for you to feed from," Markus snarled. He had sailed across the kitchen to get right up in Rocky's face. "But since it will be your own, it probably won't do you any good."

Alex didn't understand Rocky's comment any more than she understood or appreciated Sage and Markus's annoyance over it.

"Sorry," Rocky said, though without hiding his attitude. Seeing Markus's reaction he turned quickly to apologize. "I didn't mean to offend you, Alex. It was meant as a compliment." "None taken. You can retract the fangs, Markus."

Markus stepped away and headed over to the fridge. Alex looked at Rocky and shook her head. She wasn't so smitten that she couldn't see Markus's faults.

"I liked him slightly better before he fell for you," Rocky whispered, but as it was loud enough for Alex to hear, Markus clearly did. Sage didn't wait for him to ask aloud, before acting upon Markus's wish. He whacked the cereal box repeatedly upside Rocky's head. Alex laughed, but spoke up, hoping for Rocky's sake that Sage would take it as a cue to stop and listen.

"Is my essence really stronger?" she asked trying to get their attention. It worked. Sage stopped abusing his partner with Toucan Sam, and Markus stopped laughing. Rocky didn't look like he was willing to risk saying anything potentially offensive, so she turned to the others.

"Yeah, a bit," Sage shrugged. Markus nodded, but turned back to the glass of juice he was pouring.

"So, what does that mean?" Alex asked. Neither spoke, but she sensed Sage was worried, so she had a pretty good guess. "I'm getting closer," she said addressing him. She figured he'd be less likely to worry about scaring her and therefore more likely to give her a straight answer.

"We think so," he said.

She noted that he didn't make any sarcastic remark about her reading him. She wondered if it was an implication of just how worried he was.

"Don't sweat it, boys. I'll be ready, and it'll be fine." Alex was aware of the role reversal as she comforted them.

That morning she pulled up after their second lap before reaching the house. There had been a thunderstorm late that afternoon that had left the long grass wet and the air humid. Though it was clear to Alex that vampires didn't sweat like humans did, she knew Markus was too wet and flushed to leave for the night.

"You'd better go get cleaned up. Sorry I dragged you out here to get soaked." She reached up to give him a peck on the cheek. Luckily, he understood her desire and leaned down to return the soft kiss.

"What are you up to tonight?" he asked when he realized she wasn't following him back to the house.

Alex pointed to the barn. "I'm finishing my workout, first," she said. Though she still couldn't always read him clearly, she knew Markus's expressions well enough to tell he was concerned. Not knowing why, she tried to cover all the possibilities. "Briant was over just last night to check on me. Both he and Sarah agreed I could start more rigorous exercise to build my strength. And I checked with Darian. He said it'd be fine for me to use the weights and equipment in the barn—without an armed guard." She grinned, but watched Markus's expression carefully. His frown lines softened. "Go, you'll keep Sage waiting." She tried to sound casual about the fact Markus and Sage were going out to feed again.

Markus seemed a little surprised that she knew. He tried to calm the anxiety she was failing to hide.

"I'm taking my own truck, and Cormelia is meeting us a bit closer, so I should be back in less than two hours. Maybe we can watch a movie together later."

"I thought you hated television and movies?" Alex said raising a brow.

"Well, usually I lose interest. But I think with you I can find something nice to watch," he said running his hand down Alex's arm. Her whole body tingled. She was thinking he might not be the only one losing interest in the movie later. Actually, she was wondering what it would take to get him to stay home.

"Markus, I know you've all explained this before, but why do vampires really need to feed?" She regretted asking the minute the words left her mouth. She knew the answer; she just didn't understand it. Asking it only made Markus feel guilty, which she knew was unfair. She started to tell him never mind, but he answered anyway.

"It's okay. I'd rather you understand—not just to make these nights easier, but because it's crucial to our world. Sage already explained to you how we believe the world is based on balance, right?" Alex nodded. "Feeding is just another part of that. Vampires are stronger, but the Creator made us dependent on one another to staunch our individual power. Our own essence, which affects our strength, weakens after awhile unless we take in the essence of another. That exchange keeps us the stronger species, physically, but having to rely on a partner was supposed to assure our strength never overrode our compassion."

"But the Vengatti found a way around that," Alex said disgusted.

"Exactly. Don't get me wrong: we want to protect the humans. But part of what motivates us is also the fact they're spitting in the face of the Creator, purposely throwing off the balance, for their own selfish reasons."

Alex nodded, not feeling so bad about asking now that she had a better understanding. Though she was still thrilled when Markus spoke next.

"I won't lie and say it's not pleasurable. It is. But if I didn't need it physically, I wouldn't do it anymore—now that I have other . . . pleasures." Markus stroked Alex's cheek gently. The contact and the emotions which she sensed from it, both hers and his, were more than pleasurable.

There was a whistle from the house. Sage was in the front door. Alex cursed him in her mind, knowing he heard her.

"Hey, Romeo, save it for later," he called out before slamming the door.

Alex huffed, in a way that reminded her a bit too much of her thirteen-year-old students. "If he's taking his own car, why doesn't he just leave?" After Markus laughed and kissed her forehead, she was calmer, but also curious. "Who does Sage feed from? Does he have one female he exchanges essence with?"

Markus didn't answer right away. He looked at Alex, and she could sense his anxiety.

"I'm sorry, is that rude to ask?" She wished vampires had their own version of Emily Post, so she didn't keep asking inappropriate questions or making rude comments.

"Would it bother you if he had a partner or a mate?" Markus's response caught her off guard. He tried to ask casually, but Alex was too in tune to him to be fooled. She realized where his anxiety came from.

"I wouldn't have pegged you for the jealous type, Markus." Which was good, she thought, since she had dumped her last two boyfriends for being too possessive. "I was just curious, but since it bothers you, let me clarify. I respect Darian as a boss. And Rocky's become a good friend. He cracks me up, and I think he's sweet. And sometimes, when he's not being a pain in my ass, I even like Sage. In fact, Rocky and Sage both remind me of my brothers. Dave, like Sage, was a pushy know-it-all, who liked to act tough and could occasionally be condescending. But he was also super protective and caring. And he probably knew me best, because he was the oldest and most serious, so I went to him for advice or comfort. And whether either of us like to think about it, Sage and I are connected, which means he probably knows me pretty well, too." Alex stopped, watching Markus frown. She reached up to rest her hands on his shoulders. "Hey, I like not having you in my head, and I love trying to figure out what you're feeling and why. And you're usually the only one I don't seem to butt heads with, or in Rocky's case, revert back to acting like I'm twelve with. I could go on and on with why I love you, but I'm really not comfortable with gushing, especially knowing half the house can probably hear this." The words tumbled out before Alex realized their significance. It wasn't that she didn't mean them, just that she wasn't sure she had wanted to say them so soon. She felt her cheeks burning.

Markus began to smile which made Alex even more uncomfortable. "You love me?" He was deriving much too much enjoyment from watching her squirm.

"I thought vampires have perfect hearing." Her attempt at seeming more aggravated than embarrassed failed miserably. She started rolling the gravel around under her left sneaker.

Markus saw her reaction and returned to being chivalrous and tried to comfort her. He lifted her chin up, so her face met his. "I'm sorry. It was just nice to hear you say it; I've been feeling that way for days. It's a good thing, a really good thing. There's no need to be embarrassed."

"I know. I'm just not good at telling people how I feel about them," Alex said.

Markus chuckled at which Alex's scowl returned.

"I'm sorry," he said quickly. "It's just a bit ironic for a Seer to have trouble voicing her emotions."

Alex smiled. "Well, I have no trouble saying what others are feeling, so if you'd like, you can kiss me again, and I'll gladly announce to everyone in earshot what I'm sensing from you."

"Hmm, maybe later." Markus winked and headed for the door in a flash.

Alex didn't need the rest of her workout to bring her heart rate up, but looked forward to the time alone to daydream about what the rest of her evening might bring.

Unfortunately her own heart and head did not offer the peaceful respite she would have liked. With Markus gone, Sage occupied, and the others about their nightly business, Alex found herself alone with her thoughts for the first time in weeks. She should have enjoyed the privacy and the solitude. Instead she was plagued with anxiety over Markus being with another female, pain knowing Levi was out there somewhere unreachable, and fear about her uncertain future. Topping that was a strong driving desire to be able to do something useful about any one of these problems.

Though perhaps it should have been her greatest fear, her impending maturity was actually the easiest problem to push aside— for now. When she had recovered from the illness brought on by her use of her power, the others had made it clear that her projection had been strong and unusual for someone whose gift had yet to mature. Sage had explained that while a few matured Seers could project over a relatively great distance in battle, most had never learned to use that part of their gift or had been able to do it only through physical contact. She had worried it was a one-time anomaly she would never again be able to do, but Sage had heard her thoughts and calmed her fears.

"The flashes of power you have now are your gift growing to full strength. Maturity is when your powers reach that strength and release. If you didn't have the power to project in you, it wouldn't have manifested when you were upset," he had told her.

That knowledge had been a confidence boost and left her feeling stronger and optimistic. Despite her fear, she was beginning to take Darian's stance on her maturity. He told her the night after she projected that he was convinced she was the Seer of whom the prophecy spoke, which meant she was destined to reach her maturity and be able to help the coven. Prophecies were never made about ordinary humans, he had said, which Alex was until she matured. Thinking this way didn't leave her without fear or concerns, but it allowed her to focus on the problems she could do something about.

Only, in the three days since she had realized her brother was alive, she had realized there was little she could do about that, either. Alex no longer had the nagging feeling she was missing something important, but knowing the truth hadn't gotten her far. The idea that Levi was still in captivity and likely had spent a decade in hellish conditions gave her a stronger sense of purpose than anything else could have, but it also tormented her waking hours and added to her nightmares. She now spent her nights badgering Markus about the search, working with Sage to finish reading the parts of the histories she was allowed, and intruding on Darian's other work to question him about the Vengatti. And every morning before falling asleep she tried to make contact with Levi, who hadn't invaded her dreams in days. Most often, by the time she could focus her thoughts enough, her body was so exhausted from the night's other tasks that she fell into a restless sleep, waking in the early evening feeling frustrated that she had failed again.

Alone with her thoughts, that frustration was flaring. She had been blaring loud music from a radio she found on the wooden shelf along the side wall by the weights. She had completed a full body workout and punched the heavy bag that hung from a rafter until her left hand hurt too much to continue, and still she hadn't managed to clear her mind. Deciding, despite her fatigue, to make one more attempt at it, she centered herself in the large open area of the barn floor. Taking a deep breath, she opened to the beginning stance of the first form. As she worked methodically through the various karate movements, she found she could focus on her form, her breathing, and her execution, without once sensing her emotions. She lost herself in the automaticity of the movements she had performed since she was a girl.

Markus reached the barn door midway through one of Alex's katas. He had been surprised not to find her in the house and had rushed, a little worried, to the barn. But as he stood by the door, he could see she was okay. She was more than okay. He marveled at the grace her short, muscled frame exuded as she flowed through the movements. As she spun on one leg she could have been pirouetting, except that the back kick that extended from the final movement wasn't the move of a dancer but that of a warrior. Though her movements demonstrated power, Markus could tell she was calmer and more focused in this moment than he had ever seen her. And she was more beautiful to him than ever before. As she finished the final movement with a *ki-ai* that rang loud and clear even over the radio, he announced his presence.

"Impressive," he said. Alex jumped a little at the interruption, but finding him in the doorway, she smiled.

"I somehow doubt my being a black belt frightens you," she said, wiping her glistening forehead on an equally sweaty arm.

"A black belt? Really? Your father was preparing you well, then." Markus crossed the open floor wanting badly to pull her into his arms. He knew it was only a matter of time before he gave into her desires, tossing aside his careful restraint.

"Preparing me?" Alex said, her mind, for once, not on sex. "It would have been nice if he had told me what for. I hadn't even heard the word Seer until I got here."

"Your father may have been planning to tell you as you got nearer, but that didn't stop him from giving you the other traditional training." Markus could feel her tension building. He brushed aside her damps bangs, hoping the contact would distract her from an obviously uncomfortable topic.

"Traditional training?" Alex asked, undeterred. She looked confused, which Markus didn't understand; she had read the histories and seen the prophecy.

"Seers are also warriors, Alex."

"Yes, I've already had this argument with Darian. He told me the term usually just meant males, because they were the ones who fought the Others. I convinced him a woman could be a warrior, too, but he didn't mention any training."

This didn't surprise Markus. Darian was the least willing to accept the idea of a female in such a position. Not that he was any more sexist than the rest of them, as he was sure Alex would see it. Darian was just fiercely protective of females, especially after what had happened to Alia, which Markus knew Darian still blamed himself for. But Markus could tell Alex was upset about not being fully informed. He tried to explain, while holding her close.

"Seers were typically known to the coven from birth. So their parents and the warriors trained them from a very young age, right through and after their maturity. After all, an untrained human, even one with powers, wouldn't last long enough to use them in a fight with a vampire."

"Wait," Alex pushed back. "If Seers have always been trained by the coven, why am I not being trained?"

Markus cringed. He had walked her right into this. He tried to backpedal. "You came here injured, and then you needed to rest after you used your energy to project, Alex."

"Okay," she said, but Markus knew she wasn't completely convinced. "So when do you and Darian plan to start my training?" The calm control she had when he arrived had evaporated.

Markus hesitated. Lying to her was not an option, not just because she could possibly sense it and catch him, but because he felt it was wrong to lie to the female he loved. However, telling her the truth would surely set her off further. His internal debate ended when he realized it was futile; she read his hesitation as clearly as if he had answered.

"You weren't planning to train me at all, because neither of you were planning to let me anywhere near one Vengatti, never mind a battle, right? So why the hell am I here?" Alex didn't wait for Markus to answer either question before storming across the barn floor to the door to the yard. Markus cursed; he didn't need Sage's gift to know where she was headed.

Darian laid aside the correspondences he had been working on. He heard Alex's stomping as she took the flight of stairs to the second floor. He hadn't heard her and Markus's conversation in the barn, but could guess, from the attitude implied by her heavy tread and huffing breath, she was coming to argue with him about something else. Darian was learning to respect Alex's strong opinions and willingness to voice them, but after sixty years of rarely being questioned, and then never by a female other than Sarah, it was hard for him to calmly face her as she defiantly pushed boundaries. He knew human females had done a better job in recent decades of finding equal footing with men and didn't deny some of the females and most of the males in the coven could learn a thing or two from this, but vampires, including him, could be slow learners with such issues. With this in mind, he took a deep breath and tried to draw on what little patience he had as she entered the room.

"I want to be trained as any other Seer would be, Darian," she began, with no introduction. "In fact, I want to be *treated* as any other Seer would be. Period. I won't accept any more of this bullshit about me being different just because I'm a woman."

Darian wanted to point out if she hadn't been a woman, he probably would have knocked her upside the head for the insolence she just displayed, but didn't want Markus, who was in the doorway, to get his back up perceiving it as a threat rather than the honest statement it was.

"Easy, Alex," Markus said to her. She turned to face him with a look only a female could give to her male. He held her stare, but shifted slightly on his feet. Darian knew the feeling and sympathized, so he tried to bring her attention back his way.

"But you are a woman, Alex, and, like it or not, that changes things."

"Sure, it means I have needs and desires different from you, and it means biologically I'll never be as strong or as fast as you. But guess what, that'd be true if I were a male, too. Because I'm human, Darian. But I'm also a Seer, and if you want me to be useful, I need to be treated and trained as any other Seer would be."

Darian thought a moment about what she said. Essentially, she was right. Even male Seers were trained only to stay alive. No human could hope to match the speed or strength of their kind. But as he looked at the small female in front of him, he couldn't help but think it ridiculous. The idea of her anywhere near a fight was unthinkable. Training alone would be dangerous for her. He'd have to find a way around having her present for any real battles.

"No," he said with no other explanation. He knew she wouldn't accept his reasoning, so why waste his breath?

"My family has sacrificed too much for it all to be in vain, Darian. You owe it to me, to them."

Darian sighed. He knew she was referring to her brothers, whom she believed had been captured or killed by the Vengatti, something he felt was unlikely. But the fact that she believed it changed things. He could deny her the right to train if her motivation was simply to prove herself. But how could he deny her the right to avenge her family and still expect her to help the families of the coven? She had him in a corner. It wasn't a place he was accustomed to being in.

"You can't deny me without giving me a chance," Alex said with finality. "Where's Rocky?"

"What does he have to do with this?" Darian wouldn't put it past the young male to have somehow gotten involved. He was planning to ring Rocky's neck when Alex continued.

"He's the youngest among you, the least experienced and least well trained, right? I'll spar him, and if I can hold my own, you train me. That's only fair." She turned to Markus, apparently hoping he would support this plan or perhaps just warning him not to stand in her way. But before he could even shrug, another voice carried up the stairs.

"Hold up." Rocky was in the doorway pushing past Markus before Alex could respond. "Are you nuts?" he said to her, before turning to Darian. "There's no way I'm fighting a female."

"Sparring, Rocky, not fighting," Alex said. "It's just to show these two I'm perfectly capable of training to be a warrior."

"No way. Not happening." Rocky turned to Darian. "Regan, you're not going to allow this."

"Are you telling me or asking me, Rocky?" Darian's patience with those he outranked telling him what to do was wearing very thin. Alex seemed to sense the opportunity and cut in.

"Sounds like he's nervous, Darian. What can it hurt, other than Rocky's ego?" she taunted. Darian watched Rocky's face grow red and wondered how much she knew about the young vamp's temper.

"I'm worried about your neck, not my ego, Alex." Rocky was unusually short with her.

"Oh, that's right. You've got control issues don't you, Rocky?"

"I've got control enough not to flatten you right now, woman."

Darian and Markus both stepped between them. Darian knew what Alex was attempting to do, and though he admired her strategizing, he felt she had taken it far enough.

"Stop, Alex. Rocky doesn't have to do this if he doesn't want to. Just drop it."

Alex knew this next blow was low, but she also knew she needed to push the button in order for Rocky to provide her the chance to prove herself. Being able to help find and rescue Levi was more important than his ego, more important even than the friendship they had forged over the last few weeks.

"You're right. If I'm going to convince you, I probably shouldn't choose Rocky anyway," she paused, hating herself before the words left her mouth. "Since he's not a warrior himself."

Rocky's shock and hurt melded almost instantly into humiliation and then raw anger. "You name the time, human, and I'll show you who's more worthy of being a warrior."

Mission accomplished, there'd be time to apologize later.

"Fine. Now, in the barn," Alex said as she swept from the room. "And wear a cup this time," she called from the stairs.

As Alex walked out the front door, her heart fluttered in her chest. She knew she was in over her head. Even if Rocky was young and inexperienced, he was still a vampire. And he was a large, bulky, and currently angry one at that. Trying to regain her focus, she almost didn't notice Sage standing by the door to the barn.

"This ought to be interesting," he commented as she paused waiting for him to move so she could pass. She made no reply as she entered.

By the time she reached the middle of the dusty wooden floor, Sage, Markus, and Darian had filed in and were spread out around the perimeter of the open space. Rocky came in last and faced her.

"Keep the contact light. I'm not explaining any black eyes or broken bones to Sarah." Though he didn't say it, Darian was addressing Rocky. Alex noticed, and some of her earlier annoyance returned.

She nodded to Rocky and put her hands up in a ready position, guarding her face and also ready to strike. He stood dead still waiting for her to make a move.

"This isn't a staring competition, Rocky."

"Then try to hit me," he said, still refusing to put up his hands.

Alex waited for a minute, seeing if he would give in and spar her for real. When he continued to refuse, she made the first move. Her first two punches were easily blocked, so Alex moved to his side, forcing Rocky to turn in response. Rocky turned to her, shadowing her moves. No matter how quickly she spun and changed directions, Alex knew he would always be faster. Clearly this was Rocky's strategy. She would tire quickly, especially after the evening's workout, and then he would easily be able to pin her, because striking her was clearly something he was uncomfortable with. Otherwise, Alex knew this exhibition would have been over in a matter of seconds.

Alex began developing a strategy of her own.

"Are we dancing, Rocky? Because if we are, I think the male's usually supposed to lead. Have you been out of the dating scene so long you forget how that works?" she tried taunting.

Rocky tried to smile, but she could sense it was working.

"If you'd like, I could lend you those red stilettos you brought from my apartment."

She could sense Sage becoming concerned. She knew this should have worried her, but she also knew she was close to getting Rocky to react.

"Maybe you'd just prefer we switch partners? Perhaps one of the guys is more your type. We could call you Rockette, if you swing that way."

Finally, Rocky seemed fed up. Alex was discovering her adrenaline and focus had heightened her sense and her ability to control it. She tried to ignore all the tension and emotion in the room except Rocky's. His aggravation had been building as she had continued her endless assault on his masculinity. As soon as she felt a shift in his emotions, she knew he had decided to act. Since Darian hadn't put an end to this, he would. She didn't stop to register his mix of anger, anxiety, guilt, and pleasure. But knowing it had intensified gave her just enough notice to react. With a quick movement he closed the gap and swung back his hand. He couldn't hit her, even though she wanted him to try, but he apparently was willing to slap her, if it would shut her up.

Alex ducked and chopped Rocky in the groin, feeling a twinge of guilt before taking him to the ground with a kick to the back of his knee. As he lay, shocked, looking up at her, she couldn't resist one more jibe.

"I'm not your mouthy teenage daughter. Instead of trying to bitch slap me, fight back next time."

Alex was taken by surprise when Rocky didn't wait for next time. From his position on the ground, he hooked her legs, knocking her on her back. Her head hit the floor, and stars of white light blurred her vision, reminding her she had too recently recovered from a rather severe concussion. Rocky pinned her arms, and snarled, "Satisfied, little girl?"

What had started as a simple sparring exercise intensified as both their tempers flared.

"Watch it, Rocky," Darian said. He started to step in, but Alex had other ideas. She jerked her knee up, hitting Rocky in the groin again. It was enough to loosen his grip and further infuriate him. Alex scrambled to her feet, and turned to face a now empty space. Suddenly a body crashed into her, tackling her to the ground. She looked up, frightened, only to see Markus's worried face on top of her.

"Enough. It's over, Rocky," Darian said. As Markus pulled Alex off the floor, she saw Darian was where she had been standing, holding Rocky with his arms pinned behind his back, fangs fully elongated. He turned his face to Darian and snarled.

Alex knew Rocky had completely lost his temper, and if it hadn't been for Markus and Darian stepping in, she would have been the recipient of that fury. But she couldn't help but feel guilty, knowing she had put Rocky in the position he was currently in.

"You did not just growl at the Regan. Kid, I'd say you were even stupider than you look, but I'm not sure that's possible," Sage said. Alex couldn't believe it, but she sensed he was enjoying himself.

Markus, who still held Alex, looked at Sage and shook his head. Rocky seemed to come to his senses watching their reactions. He froze.

"Oh, shit. Regan, I'm sorry. I just . . . oh, screw me," he ended dropping his gaze, bracing himself for Darian's reaction.

"Just 'cause you got schooled by a girl, bro, doesn't mean you need to start batting for the other team."

"Shut up, Sage," Markus, Rocky, and Darian shouted simultaneously.

Darian dropped Rocky's arms and spun him around. Grabbing him by the belt buckle, he pulled him close. Rocky winced with obvious discomfort.

"Next time you lose control or bare your fangs at me like that, I'll make it so that female won't have anything left to aim for, got it?" He gave the belt a tug, at which Rocky let escape a whimper.

"Yup," he responded grimacing. Sage and Markus cringed in sympathy. Alex felt a renewed wave of guilt.

"What was that?" Darian jerked his hand upward again. Alex knew Darian was just being a jerk at this point.

"Yes, Regan. My apologies," Rocky said, his voice half an octave higher than normal.

Darian grinned and released Rocky with a shove that nearly knocked him over. There were a few seconds of awkward silence during which the males kept stealing glances at Alex. Finally, she spoke up. "Don't give me those looks. I'm sorry, but I told him to wear a cup. If he was too cocky, that's his loss." She winced at her own poorly chosen pun. "But clearly, up until the point I nearly had my throat ripped out, I think I proved I'm relatively adept at protecting myself."

Sage stifled a laugh, and Darian furrowed his brow. Seeing both, Alex began to protest, aiming a nasty retort at Sage. "Oh, please, at least I'm—"

Markus cut her off. "Trainable. She's trainable." The others looked doubtfully at him. "She'll never be able to fight the Others—"

Alex began to protest, but he held up his hand, and reluctantly she listened.

"—but she may be able to learn enough to get away. And she certainly can be trained to fight off their human victims if necessary. She's of more use to us if she can be out in the field."

Alex could sense how hard this last sentence was for Markus and knew he hoped that day would never come.

"She's of more use to us alive, actually," Sage muttered.

"Exactly," both Alex and Markus spoke the word. Both started to explain, but Darian interrupted.

"You'll be responsible for the training?"

"Yes," Markus replied.

"Fine. It can't hurt." Alex grinned, but Darian continued. "But Markus decides if and when you go out with any of us. And our promise as your coven is to keep you safe, so if any of us tell you to stay put, or hide, or run like hell, you'll do it, no questions asked. Or I'll have you locked up in that room faster than you can say—"

"Rapunzel, Rapunzel," Sage interjected. Darian spun around, his lips pulling back from his teeth.

"Darn it, I guess I should've rethought the short hair," Alex said. She and Sage laughed, despite knowing Darian was both serious and seriously annoyed.

"Joke all you want. I am not kidding." The Regan strode towards the door. Just before he stepped out into the yard, they heard him mutter, "Damn, those two are annoying together."

Alex, Sage, and Markus cracked up. Rocky waited until he was sure the Regan wasn't returning before joining in. Alex caught Rocky's eye, wondering if he held a grudge, but, with a shrug, she knew she would be forgiven.

Chapter 11

Alex was pretty sure she was having a good dream for once, which meant the likelihood of her remembering it when she woke was slim. But that wouldn't keep her from enjoying it. Markus was with her in her dream, lying in bed next to her, watching her with sleepy green eyes. Somewhere on the other side of her an annoying beeping was ruining the moment. But as Markus leaned over, grinning down at her playfully, the noise seemed a minor detail. Alex closed her eyes in expectation of his soft kiss. It didn't come. Instead, the beeping stopped and, with the quickest of pecks on the cheek, Markus was out of the bed, gathering his boots to head back to his room to change.

"Get up, sleepyhead." He sat on her side of the bed and tousled her hair. "Time to train."

"Crap." It hadn't been a dream, which meant the nightmarish alarm had been real. "Why are we getting up when it's still light out?" Her words were muffled by the pillow as she rolled over on her side.

"Never thought you'd say that, I bet." Markus laughed at her backwards statement. It occurred to her how easily it had slipped from her tongue.

"Well, if you vamps didn't mess with my head. . . ." Alex groaned as Markus put on the nightstand lamp. She tried to cover her eyes with the sheet.

"Technically, we can't mess with your head. That's why you're here, remember?"

Alex pulled back the sheet an inch. "Well, I guess that's a good thing, huh?" She tried to hold his stare while batting her eyelashes like some old-time movie star. He leaned over apparently falling for it. Finally, her dream could resume.

"It's very good," he whispered in her ear, taking hold of the sheet. "Now wake up, warrior." With one sweep of his hand he had stripped off all the covers, leaving Alex shivering and annoyed in just her tank top and underwear.

"Hey," she said throwing the pillow at him. But when he realized she had removed her pajama pants sometime during the day, he spun around. He stood up and was ready to leave, but Alex wasn't letting him off that easily. She jumped from the bed, landing on his back, piggyback style. If Markus had been smaller or human, the surprise of it would have knocked him over, but as he was neither, he hardly reacted.

"Is this some kind of hazing?" She tried to use one hand to force his chin around so he was facing her.

"No," Markus said, laughing. "That doesn't start until we get in the barn." Alex wasn't sure, but she had an ominous feeling he wasn't entirely kidding.

"Then why the uber early start?"

"Because one of us has to work in addition to these training sessions, remember?" He squeezed her hands. "You can take a midnight nap after I leave if you're tired."

"Are you implying I'm weak, or are you telling me you have plans for later that require me to be well-rested?" Alex knew he wasn't implying either, but loved to tease him. It had the desired effect. She could feel the heat from Markus's blush as it shot up his neck and face. She laughed as he stuttered, searching for a reply.

He apparently decided it was best not to answer. He tried another topic. "As much as I love to carry you around. You may want to change before we start. I'm not sure you'll want to walk back through the house when everyone's awake in a wet t-shirt and, uh, panties."

Alex giggled at his word choice, but disengaged her hold and slid off his back.

"Are we going to get that sweaty?"

Markus stopped at the doorway and turned around with a devilish grin. "Let's just say one of us is going to end up soaked." With a wink, he slid out the door.

It was with a small amount of trepidation Alex entered the barn twenty minutes later. Markus had sent her out to do a warm up lap alone, partly so he could 'get things ready,' whatever that meant, but also because it was still too light for him to be outside. He had used the tunnel connecting the basement to the barn to avoid the setting sun.

Alex wasn't sure what to expect when she slid in the side door, trying to minimize the amount of early evening light that entered the open room. But it wasn't having something fly past her face faster than she could blink. Her gaze darted to where she heard the thunk. On the back wall of the barn three knife shafts stuck out from the wood. As Alex walked closer she realized they were all deftly centered in a one-inch knot in the pine board. Her mouth agape, she turned slowly to face Markus, who stood at the opposite end of the long barn.

"I wouldn't have hit you," he said with a smirk. "As you can see, I'm fairly accurate."

Alex scoffed at the understatement. She reached up and tried to tug one of the weapons from where it was deeply lodged. "Is this what we're starting with?"

Markus flashed to her side, startling her with his speed, and swiped the knife from her hand swiftly. He clearly didn't want her handling sharp objects, perhaps recalling the scars on her wrists, or perhaps remembering how she had dropped her steak knife three times during last night's dinner. Of course, only Sage knew that was because she was beginning to be inundated with flashes of everyone's emotions.

"I thought we'd start with something a little more basic. The first rule of fighting—"

"Never get hit," Alex finished.

Markus seemed a bit surprised, but recovered quickly. "I forgot you're not totally new to this," he said with a smile.

"I've done avoidance techniques, blocking, all that—more than a few times," she informed him, with just a touch of cockiness.

"Right. Well, then, this should be easy for you."

Markus's smirk had her second-guessing her self-confidence. He headed to the wall where the radio was resting on a shelf. But he wasn't turning on some tunes. He bent over to take something from along the wall. Alex tried to see what it was. She was confused when she noticed a red pail by his feet.

"Your job this morning is simple," he said. He walked back to her with his hands behind his back. "Don't. Get. Wet." With each word he had swatted at her with a sponge. Knowing he was up to no good, she was ready for him and managed to mostly block and duck the three playful swipes.

"Not bad," he said. "You ready to see what you're really up against, though?" His grin was gone, and Alex knew that though the technique might be playful, the lesson Markus had in mind was no joke. Without a word she nodded.

Before she blinked, Markus was no longer in front of her. She spun towards where she thought she saw the blur of movement, but as she turned, she felt a splat of wet sponge on her back. She turned again, this time simultaneously dodging to the side, but, again, before she could decipher Markus's movement, there was a new wet spot on her shoulder. She made her next move, and he drenched both her gut and the back of her head.

"Ack! You couldn't use warm water?" Alex said as the ice-cold stream dripped down her scalp, following the line of her spine to send shivers down her back. She heard Markus chuckle to her left, but as she turned he appeared beside her and whispered in her right ear.

"Focus. React. Don't anticipate." And in another flash he was gone.

"Right," Alex said more to herself than to him. She tried to relax both her body and mind so she could react more quickly to the blurs of motion. Her renewed focus greatly improved her reaction time but did nothing to keep her from getting hit again and again. She simply wasn't quick enough to move away from Markus's continued assaults. So, completely drenched and with nothing to lose, Alex decided to switch tactics. With the next blur of movement, Alex dove into a roll, not away from where she perceived Markus to be, but right at him.

With a thundering crash, Markus came into focus. He hit the barn floor face first, a foot from where Alex was gingerly getting to her feet. All her limbs seemed intact as she self-assessed the damage, but she was pretty sure there was a brilliant bruise blossoming over her left cheekbone. She guessed Markus's boot had caught her face as he fell.

Markus was up and by her side almost instantly. When he saw the swelling red mark, his expression was one of horror.

"Are you okay? I'm so sorry. I tripped—" He was frantic, pulling her to him to examine her more closely. Alex smiled.

"You didn't trip. I tripped you. And maybe you should look in a mirror before worrying about me." She reached up to his chin and gently wiped away a trickle of blood from where he had landed.

"You did that purposely?" Markus was unconcerned about his own injury, but Alex's words bothered him.

"Dive at you? Yes. I wasn't having any luck avoiding you, so I figured going on the offensive might work." Alex couldn't make sense of his emotions. "Are you angry?"

"Yes," Markus answered in frustration at which Alex's own annoyance began to surface. He had no right to be mad at her just because she embarrassed him. She started to tell him so.

"Alex, I'm not mad at you. I'm mad at myself. I could've really hurt you. This is what Darian and I worried about," he said, shaking his head. "And obviously the point of this drill was lost on you anyway."

Instead of being comforted, this last comment inflamed her anger. "Pardon me for being so thick," she said, pushing away from his hold.

"Alex." He grabbed her arm before she could turn to leave. "You're not thick. I thought I knew how to train you. But I've only ever trained other vampires, young male vampires. You're human—tough, but human." He attempted to calm her with a grin. It worked enough that she was willing to return to his embrace.

"Well, what was I supposed to learn from that lovely sponge bath, Sensei? Other than avoiding vampires is nearly impossible?"

Markus looked at her for a moment. "That pretty much was the lesson." After a brief pause they both started laughing. When they finally stopped, a serious expression returned to Markus's face.

"It seems silly, Alex, and granted I enjoyed the method more than I should have, but it's important for you to know how we move out there. In a real fight, one blow would be all it'd take to, . . ." he couldn't bring himself to finish. Alex sensed his fear and understood the message he wanted to convey.

"I know, Markus, and I get it. I also trust you'll help me get better, so I'll stand the best chance any human can," she said. "Only, without the ice water next time, right?"

He nodded, but remained serious. "But, Alex, promise me you won't ever purposely attack a vampire again."

Alex just smiled. She wouldn't make promises to Markus she couldn't keep.

He sighed and started to lead her to the back door. "Let's get you an icepack," he said.

"Right after we get you a bandage." She smiled and headed to the side door. "It's dark out now. And this way's quicker." She was out the door before Markus could protest.

When they walked in the kitchen, Markus wished he had been more insistent on using the back entrance. Alex may not have realized it, but they were quite a sight. Markus had a streak of dirt down the front of his t-shirt from where he had skidded across the floor. He could feel the split skin on his chin and knew he was bleeding onto his collar. Alex, who had been wet before rolling across the floor at him, was now covered in a muddy substance that left smears on her bare skin and clothing. Her cheek resembled a small red plum, and the bruising was spreading, giving her a shiner.

"Markus!" Sarah said. He tried not to be bothered by her scolding, knowing it bred from her concern.

"What the hell happened to you two?" Darian shot to his feet, sending his chair skittering back across the tiles.

Markus saw Sage and Rocky attempt to hide their grins. He knew they had been awake earlier and likely had heard most of what occurred in the barn.

Sarah had rushed to the freezer and was handing Alex a towel-wrapped icepack before he could explain.

"I'm sorry, Regan, it was my fault—" Markus began, but Alex interrupted.

"It was your fault for underestimating me, but you're not alone there," Alex said turning to Darian. "But I caused my own injury, and his, by diving at his feet. So if you're going to get pissy, it really ought to be aimed at me, Darian."

Darian glared for a moment at Alex, before turning to Markus. Markus was glad to see the Regan ignored her and his anger was still directed at him. She needed to work on her authority issues, but Markus would rather he be the one to help her with that, since Darian had temper issues of his own to deal with.

"What did I warn you about . . . this. . . ." Darian pointed from him to Alex. It was clear he was referring to their relationship, as well as their injuries.

"Darian," Sarah said, "be reasonable."

"Our job is to protect her, Markus," he said getting in Markus's face.

"I know that, Regan." Markus was the last one who needed to be told this.

"Good. Don't let other . . . things distract you." Darian started for the door. Markus didn't bother to argue. He knew Darian wasn't done with this conversation, and he'd rather not bring Alex into it if possible. Darian had other ideas. He turned to her before heading into the entryway. "And can you please stop being reckless this close to your maturity?"

Markus thought the Regan said it with more exasperation and concern than anger, but Alex still glared at him. When Darian turned his back, she took the icepack off her cheek and tossed in her hand like Markus had seen the pitchers do in the baseball games Rocky watched. Before he could say anything, Sage flashed in front of her.

"His delivery sucks, but the advice is sound, twerp. Use that icepack for its intended purpose."

"I was thinking I'd like to throw it, not that I was going to," Alex mumbled, returning the pack to her swollen cheek and turning her back on Sage.

Sarah gently squeezed her shoulder as Alex walked past her. "Sage's right. He was upset because you were hurt." She addressed Markus next. "I'm sorry I snapped at you when you came in. It just surprised us because we know how cautious you are, Markus."

Markus knew Sarah was sincere, and even accepted Darian was well intentioned. "I know, Sarah. I understand. I wasn't too happy with myself either."

"Oh, please. It was an accident. I'm not some fragile doll you have to treat with kid gloves." Alex realized she was snapping at Markus and turned to him with an apologetic grin. "Will you just go bandage up your chin? Nobody wants you bleeding on their breakfast."

Sarah leaned over to look at Markus's cut. "She's right. If I don't tape that up now, it will heal open like that and leave a scar."

"We can't have anything marring that beautiful mug, right, Alex?" Rocky said.

"Shut up, Rocky," Alex and Markus shouted at him from opposite ends of the kitchen. Markus winked at Alex, then headed down the hall to the bathroom behind Sarah.

"If I had a dollar for every time I was told that," Rocky mumbled.

"You'd have more than enough money to buy yourself a muzzle," Alex replied. She laughed as Sage snorted orange juice through his nose.

"Took the words out of my mouth," he said coughing.

"Well, your mouth was full, and I couldn't let the opportunity pass."

"You know, Darian is right." Rocky dropped his bowl in the sink with a bit too much force. "The two of you together are friggin' obnoxious." He didn't wait for a reply before strutting out into the hall and down the stairs to the basement.

Alex could sense a wash of pain and perhaps something else follow him as he left. It was out of character for Rocky not to enjoy a little ribbing, so when Alex asked the question in her head, she expected Sage would answer.

"You know you're sensing them all more and more clearly, right?" he asked instead.

Alex didn't need him to state the obvious. She was trying not to think about it. She had enough to worry about. But there was no denying that dinnertime the last few nights had been almost as dizzying as trying to attend high school when her sense first started. There weren't hundreds of vague emotions to sort through, just those of five others, but her sense of them was becoming increasingly strong.

"I want to know why he's so upset, Sage," she said hoping to control the conversation.

"I heard you the first time. I always hear you, remember? Which is why I brought up the more important topic. It's only going to get worse, and you're doing a lousy job of controlling it," Sage said. "You are trying to control it, right?"

Conversations with Sage always ended up annoying Alex. He spent half the time asking questions he already knew the answers to and the other half commenting on thoughts she didn't want voiced.

"Answer my question, and we'll discuss it," she bartered.

"It sets a bad precedent, you know, me interpreting what anyone in the house feels whenever you're curious." Sage leaned back on the counter waiting for the response he knew would come.

"Am I the kettle or the pot?" she asked. "I notice how hard you work to block out everyone's thoughts. Are you even trying to control it?" she threw back at him. She was irritated by his hypocrisy, but she also knew he was right, somewhat. Her gift allowed her to sense others' emotions, which was intrusive enough. But it didn't allow her any insight into why someone was feeling a particular emotion. And as she was quickly learning, she was often mistaken when she attempted to interpret the reasons behind these feelings.

However, if she and Sage combined their gifts, it allowed them almost total knowledge of someone's inner self. In other words, it was a complete invasion of another's privacy, without that person's permission and often without their knowledge.

"So you see the dilemma, then," Sage said hearing her internal reasoning. "If I tell you, even when it seems innocent enough, they'll never feel they have privacy. Even if they wanted to, they wouldn't be able to trust us. And that would lead to resentment—fast."

Alex was sensing Sage with about as much shame as he was reading her. She knew he felt some hurt and regret.

"You know this from experience." It wasn't a question.

He frowned. "Let's just say I was lucky Darian and Markus have more patience for my talents than my family did."

Alex saw him cringe when he heard her sympathetic thoughts. "I can't help thinking about what I sense, Sage. Which means, unfortunately for them and you, there will be times you'll be doubly invading their privacy."

"It might be hard to believe, but I'm pretty good at keeping others' thoughts to myself." His accusing glare left Alex feeling like she was the one who could read his thoughts. In the last few days she had blurted out what someone in the room with her was feeling at least half a dozen times. It wasn't that she was intentionally trying to embarrass or manipulate her housemates. But the sudden invasion of someone else's emotions mixed in with her own often took her off guard.

"It'll get easier," Sage said. "But you have to work at it, which brings us back to our other topic."

Alex groaned. She knew he was right. She did need to control her abilities, as well as her mouth. But the fact was she didn't have a clue where to begin with her abilities. Every time she had tried to control her sense she ended up with an aspirin-resistant headache that lasted for hours.

"You worry about a headache, but dive headlong into a vampire moving at full speed. You are a weird one, twerp." Alex noticed Sage had abandoned midget as his nickname for her, in favor of this much more endearing term. "Yeah, well, like it or not, twerp," he continued with a wink, "our quality time isn't over. Now that we've finished going through the histories, Darian wants me to try to help you control your sense before it matures."

Alex pursed her lips. "And how does Darian know I'm having trouble controlling it to begin with?"

"I spy. That's why he tolerates me. I even get paid for it."

"Oh, that's rich, after the lecture you just gave about the moral dilemma you face knowing everyone's business. And I suppose this isn't optional?" She got up and dropped her own breakfast plate into the sink with force equal to Rocky's.

"Trust me, Alex," Sage said, "As unpleasant as it may be, this isn't something you want to opt out of."

Alex turned her back to him and hung her head over the sink. The time with Sage wasn't the prospect that bothered her. They bantered constantly, and with many years more experience, Sage almost always had the upper hand. It didn't hurt he could also hear her comebacks before she could speak them. But, if she were honest, she enjoyed working with him. Sage was intelligent and quick-witted, but also surprisingly reflective when it came to interpreting the histories and what the information in them meant for her future and the future of the coven.

She wasn't even terribly bothered by Darian's mandate. She wished he would occasionally include her in discussions and decisions that pertained to her, rather than just informing her after the fact. But she knew he had her best interests and those of his subjects at heart.

What frightened her was the possibility of being unequal to the task at hand. She wasn't afraid of failure itself. She was willing to fail a thousand times if it meant learning how to succeed. Her fear was she'd never manage to control her sense. Her fear was Ardellus's warning about living a tortured life would become her reality.

With her own emotions so intense, Alex vaguely registered Sage's sympathy and compassion as he leaned against the counter next to her. But when he reached over and touched her shoulder, the emotions filled her up, pushing out her own worries.

"You're too damn stubborn to let that happen," he said before removing his hand.

Alex lifted her head and tried to smile at him. "Is it supposed to make me feel better that you've learned how my sense works enough to manipulate it, while I haven't?"

"Yes. It means you're in the hands of a competent trainer," he said heading to the doorway. "I won't even kick you in the face, which is more than can be said for some vamps." This last comment was made with more volume and clarity than was strictly necessary in the confines of the kitchen, which told Alex Sage had intended for Markus to hear. She doubted, however, if Sage expected to be attacked by him midway across the foyer.

At the doorway she saw Sarah on the other side of the entryway, having returned from treating Markus. As they watched the two grown males tussle like boys playing Wrestlemania, they shared an exasperated sigh. They both avoided the melee and headed upstairs, leaving the males to their own violent devices.

Rocky tasted his own blood in his mouth.

"Damn it," he cursed himself as he pulled his fingertip from his teeth and saw the red seeping around his gnawed nail. He licked the skin to stop to the bleeding with his venom. He had been mortified when Sarah had left the bottle of "Bitter Nails" on his nightstand, but was starting to think the well-meaning female had a point. This habit was getting a bit ridiculous.

"It wasn't Sarah. It was Darian," Sage said tossing the stack of reports onto the back seat and sliding in behind the wheel. Rocky had been waiting in the parking lot of McNally's pub. Sage had ducked in to pick up the other warriors' weekly reports as a favor to Markus, who was home getting further chewed out by Darian for that morning's training mishap.

"It was Sarah's scent," Rocky argued. He wanted to kick himself the minute the words left his mouth. First, acknowledging Sage's comments about his private thoughts only encouraged him.

Second, he knew if Sage said it was Darian, it was. The idea of the Regan being involved intensified Rocky's humiliation.

"That's why he had Sarah deliver it. He doesn't want to harp on you like your father," Sage said, "but the scabby raw fingers are getting to him."

Rocky felt his face flush. He refused to respond, out loud at least. Internally he was telling Sage where he could stuff his gift.

"I'd rearrange your face for that, but I'm guessing by the nail biting and the highly unusual silence on the ride in, there's something even more stupid you're about to confess." Sage looked at him seriously.

Rocky wondered with a bit of trepidation, just how much time Sage spent in his head. Before his thoughts could stray to any of his other improprieties, he focused on the original reason for his uneasiness.

"I didn't do anything stupid or break any laws for this," Rocky said. Then he amended, "No coven laws, anyway."

Sage groaned.

"No, listen," Rocky started. "Do you believe Alex, that the Vengatti have her brother?"

Sage's expression changed. Rocky relaxed. It was clear Sage would be on board.

"Yeah, I do. And Markus does, too. That's why we've expanded our patrols."

Rocky took a deep breath. He hoped Sage wouldn't pass along what he was about to say, because there was no way to word it that wouldn't sound impudent coming from him.

"No offense to Markus, but I don't really see the point in that." Rocky paused as Sage's eyebrow cocked, but he remained silent, so Rocky continued. "Patrols were designed to catch the Others hunting and feeding. The whole point was to protect humans and punish the Vengatti we caught, right? How is that going to lead us to Levi?"

"New orders are to follow, not destroy, unless it's necessary to save human life," Sage answered. Rocky heard the doubt in his mentor's voice.

"Which has worked so well in the past. We either follow so far behind, we lose them, or get close enough and get noticed, which leads to high-speed chases that attract attention. You like spending your life wiping the memories of human cops and reporters?"

Sage smirked. "Okay, smartass, what's the solution, then?"

Rocky grinned. He reached under the seat and pulled out the laptop.

Sage shook his head. "No coven laws? You think lifting the Regan's laptop is sanctioned?"

"Chill," Rocky said opening it and powering it on. "I asked to borrow it three days ago. He hasn't asked for it back, so technically I still have permission to have it. Besides, you don't think he actually knows how to use it without one of us home to show him, do you?"

"You either have a lot of faith in me covering for you, kid, or you have absolutely no respect for the authority I have over you." Sage was eying him warily, but Rocky knew not to answer. He also knew his mentor wouldn't rat him out to Darian or Markus as long as he had something to back up his mouth.

Rocky turned the computer around to face Sage.

"What am I looking at?"

"A map. A map of possible residences of the Vengatti coven."

Sage looked up at Rocky. "How?"

Rocky laughed. "Darian gave me the idea, actually. I was listening in the night Alex projected on you all."

"Shocking," Sage interjected.

Rocky shrugged. "When Alex first asked Darian to find her brother, Darian told her he couldn't just look them up in the Yellow Pages. But after I thought about it, I realized—he could."

Sage furrowed his brow. He was obviously doubtful.

"Okay, they're not listed in the phone book, but even the Vengatti pay taxes to stay under the radar. And we know most of the names they use as covers. I hacked into the Bristol City Hall tax collector's records."

"Coven laws—I knew there was a reason for the distinction," Sage said shaking his head.

Rocky cringed. If that bothered him, he wasn't going to like the rest of the steps Rocky had taken to obtain his information.

"Yeah, well, as you can imagine, like us, most have their mail sent to P.O. boxes all around the city and suburbs."

"But this isn't a list of post offices," Sage said. He seemed to see where this was headed.

"Ah, no. And I'm not quite good enough to hack into the federal Post Office system," Rocky hesitated, "but Remalt was."

Remalt was the coven's technology expert, which wouldn't mean much considering how slow to progress most of the coven was, but Remalt was self-taught and super savvy. A severe injury left him unable to serve as a warrior, so he fulfilled more than his share of hours working to keep coven communications and records secure.

"And Remalt did this for *you*?" Sage had correctly read Rocky's reason for hesitating.

"Well, I chose my words carefully. It may have sounded like I was asking on behalf of Markus and Darian." Rocky grinned. "I believe you call it carefully maneuvering the truth."

Sage scowled. The I-learned-it-from-watching-you excuse was hard to swallow, even if it was accurate.

"Half of them are probably abandoned properties or empty lots," Sage said.

"Half of them were. Those are the yellow dots. The blue dots are occupied properties. I cross-referenced using records from the utility company."

Sage nodded. Rocky could tell he was impressed.

"You did your homework. Now what?"

"Well, the intention was we'd systematically rule out places. I added a record-keeping feature so we can track who and what we find at each property, so we could use it again. The dots turn red when data is entered, so it's easy to see which addresses are confirmed."

"And was your intention to tell Markus about this before or after we tested it?" Sage had his hand on the keys in the ignition.

"Can I defer to you on that, Mr. Authority Figure?"

Sage grinned, but shook his head. "Nope. You want to play with the big boys, Rock-o, you need to be willing to call the shots."

Rocky sighed. He knew what Sage was saying. He couldn't expect to take credit for this if it worked but pass the responsibility on to Sage if it flopped, or worse, led to some unforeseen disaster. But Sage didn't have the added burden of being in Rocky's position. Rocky had the most to lose.

"You also have the most to gain," Sage said, listening in on Rocky's thoughts again.

"Actually, I think Alex and Levi have the most to gain," Rocky said. He glanced into the back and remembered the first night, when he had carried her to this car, laid her across the back seat, and marveled at her strength, her ability to fight. His respect for her had only deepened since that night, even after the sparring incident. He was pissed she had manipulated him into it, and jealous she got her way, but he admired her willingness to risk her friendships, her body, her life, to learn to fight so she could save her brother.

"It's worth the risk," Rocky said to Sage. "Let's go. We'll fill Markus in later."

"We?" Sage asked, eyebrows cocked.

"I will." What the hell, the lead warrior couldn't like him any less.

Having survived another night's dinner without being overly distracted by her growing sense, Alex sat in the living room waiting for Sage, whose turn it was to do the dishes.

Rubbing her hands over her aching shins, she cursed him mildly in her head, hoping he could hear. Though she had remained relatively focused during dinner, she did have a few close calls where she almost commented on someone's emotion. *Lucky* for her, she had been sitting across from Sage, who felt it was helpful to kick her whenever he heard in her head she was about to speak. She was happy not to frustrate the others, but she wondered whether Sage knew or cared how hard the toes of his boots were. Between dinner and this morning's accident, she was thinking sneakers would make great Christmas presents. Assuming she made it to Christmas.

"Is your mind ever quiet?" Sage muttered as he entered the room. "Creator, I think some days I hear you in your sleep."

Alex glowered at him, but not because she was annoyed that he was constantly listening. She knew, technically, that couldn't be helped, but his constant listening meant he knew exactly what she was attempting to do every morning before she fell asleep. And he knew the unremitting pain she had been suffering since she first realized Levi was alive and captured.

"This may help you make contact," he said. He sat in his usual spot, in the chair to the right of her.

"How?" She sat up, more eager to learn than before.

"Well, I don't really know how the connection works, but it seems likely you'd both have to be focused on each other's sense in order to communicate."

"Then how did Levi make contact to begin with? I was asleep the first time."

"You were asleep every time, which is how I didn't hear it. Like I was saying, it's the only time you manage to calm your mind. He's obviously learned to focus enough to break through even when you're not fully conscious," Sage said.

"So why did he stop?" A dozen possible and equally horrific reasons seeped into her thoughts.

"Your guess is as good as mine, kid, but don't get ahead of yourself. He could still be fine," Sage said hearing her worry.

Alex tried hard to ignore the doubt she sensed from him. "Right. Well, let's start. Maybe if I can figure this out, it'll work again."

"The first thing you need to master, if you're not going to go nuts after you mature, is focus. Your thoughts at any given moment are as jumbled and incoherent as Rocky's constant blathering. It's a wonder either of you can function."

Alex shot Sage a slew of comebacks that would have made any truck driver proud.

"Nearly three centuries, and the swears never really improve," he muttered. "You done? Good. You ever do any of that yoga or meditation crap that's become so popular lately?"

Alex cringed. She had tried both, but, as Sage had just implied, she never found she had the focus required. Meditation usually ended with her twitchy or asleep, and the only yoga class she ever attended came to an embarrassing end when she became too interested in the emotions of the women around her and fell out of some animal-named pose onto her rump.

Sage smiled. Alex wondered if he could pull pictures out of her mind as well.

"Well, guess what, that's the kind of focus you're going to have to learn," he said, ignoring the question he no doubt heard in her head.

"And how do you suggest I do that?" she snapped. This was precisely what she had feared earlier that morning.

"Practice, patience, and motivation," Sage said. "You do like the smidge of sanity you have now, right?"

"Fear is a great motivator," she said sarcastically. "You really should have gone into education rather than become a warrior. It seems a real waste of your talent, not to mention your superior people skills."

"Mothers tend to keep their young away from me," Sage said tapping his mark with a grimace.

"Shocking," Alex said, though she did feel some sympathy. Sage's world knew just by looking at him what he could do. She imagined it made more than a few coven members avoid him. Her own gift was equally intrusive, but invisible. She wondered how many of her friends and coworkers would want to be around once her gift matured if they knew what she'd be able to do. She wondered how many parents would want their children in her classroom.

It occurred to her that that part of her life was probably over, so there was no need to worry about it. What she needed to worry about was discovering a way to find and save Levi. And to save herself.

"What do you want me to do?"

Sage looked devious for a brief moment, before deciding to be serious. He suggested she start with a simple focusing activity in which she attempted to focus on a single thought for a prolonged period of time.

"Should I be picturing a babbling brook?" Alex asked as she crossed her legs and closed her eyes.

"You can picture Markus's naked ass for all I care. As long as you can stay focused."

Alex opened her eyes, her cheeks flushing. "Since you'll be hearing my thoughts, you may want to rethink that." Sage seemed to regret the comment as he tried to suppress his own embarrassment.

Alex decided instead on a beach. She could vividly see the rocky jetty and the dark green seaweed strewn across the beach of her childhood. She tried to remember the smell of the saltwater, sand, and seaweed and the sound of the small waves tumbling into the shore. It wasn't hard to visualize. She had spent so many summer days there with her brothers and mother while her father worked. It was the place she went to for solitude once she was old enough to ride the bus on her own. It was the place she ended up the evening after Levi and Dave's funeral. She had sat out on the very edge of the jetty watching the tide come in, wishing it would sweep her away. As she remembered, she relived the pain of that night. Pain that was suddenly mixed with frustration. Somebody else's frustration.

"Crap." Alex opened her eyes and saw Sage shaking his head. "Maybe that wasn't the best place to focus on. But I did okay at first, right? How long?"

"Less than half a minute before your thoughts strayed. Try again," he commanded.

For the better part of an hour this was repeated. Each time, Alex tried to choose a different topic or visual to focus on, ideas she thought were unimportant or impersonal enough not to distract her. She tried with her eyes closed, eyes open, standing, sitting, pacing. Each time with the same result. In fact, the longest she managed to maintain focus—just over a minute—she was staring at her own feet. But even this ended with a strange, but apparently humorous mental tirade about the ugliness yet necessity of toes. It was Sage's laughter that made her realize she had once again failed.

"That's enough," Sage finally said. "I can only handle so much weird in one night."

Alex frowned. It wasn't that she wanted to continue this task indefinitely, but she had at least hoped to see some improvement, to have a small success with which to salvage an otherwise rotten day.

"It'll come," Sage said. "In the meantime, when you're around the others, at meals especially, because there are so many of us, try to block out all but your own emotions. Focus on the conversation, the food, the charming male kicking you under the table." He winked.

Alex scowled at him. But her expression morphed into one of confusion. "If Darian wants me to learn to use my gift so I can help the coven, shouldn't I be trying to focus on sensing them more, not less?"

"No. When your powers mature, Alex, you will sense everyone without having to try. If you're going to be of use, you need to learn to still be able to sense yourself." Sage was eerily serious, and Alex knew he was both worried and determined for her to understand. He had started to get up, when she stopped him.

"Sage, what's it really going to be like when my gift matures?"

Alex sensed his immediate hesitation. She stood blocking his way, to make it clear she wasn't going to let him evade the question.

"I'm not a Seer, Alex," he said trying anyway. "How can I know?"

"But your gift is similar. Before it matured, you had occasional insights into people's thoughts. How much stronger was it after?"

Sage examined Alex as she stood in front of him, as if she could contain him and force an answer from him. He admired her spirit, even though she sometimes overestimated her own strength. He hoped for her sake, for everyone's sake, that she could be as strong as she thought when it came time for her to mature.

He debated whether it was wise or even right to tell her what it was like for him. He didn't know for sure her experience would be the same, though he doubted it would be much different. He thought about what he had told Darian the night they explained her gift to her. He had said it would have been better to know what to expect. He wasn't convinced that was true. But he knew it couldn't have been worse.

"It'll be like when I touch you, except. . . ." he could see from the look on Alex's face she knew the rest.

"Except it will be multiplied by the number of people in the room," she finished, her voice soft but steady. Sage knew this had occurred to her before. Early on when she was studying the histories and learning about her gift, he had heard her worries. But as she became closer to her maturity and her senses grew, she had a better understanding of what this would feel like. And he knew it terrified her, as it rightfully should.

"Do you remember those first days?"

"No," Sage answered, not to her question, but to the request forming in her head.

"Sage, you do, right? You remember exactly how it felt," she pushed.

Sage continued to shake his head. "It's not something you forget. Nor is it something you need to feel before it's necessary."

"Were you in the same room as me for the last hour? It's never been more necessary." Alex held out her arm to him.

Sage was uncertain.

"I'm sure, Sage, please."

He knew she was determined, but he worried it was the wrong decision. She had no idea what she was asking. She pushed her arm closer. Realizing she wouldn't fold, Sage sighed. He closed his eyes and remembered. Then he reached out and wrapped his hand around Alex's forearm. There was a sudden intake of breath as she was hit with his emotions. He maintained the contact longer than any other time he had touched her, not to torture her with his feelings but because he had become lost in the memory of them. He broke contact only when someone entered the room and jolted them both from what they were experiencing.

"What are you doing to her?" Markus demanded from the doorway. He stormed across the living room.

Sage dropped his arm and opened his eyes. He saw the cause of Markus's concern. Alex was standing before him pale and shaking, she fell back onto the couch the minute Sage disengaged.

"Answer me, Sage," Markus snarled, having gone astray from his usual calm character. Sage noticed with amusement that this was becoming a habit where Alex was concerned. It was about time the warrior showed his true colors.

"Just give her a minute." Sage didn't snap back, but sat at the edge of the seat opposite Alex to watch her color return.

Markus seemed more concerned by this response. "Why? What happened?" He knelt down next to Alex.

She became aware of his presence and took stock of her own appearance. She took a deep breath and wiped the tears from her cheeks.

"I'm fine," she said. "I had to know, though," she added looking from Markus to Sage.

It took Markus a minute, but finally Sage heard his thoughts come together. Sage nodded to confirm. He knew his friend was furious with his decision, but it was too late now.

"But it won't be that bad for you, Alex," Markus said. "You'll be prepared, and we'll be there to support you." Markus didn't turn to look at him, but Sage knew he doubted his own words of comfort.

Sage started to speak. Misleading her was both unfair and potentially harmful. But Markus cut him off.

"That's enough for tonight," he snapped at Sage. To Alex, he said, "Let's go to bed."

She nodded and allowed Markus to help her off the couch and hold her arm as they walked toward the hall. Before they reached the door, she stopped him.

"Sage," she said turning back, "Thank you."

Sage nodded. Then, as the thought occurred to him, he spoke up. "Alex, try the middle of the day next time. They won't be watching him as closely then."

Markus looked confused, but Sage knew Alex understood exactly what he was referring to. She smiled and nodded before heading out of the room with Markus.

Chapter 12

Alex rolled over the next evening and reached for Markus's hand. He almost always slept on his back with his hands by his side. Alex had teased him the first few nights, telling him if he was going to sleep looking like a corpse he ought to get a coffin and fulfill the whole vampire myth. But, in truth, she had grown to like it. She always knew exactly where he was in the bed, which made it easy to reach for the appropriate body part in the dark or with her eyes closed. And considering they hadn't moved beyond a few innocent body parts, it meant her aim was usually flawless.

But this evening as she skimmed over the covers in the usual spot, she came up empty. Opening her eyes slowly, expecting to be assaulted by the late afternoon light that peeked in around the drapes, she realized something was amiss. Markus had already left, and the room was mostly dark.

Throwing on running shorts and a sports bra and tank, she grabbed her sneakers by the dresser and headed for the door. Halfway down the hall, Markus was heading into Darian's office.

"Hey," she called approaching him. She noticed Darian waiting in the doorway with his hand on the knob, ready to shut the door behind Markus. In the office already sat Sage and Sarah. Alex was curious, but continued her question, a little awkwardly knowing she had an audience.

"Why didn't you wake me?" she asked leaning in close to him.

"I thought you needed a day to rest." He gently traced the deep purple bruise on her cheek. The skin was more tender than she had realized. She involuntarily flinched at even his light touch. He pulled his hand away with a pained expression.

"I'm fine." Alex didn't want to start the day angry with him, but wanted him to understand. "I can't afford a day's rest."

"Let's talk about it later, okay?" Markus gestured to Darian and the others to imply he was holding them up. Alex might have continued to argue, but he quickly leaned over and kissed her undamaged cheek before heading into the room.

Darian's look made it clear she wasn't any more welcome to remain outside the door, than she was to enter. She stepped back, and he closed the door in front of her.

Alex made her way down the stairs and found Rocky standing in the doorway to the kitchen. She realized it must have been later than she thought when she saw he was already shaven and wearing shoes, two things he never did before breakfast.

"Day off?" she asked, seeing his mesh gym shorts and sneakers instead of the usual jeans and boots.

"Yup." He let her pass, but remained in the doorway. Alex noticed he was uncharacteristically quiet and worried for a moment he was still upset with her over the teasing at breakfast the night before. But when she focused on his emotions she discovered he was curious and a bit nervous. She examined him more closely as she started in on her yogurt, following his gaze back up the stairs.

"Anything interesting?" Alex asked, pointing up. She knew if she wasn't careful, she and Rocky would be overheard the same way he hoped to hear them.

Rocky looked at her and shook his head. "Oh, no," he whispered, "I'd be foolish to spy on one of them for you. To eavesdrop on all of them would be suicidal."

"So it's a coincidence that while they're all meeting up there without you, you happen to be standing at the bottom of the stairs?" He smiled. "The basement too far to hear from?" She moved closer so they could speak more softly. Rocky nodded, then put his finger to his lips to tell her to keep quiet.

"It was stupid, Sage," Markus snapped. "I practically had to carry her to bed, Darian."

"You should talk. See her face this morning, loverboy?" Sage said cutting in.

"Stop." Darian put an end to the bickering and turned to Sage for an explanation.

"She asked me to. And she has the right to know what to expect," Sage said. His jaw was set as Darian examined him, likely trying to detect the bullshit Sage sometimes relied on when his decisions were questioned. "If you want me to help her, you have to trust me," he told the Regan.

"I do trust you," Darian answered. "We all do. We're just worried about what she can handle."

"She's taken on too much," Sarah spoke up. "Trying to find her brother, training for battles, learning to control her gift—she's stretched too thin, and it's not healthy. Ardellus agrees. He's afraid it'll push her into her maturity before she's ready."

"You spoke to my father about this already?" Darian asked incredulously.

"Seeing you don't answer his calls, and he has asked to be kept informed about Alex's progress, yes." Sarah maintained calm, but Darian didn't continue. Instead he started pacing the room, running his hands through his hair.

"Maybe he's right."

"Well, no one's going to stop her from trying to contact her brother," Sage said. "And it would be dangerous to have her go into her maturity without any practice controlling her sense."

"I agree," Darian said.

"Then are you going to tell her she's too fragile to train?" Markus asked.

"Would you have a problem having that conversation if you weren't sleeping with her, Markus?" Sage asked sardonically.

"Sage," Sarah scolded.

"No. He's right," Darian said facing Markus. "I don't care what role you want to play outside my office—lover, mate, whatever—but in here you are my lead warrior and my advisor. So either you start acting like it again, or I'll find someone who can."

Rocky looked nervously at Alex to see what, if any, of the ongoing conversation she had heard. Her look of intense curiosity left him thinking she had made out none of it. He thought it was probably best if it stayed that way. Knowing that the conversation concerned her would lead to her forcing her way into an already overheated argument.

"Want to watch a movie today?" he asked hoping to lure her away. It had the opposite effect. He always forgot how sharp she was. Humans on TV were much dumber.

"It's about me, isn't it?"

Rocky remained silent.

"What's it about, Rocky?"

He just shook his head. He tried to grab her as she slipped off her sneakers and tiptoed to the bottom of the stairs. He heard when the conversation above faltered and knew, before he could stop her, what would happen.

Alex hadn't made it past the second step when the door swung open. Darian glared down at her. She tried to sneak a look back at Rocky, only to discover he had fled. The door to the basement stairs was open just a crack. *Coward*, she thought.

"Now would be a good time for your run, Alex," Darian said with a little too much force for a mere suggestion.

Alex tried not to look like a kid with her hand caught in the cookie jar. After all, if they were discussing her behind her back she had every right to listen. Didn't she? Darian seemed to guess what she was thinking. He squashed the argument before she could make it.

"It's as much about them," he said pointing into the office, "as it is about you. Therefore, you have no place in this conversation."

Alex nodded, both annoyed and embarrassed. She dropped her sneakers so she could slip her feet into them and then headed for the door.

"And you can escort her, Rocky, unless you'd like me to find other jobs to keep you busy tonight," he said addressing the crack in the doorway.

"Love to," Rocky said, opening the door with an apologetic grin. He grabbed Alex's arm where she had paused on the way to door. Even with her back turned, Alex knew Darian had waited for them to leave before returning to the office.

Alex fixed her laces in the driveway before starting out across the dewy lawn, leading Rocky on her and Markus's usual route.

"It was more an argument than a conversation, wasn't it?" she asked halfway across the field to the right of the house.

"I think Darian made it clear he didn't want you to hear it," Rocky said. Alex noticed he jogged more easily beside her than Markus and wondered if being closer to the time when he didn't move at light speed made it easier for him to match her comparatively slow pace.

"I don't need a replay. A yes or no will do," she said still more out of breath than him. "It'd be nice to know what to expect from them later tonight."

"Yes, then," he conceded.

"Because they're worried after Alexandra's terrible, horrible, no good, very bad day?"

Rocky looked puzzled. Apparently his knowledge of pop culture didn't apply to children's literature. Alex wondered vaguely what types of books vampires read to their young. But before she got sidetracked, she explained.

"It's a book title, about a bad day, which I had yesterday with Markus, Darian, Sage—and you, for that matter."

"Me?" Rocky asked, surprised.

"Yes, but answer my question first. I'll come back to that. They were worried about everything that went down yesterday?"

"Yes."

"And Sage and Markus were having a big-brother-versus-boyfriend head-bashing session?" she asked, as they rounded the corner.

Rocky looked at her as he ran. "I thought you didn't hear any of it?"

Alex laughed through her heavy breathing. "I grew up with brothers and had a few boyfriends in my life, Rocky. It's not that hard to imagine."

They ran in silence for a few minutes. Alex noticed Rocky was still watching her, probably waiting for her to continue. But she didn't want to get him in trouble, and she wasn't entirely sure she wanted to know more.

"Are you upset?" he finally asked, breaking the silence.

"Yes," she answered. "And no. I'm upset I caused tension between them, and because my relationship with Markus makes his job harder. But the fact they all care enough to argue is kind of flattering, comforting even."

Rocky nodded, but then allowed her time to run in peace. He didn't know her mind was almost never quiet. Sure enough, after half a lap her thoughts returned to the topic she had put off.

"Don't you want to know why you were part of my bad day?"

Rocky frowned. "I'm guessing it involves me saying or doing something stupid. Whatever it was, I'm sorry."

His sincerity took Alex off guard. She slowed to a walk to take in both his expression and his emotions.

"What?" he asked, clearly feeling insecure by the close examination.

"Rocky, you know you're not stupid, right?" She realized too late it was an awkward question to pose, but an honest one. "Just because you have the misfortune of having to spend all of your time with three ancient know-it-all males who love to rag on you doesn't mean you should take their comments to heart."

"Isn't your mate one of those ancient know-it-alls?" he teased.

"He's my boyfriend. And I'm training him still," Alex said. "Seriously, though, you have a better sense of humor and more social skills than the three of them combined."

"I'm funnier than Sage?" he asked, cocking an eyebrow.

"Please, he can dish it, but he can't take it. And half of his witty one-liners he probably plucks from other people's heads."

Rocky laughed at this, and they both resumed their running pace. "So what did I do?" he asked, not looking back as he ran ahead a few paces.

"You didn't do anything. I thought I did, because you were upset after breakfast yesterday when I was teasing you. I felt bad, but Sage wouldn't tell me why you were feeling what you were. He actually lectured me on the immorality of using him to spy on you." Alex smirked, knowing Rocky would enjoy the irony of this. He weakly returned the smile, which told Alex he remembered why he had been upset.

"It was no big deal. It was stupid, really," he said. "I'm glad Sage kept his mouth shut for once." He apparently hoped to change the course of the conversation.

"Rocky," Alex began, not buying it, "You don't have to tell me, but if it was something I said or did, I am sorry." And she was. It was Markus she had fallen in love with and Sage whom she turned to for help her with her gift. But she and Rocky had fallen into an easy friendship at a time when a good friend was never more appreciated. She didn't want to do anything else to jeopardize that.

Rocky turned, jogging backwards to face Alex. "It wasn't you," he said. "I was upset with myself because . . . well, it sounds stupid, but I was jealous." Even in the dark Alex could see he flushed as he finished speaking.

"We all get jealous, Rocky. No shame in that." She wanted to drop it, but her curiosity got the better of her. "But, why?"

Rocky turned around so he was no longer facing her. "You're a human and a female," he started, keeping his eyes focused on the tree line in front of them, "and yet you can be trained as a warrior to serve the coven, my coven. I'll never have that." He stopped and turned to her. "My sons, if I ever have any, will also probably not be allowed to have that. Because of me."

Alex felt awful. She hadn't realized how much Rocky wanted what she had bullied her way into getting, even using him as a means to get it.

"Darian wouldn't deny them that, Rocky. Not if you continue to serve him as loyally as you do. He'd want nothing more from his warriors than a heritage like that." Alex wasn't just trying to comfort him. She knew she was right.

"It's hard to prove you're loyal when everything you do is out of obligation," Rocky said kicking a stone on the path.

"But it's not just obligation. You want to serve."

"I'm not sure my intentions count for much," Rocky answered.

Alex looked at the male in front of her, and hated with a passion the father, sister, and coven members who had stripped him of his future and his dignity.

"I think they count for everything, Rocky."

Later that night Alex stepped out of the shower, the hot water having done wonders for her aching muscles. After her run with Rocky they had retreated to the barn to lift. Alex even taught Rocky the first two karate forms when he had refused to spar with her.

As she threw on a clean outfit, one that didn't involve a sports bra, and ran over her lips with a thin coat of gloss, she felt good.

Markus and Sage had left for their patrols by the time she had returned to the house. And Darian had avoided speaking to her by asking Rocky to help him with something on the computer. Alex knew one of them would eventually have to face her to relay the outcome of the earlier argument. She was ready for that, and ready to accept whatever overprotective measures they had in mind. Her conversation with Rocky had put things into perspective. She knew she was getting everything she wanted, even if some things had to wait. If Rocky could put his life on hold to serve a two-hundred-year sentence he didn't deserve, she could wait a few weeks until she matured to prove to them she was strong enough to handle everything.

Determined to enjoy her good mood, she flitted down the staircase, hopping over the last step. She headed for the kitchen hoping to find Sarah. Sure enough, she was at the counter stirring a pitcher of iced tea.

"Want help with dinner?" Alex asked, returning the smile Sarah greeted her with.

"In a bit. Would you like some tea?" she asked, already taking down two glasses and heading to the freezer to fill Alex's with ice. Alex had never seen any of the vampires use ice in their own drinks, even on the hottest of nights.

"Sure." Alex sat on a stool at the island instead of at the table. It had become her and Sarah's usual place to share a late-night glass of wine or cup of coffee. Alex usually treasured these rare moments of normalcy, but tonight she was wary. Sarah had placed the two glasses, two spoons, and the sugar bowl on the island and sat across from her without saying a word. Alex sensed some anxiety and knew this would be more than a friendly chat.

"Alex," Sarah began, "Can I talk with you about the conversation we all had this morning?"

Alex laughed. "Oh, Sarah, I'm sorry they put you up to this, because they didn't have the . . . nerve to tell me themselves," she chuckled. "I promise I'll remain calm—at least until I see one of them."

Sarah smiled. "Good, but just remember none of those males ever put me up to anything. Though I do think they were more than a little relieved when I volunteered."

"Noted," Alex said. "So what executive decision did Darian make about me while I was banished from the house?" Seeing Sarah's frown, Alex instantly regretted her word choice. "I'm sorry. I know he's just trying to help," Alex said. "And I was skulking up the stairs like a nosey child." Alex blushed. It seemed silly in hindsight.

Sarah seemed to sense her embarrassment. "Oh, don't worry about that in this household. We're all guilty of it, only vampires don't have to skulk. We eavesdrop from anywhere while pretending to do innocent things, like make tea," she said, raising her glass with a coy smile. They both laughed and enjoyed the moment, taking time to stir sugar into their glasses and drinking a bit before continuing.

"In all honesty though, Alex, we all do have your best interests at heart," Sarah said. "And though I'm sorry the decision was made without your input, you don't need to witness any more of their ugliness than you do already."

"Probably true. Especially since I have the bad habit of matching it with my own ugly," Alex said. "So what do you all suggest? Or it is more than a suggestion?"

"It's part mandate, part suggestion, to be honest," Sarah answered. Alex didn't need her to say the last part; she knew she could expect total honesty from Sarah.

"Markus has been ordered to stop your training, just until after your maturity," Sarah said, hoping to head off any argument from Alex. But she gave none. "Sage, on the other hand, has been asked to fit in as much training as possible."

"After last night, I'm not arguing with the need for that," Alex answered, aware her body involuntarily shuddered. Sarah leaned forward and patted her hand. "And the suggestion part?"

"Is that outside of that training you take it easy," Sarah answered. Alex sighed. "How many hours did you work out today?" Sarah asked after this reaction.

Alex hesitated. "Three, maybe three and a half?"

Sarah raised an eyebrow. "Try over four, which is enough to leave anyone physically exhausted. Then you spent another hour trying to contact your brother, which is mentally exhausting. You'll spend at least an hour with Sage after dinner. And that's not mentioning the strain of just sitting with us all at dinner."

"Did he tell everyone that?" Alex asked, cringing. She wished she hadn't as the movement sent a spasm of pain through her cheek. Sarah saw the flinch and crossed the kitchen to retrieve a fresh icepack.

When she returned, she answered. "The more we understand, the more we can try to help, Alex. That's all Sage is trying to do. But he won't have time if you exhaust yourself and mature too soon."

Alex understood their concerns, but knew she needed the physical relief now more than ever. "I've always used exercise to quiet my thoughts, drown my sense. When I'm running I can focus on just that, running," Alex tried to explain. She looked up at Sarah, who seemed sympathetic but still concerned. As she began to speak, Sage banged open the front door and entered carrying half a dozen pizza boxes.

"Maybe we ought to take loverboy out of the equation," he said commenting on a conversation he was not intended to be a part of. "Because clearly your recent runs have done nothing to help your focus."

Alex sneered at him as Markus entered behind him.

"I'd take him out for the second time this week if he weren't carrying dinner," Markus said shooting Alex and Sarah a wink.

"I guess we don't need to cook tonight," Alex said to Sarah, who returned a guilty grin. Feigning offense, Alex asked Sage, "You planned to placate me with pizza?"

"Did it work?" Sage asked, opening a box and sliding it on the counter of the island so it was right under her nose. She inhaled deeply.

"Pizza always works for me." She grabbed a steaming slice straight from the box.

"Remember that," Darian said to Markus as he entered the room with Rocky. "Pizza and diamonds, right babe?" He leaned over and kissed the part in Sarah's hair.

"I'll take the diamonds," Sarah said, slapping at him playfully.

"Pizza's fine," Alex said to Markus. "Diamonds would be a bit ridiculous at this stage," she teased. Markus frowned, and Alex thought she sensed hurt, but couldn't be sure with all of them in one room.

Sage handed a box to Rocky.

"Sweet, a whole one?" he said with a grin.

"No one else wants your nasty anchovies," Sage answered. He was at the fridge tossing beers to Rocky, Darian, and Markus. He then pulled up a stool opposite Alex. She smiled. There'd be no bruised shins tonight; the island was solid cabinet below. She looked over and saw Rocky heading back to the basement.

"Hey, Darian," she spoke up over the bantering occurring between him and Markus. "If we're not doing a sit-down dinner, why not all eat together?" She nodded to Rocky, who had paused at the door. He shook his head, apparently not wanting to repeat this conversation.

"That's fine," Darian said to her surprise and to everyone else's. The room was quiet for a minute, before he continued. "We're short a stool, though."

"I'll stand," Rocky offered immediately. When Darian resumed heckling Markus, Rocky returned to the counter with a look of amazement and gratitude. Alex caught his eye and winked. He offered her an anchovy in return.

"Ick," was all she replied before starting in on her second slice. She was happily sucking in all the emotions around her.

Sage caught her attention and shook his head. She knew what the admonishment was for and could have cared less.

I'm not passing up these feelings, she thought. She stuck her tongue out at him for good measure. He rolled his eyes at her immaturity, but then flicked his bottle cap at her face. She returned the gesture, but overshot and hit Rocky. Within seconds, an all-out battle had begun.

Markus was sitting up on the edge of the bed waiting for Alex when she returned after her session with Sage. Her look of exhaustion and sigh of relief as she kicked off her shoes and crawled onto the bed next to him told him how well it had gone the second night.

She laid her head on his lap and looked up at him.

"Was it that bad?" he asked running his fingers through her short, spiky locks.

"No, just tiring," she explained. "I was trying to figure out how to block people's emotions, or at least dull them. Since Sage is so hard, we used Rocky as my guinea pig. He was in a good mood after dinner, so it made it bearable. At least when I failed, I was sharing his happiness," she said. "I felt a lot of happiness. None of it mine or Sage's."

She closed her eyes and sighed again, but this time it seemed a sigh of relief. Markus could see the strain on her face fade as he continued to twirl her strands. He wondered how she could be this content. Could she possibly be so tired she didn't sense his emotions?

"I could fall asleep right here," she said, as if answering his unspoken question.

"Actually, Alex, I was hoping we could talk first." Markus removed his fingers from her hair.

Alex looked up at him. "No offense, hun, but if it can wait, I'm really tired."

Markus slid his leg out from under her head. "Sure. Fine." He walked around to the other side of the bed, where he usually slept, and roughly kicked off both boots, letting them drop heavily to the floor.

Alex sat up and spun to face him. "You're upset." She appeared genuinely surprised, but Markus no longer wanted to discuss it. He turned his back to her and began to undo his belt buckle.

"Hey, if something's bothering you this much, we'll talk now. I'm awake," Alex said.

He could hear the edge to her voice and knew he had upset her. It hadn't been his intention, no matter how hurt he was.

"It's fine. Get some sleep." He turned and attempted a grin. He should have known it wouldn't work; Alex was now tuned in to his emotions and wasn't likely to let it rest.

"Oh, come on," she said scooting over to him. "I hate when guys do that—say they need to talk, then refuse to actually say what's bothering them."

Markus dropped the fake grin. He didn't know why, but her words incensed him. "Excuse me if I don't have the relationship experience you obviously do," he snapped.

Alex sat back as if he struck her. "What's wrong, Markus?"

He noted the ironic twist. It was usually Alex whose temper flared easily and Markus who remained the voice of reason. But tonight he was the one flying off the handle.

"Maybe I should ask you that. What's wrong with me, Alex? Or are you too tired after hanging out with Rocky and Sage to answer me?" He began pacing the rug at the foot of the bed trying to calm himself. But he had already succeeded in angering Alex.

"Stop. You know damn well I wasn't with Sage and Rocky for my own pleasure. I'm asking you what's wrong because I don't understand why you went from Romeo to Godzilla in less than two hours. And for your information, I've had about four relationships in my whole life, and none of those guys could even compare to you until about two minutes ago."

Markus stopped pacing and leaned over, his hands on the footboard. His anger dissipated.

"Then why did you say what you did at dinner tonight?" he asked her.

"What?" Alex seemed confused. "I hardly spoke with you at dinner tonight. The only thing we said—oh. The diamond comment?" Markus was glad she remembered, until she began to laugh. "Markus, I think we're arguing over a cultural misunderstanding. You can feel free to buy me gifts, but in my world a guy usually only gives his girlfriend a diamond for one reason—"

"I know the tradition, Alex!" Markus cut in, frustrated by her suddenly calm demeanor. "Vampires have used it ourselves for as long as humans."

He watched as Alex's jaw dropped. She stuttered as she spoke. "But . . . Sarah . . .

doesn't. . . ."

"She wears a sapphire. She's the mate of the Regan. That's our coven's tradition."

"Oh," was all she responded.

Markus tried to control his voice as he examined her shocked face. "You said you loved me."

"I do," she said.

"And you've made it clear you want to make love to me."

Alex blushed, but then responded. "And you made it clear you don't. I thought that meant you wanted to take it slow. But now you're talking diamonds?" She sat back on her heels and bit at her lip. "It may be backwards from how you were raised, but in my world, my generation usually get a little more intimate before getting engaged."

Markus didn't understand. "Do you doubt I love you because I won't make love to you?" He knew Alex was smarter than that—which meant there was more to her uncertainty.

"No," Alex said. "I guess people just like to make sure they're compatible . . . in every way, before they make such a big commitment."

"So you have doubts." Markus was no longer angry. But hearing this confirmed his fears from earlier. Alex didn't deny it.

"I've got a lot on my mind right now, Markus. My whole future is one big question mark. I didn't expect this to come up so soon," she offered as way of an answer or explanation.

Markus nodded. "I understand," he said. Though he wasn't sure he did. He knew he loved her, and he knew that would be true for however long they had together. He didn't understand her doubt, but knowing it was there changed things. He picked up his boots and headed to the door.

"Where are you going?" Alex asked sliding off the bed and following him to the door.

"You need time alone to work things out," he said. "And it's not proper for me to stay here with you if we're not in a serious relationship."

"Who said we're not—" But he wouldn't stay to hear the rest. He flashed to his room and closed the door behind him.

Alex wanted to crumple on the floor where she stood and sob, but in addition to her pain, she was too angry with herself and him. She wouldn't give Markus the satisfaction of hearing her cry in the room right next door, the room they usually shared.

She stumbled down the stairs, her eyes welling over. She hoped she could crash in the only unoccupied floor of the house. The last thing she wanted was company. Seeing the light on in the living room, she cursed and headed for the basement. If distance couldn't provide privacy, she hoped technology could. Mercifully, she found the doors to both Sage's and Rocky's rooms closed and the far office, Markus's office, open and empty. Grabbing what she hoped would be a loud, guns-blaring action film, she popped it into the DVD player and turned the volume up loud enough to drown out her sobs. She collapsed onto the leather sofa. Despite Sarah's earlier warnings, tonight it was a blessing that her body and mind were exhausted. Despite the heartache, she fell asleep before the opening credits ended.

Dave Matthews was playing on the stereo as Alex opened her puffy eyes. She remembered falling asleep in her jeans and blouse, but awoke covered in a fleece throw. As her eyes adjusted, she made out the Mets logo in the soft fabric. She didn't have the strength to sigh with distaste.

She sat up slowly, trying to detect a clock on any of the machines in front of her. The stereo read the track number and the display of the DVD player was flashing 12:00. Hoping it was still late afternoon and she could retreat to her room in peace, she made her way quietly into the hall.

At the top of the stairs, she glanced across the foyer and saw Rocky watching her from the kitchen. She debated ignoring him so she could dash up to the second floor but felt guilty. It was no doubt Rocky who had checked on her during the day. So, trying to look somewhat dignified, even in last night's cloths, she walked across the entryway and into the kitchen to thank him.

"No problem," he said trying to lighten her mood, "It was a little hard to sleep with Terminator blaring next door. I figured you wouldn't mind."

"I didn't look at what I put in, to be honest. Dave Matthews was a much better listening selection. As for the Mets, well. . . ." She tried to grin.

"Yeah, well, they're not the Yankees and not the team my father likes, so they seemed like the obvious choice."

"You're forgiven, then," Alex said heading to the cabinet. Forgoing her usual healthy selection of fruit for a frosted Pop-Tart, she started back out of the kitchen. Before she was halfway to the door, Sage entered. If she was lucky enough to have anyone in the house not listen in to the entirety of last night's nightmare, Sage would not be the one.

"Ah," he stammered for a moment, not sure how to greet her. Deciding against it completely, he nodded and slid past. Rocky shot her a sympathetic look before she could dart out and up the stairs.

At the top she met Darian and Sarah leaving their bedroom. Alex wondered if things could get any more awkward as Darian also stammered to say good morning. Then as Sarah started to reach forward to comfort her, Alex heard the knob of Markus's door turn.

She shot down the hall as fast as her human legs could carry her and shut the door, a little too hard, behind her. When she thought she had heard three sets of shoes go down the stairs, she leaned against the door and slid to the floor. With a day's sleep, her body now had the energy it needed to continue crying.

The truth was, she didn't need time to think, not when it came to Markus. She loved him and he loved her. And even without making love, she knew they had plenty of physical attraction. Even when he had found the strength to say no, his body made it clear he was interested. But it had been a ready excuse, the easiest one to put words to.

As for commitment, she guessed deep down that she knew she was ready for that also. Even though such a permanent leap terrified her, she knew it was right. She hadn't had a fantasy or daydream since she arrived that didn't involve the two of them together, not just sexually, but as partners. Her previous relationships were plagued with doubts from their very beginnings. She had tried with a few to convince herself it was from her own fear of getting hurt. But now that she understood her sense, she was pretty sure those doubts were from a deep knowledge of who she was and who was right for her. Despite knowing him for less than a month, she had no doubts about Markus.

And her future? Futures were always unknown. Her own predicament didn't make her unique in that way. So why was she hiding behind a door from the one thing in her life she was sure about? She hurt him deeply by denying she wanted exactly what he did. Alex stood up and wiped the tears from her face. There wasn't much about her current situation she could make right on her own, but this she could fix, hopefully.

In less than half an hour she was cleaned up and back at the bottom of the stairs. She was relieved to see he was still in the kitchen, having not yet left for his patrols.

Markus looked up at her as she reached the bottom step. The others pretended to occupy themselves with other tasks.

"Can we talk?" she asked quietly. He nodded and walked out of the kitchen to meet her.

"Um, not here," she whispered. "Could we go for a drive or something?"

"I have to work soon." His lack of expression scared Alex. Was she too late?

"That can wait. Can't it?"

"We'll need Darian's permission for you to leave," he continued.

"Oh, please, Markus," she said forgetting to whisper, not that it mattered. "If your morning has been as awkward and uncomfortable as mine was, I'm sure you've gathered no one wants to witness a repeat of last night. In fact, if we asked, I bet they would all pile into a single vehicle and happily flee like some messed-up episode of *The Partridge Family*."

"Like who?" he asked confused.

Alex couldn't help but roll her eyes. "When we get married, my first task is going to be to get you some modern cultural literacy."

It took him a minute before the significance of her statement sunk in. When it did, he reacted immediately. With his change in expression the tension in Alex's shoulder muscles eased.

"Let me just—" Before he could finish, a set of keys bounced off his shoulder and landed on the tile by his feet.

"Get the keys from Sage?" she finished, picking them up off the floor. She managed a smile as she dropped them into his palm. Before closing the door on their way out, she called back, "Thank you," to whoever was still listening.

Chapter 13

Out on the open road Alex rolled her window all the way down and stuck her arm out into the damp night air.

"Any place in particular?" Markus asked as they neared the first intersection.

Alex realized she still didn't know where the farmhouse was located in relation to anything else. Despite Sarah's arm-twisting, Darian had refused to allow Alex to return home to collect the rest of her belongings after it was confirmed the Vengatti had been watching her. The best he had agreed to was to escort Sarah to pack for Alex. She wasn't even sure she was still in the Bristol suburbs.

"Are we too far from the ocean?"

"Nope." He turned the Jeep left. They continued to drive in silence. Alex watched the country roads turn more congested, though still residential. He was skirting the city. When the front yards started to be dotted with hydrangeas and beach rose bushes and the family homes became outnumbered by summer cottages, she knew they were close. She breathed deeply, trying to catch the first scent of the ocean. Despite the daunting conversation that loomed, she found the salt air calming.

"You miss this," Markus commented, watching her. "Why didn't you say something before?"

"I was so overwhelmed with everything, I guess I hadn't realized I missed it." She vaguely wondered whether it would have mattered, whether a drive like this would be an option on an ordinary night.

Just then he turned off the main road onto a side street whose sandy shell-embedded pavement crunched under the tires. With a final turn the ocean was before them. The crescent moon reflected in the waves.

"Beautiful," Alex said, kicking off her sandals and leaving them by the entrance to the beach.

"I think so," Markus said, but when Alex looked back, he was staring at her instead of the view.

"Back to being Romeo?" She teased him for the cliché line.

"Back to being reasonable," he answered.

"Yeah, me too." Alex realized he was trying to start the conversation they had come here to have, but didn't say more.

When they made it down to the water he took her hand, and they began walking up the empty stretch of beach with their feet in the surf.

"Markus, if the topic hadn't come up at dinner, how soon were you planning to mention it?" Alex began.

"I don't know," he answered. "I knew it was inevitable, but . . . well, I also knew what you said last night was true, that you had too much on your mind to worry about choosing a mate."

"It's not a matter of choosing, Markus." She stopped and tugged his hand gently. "I've chosen you. I have no doubts about that. I never did."

Markus smiled and pulled her into his arms. "That's all I really need to know. And I understand, Alex, about wanting to wait until after your maturity when things settle down."

Alex pulled back and looked at him anxiously. She was kicking herself. She had told him exactly what she wanted to, what she felt, and he understood. But something else was bothering her.

"It's not just my maturity or finding my brother, though," she said, dropping his gaze. She watched her feet as she drew figures in the sand with her toes.

"I guess I don't understand, then," Markus said. Last night's frustration was resurfacing, and Alex knew he had every right to feel it.

She peeked up again and met his eyes. "We've spent every night on our runs and every morning in bed talking about everything under the sun, or moon, I guess. But I still feel like I only know a fraction of your life. And though there's much less to know, you only know a fraction of mine."

"We know all we need to know, Alex. We want to be together. What else is that important?"

She thought of the million trivial things she didn't know. And she realized Markus was right, none of them were significant. But it couldn't be that easy.

"I don't know," she answered. "You've done this before. Aren't there certain topics couples should discuss first?"

Markus looked perplexed. Perhaps however many decades or centuries ago it was he had last married, it really was that simple.

"Like religion?" she asked, sounding as unsure as he looked.

"I believe in the Creator, and that our spirit is within our essence, and I believe in an afterlife. Vampires don't have ritualized organized religions like humans. Is that important to you?"

"Um, not really. I'm not a fan of organized religion; it causes too many arguments among otherwise good people. But I believe in a God, or a Creator, and in the human spirit—or vampire spirit." She smiled. "And I like to think there's someplace for that spirit to go after this life."

"See, we're more than compatible." Markus paused with a hopeful look. But Alex continued.

"What about children?"

"I've always wanted young, but I'd understand if you didn't—"

"No, I do." She only paused a second. "Finances?" she continued. "I'll be honest, I've got student loans up to my ears."

Markus laughed. "Alex, you're the coven's Seer. All your needs will be taken care of, but additionally, I will provide for you."

Side-tracked from the original conversation, Alex spoke up, annoyed. "I won't take hand-outs from the coven. And I won't let you pay my debts either."

Markus sighed. "Fine. We'll arrange for you to receive payment from the coven for your service, just like the rest of the warriors get. That should solve both problems, yes?"

"I guess." Alex remained still, racking her brain for other important topics she was forgetting. Markus stopped her. He lifted her chin so he had her undivided attention.

"Stop looking for problems, Alex. They'll arise on their own. All relationships have them, but we'll work through them—as they occur. We don't need to tackle everything in one night." He paused and smiled down at her. "You date like you spar. You spend so much time anticipating, you miss the chance to just react."

"I guess it's good I have you to train me in both areas," she said, grinning.

"Should we work in a little now?" Before Alex realized what he meant, Markus kicked a spray of water that hit her thigh and dripped down her bare leg.

The ensuing water fight left them both wet, but Alex was drenched. She decided as a last ditch effort to use her own dripping body as a means of soaking Markus. As he turned to reach into the tide to splash her again, she dove onto him. The soft footing and his off-center position led them both to land on the wet sand.

Alex laughed and shook the water dripping off her short hair into his face.

"Truce," Markus said, pulling her face closer so he could kiss her. Alex let her body fall completely onto his as their kissing became more intense. The cool water washing over their feet did nothing to temper the heat she felt as she lay across his chest.

Eventually she managed to pull away. As she ran her finger along the collar of his t-shirt, she decided to ask again, promising herself she would stop until he pursued if he once again said no.

"Any chance it would be proper to pull this shirt off of you now that I've agreed to marry you?" She blushed a little, not used to being so persistent in this area.

Markus frowned. "Probably not," he said. Alex tried to hide her disappointment. She had Markus's total devotion and commitment; she knew she should be content with that, but it didn't keep her whole body from tingling when he pulled her onto him again and whispered in her ear.

"But I'm not all that interested in being proper with you anymore."

And with the speed at which Markus stripped off both his clothes and hers, Alex was quite sure he had never been too interested in being proper. She was glad her tank top was stretchable cotton and her denim shorts were both loose and sturdy, or she was sure she wouldn't have had any clothes left to return home in. It seemed a few weeks of restraining himself against her frequent come-ons was all the foreplay Markus needed.

He held her on top of him, so it was his back not hers on the wet sand. But he made it clear he was the one in control, which was fine by Alex. She didn't fight him as he held her bare hips with his large hands and guided her onto him. Alex sucked in a breath and squeezed Markus's shoulders as her small body adjusted to his large size. He waited just long enough for her to exhale before starting to rock his hips, pushing himself deeper inside. He started slow and gentle, but even that control didn't last long. Alex was realizing the added pleasures that came with making love to a species with such speed.

She tried to hold back, to slow her body's response, but it was a battle she wouldn't win. Markus flashed her a fangy, triumphant grin as she cried out, her warm wetness contrasting with the cool waves lapping their entangled bodies. Their first time was too fast and over too soon. But as Markus carried her deeper into the water, still inside her, Alex remembered, if she was lucky, very, very lucky, she'd have centuries to get it right.

"Nice ass. You have something against underwear? Because I know your mother packed some in the box of clothes she sent over." Sage knew it was coming, so he easily ducked the jeans Rocky whipped at his head.

The young vamp was stripping out of his own clothes to put on a pair of jeans and t-shirt they had salvaged from a Vengatti male they had taken out a few nights earlier. It was a good thing Sage had parked the Jeep along a dark side street, because the open door Rocky was using as a privacy screen wasn't hiding much.

"If I had known I'd have to change into this crap in the middle of the street, I might have asked her to pack a full body suit. I smell like baby vomit."

Sage concurred, crinkling his nose. Vengatti vamps who fed exclusively from humans tended to have a nasty sour milk scent. "I'd be more worried about catching something from the dead S.O.B. we pulled those from."

Rocky squirmed at the thought as he pulled the t-shirt over his head. He couldn't complain much, though. This had been Rocky's suggestion when Markus's only complaint about his program and plan to use it had been that leaving their scent at Vengatti residences all over Bristol might cause them to panic. He worried they'd react brashly, possibly further endangering Levi or other innocent humans.

"I suppose it was a coincidence this dude happened to be closer in size to Markus and me than to you?"

Sage smiled and shrugged. "Got the two addresses?"

"Yeah," Rocky sighed. He was tucking his weapons into the waistband of his new digs. "Let's hope we have better luck than you and Markus did last night."

Sage knew Rocky was disappointed that the first night Sage had taken the lead warrior out to show him the program in use, they had stumbled onto two abandoned properties and the home of one human whose name just happened to be the same as one of the cover names used by the Vengatti. The man's pit bull had been sleeping just inside the fence Markus had hopped to check out the property. Had he been human, he might have lost his junk. It seemed any kind of truce between Rocky and Markus was destined to fail.

"Markus had a bad night all around. It wasn't your fault," Sage said. "Anyway, I think he may be making up for it tonight."

"You think?" Rocky looked skeptical.

"There are certain things I really don't want to hear—and with Alex that's not easy, so if we could get moving, so I have someone else to focus on, I'd appreciate it."

Rocky rolled his eyes. Sage smirked. It was Rocky's head he'd be in for the next few hours as he listened and recorded what the young vamp discovered as he searched the Vengatti properties.

The first address was empty. There was a faint smell, but it was over a month old. At the second address, a small two-storied home, they had some luck.

Two females, both matured. The older one feeds directly from humans, by the scent. Shit, even their females are despicable, huh?

Sage shook his head, though he knew Rocky couldn't see it from where he was, half a block away.

One unmatured male, Rocky continued. *He's home, too. Looks about sixteen, seventeen. And Daddy dearest is away, but that bastard is definitely feeding from humans. His scent is as nasty as these shitty clothes I'm wearing.*

Great, Sage thought. *Just get your ass out of there, then.* But of course Sage's gift only worked one way. He knew Rocky was circling around back to check the property for any signs of a human captive, despite agreeing with Markus and the other warriors that Levi was unlikely to be held in a house with females and young. The property they were looking for would reek of males, strong males who fed from humans.

From his spot down the street, Sage saw the car approaching before Rocky heard it and had time to flee. Sage flashed down the street, darting from tree to tree, dodging streetlights to remain unseen.

I got this, Sage. Don't jump the gun, yet. Rocky hoped his mentor heard this and would stay hidden unless things went south.

He had made it to the sidewalk before the car pulled up to the curb outside the house. He put his head down and pretended to be walking away.

Two Vengatti males got out of the sedan. One was the male who lived in the house; Rocky recognized the scent. The other smelled unfamiliar, but just as strong, and just as unpleasant. They both stopped at the end of the driveway to watch him. There was no chance they'd mistake him for a human. The question was which scent they would pick up—his own, or that of the male whose clothing he wore.

"Hey, you, what the hell are you doing out here?"

Rocky sighed in relief. If they smelled Rectinatti, they wouldn't have wasted time questioning him. He turned around and shrugged, keeping his eyes cast down. He was young enough that there was a chance they wouldn't have run into him on patrols and be able to recognize him.

"You here for Mallory?" It was the male who lived there, the father. Perfect—Rocky could play the dumb boyfriend well enough.

He nodded.

"I told you on the phone, she's already feeding someone—someone much, much higher up the food chain than you. Do I need to make that any clearer?"

"No, sir," Rocky answered, playing along.

"Good. I don't care about your crushes, you come around here again and you'll be an appetizer for him, got it?"

"Yes, sir. Sorry." Rocky was backing up. He noticed the second vampire sniffing the air, a look of confusion on his face.

"He smells funny," he said, turning to his partner.

"He's feeding off females instead of humans, of course he smells funny. It's the smell of a coward. Let him go. We need to get Mallory back to the house."

Rocky didn't hang around. He flashed down the street. He nearly choked on his own stomach when someone grabbed him from behind and pulled him into an overgrown pine.

"Calm," Sage whispered, his hand over Rocky's mouth. "And sheath the knife, please." Rocky put the knife back into the holster on his jeans and clutched his pounding chest.

"I could've killed you."

Sage scoffed. "I took my chances."

"Did you hear all that? Do you know what it means?"

"It means even the Vengatti girls won't feed you," Sage teased. It would have been in poor taste on a normal night. Tonight it was just obnoxious.

Rocky was about to tell Sage who *he* could bite, when they heard voices return to the yard.

"You'll do it for as long as he asks you to. It's an honor and your duty."

"Then some other female can volunteer." This was the voice of the young female Rocky had seen inside the house. "It makes me feel cheap and dirty."

Rocky heard the slap and the female's cry of pain. He spun around, fangs elongated, and started back the way he came. Sage tackled him and quickly dragged him back out of sight. Rocky released a growl, but his mentor responded by boxing his ear hard enough to snap him out of it. Rocky looked up at Sage's enraged expression and realized he had done it again.

"What's your job tonight?" Sage snapped. "You rush to her aid and what's the best that can happen? You kill her father in front of her, giving her and her family another excuse to hate us, and you ruin our best chance to find their Regan, and possibly Alex's brother. Think, Rocky!" He shoved the young vamp into the chain link fence behind him.

"I'm sorry. I know. I just snapped," Rocky said, pulling himself together. "They're moving," he said pointing down the street to where taillights cast a red glow on the pavement.

"Jeep's right there," Sage pointed across the street. They waited until the sedan had turned the corner before flashing from their hiding spot to the car. They would pursue from a distance.

Rocky knew Sage wasn't entirely focused on the vehicle a block ahead of them. He could follow a car in his sleep. Instead, his glare kept returning to Rocky.

"I said I'm sorry."

"That wouldn't have done you much good if it had been anyone else with you."

Rocky wasn't sure if Sage was referring to the fact his gift gave him the split-second notice he needed to prevent Rocky from bolting, or the fact any other warrior would likely have beaten him senseless and refused to work with him again.

"If a warrior lost control and acted without thinking, endangering himself, his mission, or his partner, he'd be reprimanded, severely, if not let go on the spot," Sage said.

"Lucky for me I won't ever have to worry about that," Rocky retorted. He knew Sage was trying to help, offering sound advice about how to act if he ever wanted to be a warrior. But despite his and Alex's belief that Darian wouldn't keep Rocky from serving once his sentence was over, Rocky was convinced this was as close as he'd ever get.

"I know it seems like an eternity to you now, kid, but it's a small fraction of your life. Don't ruin any chance you have of getting what you want afterward by being reckless now."

Rocky turned to face his mentor. He wondered how many vamps Sage fooled with the tough-guy routine and how many knew being an ass was just an act.

"Watch it," Sage called.

At first Rocky thought the warning was related to his thoughts, but Sage slammed his head down, smashing his forehead into the dash just as Rocky heard the first shot hit the windshield. Rocky pulled his own gun from his waistband and was ready to return fire. The Vengatti males had realized they were being tailed and slammed on the brakes as the Jeep closed in. But Sage spun the vehicle around and tore off down the next street.

"What are you doing? There were only two of them," Rocky said, turning back to Sage, rubbing the welt forming on his head.

"And an innocent female. And soon, because of the gunshots, half a dozen cops." Sage sped down a parallel street. "Mark down this street. We'll start working our way out from here tomorrow."

Rocky brushed the glass off his lap and opened up the laptop. As he zoomed in on their location, a grin spread over his face.

"There are five addresses in or around these neighborhoods. One is home to a Reginald Vendetti."

Sage turned to Rocky and raised a brow. "You don't think their Regan is that stupid, do you?"

"Stupid, yes," Rocky laughed. "Humorless, apparently not."

"It's got to be a decoy."

Rocky shrugged. "It's a good place to start."

"Keep this up, and Markus is going to have to find more reasons not to like you." Sage smirked at Rocky, who returned his mentor's grin.

When Alex and Markus pulled into the driveway they were both completely content. But when it occurred to Alex they'd have to face their housemates in their current condition—wet, sandy, and flushed—a bit of anxiety crept in. She tried to use her sense to figure out who was in the house, but found her own intense emotions were getting in the way. Markus, seeming to have similar concerns, sighed a little in relief when he parked next to Sarah's sedan.

"Rocky and Sage must have taken my truck and left already."

"I should hope so." Alex pointed to the clock on the dash. "Did you see how long we've been gone?" It was already 2:45, and the males usually returned for dinner a little after four.

"Oops," Markus said with a grin. "I guess I better stop in and apologize to the Regan for playing hooky, huh?"

"No," Alex said, shaking her head. "You thank him for the night off. But, you might want to shower first." She laughed as she brushed sand out of his short wet hair. "I could help you with that if you'd like."

"It's tempting," he said, getting out of the car and coming around to open her door. "But maybe we ought to wait for a time when my boss and best friend isn't in the room right next door."

When they reached the front porch Alex felt her blush deepening.

"Wouldn't the basement entrance be better?" she whispered as Markus reached to open the door.

"There's only one way past his office," Markus said, shrugging.

"I have a funny feeling that's not a coincidence."

But Darian had the decency not to look up as they walked briskly past his partly open door. And since Alex wanted nothing to do with witnessing Markus's explanation of their late return, she gave him a lingering kiss at his door before returning to her own room.

After a long shower, during which she relished every memory of the evening, Alex had returned to her closet to find the second clean outfit of the night. Deciding against her usual jeans-and-tank routine, she pulled out a short denim skirt, floral-print baby doll blouse and leather sandals rather than sneakers or flip-flops. Markus met her at the door to the office and looked her up and down, wagging his brows approvingly. She shook her head as he followed her down the stairs. When they were halfway to the foyer, Alex heard the doors of the truck slam in the driveway. Markus, apparently occupied with other things, didn't notice. If he had, he may have checked his comment, knowing they'd soon have an audience.

"You know, I really like that skirt," he said, staring at her ass as they reached the tile.

Alex turned to shush him when Rocky and Sage came through the front door.

Rocky looked a little worse for wear with cuts on the back of his neck and a lump on his forehead, but he still grinned at Markus's comment—at least until Markus began to scrutinize him. Sage, however, took less than a minute to register both their expressions and no doubt their thoughts.

"Oh, please." He shook his head like it was an Etch A Sketch he could magically clear.

"Wow, Sage, I didn't know you were even capable of feeling embarrassment," Alex said, doing some sensing of her own.

Sage just glared at her before heading to the basement stairway. The door slammed behind him.

"No offense, Alex, but that was stupid," Rocky said.

Instead of snapping at the young vamp, like he often did, Markus nodded in agreement. "Sage doesn't get mad without getting even," he said with a grimace.

"I really didn't want to know what he heard in your two heads, but now I'm guessing, by the end of dinner, the whole house will know," Rocky said with a look of obvious distaste. "At least I won't have to be in the room."

Alex cringed. Living with vampires had some serious drawbacks.

Sure enough, Sage made sure dinner was as uncomfortable as possible. He started with seemingly innocuous comments.

"I like that shirt, Alex," he said with mock sincerity, passing her a dish of peas. "You didn't have that on when you left earlier, did you?"

Alex ignored him and tried to start up a conversation with Sarah. It didn't stop her from hearing him start on Markus.

"So, you score anything tonight?" He left a dramatic pause before adding, "On patrols, I mean."

"As I think you know, I didn't make it out tonight," Markus answered curtly.

"That's right. You were busy with Alex on the beach," Sage continued.

"Cut it out, Sage," Darian ordered. He followed up with a question about what had happened that evening before Sage could continue and push Markus over the edge.

When dinner was over, Alex wanted nothing more than to escape to her room to be with Markus. However, Sage was intent on making her miserable one way or the other before that could happen. He was heading into the living room, feeling much happier than he should be, Alex thought, as she trudged along behind him.

"Sage," Markus called, seeing his grin.

"Yes, loverboy?" Sage stopped and let Alex pass, but she paused at the doorway.

"Don't you dare mess with her tonight," he said in a tone that was deadly serious. At times like these, Alex liked being reminded Markus was not simply a warrior. He led the warriors.

"I'm just training her," Sage answered innocently. Markus nodded and started up the stairs.

"Hey, Markus," Sage called, "Don't forget your boots outside on the porch."

Markus looked at him suspiciously before turning back to the front door. "Right. Thanks," he said, never looking away from Sage.

"You might want to bang them before bringing them in. You know how sand can get stuck in all the crevices."

Markus was inches from Sage's neck, fangs out, when Darian flashed from the kitchen and crashed into him, stopping what no doubt would have been a blood bath.

"Markus," Darian pulled him to his feet and spun him around, not letting go of his grip. "Rocky's got the program up and running in my office. He wanted to show you what they found tonight. Go check it out. Now, please."

Markus shook him off and tried to regain his composure. "Sure," he said, glaring at Sage as he went up the stairs.

"And you," Darian said to Sage, who had begun to edge his way into the living room, "will do your job without the added commentary. And maybe while you're working with Alex, you can freshen up your own skills. You seem to be having trouble staying out of others' heads lately."

"Hers I can't help," Sage said, having the audacity to sound defensive.

"All the more reason to keep quiet when you hear her private thoughts." Darian turned to Alex, who was still in the doorway to the living room. She mouthed 'thank you,' and he nodded.

When Sage and Alex had taken their usual places in the living room, Sage addressed her.

"I'll keep my comments to myself, if you at least attempt to tone down your little fantasies when I'm around, deal?"

Alex wanted to be done with this conversation immediately. "Deal. Let's just work. The sooner I can learn to focus, the happier we'll both be."

But at the end of another hour of more failures than successes, it was clear neither of them was too happy.

"I hate to break this to you," Sage said as Alex rubbed her temples, "but we're going to try again tomorrow before breakfast."

"I thought no one had issues with my running?" Alex said, getting more annoyed.

"We don't. But Darian wants us to focus on this now, and it's the only time I have. You can run after we leave. You don't need an escort; no one's worried about you taking off anymore."

"You all keep making decisions about me without my input and you will need to worry about it," she mumbled.

"Yeah, well, feel free to do as the rest of us do and leave a note in the complaint box. It's the round metal bin next to Darian's desk." Sage got up and headed for the door, but Alex stayed where she was on the couch. She closed her eyes and tried to calm her aching head. She hardly remembered when Markus came into the room just before sunrise and carried her back to bed.

What seemed like moments later, Alex awoke to Markus gently playing with her hair.

"Morning, sleepy," he said.

She groaned and rolled over, pulling the covers with her. She only vaguely registered the ease with which they moved, meaning Markus was under them with her as opposed to on top of them.

He chuckled at her and slipped out of bed.

"Come on, don't you want to get up?" He had come around to her side of the bed to kiss the top of her head.

"What's the rush?" She sighed, remembering what was facing her instead of their usual morning run together.

"It's still early," Markus said quietly. "I think Darian and Sarah are still asleep."

Alex was too groggy to catch on. "It's not them I don't want to see," she answered.

Markus sighed. He sat on the bed and pulled the covers down so she could see his face.

"I was implying that while we had some privacy, I'd like to take you up on your offer from last night—to help me wash up?" As his grin spread, Alex's eyes widened in comprehension.

"That I'll get up for," she said, pushing him off the mattress so she could crawl out after him.

When Alex and Markus came downstairs awhile later, they found Sage already up and in the kitchen with Rocky. Alex waited by the door for Sage to get up, but instead he beckoned for her to come in.

"Good, you brought lab rat number two," he said as Markus entered ahead of her.

"Do we really need to involve other people in my humiliation?" Alex slumped into a chair at the butcher-block table.

"You're technically the only person here, by definition. But, yes, as your gift involves sensing others' emotions, it does help to practice with others present." Sage reached behind him to get her a bowl from the cabinet, as if Cocoa Krispies would somehow make the experience more enjoyable.

"So, what's the goal?"

"To read only one of us at a time," Sage answered.

"With you in the room, that's pretty impossible." She grabbed the cereal box from Rocky, deciding a little chocolate couldn't hurt.

"Soon enough they will all be that strong," he reminded her.

She was fairly certain he wasn't trying to taunt her, but it riled her just the same. She was unlikely to forget what Sage had let her feel the other night.

"What do you need us to do?" Markus asked.

"Nothing. Unless you want to try to whip up a slew of mixed emotions to mess with her," Sage said.

Markus glared back. "I think what I'm feeling now is just fine."

"Yup, that'll do." Sage smiled. "Whenever you're ready, Alex. Probably best to start with sensing me and blocking them. It should be easier."

Alex closed her eyes for a minute and inhaled slowly. Before doing as Sage asked, she tried to focus on her own emotions, pushing the others to the back of her mind. She was getting slightly better at this part, though she was never totally able to eliminate the buzz of the others' feelings.

She opened her eyes. She attempted to let in just Sage's mood, which was by far the strongest. For a brief moment she thought she had it, as only a growing sense of pleasure mixed in with her own doubt. But as soon as she realized it, the others' emotions flooded in as well.

"Ugh," Alex groaned. She was like a little kid learning to ride a bike who fell over as soon as she realized she was pedaling on her own.

"It didn't work?" Markus asked.

"No. You are still annoyed, probably with Sage. You," she said turning to Rocky, "are amused, probably also by Sage, and please don't be, it only encourages him. And you," she said to Sage with a tone of accusation, "are smug, probably because you enjoy watching me fail in front of an audience."

"Two out of three, not bad," Sage said.

"You're not pleased with yourself right now?" she asked, cocking an eyebrow.

"No, I am," he answered. "But I was actually pleased because before you failed, I noticed you had gotten better at focusing on your own emotions. And I was thinking what I fine teacher I must be if I'd managed to teach you the most important lesson."

Alex rolled her eyes and returned to her soggy cereal. Markus asked if he needed help patting his own back, though Alex doubted a pat was what he had in mind.

"How do you know who's feeling what?" Rocky asked. Alex was glad the conversation had turned serious again before Markus and Sage could go at it. "I mean, you don't hear us the way Sage does," he continued, "so how can you tell?"

Alex thought about it for a moment. Rocky was right in the sense she was only feeling emotions, not hearing each of them say how they felt.

"Each emotion has a distinct feel," she explained. "When one of you is feeling many emotions at once, it's harder to distinguish them, but I always know who I'm sensing. Your emotions have a certain tenor, like your tone of voice."

Rocky looked at her for a minute. "You know, I don't know whose gift is weirder, yours or his."

"Thanks, Rocky," Alex said, "I love your honesty."

Sage cracked him on the skull with the spoon he had used to stir his coffee.

They finished breakfast and continued with Alex's training, which, after numerous more partially successful tries, left her with a dull headache again.

"You going for a run?" Markus asked as he grabbed his keys from the porcelain dish on the entryway table where the males often left them.

"Yeah." She rubbed her temples, distracted.

"Maybe you should take a nap later," Markus said concerned.

Alex hated to worry him before he left. She managed a smile. "You want me rested up when you come home?"

"That wasn't why I said it, but. . . ." He returned the smile.

"Maybe we can try something wild and crazy tonight," she whispered.

He raised an eyebrow with an expression that seemed both intrigued and turned on. "Like what?"

"The bed."

Markus laughed loudly and kissed her goodbye.

Chapter 14

In just a few days Alex had fallen into a new and equally exhausting routine. But things were starting to turn around—for the better. Her early evenings and late nights with Sage were slowly starting to lead to progress, but the headaches they almost always led to still left her dreading the time. She was still running, on her own now, after the males left for the night. But her additional workouts were cut back to an hour. This shorter routine wasn't a conscious decision by Alex to take it easy. It just seemed, coincidentally, that Sarah or Darian or whoever had the night off happened to need to show her something or ask her a question that required her to go back to the house. Alex found she wasn't upset by these interruptions. Usually her energy was petering out anyway by the time they occurred. Not usually one who required much rest or sleep, Alex wondered if her increased need was due to her approaching maturity or simply a combination of long nights training and late mornings making love, which, thankfully, had remained uninterrupted since her and Markus's night on the beach.

When Thursday came and Markus suggested they take it easy on his day off, Alex found that her body and mind relished the idea of just relaxing with him. So Markus and Sage headed out early to feed, again taking separate vehicles so Markus could return as soon as possible. And Alex skipped her run to indulge in a few hours of reading. It was something she had done very little of this summer and, like the beach, she didn't realize how much she missed it until she was back enjoying it.

Markus entered the living room and found her hungrily turning the page of the new summer thriller, which she had bought and started the week before school got out—the week before her own adventure started. She looked up when she noticed him standing over her.

"Hold on," she said putting her finger up, "I'm at the second murder—let me just finish this chapter."

Markus grinned and snuck in a quick kiss despite her request. "Take your time. I've got to check in with Darian about something, anyway. I'll be back in a bit."

Engrossed in the world of her book, Alex just nodded. As her eyelids started to droop at the end of the next chapter, she looked at the small mantle clock. She had been reading since Markus had left to meet Cormelia almost four hours ago. It was no wonder her eyes were tired. She put her book on the cherry table next to her and closed her lids, figuring Markus would be returning any moment.

Sure enough, moments later he was running his fingers along the side of her face.

"You going to wake up to get something to eat?" he asked quietly.

"Mmm," Alex moaned opening her eyes. "Want me to make you lunch?"

Markus half smiled and half bit his bottom lip. "It's dinner time, Sleeping Beauty, and Sarah's already done cooking. They're waiting for us."

Alex sat up quickly, giving herself a head rush. She leaned around Markus to see the mantle clock. The small brass hands had read just after midnight. But as she looked again, it was almost five.

"I slept five hours?" She swatted at him in frustration. "Why didn't you wake me? I wasted our whole day together."

"Hey," Markus said in a tone meant to soothe her. "You obviously needed it. Don't worry about it. I got a lot of work done with Darian tonight. Which means after my meeting with the warriors tomorrow night, I'm sure I can come home early, okay?"

"Meeting?" Alex was heading to the hall with him and was awake enough to be curious.

"Just rearranging a few patrols," he answered. She was also awake enough to register his reluctance to say more.

Alex had been willing to forgive Markus for allowing her to nap away their day together. He had meant well and had already arranged to make up the lost time with her. However, as she lay in bed wide-awake staring at the ceiling midmorning, she was beginning to rethink it. It had taken her over a week to adjust to the vampires' schedule of sleeping days and waking nights, which she had followed for a month. After one long nighttime nap, she felt it had all been undone. When her restlessness reached its peak, she gave in and slipped out of bed. Remembering her unfinished book on the coffee table in the living room, she threw on some sweats and headed downstairs.

She debated as she picked up her book whether remaining in the dark house would help lure her back to sleep. Deciding it was probably futile, she headed for the front porch to enjoy the rare opportunity to soak in some sun. She pulled one of the oversized wicker chairs into the far corner where, despite the overhang of the porch roof, the angle of the sun left a sunny spot for her to read. As the sun soaked through her clothes warming her, she wondered whether Seers typically suffered from Vitamin D deficiencies. It might make for a good excuse to do this more often. She understood vampires' inability to leave the windows and curtains open, but the constant air-conditioning sometimes made her feel confined in the house. Then again, her brief jaunt on the beach had made her realize she had been confined to the house—all summer. With a sigh she knew this was yet another argument she would have to have with Darian. For now, though, she would be content with sunshine and fresh air.

It wasn't long before she had pushed up the legs of her sweats and removed the long-sleeve top she had on over her tank. Though she wasn't tired, she delighted in the complete relaxation and used the moment to daydream.

Her mind seemed to be pulling her backward through her most vivid memories. She was on the beach making love to Markus, the sound of the waves drowning out their ragged breathing. She was in Darian's office, scared and confused, being told she was a Seer, a gift that could kill her or give her power. Flinching, she was back in the alley being attacked, her heart racing even in her memory. Then she was in her apartment holding Brady's collar, rubbing her fingers over the smooth metal nametag, tears dripping from her nose.

As older memories came, it occurred to her how many were painful: her father's stroke, his slow progression into depression, her cutting, the accident. It wasn't until her memories were focused on times before the crash that she remembered sustained periods of happiness. She watched again as Dave walked across the stage at his high school graduation, accepting his diploma and a scholarship to play football at the top state university. She recalled Levi taking her out for ice cream the day after he got his license. She remembered her father's look of pride as her brothers carried her out to the car on their shoulders after she had won her first karate competition. These times were full of such pleasure and innocence.

Though she realized it was probably her naiveté at the time that led her to remember them that way. By that time, surely, Dave, if not both he and Levi, would have been experiencing some of the same changes Alex was undergoing. And if her father knew, which he must have, then he had been experiencing the worry and fear that came with that knowledge. Alex wasn't a parent yet, but she could imagine how taxing that fear could be. It made her reexamine her view of her father and his actions at the time just before and after her brothers' accident. Where once she held resentment, even disgust, now she felt what she had thought she never would: sympathy and empathy.

Rethinking how her father must have felt also made Alex wonder about what her brothers had gone through. Though her father never made allowances for her being younger or a girl, she knew her brothers and mother had done the best they could to maintain her innocence and protect her from the unpleasant realities of life. What she didn't know then was how unpleasant those realities were. Here she was as an adult with over six years more life experience than either of her brothers had before their accident—or abduction, as she now believed it to be—and she still struggled to deal with her current situation. Both may have known what to expect from the preparation and training their father had likely given them, but she was pretty sure neither had fully matured prior to being captured by the Vengatti. She shuddered to think what it must have been like to undergo such an experience without the support of people they could trust.

"It was nightmarish," Levi answered. Once again Alex's dreams had brought her back to her family's basement. Still conscious enough to realize she had succeeded in contacting him again, she cried out, elated.

"Levi! Oh, thank God. I've been trying to reach you. I was worried when you stopped—well, what is it exactly we're doing?"

"You were worried? You were trying?" The look he shot her was chilling. "Yet I'm still here, and you're still ignoring my advice."

"What advice?" She speculated about his drastic change in mood. He hadn't seemed happy during her previous dreams, but for the most part he had been patient, and underneath his pain there had still been a hint of the warmth she had remembered him having.

Now he was completely cold and angry. She realized it at the same time she registered her sense of him wasn't as strong as she would have expected, considering her growing sense of the others. She attributed it to not physically being in the same room with him.

Levi had turned his back to her and was once again facing the dartboard with a fist full of darts. "I can't really spell it out for you," he said tossing the first dart.

"Because you're being watched. We figured that. And you don't know exactly where you're being held, do you?" she asked. He didn't turn around, but shook his head. "But there has to be a clue you can give me, something that will help us know where to look."

"Look around you! This is the clue!" He shot the final darts at the board in close succession.

It hit Alex hard and fast.

"Home?" She looked doubtfully around the dated family room. She had thought her mind pictured this place when he spoke to her this way because they had spent so many hours playing there as children. Now she realized it hadn't been her subconscious leading her here. Levi had somehow intentionally conjured up this setting. The pieces started to fit.

"You told me I was looking for answers in the wrong place. I thought you meant I was asking the vampires I'm with the wrong questions," she said. "But you meant it literally. There's something at the house, something that will help me find you?"

Levi anxiously turned to face her. She could see the desperation in his expression as he nodded.

"They can hear you, but not me right?" There had to be a way to get more information without putting him in danger.

He nodded again, then looked behind him distractedly. She couldn't tell whether he was looking back at the wall with the dartboard in the imagined room they shared or whether he was hearing something in the actual space he was being held.

"So when we talk, are we saying these things aloud?" Alex didn't think that could be possible. The first time she remembered dreaming of Levi, Rocky had been guarding her.

Levi shook his head. He continued to look back frequently. Alex thought about how else someone could know what he was telling her, if no one could hear him speak. *Hear* him. Crap.

"The Vengatti have a Knower. He can hear your thoughts," she said, shaken by the idea.

Before Levi could confirm, he spun around. Alex felt as if she, too, had turned abruptly, as the room seemed to spin with Levi's motion. She closed her eyes to steady herself.

When she opened them, she was on the porch. The sun had moved, so she was mostly in the shade, but that wasn't why goose bumps rippled over her skin. She leapt out of the chair and dashed for the house. Midway across the foyer she realized she was still holding her book. She let it fall to the floor with a soft thud as she darted down the stairs. Despite the chaos of thoughts bombarding her, she knew exactly what needed to be done and whom she needed to help her.

The blow sent Levi crashing to the floor of the windowless room in which he had spent the better part of eleven years. The blood that gushed from his nose wasn't the first to stain the concrete floor.

"You're supposed to be getting information, not providing it." Leonce nudged him hard in the rib to force him to roll over. Levi wanted to destroy the black boot that had bruised his body so many ways over the years almost as badly as he wanted to destroy the blood-sucking bastard who wore it. Leonce heard the thought and raised his foot over Levi's face; he stomped down. Levi flinched, bracing for the pain, yet welcoming the numbness that would come from both the head blow and the loss of blood.

Leonce wasn't in the business of giving people what they wanted. His foot stopped just centimeters from Levi's face. The large male pushed his brunette waves from his forehead and sneered. "Do you have anything useful, or just more of your bullshit?"

"You heard it all. You don't need me to repeat it," Levi said defiantly. He turned his head and spit out a mouthful of the blood that ran down his throat from the broken nose. He purposely sprayed in the direction of Leonce's other leg.

"I heard what you allowed me to. I want the rest of it," Leonce demanded.

Levi and Leonce both knew this was only partly true. Leonce apparently couldn't hear the conversations Levi was able to hold with his sister in the form of communication only two Seers could utilize. Levi wasn't sure why, and Leonce knew this. But it didn't stop the vampire, who was accustomed to hearing everything in the Seer's head, from being annoyed—and, Levi sensed, threatened.

"She still doesn't have it, which means she doesn't know any more than I do, probably less."

"But she's living with them, so when she finds it, they'll have all the information—the whole prophecy. And we won't." Leonce cursed, but walked away without further harming Levi. The Seer sat up, tucked his chin-length blond hair behind his ears, and wiped the blood from his face the best he could with his dirty sleeve.

"She still doesn't know what she's looking for?" Leonce asked.

"Nope. She thinks she's looking for information about where I am," Levi answered honestly.

"And is she any closer to finding it?" Leonce was becoming intolerable with the slow pace. Levi ought to have been, too. It was his body, after all, which bore the scars of the Vengatti Regan's impatience.

"Yes, assuming it's still with my father." Levi was careful not to avert his glance. It was a common tell, one Leonce would jump on. Levi's gift allowed him to feign concern easily. What was harder was refocusing his thoughts. He'd already spent many hours this summer, while the monsters slept, analyzing what he had overheard about the search at his parents' home. Returning to it now would only heighten Leonce's suspicion.

Leonce had grudgingly accepted that what his males had told him was fact, but only after forcing them to make eye contact. He trusted no one, so he used his gift on everyone. No one dared refuse. It was as good as admitting to hiding something from him. It was as good as signing one's own death certificate.

But Levi didn't need permission or contact to use his gift. He sensed everyone, whether they liked it or not. He had sensed the two males, who had been sent to look for Alex and her father at his childhood home, as they reported to Leonce a few weeks earlier. Neither of them believed they were lying when they told their Regan the elder Crockers had moved and left no forwarding address with the middle-aged man who claimed to live there alone now. But the Seer had sensed otherwise; the males' conviction felt muddled, tampered with. Levi was glad he was the spitting image of his mother; it meant nothing of his father's appearance had connected him to his captive son as he fed the two vampires the lie and then made sure they believed it. He knew his father's gift was weak, but was proud his old man had pushed it to the limit to keep the secrets of their kind safe. The longer it took for Leonce to acquire the histories, the better.

"Convenient for you isn't it, that the girl and your parents are apparently both in hiding, protected by the Rectinatti, and the Seer histories remain out of reach?" Leonce stopped his pacing and examined his Seer. Levi sensed his suspicion. The Vengatti Regan hadn't bothered to hide that when Alex was captured and the full prophecy found, Levi would be useful for little more than an occasional snack, and certainly not worth the effort of keeping him alive. If Levi wanted to survive, he'd have to convince Leonce otherwise.

"You're not at all curious to see what the combined power of two Seer siblings could do for you, for your coven?" Something tugged at Levi. A memory flashed before his mind's eye of when he used to fight to keep Alex out of his thoughts, when he would suffer anything to protect her. And he had suffered. But for what? So she could live her life blissfully ignorant of his pain? So he could keep her from this world—only to have her fall into the hands of the other monsters anyway? She didn't even seem bothered by it. Fine, then she could take his place. "She'll find them—and when she does, I'll see to it you can find her."

Leonce sneered at Levi's statement, or perhaps his thoughts. "Such concern for us, such willingness to self-sacrifice. One might think your essence was still pure and strong. Should we test that theory? See how much good you still possess?"

"Back the fuck off, Leonce," Levi said, though he was the one inching toward the wall. "I can hinder your plans as much as help them. And you'd never even know—because you can't hear what I tell her." Levi knew no threat would stop what was coming. But he also knew his body could handle only so much more. He wouldn't give himself willingly, even if fighting it would amplify his pain.

"Threaten me again and I'll drain you dry, you little prick. Follow through with that insane scheme and I'll keep you alive just to have you watch me torture your sister night after night, at least for as long as that still bothers you," Leonce growled. His gift meant he knew Levi better than the Seer wanted to admit. "Ty," he called through the door. The large dark male appeared filling the doorframe. "Our human needs to be reminded whom he serves."

Ty ran his tongue over his fangs. "My pleasure."

He was across the room before Levi could blink. As Ty tore into his neck and began to feed from Levi's essence, to suck out what was left of his goodness, the Seer didn't bother to repress his scream. He had long ago lost his last scrap of dignity.

Alex ran right past Sage's closed door. When she reached the second door, she threw it open without knocking. Rocky slept through the invasion, forcing Alex to rush to his bed and shake him violently.

"Rocky, get up! It's an emergency, wake up!" Sarah hadn't been exaggerating when she had told Alex vampires slept soundly during the midday. After a final desperate shake, Alex tugged the covers he had wrapped around his neck right off the bed.

Instantly she wished she hadn't. Rocky woke with a snarl, fangs out, only to find Alex with her back turned to him standing by his bed.

"Alex?" He realized he was uncovered and completely nude and pulled back the sheets she had removed.

"Um . . . yeah." Alex couldn't let her embarrassment deter her, but she didn't turn around. "You need to get dressed and meet me in the foyer, Rocky. I need to go to my folks, now, and it's still light out."

She tore out of his room, closing the door behind her. She sprinted up both flights of stairs, but crept down the upstairs hall. She knew an immediate departure was absolutely necessary, but she had her doubts about Markus or Darian sharing her opinion.

Luckily, Markus slept as soundly as Rocky. Alex was able to put on clothes and shoes, the first she could find, and even steal one of his baseball hats before sneaking out of the room without him so much as rolling over.

Just as she had asked, Rocky was dressed and waiting for her in the foyer.

"Where are the others?" he asked as she hit the landing.

"Asleep," she answered breathlessly from running frantically through the house. To remind him why she had chosen him, Alex yanked open the front door, letting in all the midday sun. She scooped a set of keys out of the dish near the door. She didn't care whose they were or what vehicle they went to. But when she went to hand them to him, he stepped back.

"You mean they don't know?" Rocky asked. Alex knew she had hit a snag. She needed Rocky on board.

"I came to you, because they couldn't help if they did," she said pointing outside. "And as I'm only going to my parents' house, which is perfectly safe, they couldn't stop me either."

Rocky opened his mouth to argue, but there was no need. An answer came from the top of the stairs.

"You want to test that theory?" Darian's irritation was evident even as he rubbed the sleep from his eyes. It seemed Alex could no longer postpone this discussion.

"It's not a theory. I have a right to come and go as I please. Unless your agreement that I was no longer your prisoner was bullshit?" Alex, with keys still in hand, backed into the sun-filled doorway. Darian saw the move and stared her down. Alex held his gaze. Each was trying to gauge the other's resolve.

"Rocky," Darian said, never looking away from Alex.

Rocky gave her a quick look of apology before pushing her aside and shutting the door. She tried to fight against him, but it was futile. She was pissed, and started to tell both of them before Darian interrupted.

"How many times do you think you can set the alarm off before waking one of us?" Darian asked, coming down the stairs once the entryway was dark again.

Alex was distracted by his comment. "I punched in the code."

Darian scowled at Rocky, and Alex realized the young vampire hadn't told the Regan he had given her the code.

"It beeps anyway," Rocky explained quietly, his guilt two-fold, since he also hadn't told Alex about this feature of the alarm. "Every time the door opens."

Alex was thinking she hadn't ever heard the alarm beep, when the crowd in the foyer doubled.

"You wouldn't," Sage said more in a growl than a yawn as he came up from the basement. "Only those of us able to hear pitches that high are lucky enough to be woken up by your midday roaming."

By this time Markus had made his way down the stairs in a flash. "What happened? What's the matter?" he demanded.

They all looked to Alex for an answer. It was the reminder she needed to jolt her back on track.

"I couldn't sleep, so I went out on to the porch to read. I must have zoned out, because Levi was able to make contact again." She continued at high speed to explain what she had learned and why she needed Rocky to take her to her parents' immediately. She got a spark of interest from Sage when she informed them the Others also likely had a Knower. Darian didn't react to this, but was full of doubt in general. From Markus she registered mostly concern.

When she finished, Darian addressed her. "And you 'contacted' Levi when you fell asleep—while reading this?" He had walked to the middle of the floor and picked up the book she had dropped on her way to wake Rocky. The title along with the shadowy figure on the front cover made its genre evident.

"I know what you're implying, Regan." Alex was angry even though the accusation hadn't yet left his mouth. "As I've told you before, these are not just dreams."

Before Darian could argue, Markus spoke up. "We believe you, Alex," he said, shooting Darian a look, "but that doesn't mean you can take off in the middle of the day unprotected."

"She wasn't going unprotected," Rocky said before Alex could. "I wouldn't have taken her without asking, but now that you know, there's no reason not to let her check it out. I'm perfectly capable and more than willing to protect her." Alex could sense his uncertainty about questioning both Markus and Darian, but he held his chin up and looked them both in the eye.

Darian stared at him for a minute, but responded calmly. "I don't doubt your ability, Rocky, but you're not supposed to be off the property without an escort, which poses a problem at noon."

"He has an escort," Alex cut in. "I'm the coven's Seer and a warrior—or I will be soon. Who's going to be around at noon to verify the finer points?"

"Fine," Darian sighed.

"No," Markus said.

The two males looked at each other in disbelief.

"It's too dangerous, Darian," Markus argued.

"It's your patrols, made up of the males you've trained, who have reported there's been no activity there since the night after Alex arrived here," Darian countered.

"You've been watching the house? Someone was there—?" Alex was shocked and upset she hadn't known. But Rocky nudged her arm to silence her. She stopped, knowing, as he did, her fear would only keep them both home.

"He's only had a year of training," Markus said.

Rocky clenched his jaw and looked ready to argue, but Sage stepped in.

"I'll vouch for him, Markus. I trained him, and you trained me. You had me running patrols with little more than a year's training. Besides, any of the Others out at this time couldn't have any more experience than he has."

Markus looked like he would have continued to argue, but Darian cut him off. "Enough. They can go if they want to. The sooner she gets it out of her system, the sooner we can all get back to bed." He turned to Rocky. "Be quick, and check in every thirty minutes."

Markus looked to Alex. She could feel his love and concern, and it overwhelmed her.

"Please, Alex. Wait until I can take you later."

It hurt her to deny him, but it wasn't enough to keep her from going. "Sorry, Markus." She turned and handed the keys to Rocky who now accepted them. They both started to the door.

"Rocky." Markus tried to hide his pain behind his fierce expression. "You bring her back injured in any way, and you'll be lucky if I let you clean a warrior's weapon for the next two centuries."

"If she comes back injured, warrior," Rocky said, holding his fist over his heart in a gesture Alex didn't recognize, but Markus and the others seemed to, "it'll be because the bastard who tried to attack her killed me first."

Markus nodded gravely at him, his look displaying more respect than Markus usually showed the young vampire. He stole a quick kiss from Alex before backing up to allow them to walk into the scorching sunlight.

Alex walked to the car in a daze. It wasn't until Rocky was peeling out onto the main road that she realized she should say something.

"Um, thanks, for what you told Markus," she said. It was a bit mild for the intense loyalty he had just shown, but she didn't know how else to express her gratitude.

Rocky blushed and kept his eyes on the road. "You're welcome. I meant it, you know."

"I know," Alex answered.

They rode in silence for another mile, but as Rocky approached the second intersection and correctly put on his left directional, Alex remembered what she had learned back at the house.

"You've been there before, with Sage."

"Yes," Rocky confirmed. "We didn't tell you because the Vengatti never went in the house. Your parents were fine, and the Others have never come back. Markus has had patrols there to be sure ever since the second night you were with us."

Alex nodded. Part of her was frustrated she hadn't been told. Information about her parents and their safety was her business, even if it worried her. Another part of her was somewhat surprised Darian hadn't told her this early on to gain her trust. Knowing he had seen to her family's protection would have bought him some respect and forgiveness during those tough first days. She was glad to have more evidence he made decisions based on what was right, not just what benefited him or his coven.

Rocky allowed Alex to ride in silence for most of the ride. Thirty minutes in, he called home as ordered. Alex rolled her eyes at the ridiculousness of checking in when the others knew they couldn't have possibly arrived yet. She heard Markus answer the phone. When the brief conversation was over, Rocky spoke to her.

"Do you know what to look for?"

"No, but I have a good idea where to look," she answered honestly, pulling her hand in from the open window of the Jeep. The dark green paint was scorching after absorbing the midday sun.

"That's a start," Rocky said. Alex wished she couldn't sense his doubt as he tried to sound hopeful.

When they turned onto her parents' street, Alex felt a twinge of guilt. Christmas day was the last time she had taken a cab from the city to visit her parents. Then the lawns had been covered in half a foot of snow. Now most were burnt due to the lack of rainfall and hot July temperatures.

"My mother's car is gone," Alex said with relief. "But you should probably park down the street just in case."

"No, I'm leaving it right out front," Rocky answered. Alex registered the business-like tone he had assumed since they left. He was serious about protecting her, and that meant assuring a quick retreat if necessary.

"Whatever you think's best," she answered with an appreciative nod.

He pulled up to the curb and shut off the engine. He left the keys in the ignition, though, as he started to get out.

"Stay here for a minute. And keep the doors locked," he told her before shutting the driver's door. Alex watched as he walked the perimeter of the yard, crossing the front door as well as the side entrance to the garage. He strolled back to the car coming around to the passenger's side.

"Nothing fresh," he told her as she opened her door and got out.

"You know, the neighbors are going to wonder what kind of over-protective boyfriend I'm bringing home," she smiled.

"Let them," he said with a shrug.

She led Rocky back up the path to the front door. She tried not to notice the ragged state of her mother's once pristine front-door garden. She reached into an overgrown holly bush and pulled out the hide-a-key rock that had been there since she was a kid.

"Ouch." She pulled a dried thorny leaf from her finger.

"People really use those things?" Rocky asked watching in disbelief as she pulled the rusted key from its hiding place.

"Yes, and most people don't even hide them in thorny shrubbery," Alex said, unlocking the door and replacing the key. "My father claimed he hid it there because it was the last place a robber would look, but my brothers and I thought he did it as a means of punishment for whichever of us was irresponsible enough to lose our house key." She started into the entryway, but Rocky held her arm.

"Me first, just in case."

Alex rolled her eyes, but held the door for him to enter. When he seemed satisfied the house was truly empty and safe, he motioned for her to come in.

"Where do we start?" he asked.

Alex led him through the living room and into the kitchen. There she opened a door leading down to the family room in the finished half of the basement. As she walked down the gold-carpeted stairs, she felt her legs shaking beneath her. The room, which she always avoided when she visited, looked just as it had when she was growing up, just as it did in her dreams with Levi. There were new boxes against the back wall, and a layer of dust, or possibly mildew, covered the foosball table. Everything else remained painfully untouched, as if by maintaining the room her parents had hoped to hold on to a sliver of its shattered past.

Alex remained at the bottom of the stairs absorbing all this until a hand rested on her shoulder. She jumped, even at Rocky's gentle touch.

"Sorry, Alex, but we don't have much time. Darian and Markus want us in and out quickly."

"Right," Alex said, shaking herself from her thoughts.

She walked directly to the dartboard, hoping her hunch was correct. Lifting the board from the wall, she sucked in a breath. Where there should have been blank wall there was a wooden box, just small enough to be hidden by the dartboard, squeezed tightly into a hole cut in the plasterboard.

"That's it? You found it?" Rocky asked, crossing the room after her. They were both amazed she had discovered something so quickly.

"Help me get it out. Do you have a knife on you?" she asked, unsuccessfully prying at the box with her non-existent fingernails.

Rocky laughed, lifting his baggy t-shirt. He had a knife handle sticking out of a holster on each side, and as he turned she saw what she thought was the handle of a handgun tucked into the back of his jeans. If he packed this heavy going to her parents, she could only imagine what he had on him when he went out looking for Vengatti.

"I'd offer you a Boy Scout badge for preparedness," she said as he slid out one of the large knives, "but I think they might have a policy against carrying concealed weapons."

"Their loss," Rocky said, prying the box partly out. It was proving difficult, so Alex tugged the loosened corner as he began to use the blade to dig out the opposite side.

"Nothing's there."

Rocky spun around so fast Alex only saw a blur of movement as she was shoved into the wall. When the blur came into focus, Rocky stood in front of her with the knife held out in front of him.

"Careful, Rocky, it's just my father," Alex said, rubbing the back of her head.

Rocky cursed, and Alex knew the reason, as she shared the sentiment. In their excitement, neither her sense nor his enhanced hearing had alerted them to another's presence.

"They've found you, Alexandra," her father said. She noted his speech was more fluid than it had been at Christmas. She wondered whether his therapy was finally working. "You're in danger," he continued. He was looking at Rocky. Alex muscled her way around her guardian, so she could approach her father. Rocky shadowed her movements.

"No, Dad, I'm okay. The Others haven't found me. Rocky's with the Rectinatti. They're protecting me, training me." It took all the control she had not to remind him this was a job he should have formally started years ago.

"Using you," her father answered.

"We rescued her from an attack and have promised to keep her safe. She's offered to help us in return. That seems like a fair exchange to me," Rocky snapped. "You didn't even bother to tell her she was in danger." He had stepped in front of her again, as if he could protect them both from her father's accusations.

"Shh," Alex stopped him. She didn't know how fragile her father was; his moods could change hour to hour since the stroke. She wanted to get any information she could while he was still lucent. "Go call Markus and tell him we're fine, but need more time," she ordered. Rocky glared at her, but when she didn't back down, he pulled the cell from his pocket and began to dial.

"He's right, Dad. They're helping me with everything. But there's something else I need. Something that may be in that box," Alex said, indicating the half-extracted box in the wall behind her. She didn't mention Levi because she knew it would upset him. Once set off, he could take hours to calm down.

"It's empty," he said. She was going to ask how he knew for sure, when he continued. "I emptied it after they came looking for it." He stared blankly at the box.

"Who came for it?" She turned on Rocky who had just closed the phone. "You said they never got in the house."

"They didn't," he answered. "Sage, Markus, and I checked ourselves. The scent never went past the front steps. Maybe he sensed them."

Alex shook her head. Her father couldn't have been a Seer himself or he would have sought out the coven, or they would have sought out him.

"I sent them away," her father said. "I'd rather see it destroyed than in their hands."

"Sent them away?" Rocky questioned. He looked at Alex and raised an eyebrow. Apparently he doubted her father's ability to fight off two male vampires as much as Alex did. But she was more interested in the second part of his statement.

"You destroyed it?" she asked with despair. She rushed back to the box and wrenched it from the wall. It fell to the floor, its cover falling off as it crashed on the carpet. Alex stared in shock at the empty box.

"They couldn't know. None of them can know," her father said. Alex's hands shook as she knelt by the empty box. She looked up at him despondently.

"Know what, Dad?" She sprang to her feet and crossed the room. She clutched at her father's shirt. "What was in there? I need to know. I need it to save Levi!"

Rocky rushed to intervene. "Calm down, Alex," he said prying her fingers off the flannel fabric. "Back off; you don't want to hurt him." He pulled her back and pinned her arms by her side.

"You have all you need, Alexandra. The last of three will yield more power than them all."

Alex was frustrated with her father's apparent gibberish. "I don't have what I need. I don't know how to find him," she shouted, fighting against Rocky's hold.

"Quiet, Alex," Rocky urged. "You'll have the whole neighborhood here."

"You've always known. You can find him, but not save him. They take too much," her father said. For the first time since he started this double-speak, he looked up into Alex's eyes. If Rocky hadn't been holding her, she would have collapsed as a wave of pain, then fear, worry, and finally—oddly—pride washed over her. It drowned out her emotions much the same way Sage did when he touched her. For a moment she was lost in her father's feelings.

"Oh, my God," Alex said as she regained her sense of herself. Rocky steadied her.

"What is it?" he asked concerned.

"He just projected on me," she said, looking at him confused. "My father is a Seer, too."

Rocky actually chuckled. "Of course he is, Alex, or was before whatever happened to him weakened his essence. If he hadn't developed some Seer powers, you and your brothers would never have been full-blooded Seers."

Alex was still wondering about this when a loud crash caught them both off guard. They turned to see her father had fallen down the last two stairs and was trying to get up.

Rocky rushed to his side and helped him to his feet, then guided him to the couch, where he helped him sit.

His focused look was gone, replaced with the glassy stare and shaking hands Alex had come to expect since his stroke.

"El—Ellen?" he asked looking quizzically at Alex.

Rocky looked at Alex for an explanation. "It's my mother's name," she said.

"It's like he doesn't remember just talking to you," Rocky said. Alex nodded, admitting Rocky was probably right. "We should leave now, before your mother returns. I think I heard two women talking in the yard next door."

"Makes sense. She wouldn't leave him long," Alex said. She was numb, but conscious enough to reply with a practical response. She stood staring at her father as Rocky quickly replaced the box, covering it with the dartboard.

"Out the back," he said, pulling her arm as they both heard the front door close.

"Tim? Where are you? Susan made some of your favorite cookies for us," her mother called from the first floor.

Alex glanced back at her father one last time, hoping for a look of recognition as she blew him a kiss goodbye. She was met with a blank stare.

Chapter 15

Driving as fast as he could without drawing attention, Rocky sped back toward the center of town. He kept stealing glances at Alex, watching, hoping for a reaction. He had to remind her to put on her seatbelt twice before it seemed to register. It would have bothered him if she were sobbing or screaming in frustration and anger. But her tostal lack of emotion was beginning to frighten him. He remembered how sick she had become after she had expended her energy accidentally projecting on them two weeks earlier. He wondered if having her father project on her could have done similar damage. He tried to repress it, but he also couldn't help but feel worried about Markus's reaction when they returned home. Physically Alex was fine, unharmed as promised. But Rocky doubted any of them would look at Alex in the state she was in and think he had adequately performed his duty.

As he passed through the business section of town, he cursed every red light. After being stopped at the third intersection in a row, he contemplated running the next one. As the light turned green and he started to gun it, Alex shouted from the seat next to him.

"Stop! Rocky, pull over."

Oblivious to all that passed, Alex had been sitting numbly in the passenger's seat. She was trying to sort through the mess of questions, disappointments, and emotions that plagued her as she left her parents' home. She realized she was doing a poor job of it when she sensed Rocky's fear and anxiety. Jarring herself into the present, she had called out to him.

Rocky swerved into the next parking lot at a dangerous speed and slammed on the brakes so hard it was a good thing he had reminded her earlier to buckle up or she surely would have broken her nose on the dash.

"What's the matter? Are you okay?" He threw the Jeep into park and pulled out his cell.

Alex unbuckled and opened the car door. She put her head between her knees for a moment then slowly sat up. When she saw the building they had parked in front of, she managed a weak grin.

"I'm shitty to tell you the truth." Somehow her cursing seemed to lessen Rocky's anxiety. Alex's grin grew as she sensed this.

"I'm sorry, Alex, that you didn't find whatever it was your father had. Let's just go home, okay?"

It was obvious to Alex that her mood swings had riled him. Still, she shook her head. "I need a few minutes," she said, sliding out of the car. "Call Markus and tell him we're almost done at my parents' and we'll call when we're on our way."

"Alex, I can't lie to him," Rocky said.

"Then bend the truth," she said, "Please."

Rocky sighed. "You chicks ought to be required to have a license to uses faces like that."

Alex pushed her bottom lip out farther and looked up at him from under her eyelashes.

"Fine," he said, dialing. Alex smiled as he managed to maneuver his way around an all out lie. "Yeah, we're still here. Just need a little more time. We'll call you when we're on the road again," Rocky said into the phone at lightning speed.

"Is that an engine running? Are you in the car without her?" Alex heard Markus's question. Rocky looked to her for help, which she gave in the form of ripping the phone from his hands and snapping it shut.

"Oops, bad reception, I guess." She tucked the phone into her back pocket as she shut the door.

"Hey, where are you going?" he asked jumping out of the Jeep and following her as quickly as possible without drawing attention to his speed.

"You have cash with you?"

"A little, what do you—?" Rocky stopped and followed her gaze. "Ice cream? Markus is going to kill me because you want ice cream?"

Alex looked at the ice cream shop in front of them. It hadn't changed its overall appearance since she was a kid. Sure, it now had neon signs advertising twenty-four flavors of soft-serve, but essentially it was the same place she and her brothers rode their bikes to every time they found enough money to buy a cone. It was the same as the day Levi, wanting to show off his new driving skills, had driven her the two and a half miles to buy her an entire sundae, so she wouldn't tell their father he had hit two curbs and nearly killed the neighbor's Lab on the way there. Her life had changed drastically and dramatically in the years since, but somehow seeing that some things remained the same gave her an enormous amount of comfort.

"Ice cream heals all wounds, Rocky, especially chocolate ice cream," Alex said, heading toward the line.

"I think that's time, actually, something we don't have much of," he answered, but reluctantly he followed her.

Alex stepped up behind a family of five. She smiled as she watched the three girls twirl around their parents' legs, their emotions nothing but pure joy. After a moment she looked up at Rocky. When he saw the sudden change in her expression, he panicked.

"What is it?" he whispered.

"I can sense them," she answered. Rocky looked around frantically, his hand going to his back. "No," she said, reaching to stop him. "I just mean the humans. All of them."

"Oh," Rocky said relaxing his shoulders. "Well, why does that surprise you?"

Alex thought about it for a moment. She wasn't sure why it surprised her, but it was the first time she had been outside the house near other people since her powers had strengthened.

"I don't know," she answered, "I guess I thought I was sensing you all more clearly because I had gotten to know you better. And it made sense I could feel my father's emotions that way, too. But to be able to feel total strangers right away—it's just weird."

"I don't know much about it, Alex, but, from what I gather, your power isn't limited like Sage's is. That's why Seers are so valuable."

"Right." The word "hunted" popped into her head. That was how Darian had first described it. "I guess it just startled me to be able to feel them all so distinctly," she finished. She hoped to guide the conversation away from this topic.

Rocky's eyes lit up as she spoke. He looked excited for the first time since they found the box. "Close your eyes," he said reaching forward to cover them.

Alex backed away. "Why?"

"Just trust me. I want to try something." She crept forward and allowed him to hold his hand over her face. "How many people are behind us in line?" he asked.

"I don't know, Rocky. This must look ridiculous," she said, wriggling under his sweaty palm.

"That hat of Markus's looks ridiculous on you, but who's watching. Now how many?"

Alex attempted to find his feet so she could step on them. She didn't need to focus to answer his question. "Four," she said, pulling away. "And the hat looks cute." She adjusted the brim before looking behind her.

"Four," he confirmed. He grabbed her arm and pulled her out of line.

"Where are we going? You just lost our place in line."

He spun her around and dragged her ten feet to the left, his hands over her eyes again. "We're in front of the coffee shop. How many are inside?"

Alex frowned at him, but kept her eyes closed. Despite pretending to be annoyed by this test, Alex was actually as curious as Rocky about her ability. As she sorted out the emotions she sensed coming from the shop, she was beginning to see how her ability could be useful to the coven.

"Eight," she said after a brief pause. She opened her eyes to check.

"Seven," Rocky was saying, "close enough." But then a worker stepped out of the back with a stack of paper cups. Rocky looked at Alex and let out a low whistle. She tried to hide her look of self-satisfaction.

"Can we just go get ice cream now?" she asked, heading back to the end of the line again.

When they made it to the counter, Rocky stepped in front of her. "Two large hot fudge sundaes—with chocolate ice cream," he told the teenage girl with braces and a curly ponytail.

"Are you hungry?" Alex asked, shaking her head. "Because I'm never going to eat an entire large sundae."

Twenty minutes later, Rocky inspected her dish. The half scoop of melting chocolate ice cream hardly qualified it as unfinished.

"It was a crappy afternoon," she said, pushing the last bites toward him. He smiled, but remained silent as he reached across the picnic table with his spoon and shoveled the remainder of her ice cream into his mouth in one spoonful.

"Ow," he said covering his mouth. Alex raised an eyebrow. "Fang-freeze," he answered after swallowing.

Alex howled at what she assumed was a joke.

"It's not funny," he said. "That's why there's never ice cream in the house. Vampires don't eat it; our fangs are too sensitive to the cold."

"Hey, watch the v-word. We're in public," she hissed. Rocky shrugged, which Alex supposed was a valid response. Most people, including herself until a month ago, would never believe their ears even if they were listening in. "I don't buy the cold-sensitivity," she told him quietly. "I've seen those things up close. There is nothing delicate about them."

"Oh, they're tough as nails," he said with a grin, "they're just used to sinking into warmer . . . food."

Alex rolled her eyes and began wiping her hands and mouth with her napkins.

"Good idea," Rocky said. "Get rid of the evidence."

Alex laughed and pointed to a stain on his shirt. "How are you—" she stopped when the theme song to *Rocky* started to buzz from her back pocket.

"Oh, crap," Rocky said looking at his watch. "It's seven past."

"Seven minutes and he's freaking out?" Alex sighed, pulling the phone from her pocket. Rocky tried to grab it, but she backed out of reach and opened it.

"Pollyanna's Patience Apothecary. We specialize in patience potions and chill pills. Which can we interest you in?" Alex asked in a sugary sweet voice that was an odd cross between Mary Poppins and Paula Deen. Rocky's jaw dropped in horror, but Alex winked at him.

"Not amusing, Alex," Darian's voice, rather than Markus's, called out. His fury was evident even through the phone. Alex crinkled her nose and looked apologetically at Rocky whose face had lost all color. His enhanced hearing made it unnecessary for her to hand the phone to him. He heard Darian's order with chilling clarity. "Get home, now. You even pause at a stop sign too long, Rocky, and I'll file your fangs down to toothpicks."

There was a click, and Alex knew he had hung up. She looked back at Rocky who was still frozen. As she started to worry that he might have gone into shock, he jumped up, a little faster than was humanly feasible.

"Car, now," he said. Alex nodded and hurried behind him. She needed no reminder this time to put on her seat belt as he spun the tires pulling out.

"Let me handle this—" Alex and Rocky couldn't help but laugh at their simultaneous suggestion.

"Jinx, no returns?" Alex playfully suggested as Rocky parked the Jeep next to the barn.

"I'll be the one having my face rearranged if this goes poorly," Rocky said, turning off the engine.

"Something they're unlikely to do to me, no matter how pissed they are," she said. He paused before getting out. She knew he was considering the possibility she was right.

"Funny how you don't mind playing the female card when it benefits you," Rocky jeered.

"There's a reason we're considered the smarter sex." Alex pretended to toss the long hair she didn't have. Rocky shook his head. "Since it'll benefit you too, tonight, best just let me work my magic," Alex said.

She hopped out of the car and headed to the door. He beat her there and they exchanged a quick look before he opened it. They walked into the foyer. The entryway was empty. Alex was about to say that seemed like a good sign, until she looked up the stairs. Sage stood at the top leaning against the railing. The look he gave Rocky as he pointed for him to go into the office was a mixture of exasperation and sympathy. Alex hurried up the stairs ahead of Rocky, but Sage stopped her at the top.

"Not you. Not now."

"Rocky's report can wait. I have questions," she said, slipping under his arm before he could grab her. There were benefits to being small. She heard him curse as she entered the office. He and Rocky trailed behind.

"I'd like some answers first," Darian said. He attempted to address Rocky, but Alex held her position sandwiched between the two males. She realized if Darian wanted to sock Rocky, he could manage to do so without so much as skimming the top of her head with his fist, but she hoped the mere gesture of putting herself between them would suffice.

"Yes, we made an emergency pit stop on the way home because I wasn't feeling great. Yes, I hung up on Markus before Rocky could inform him of that. And sorry I got a little feisty on the phone with you, Regan, but I'd had a really crappy afternoon and thought I was having a little fun with Markus." She looked over to where Markus stood and gave him a grin and a one-shoulder shrug. He let one corner of his mouth curl up.

Alex turned back to Darian ready to continue, but he cut her off.

"Ice cream is an emergency?" Both hands in fists rested on his hips.

Alex looked back at Rocky quizzically. Turning to Sage, her eyes narrowed.

"I didn't have to tell him," Sage said. "I told you convincing him to get the GPS software would come back to bite one of us in the ass," he said to Rocky. Perhaps Sage had been correct when he told Alex Rocky underestimated the older vampires; at least one of them was savvy enough to work such technology.

"Chocolate elevates serotonin. Think of it as a resuscitative measure," Alex said to Darian. She bit her cheek to keep from smiling. "Now, can I get help making sense of what happened at my parents', or do you want Rocky to tell you about my new parlor trick first?"

The question had the desired effect. The anger in the room diffused as they all looked curiously between Alex and Rocky. Seeing the sudden opportunity, Rocky seized it. Alex smiled as he began.

"It's nothing you probably didn't expect. It was just surprising she can do it already," Rocky said. He explained how he had tested her ability and the success she had determining the exact number of people around her without seeing any of them. Sage agreed it was something to be expected, but was pleased she already had the control and power to sort out the emotions of strangers.

"Maybe we shouldn't be all that surprised by her," Rocky said, flashing Alex a grin. "Her father did say she'd be the most powerful Seer."

Rocky obviously felt this information was something Alex would be proud to share. But as the others looked at her in surprise, she turned to him throwing up her hands.

"What?" Darian asked first.

Rocky hesitated, finally seeming to understand Alex hadn't wanted to share this.

"He was only making sense half the time," Alex answered.

"But what did he say?" Darian pressed. He turned to Rocky when Alex avoided his eyes by watching her feet.

"He said, 'The last of three will yield more power than them all' or something like that," Rocky said. He dropped his gaze as Alex scowled at him.

"'The last of three' is from the prophecy, but where's the second part from?" Darian wondered aloud.

"Maybe he just made it up," Alex said. She had nowhere to look because from every direction one of them was staring at her.

"Or maybe Seers have their own histories and prophecies," Sage offered.

Alex spun around to face him. Of course. She should have thought of it. Levi said what was hidden at the house would give her answers. He didn't mean it would tell her where he was; if her father had known that, he would have rescued him or been killed trying. But if Seers had kept a record of their own histories, their own powers, it would likely explain more clearly than the vampires' histories how to control them. Her father, who wasn't a full-blooded Seer, may not have been able to utilize them fully, but a book like that would be invaluable to her. And it would be dangerous if it landed in the wrong hands.

"He destroyed them," Alex said, collapsing onto the couch, her chin dropping to her chest.

"He never actually said he destroyed them, Alex, just that he would in order to keep them safe." Alex knew Rocky was trying to comfort her, but she didn't think it was a matter of semantics. If the histories still existed, why would her father continue to hide them from her?

Markus moved over to the couch and sat next to her rubbing her back, while Darian paced the carpet.

"They weren't there. The spot Levi told me to look was empty," Alex said looking up.

"We'll keep searching for him, Alex. If he's out there, we'll do our best to rescue him," Markus said.

Alex looked back at Rocky, who was biting his lip. He seemed to be remembering her father's words just as she was.

"What would happen to a Seer if he were fed from?" Alex asked. She tried to stop twisting her hands. But Sage must have heard the worry in her head. His sympathy allowed her to prepare for Darian's answer, which he seemed to give reluctantly.

"A Seer has more essence than a normal human, Alex, but not as much as a vampire."

"Which means they can't be fed from regularly without being harmed, right?"

"Yes," Darian said. He didn't continue at first, but Alex pleaded with her eyes to be told the truth. "They'd be drained of their goodness, eventually. They could be dangerous, because they'd wield their power with no concern for others. They'd have no allegiances and no compassion."

Alex's thoughts turned to the cold expression Levi sometimes had in her dreams. She pushed the thought aside.

"But if the Others wanted to control him," she started, openly admitting she wasn't dealing in hypotheticals, "they'd be careful not to feed from him that frequently, right?"

Darian shrugged. "They could feed from him only when they needed to manipulate him. Right after a feeding, when his sense of right and wrong was weak, they could probably use him to do just about anything. If they demonstrated control and allowed him to recover fully each time, it might not have any lasting effect."

Alex looked up at him, hopeful.

"But, Alex," he said grimly, "the Vengatti aren't known for showing any form of control."

A slightly sleep-deprived Sage and Rocky had left after breakfast as usual for their patrol. Darian had decided last-minute to accompany Markus to the meeting with the two dozen other full-time warriors who worked for the coven and helped Markus lead and organize the other males who served only the mandated hours. About the same time, Sarah had left for a meeting with a group of females from the coven to begin planning that year's Creator's Day ball. She tried to amuse Alex before she left by ranting about the irony of planning for a winter ball during the hottest week of the year. Alex tried to smile, but secretly was glad when the door closed for the final time, leaving her alone in the house.

With no one left to hear her sobbing or raving, no one trying in vain to comfort her or distract her, she was able to deal with the day's disappointments in her own way, in her own time. With Sage far enough away for his emotions to be just a distant buzz, Alex could allow herself to feel only what her heart felt. Unfortunately what she felt was numb. The rollercoaster of first thinking she had found what she needed, then learning it had likely been destroyed, and finally realizing that the very reason she sought it to begin with might no longer be worth the risk had left her drained.

Instead of relishing the alone time, she found herself sitting on the stairs watching the front door, waiting for someone to come home. It was there Markus and Darian found her when they entered a little after midnight.

"What's wrong, Alex?" Markus asked the instant he saw her sitting alone halfway up the stairs. She had her arms wrapped tightly around her legs; her chin rested on her right knee.

"Nothing," she said sitting up. "Just glad you're back."

"I brought him home early, as promised," Darian said. Alex looked from the Regan to Markus while biting the right side of her lower lip.

"But it's Darian you want to talk with, isn't it?" Markus had correctly read her expression.

"I need to know more about what I learned today," she said to Darian. "I don't know if you'll have answers. I'm not even sure what my questions are. But if you have some time—"

"Of course, Alex," Darian said, walking up the stairs. He offered her a hand to help her up. "And Markus is welcome, too. He doesn't have to have read the histories. As your future mate and my friend, his input is important."

"Agreed." Alex reached her hand out to Markus who didn't hesitate a moment to come up the stairs and take it.

Inside Darian's office, Alex spoke for the better part of an hour describing the details of her conversation with her father and her thoughts about it. Markus and Darian mostly just listened, but also offered comfort, clarification, and their own speculations.

She told them how she was bothered by her father's strange behavior. It had been almost as if his stroke symptoms had disappeared when he spoke to her about her gift and her life as a Seer. When Darian spoke up, his words matched her thoughts,

thoughts she didn't want to admit to, let alone voice, because of what they implied about her own future.

"Alex, your father wasn't a full-blooded Seer, which meant any powers he had would have been weak or sporadic. And when the line is diluted, the person's essence would likely be weaker as well. He would have found it difficult to control the powers he did possess," Darian said. This explained her father's ability to project, but it was the next piece of information that shook her. "It's possible your father didn't have a stroke. If a Seer's essence is weak, his power could be dangerous to him. If your father pushed himself to use powers he couldn't really control to find your brother, it could have damaged his sense of self. As my father described it to you, a Seer needs that anchor to function."

"In other words, using his powers drove him mad," Alex said. She swallowed hard.

"He sounds broken, not crazy," Markus said. She processed these words for a minute. It was exactly how her father acted: broken. She shuddered, thinking about ending up that way. Would Markus be willing to care for her the way her mother tended to her father's every need? Would she want him to?

She changed the subject to another unpleasant but nagging question. "What's the likelihood my father married my mother not knowing she also was descended from a Seer?"

From what she gathered from the histories, if her father wasn't a full-blooded Seer, which he didn't seem to be, there was only one way for her and her brothers to be born full-blooded Seers: both their parents would have to have the gift in their blood. Ardellus had implied the coven had been without a Seer for centuries, which meant either their families kept them hidden or no full-blooded Seers had been born and lived to maturity.

Darian hesitated, but when Alex continued to wait for an answer, he gave it. "Unlikely," he sighed. "Probably impossible. But that doesn't mean they don't love each other," Darian said. "Sarah and I were an arranged mating, and I couldn't love anyone more."

Alex tilted her head and examined Darian, who sat at the other end of the couch. She didn't need her sense to feel his sincerity. She didn't know if her parents loved each other as deeply as Darian and Sarah loved one another. And she'd never know, because she'd never ask her mother in case she was unaware she was chosen for anything other than herself. But it was nice to think it was possible their marriage was based on what a marriage should be.

"Thank you," Alex said to him.

"Anything else?" Darian asked with a crooked grin. "I've never seen you run out of questions."

Alex pretended to ignore the last comment. She had exhausted just about all her questions and addressed her concerns, even the two she hadn't been sure she wanted to talk about at first: Levi's ability to be saved and her father's belief she would have more power than the others. In both cases she knew Darian and Markus had let her convince herself of the best-case scenario. She had concluded Levi had to be capable of recovery or he wouldn't have bothered to seek out her help. Her father's comment she passed off as simply meaning she would be more powerful than her brothers, not all Seers, as Rocky had erroneously implied. And even then, she attributed any greater power she might develop to the fact she would be protected during her maturity and would receive better training. Dimly aware she could have been deluding herself on both accounts, she still felt in better control of her emotions after talking with the males.

"I think I'm good," she assured him.

Just then, Sarah entered the office carrying with one hand a tray stacked with sandwiches and glasses and holding in the other a full pitcher of tea. Alex, still not used to seeing a female with such grace and physical strength, marveled at the ease with which she maneuvered the loaded tray onto the coffee table in front of them.

"I hope everyone's good and in a good mood," she said, eying her mate warily. "Because we're having a visitor tomorrow." She smiled and mussed Darian's hair as he groaned at the news.

"You ran into my father at the club?" he asked in a tone usually reserved for the discussion of necessary but painful dental work.

"He doesn't stay home too many nights, I think," Sarah answered, handing the first plate to him.

Darian examined the sandwich as if accepting it would somehow mean he was pleased with her news, but eventually he gave in and started eating.

"He wants to see you, mostly," Sarah said, handing Alex the next plate, for which Alex thanked her.

"Why?" Alex hadn't been sure she made the best first impression on the Elder Regan and was equally unsure whether his opinion of her should concern her or not.

"He's intensely curious about having a Seer, and a female one at that. Your maturity is going to be the highlight of the decade for him," Darian said, rolling his eyes.

Alex didn't like the idea of being a curiosity and liked even less the feeling that Ardellus viewed her as a fine piece to add to a collection. "Gee, I hope I don't disappoint him and croak or anything," she muttered.

Markus inhaled a large bite of ham and cheese and needed Sarah to hit him hard on the back. Alex was pretty sure, though, that the pain in his eyes was more from her words than Sarah's strike.

"Sorry," she said.

Markus tried to speak, but was still coughing. Sarah handed him a glass of tea, then glared at Darian.

"It's okay, Alex, Darian should have been a little more sensitive about the way he worded that."

"It's not how I feel—" he started, but stopped under Sarah's continued stare. "Right, sorry."

Alex shrugged. She didn't see the sense in pretending it was something it wasn't.

"Anyway, he'll be staying the night. I hope you don't mind giving up your room again, Markus," Sarah said with a devilish grin.

Markus may have blushed, but his face was still red from coughing, so it was hard to tell.

"No problem," he said when he finally was able to speak again. He winked at Alex. Darian apparently caught this and felt the need to seize the opportunity.

"Just remember he's right next door, and his hearing is as good as ever—even with the shower running."

Alex was sure from the heat in her cheeks that her coloration matched Markus's.

Sarah shook her head and sighed. "I may have mated the Regan, Alex, but you're getting the classier of these two friends, trust me."

The two couples shared as many laughs as sandwiches, of which the males ate plenty. Alex realized with a bit of humor and satisfaction that the meal she shared with this trio of three-hundred-year-old vampires was as close to a double date as she had ever come. Two months ago no one could have convinced her that vampire mating rather than online dating would be how she found 'the one.' Life took some odd twists sometimes.

Chapter 16

"I hate Mondays," Rocky said, jabbing his spoon into a bowl of plain flakes. It was the only cereal left after Alex and Sage had each eaten two bowls of the sugary junk Rocky normally ate, finishing off the box before he had gotten up.

Thinking his lack of junk food was the cause of his morose mood, Alex teased him. "You snooze, you lose, Rock Star. A few bran flakes won't kill you."

Instead of flashing her his usual fangy grin, Rocky actually growled. Alex was surprised, but not highly offended. Markus, however, who was about to sit down across from him with his own breakfast, slammed down his plate and growled back.

"Whoa," Alex said. "Kill the engines, boys. There's no sense fighting over Fruit Loops."

"That's not why he hates Mondays, or, to be specific, this Monday," Sage spoke up.

Rocky turned around and glared at him. "Tomorrow's my night off," he said, turning back to Alex. He offered the statement as if it explained everything. Alex didn't see how it explained anything.

"So, shouldn't you be pleased it's Monday?"

Rocky pursed his lips, obviously frustrated by her lack of understanding. Alex was becoming equally annoyed with his lack of explanation and his attitude.

"What Rocky is trying to say, but won't, because he's finally starting to realize I can hear him all over the house, is that he's not thrilled my father is coming and will likely still be here tomorrow night," Darian said, entering the room. He was wearing an ironed pair of khakis and a button-down instead of his usual cargo pants and Rugby shirt. "Right?" he said, addressing Rocky. The younger vampire didn't look up. He returned to eating his cereal instead of answering.

"Getting smarter by the day, kid," Sage said, swiping at him with his baseball cap.

"If he exercised that much control when the Elder was around, Ardellus might stop making snide comments," Markus muttered.

"Hey," Alex said, whacking her partner in the shoulder.

Rocky's temper had been pushed to the limit. He got up from the table and dumped his bowl into the sink. "No, Alex, he's right," he said. "I seem to have problems with people who feel the need to pretend to be proper all the time." Alex watched as Rocky sneered at Markus, and she felt perhaps he was no longer solely referring to Ardellus. "I guess they remind me too much of my father."

Markus stood as Rocky flashed across the foyer and stormed down the stairs. It was obvious Markus had taken the comment as the rather nasty insult it was intended to be. Darian put a hand on his shoulder to keep him from pursuing.

"I'll handle it. It's really me he's ticked at," Darian said.

"It doesn't give him the excuse—" Markus began.

Alex cut him off before he could convince the Regan of this. "Why you?" she asked Darian. She shot Markus an annoyed sideways glance.

Darian hesitated, but decided to answer her. "Rocky created a computer program to help . . . with some of our patrol work. It's turning out to be useful, and I wanted to show my father to get some advice about how best to utilize the info. Last night I asked Rocky's permission for me and Markus to present it my father—without him."

"Well, I'd be pissed at you, too," Alex said. "If he created it—"

"I understand it's unfair not to give Rocky credit up front," Darian said, "but I need my father's advice to be untainted by his . . . attitude towards Rocky. He may listen more objectively if Rocky's not in the room."

Markus nodded in agreement, which aggravated Alex, but she was glad to sense Sage shared her indignation.

"Your father has a problem with Rocky, Darian," she said, "but you have a bigger problem setting him straight."

"Alex." Markus's tone of voice made it a chastisement at which Alex narrowed her eyes. She turned back to see Darian running his hands through his hair. Between her, Sage, and Rocky, it was a marvel he wasn't balding from this habit.

"I'm not trying to be insolent, Darian. I'm telling you as a friend and as Rocky's friend." She looked at Sage, wondering whether he was willing to throw in his two cents as well. He sighed and shook his head at her thought, but spoke up anyway.

"She's right, D. One of the reasons Rocky respects you so much is because you stuck up for him against half the coven, yet. . . ." Sage didn't finish, but the message was clear.

Darian didn't respond as he made his way across the kitchen, but when his back was to them, pouring what was likely his third cup of coffee since waking up, he answered. "I'm working on him." His voice was tight but controlled. "If the program works and I can give Rocky credit, that'll help. But it takes time. As you've been told before, Rocky understands."

Alex wanted to point out that the outburst of a few minutes prior put into question how well Rocky understood. But Darian downed the hot liquid in a single swig and left the kitchen. He grabbed his keys on the way out of the house and slammed the front door.

"I've got to get going too," Markus said. He started across the kitchen without saying goodbye to Alex.

"Hey," she said hurrying after him. He stopped at the front door. "Are you mad at me?"

"Actually, I thought the looks you were giving me in there meant you were mad," he said.

"I disagreed with you, but that doesn't mean we need to stop talking or that you need to leave without saying goodbye," Alex said.

Markus looked at her for a minute. She sensed his uncertainty.

"Whatever it is, just say it." She noticed the frown he tried to erase. It was the same look everyone gave Sage when he made it obvious he was listening to one of them.

"I like your feistiness. It was one of the first qualities that made me fall in love with you," he began.

"But?" Alex asked. She knew there was a second half to this statement.

"But I'm still learning to handle it when it's aimed at me," he said, not meeting her eyes. He looked up to explain. "I've been single and in a position of leadership for a long time. The only ones I've butted heads with in centuries are Sage and Darian—and somehow it doesn't seem right to argue with you in the same way."

Alex laughed. "Yeah, I'd probably take issue with being tackled or given a noogie."

"Noogie?" he asked confused. Alex rolled her eyes.

"Really, you need to mingle more with the humans you protect, or at least watch some television," she said. "But to get back on topic, Markus, you're allowed a learning curve. God knows I need one concerning all things vampire, including how to date one."

A husky chuckle escaped Markus, and he kissed the top of her head. "You seem to have expertise in certain areas," he whispered.

"I don't think those are technically specific to vampires, though. And until Ardellus leaves, we need to put them on hold."

"True, but as Darian just left to get him, no one can object to my 'saying goodbye'." The rest of the house may have disagreed had they been around to witness the obscenely passionate kiss that followed.

Other than taming Alex and Markus's nightly routine, Ardellus's visit had been painless. Alex managed to answer his questions about her sleeping and eating habits politely. He seemed to expect the increased number of naps and growing appetite to which she admitted. Dinner Monday night had been pleasant. Darian joked easily with his father, Markus, and Sage as they reminisced about his antics as a young vampire. Sarah told Alex her own versions of these stories, often with very different endings. And only twice during the twenty-four hours did Sage have to step on her toes to keep her from accidentally spilling someone's emotions. Both times it was Ardellus's, as her sense of him was new and therefore most interesting to her.

It was only Rocky's mood that had not improved. In fact, it seemed worse on Tuesday after breakfast when he returned from the basement with his cereal bowl. Alex felt sympathetic. Ardellus's presence at the table meant he wasn't even welcome to eat with any of them for breakfast or lunch, the two casual meals when Darian often wasn't around and the rule was usually bent. She convinced him to work out with her after Sage and Markus left for work, but even then he was distracted and moody. Alex wasn't too upset when he didn't return after lunch to look for her. They often spent late nights watching marathons of bad reality TV shows on cable. Not because they liked them, they convinced themselves, but because "somebody has to make fun of those losers," as Rocky explained it.

With those plans cancelled, Sarah running out to pick up Darian's suit jacket from the cleaners for their usual date night, and Darian busy discussing business with Ardellus, Alex curled up with her book. As usual, lately, this led to her falling asleep.

Markus woke her a few hours later when he and Sage had returned from work a little early due to Ardellus's departure.

"You should go say goodbye to the Elder Regan before Darian and Sarah leave to take him home," he said, sitting next to her as she sat up and stretched. "Then I need your help in the kitchen. Sage has threatened to make chili again, and my taste buds haven't grown back from the last five-alarm catastrophe."

"On it," Alex said, patting his arm and heading out into the entranceway.

Ardellus was already on his way down the stairs, Sarah ahead of him in a royal blue cocktail dress that looked stunning on her and Darian behind, carrying his father's bag with one hand and loosening the tie Sarah had obviously chosen with the other. Sage had come out of the kitchen to respectfully see them off. Even Rocky made a polite appearance, though he hung close to the basement door. With their goodbyes said, Darian grabbed the keys to Sarah's sedan and headed out.

"You joining us for Sage's spectacular cuisine?" Alex asked Rocky.

"Ah, I'll pass," he said. But he remained in the foyer as Alex, Markus, and Sage started into the kitchen.

"That's right, he fasts on Tuesdays," Alex teased. "Maybe that should say something about our cooking when Sarah's not around?"

"I think it has more to do with the junk food you two eat while watching those stupid humans on television," Markus razzed her.

"Watch the stupid human jokes—we're not all as dumb as the pregnant housewives of Survivor Island," Alex said. She smiled at Rocky, the only one who understood the mixed reference, before following Sage to the pot on the stove. "And it was a junk-food-free afternoon, so I'd actually like to be able to swallow that. Can you lay off the jalapeños?"

Markus opened three beers as Sage and Alex fought for control over the pot. Rocky apparently returned to his room. So when the three of them heard voices in the foyer, they were somewhat startled.

"You don't need to come in, Father, I'm just getting the other keys," Darian was heard saying, but as Sage, Alex, and Markus turned around they saw both Darian and Ardellus enter. Darian put Sarah's keys back in the dish and fished through the other sets for the keys to his pickup.

"Crap," he muttered. His father raised an eyebrow either at his cursing or the fact he had come up empty handed. "I must have left them upstairs," he said. "I'll have Rocky go grab them."

Darian called down the stairs to Rocky, louder than was probably necessary considering how well they all heard. Alex realized what Darian wanted, wiped her hands on a dishtowel, and headed for the door. Sage reached out a hand to stop her for some reason, but she had already slipped past.

"He probably has the TV or radio on, Darian. I can go look if—" Before she finished, Rocky was in the doorway. He had his hands in his pockets apparently trying to look casual, despite the fact they all knew he had flashed up the stairs after Darian's call.

"Sarah's car is low on gas, so we're taking the truck," Darian explained. Rocky nodded, but Alex strangely sensed a strong wave of anxiety from him. "I think I must have left the keys in my office. Go grab them for me."

"Sure, Regan," Rocky agreed, releasing his breath. Alex had to bite her tongue not to remind Darian it was Rocky's night off. It bothered her that due to his father's presence he would ask Rocky to look, when on any other night she was sure he would have retrieved them himself.

Sage, who had come out to the doorway of the kitchen, caught her eye and shook his head.

"Son," Ardellus spoke, as Rocky was halfway up the stairs. It was clear he was addressing the younger vampire, rather than Darian. Rocky stopped and turned around anxiously. Both he and Darian seemed to hold their breath waiting for Ardellus's comment.

"I should have mentioned it earlier when we were leaving, but I wanted to let you know I was impressed with the program Darian showed me." Ardellus looked Rocky in the eye for the first time Alex had ever witnessed.

Darian sighed and gave his father a small smile. Rocky still seemed unsure and stood on the stairs in silence.

"Rocky, that was a compliment," Alex whispered teasingly to break the tension, "just say thank you and lose the guilt."

"Guilt?" Ardellus questioned, turning to Alex, interested as always in her sense. But after a brief moment he turned to Darian. Finally his eyes rested on Rocky, whose left hand was still hidden in the pocket of his baggy jeans.

Sage had been too far away to kick her, but his intense cursing, Darian's sharp intake of breath, and Rocky's look of horror told her she had made a serious slip of the tongue, before she could even register the suddenly overwhelming wave of mixed emotions shooting at her from different points in the room.

Too late, Alex surmised the possible reason for Rocky's hand position—to muffle the sound of the metal keys clinking as he made his way up the stairs.

"What's in your pocket, boy?" Ardellus asked, motioning for Rocky to return to the foyer. Rocky looked helplessly to Darian, but the Regan had no choice but to demand he answer.

When Rocky reached the last step he pulled out the key ring and handed it to Darian.

"Were you planning to leave—in the Regan's vehicle—against the terms of your sentence?" Ardellus demanded. The Elder stepped forward.

"I can handle this, Father," Darian said, rage evident in his voice. Though as Alex sensed it, she wondered if it was aimed at Rocky, Ardellus, or her.

"Yes," Rocky answered honestly. His voice didn't tremble, but Alex ached as she felt his fear. "To feed," he explained.

Rocky hadn't seen him shaking his head, again in vain, but Alex realized what warning Sage had been trying to give to his protégé. Feeding was done on a regular basis.

"For how long?" Ardellus asked, making the same connection Sage had.

"Father," Darian snapped.

"He's been doing this under your nose. You have the right to know how often."

Darian looked at Rocky. They were both in a corner. Rocky took a deep breath and managed to answer so Darian wouldn't have to ask.

"Almost every Tuesday since I was released." It was Rocky's usual night off and the night Sarah and Darian typically went out together.

Ardellus seemed outraged, but Darian just nodded. Sarah slipped through the door. Whether she had heard everything or not was hard to tell, but as she scanned the faces of the five vampires and one human who stood in the foyer, she seemed to gather that

Darian needed her calming effect. She crossed to where he stood and gently took the keys from her mate's hand. She squeezed it lightly before turning to her father-in-law.

"I'll drive you home, Ardellus. Darian can deal with this," she said quietly, but firmly. Ardellus didn't respond, but followed her out the front door. For a moment after the door closed all that could be heard was the uneven breathing that seemed to come from each of them.

Finally Darian spoke. "Markus, escort him downstairs, please." He reached into his pocket and pulled out a key ring that never went into the dish by the door. "Then meet me upstairs."

"Yes, Regan." Markus took the keys from Darian, but as he reached out to grab Rocky's arm, Rocky stepped back.

"I'll go on my own," he said, his voice unsteady. He paused briefly to look at Darian, but then walked to the door without saying a word.

Darian's heavy footsteps on the stairs to his office snapped Alex out of her trance.

"Wait, Darian, I'm so sorry. I didn't—"

"The damage is done, Alex. Leave us alone to deal with it."

Alex watched in silence as he stormed up the remaining stairs and disappeared into the office. Left alone with Sage, she turned to him, but he hardly gave her a glance as he spun around to follow Darian. Not wanting to face the same look of anger and disappointment from the one from whom it would hurt the most, Alex stumbled out the door onto the porch. She only made it as far as the front steps before collapsing. She sat on the top step, her head in her hands and began to cry. As the minutes passed her sobbing increased in intensity. Though she didn't have the vampire senses required to hear the discussion or decision about Rocky's punishment, she was in tune with Rocky enough after hurting him to feel his anger, fear, and pain. It was sufficient to know Darian ruled as a Regan must.

She jerked when the front door slammed behind her, but didn't bother looking up. She knew from her sense who it was.

"I'm going to offer you this advice for the last time, Alex," Sage said, his volume rising with each word. "If you want to keep a single friend in this world after your sense matures, you need to learn to shut up."

"I know. I'm sorry." Alex tried to cease her sobbing as she looked up at him.

"Tell it to Rocky when he's half-starved in a couple weeks," Sage shot back at her.

"Oh, God. Can I see him? To apologize?" Alex pleaded.

"I don't think he really wants to talk to you right now, Alex. In fact, I don't think anyone in the house really wants to see or speak to you for awhile."

Alex nodded and tried to wipe her cheeks on her already soaked arms. "I could go to my apartment for a few days," she offered.

"So you can hide out and avoid having to feel any of this? That's not how it works, sweetheart."

"That's not why I said it, and you know it." His righteousness was beginning to get to her. "You knew what he'd been doing every Tuesday night. And I'm pretty sure Darian did, too."

"Yeah, I'd just about figured it out. And Darian had a hunch. For everyone's sake, there are things that happen in this house and in this coven that Darian, as Regan, needs to be able to remain ignorant of. If you and I can't keep our mouths shut, those things are exposed, and he has no choice but to act upon his knowledge." Sage had come down the steps so he could face her as he drove home his point. "Your gift is a power, Alex, and with power comes responsibility. If you lack control, people will get hurt. And more likely than not, it'll be the people you care most about. Do you get that now?"

"I get it," she said, standing up and shoving his chest, "but I never asked for this gift. I never wanted this power. So I'm sorry if I suck at self-control, but it would be nice if you, of all people, could try to understand and make a few allowances for me."

Sage shook his head. When he responded it was quietly and without anger or sarcasm.

"It's time for you to grow up, Alex. The world doesn't make allowances for you just because you've been dealt a lot you're not happy with. Either learn to control your gift and your mouth, or learn to deal with the consequences."

Sage walked past her up the steps and slammed the door behind him.

Alex stumbled onto the walkway and took off across the yard at a full sprint. Her tears were blurring her vision and her runny nose impeded her breathing, but she didn't stop. She ran all-out as if she hoped she could run fast enough to rewind the events of the last hour. Instead, she sped on closer to sunrise. Somewhere in the middle of her fourth lap, in the field behind the house, she tripped over an uneven patch of ground and hit the path she and Markus had worn into the field over the last few weeks. She lay where she landed, the dry dirt sticking to her tear-streaked face and sweaty arms.

As the sky to the east began to lighten gradually, she wished she were a vampire. She wished the sun would come up and burn away a layer of herself, the layer she had been hiding behind since she learned what she was. Because Sage was right. Whether she wanted this power or not was irrelevant. She had it. She could find a way to control it and put it to good use, or she could allow it to torment her. She had been down that road before with her grief over her brothers' deaths. She had chosen the wrong path then, and it had taken months to reverse course. Despite Sage's accusation of immaturity, she was older now, and hopefully a smidge wiser.

With the sun rising, she realized with just enough humor left to appreciate the metaphor, that there was nobody able to pick her up off the dirt but herself. So she pushed herself to her feet and attempted to clean off her face, at least, by wiping it on her shirt. And she headed back across the yard to the house with dry eyes.

Inside the foyer, Alex shut the door and set the alarm. She hadn't expected anyone to be waiting for her. Sage made it clear everyone was upset with her. So she headed up the stairs expecting to spend the first of many nights alone.

But at the top she was met by Markus. She noticed his right hand was red, like he had scalded it in hot water.

"I was worried you hurt yourself," he said, rushing to her.

Alex realized he must have tried to look for her out the windows of the house, burning his hand in the sunlight that came in as he pushed aside the curtains. Her first instinct was to feel guilty. She should have known that no matter how upset he was, Markus would also have been worried about her being out after sunrise when there was no one left who could protect her. But part of accepting responsibility for what she could control meant learning also to accept that there were things she couldn't.

"I'm fine, but you're not," she said. "Can I get you ice?"

Markus shook his head. With his other hand he reached out to her face, rubbing his thumb over the muddy streaks that remained. His silence made Alex uncomfortable. His emotions made her curious.

"You're not mad."

"No."

"Why?"

Markus put his hand down and sighed. "You won't like my reasons, and I don't want to argue with you. There's been enough of that tonight."

Alex hardly considered her conversation with Sage an argument. He had lambasted her, which she mostly deserved and therefore had little with which to ague. And she knew Rocky wouldn't have argued with whatever Darian's decision was. He could be impulsive, but he took the blame for his own actions. It left her wondering and worrying about what other arguments had arisen. But, like Markus, Alex didn't want to argue or get upset about conversations that were over and done with.

"No arguments, then. But I'd like to understand," she said, "if you want me to."

"Then I'll just tell you one reason, one you might understand, one you might even like," Markus said, taking her hand. "I love you, flaws and all."

"That gives you a lot to love some days." She mustered a weak smile. She couldn't find the words to tell him the comfort this knowledge provided. So they walked back to her room in silence. And when he followed her into the bathroom and took the washcloth from her so he could wipe the dirt from her face, tears once again left trails on her cheeks. Only these tears, she welcomed.

Wanting to prove she could face him and by doing so face her culpability in the previous night's events, Alex met Sage in the kitchen at their usual time. He didn't look up from his coffee when she entered. He didn't respond when she greeted him.

"Now who's being immature," she mumbled, plopping heavily into a chair opposite him.

He did react to this. Leaving the still steaming cup behind, he stormed out of the kitchen, his black boots vibrating the floor and causing ripples in his coffee. Ripples that on a miniature scale mirrored the wave of emotion he sent at Alex. Having the control and focus that came with centuries of practice, Sage had very precisely honed in on one feeling Alex hoped she would never have to feel being aimed at her again: disgust.

When she caught her breath, she stood up from the table. In the glass-front cabinet to the right of the sink she spotted what she wanted—on the top shelf, of course. She went back to the table and dragged a chair across the floor. As she was hopping down with the oversized soup bowl, Darian entered the room. He took one look at what she held in her hand and shook his head.

"Sarah does that."

"I'd like to this morning," Alex answered.

Darian looked as if he were about to argue, but stopped. "Fine," he said, his voice cool. "For the next twenty-six days it can be your responsibility." Then he, too, left the kitchen.

Alex finished putting everything on the tray and carefully headed down the stairs to the basement. Halfway down the hall leading to the passageway to the barn, she froze. Twenty-six days. It was an odd number to choose. Not the number of nights Rocky broke the boundaries set by his sentence, which would have been over fifty. Not a set number of weeks, which would have translated to twenty-one or twenty-eight days. But twenty-six. It seemed random. But Darian's decisions were never random.

It was the exact number of days until Alex's twenty-sixth birthday.

This may have been Rocky's punishment, but Darian's message to her was as clear as Sage's had been when he spelled it out last night. Only Darian's means of delivery was even more difficult to swallow.

Alex readjusted her grip on the tray and tried to brace herself for what she thought would be the most difficult part of this lesson. When she entered the passageway she realized, having not been down it before, she wasn't even sure where the room was. But as soon as she found the light switch and flipped it with her elbow, she discovered there was only one door other than those at each end. And the heavy metal structure with the eight-by-five-inch sliding opening in its center left no doubt this was the room Rocky was being held in.

Guessing he could hear her already and feeling awkward about approaching, Alex called out. "Rocky, it's Alex. I'm bringing you breakfast."

She could have sworn she heard a chuckle. Putting down the tray when she made it to the door, she attempted to slide open the port in the center through which she assumed she was supposed to pass him his food. It was stuck. She tugged on the handle with greater force and finally it slid. She had been pushing so hard, she nearly fell over when it wrenched free. This time she was sure Rocky had laughed at her. She should have known Rocky would be the easiest of them to face. At least he was trying to be. Alex couldn't block out his pain, embarrassment, or fear, and she figured that even if it would be good for her training, it wouldn't have been fair for her to try. But she could try to ease some of it.

"Are you laughing at me?" she said looking in at him. He sat in the middle of the room in just his jeans. Balled up on the floor behind him was what she assumed was his shirt. With a jolt of deeper guilt and sympathy, she realized he had likely been using it as a pillow. The room was bare concrete as far as she could see into the dark corners.

"I can't help it if you're funny," Rocky said. She thought he saw her look of compassion as he tried to turn the conversation back to humor. "First you identify yourself, like there's another human chick in the house I might confuse you with. Then you nearly fall into my Fruit Loops just opening the hatch. And speaking of Fruit Loops, you going to give me that tray or is part of my punishment to watch you eat?"

Alex tried to smile as she slid the tray to him. He met her at the door to take it, but he avoided meeting her eyes. She wondered if it was because his seemed as bloodshot and puffy as her own, or if he wasn't ready to face her and her attempt to apologize. She waited to speak until he was done eating, a shorter time than she would have expected considering the oversized bowl of cereal, two clementines, and bagel that had been on the tray. When he drained the last of the OJ from his glass, she figured she couldn't procrastinate any further.

"Rocky—"

"Alex, please don't apologize."

She was upset, but understood. He didn't want to hurt her by not accepting it, but wasn't ready to forgive her, either.

"Okay. I'll wait," she said.

"No," Rocky said standing back up and coming to the door. "There'll never be a good time, Alex, because you're not to blame. And neither is Sage or Darian."

Alex furrowed one brow, wondering how he knew this had been on her mind the night before.

"I'm a year and a half older; my hearing is better, even from in here. Although I wouldn't doubt half of eastern Mass heard the two of you last night. But that's not the point. Point is, I chose not to ask any of them for help. Instead I took advantage of their trust knowingly and continuously." Rocky paused, and Alex sensed his deep remorse and shame. "Believe me, I feel I deserve this more than I ever deserved to be locked up last time." He turned away from her as he finished, and Alex's arm was too short to reach out to him.

"I'm still sorry my big mouth got you caught, though," Alex said. "You may have stopped or at least come clean on your own terms."

"Or I may have been caught by someone else in the coven, which would have been disastrous for me and Darian. I'm not stupid enough to criticize someone else for their lack of self-control, Alex."

"Good thing the others are, then," she said, "because it is something I need to work on."

"I think they're more concerned than mad," Rocky said.

Alex tilted her head. "Is that why they chose to release you on my birthday rather than yours?"

"Well, mine's in February, so I'd be dead by then," Rocky joked. Alex shuddered, remembering that even three and a half weeks would be an excruciatingly long time for him to go without feeding, particularly when, as best she could remember, it had been two weeks already since Darian and Sarah had gone out together.

"Sorry," Rocky continued, watching her face. "I'm sure you're right. It wasn't a coincidence, but I'd bet it was done as much to scare you, as to punish either of us." Rocky paused again. He bit his lip. "Alex, this is going to sound bizarre coming from the vamp behind bars, but I'm going to say it anyways, because having lived through it for the last year and half, I'm probably the best one to explain."

"I welcome your advice, Rocky, no matter where you're standing while you're giving it."

Rocky nodded. "In your old life being impulsive or losing control might lose you a job or even a friend. Both of which would suck, but people recover from those. But in our world, especially in the role you say you want to take on, our enemies will take advantage of one slipped piece of info, one rash decision, and people could get hurt, even killed. Markus and Darian and Sage understand that because they were all trained as soldiers in a time when all-out battles were far from rare and casualties weren't covered up. In my lifetime—yours too, though you were unaware of all this until recently—everything is small-scale and covert. Otherwise, we risk exposure. But the victims are just as real. And though they may suck at articulating it, Sage and Darian are just trying to keep you, and me, too, probably, from becoming a victim—or worse, in my opinion, from being the cause of another victim."

It took a minute for Alex to respond. Finally she looked up at him. "It's hard some days just to remember there is a world beyond this house, never mind that it's dangerous now."

"It won't be long before you won't need reminding of that. If they let you on patrols, it's obvious."

"I hope your timetable is right," Alex said. "I'd rather just have it happen than wait, not knowing."

Rocky flashed her his cock-eyed grin. "Well, your essence has gone from fast-food hamburger to steakhouse tenderloin, so you got to be close," he teased.

Alex wondered, though, if this was also a hint. "You'll tell me when I hit Kobe filet and get too tempting to have around, right?"

"You're human; it'll be a couple weeks, at least, before I get that desperate. In the meantime, though, I think someone else may kick you out."

Alex would have teased him about the desperate comment, but Rocky had turned to retrieve the tray. As he slid it through, they both heard the door open at the end of the hall. Alex put the tray on the floor and said a hurried goodbye to Rocky before she once again attempted to fight the hatch closed. Rocky didn't laugh this time when Darian's large hand brushed hers aside and slammed it shut.

"Twenty minutes for breakfast and lunch. And dinner he eats alone. You eat upstairs." Darian looked down at Alex, who realized how much she hated being short some days.

"Fine. That's fair," she said, knowing fair wasn't at all his concern.

He pounded the door twice. Alex gathered this was the only greeting Rocky was getting this morning.

"Yes, Regan," came the reply.

Darian nodded, though Rocky couldn't see it, and headed back toward the main hallway. Halfway to the end, he turned around and came back to take the tray Alex had picked up off the floor. He carried it back up stairs for her without another word.

Chapter 17

Chopping vegetables on the wooden cutting board in the kitchen, Alex could almost forget the strain of the last two days. Sarah teased her about the tears streaming down her face from the pungent odor of the onions. Using the dishtowel to wipe her cheeks, she laughed easily, glad as always to have Sarah's company.

"We're just in time," Sarah said, dumping the last of the ingredients into the pan and giving them a quick stir.

Alex listened for the car Sarah must have been able to hear, but it was another thirty seconds before she heard the crunching of pebbles under the tires. With the windows open for once, enticing the cool air of the rare rainy night into the house, the women could hear Markus and Sage's voices as soon as they opened the car doors. Alex couldn't make out the words, but from the volume and intensity of the conversation, she guessed they were arguing again.

"It'll be a miracle if those two don't kill each other before Rocky's released," Alex said. She hid her twinge of guilt with a forced smile. For some reason, Sage and Markus had gone out on patrol together the last two nights, despite their very different approaches to work. She turned to Sarah, who hadn't commented. Her friend seemed to be intently listening. Sarah wiped her hands on the towel she was holding, dropped it on the counter, and rushed to the door.

"Sarah, what's the matter?" But as Alex said this, she was tuning in to Sage's emotions, the easiest for her to separate from her own growing anxiety. Before she could make sense of the layers of Sage's mood, the front door opened and the two males entered.

"It'll be healed enough. We go tomorrow," Markus was telling Sage.

"We'll see," Sage answered. "Darian won't want to go if it's not."

"As Regan, Darian shouldn't be going at all. It's my call." Markus would have continued the conversation, but Sarah flashed to his left side.

"Let me see it. Is it deep?" Alex hardly had time to register her words. As Markus removed the black wad from his upper arm, Alex saw what the dark fabric hid: the color of blood. She gasped as the exposed wound gushed.

"I'm fine," Markus said seeing her expression.

Alex looked to Sarah for reassurance. "It's deep, but he'll heal quickly," she said. "Sage was right, though, Markus. You should have gone with the twins to Briant. I'm likely to leave you with a scar." Sarah must have been referring to the part of the conversation Alex hadn't heard. If Markus hadn't been hurt, she would have wondered and worried about who else was wounded.

"You're being modest. You stitch better than anyone. Besides, we need to see Darian. Can you do it in the office?" he asked, pressing what Alex realized was a torn off sleeve of his sweatshirt back over the wound.

"That rug has seen enough abuse. Sit in the kitchen. I'll go get him and my supplies." Sarah sped up the stairs. Sage called after her for Darian to bring the laptop.

Alex tried to take a deep breath. She reassured herself; if Sarah was able to worry about blood on the rug, Markus wasn't seriously injured. Despite that, she felt better when he moved to her side.

"I'm okay, really. It happens. Can you please speak, so I know you're alright?"

Alex finally nodded. She wrapped herself tightly around his uninjured side. "Sorry, you just scared me."

As they made their way into the kitchen, Alex realized she had never really asked for the details of what Markus and the others did when they went out every night. She cringed when she recognized it as another example of how self-absorbed she had been. Of course there was danger; of course there were injuries, even deaths. A vampire had died the night she was brought to the coven. That bastard had been a Vengatti. He had been attempting to capture or kill her, so Sage and the coven felt it was justified. But she was sure the Vengatti would feel as little remorse about killing a member of the Rectinatti coven—her coven, with her friends, and her lover.

"Alex, you don't have to watch this," Markus said, shaking her from her thoughts. She guessed her face portrayed a hint of the horror she was feeling. Markus must have mistaken this for uneasiness about watching Sarah stitch his wound.

"I'm fine, but doesn't that hurt? Shouldn't you have some kind of painkiller or local anesthesia first?"

Darian, who had entered the room a moment after Sarah, chuckled. But Alex was almost sure she could see Markus flinch each time Sarah's needle pierced the skin and tugged the suture thread to close the gap in his flesh.

"Are they always this stupid?" she asked Sarah.

"They call it brave." Sarah didn't look up, but Alex saw her lips press together trying to repress her grin.

"No pain, no pride," Sage said, sitting at the island with Darian. He didn't look up from the screen of the laptop, so he missed Alex's exasperated headshake.

Deciding she had seen enough of Sarah's handiwork, she squeezed Markus's other hand before heading over to see what Sage and Darian were examining.

"He put a password on it? I'll kill him," Darian said, glaring at the dialog box requiring a password that had popped up on the screen.

"I tried all the obvious ones—your name, his name, Rectinatti. No luck," Sage said trying a new combination with no success. "I'll go ask him," he said after a few more failed attempts. He had his hand on the screen, about to slam it closed. Alex reached out to stop him, carefully avoiding his touch. She could already feel his mixture of emotions concerning having to approach Rocky, now imprisoned, for help with the program he had created and protected.

"May I?"

"You a computer geek as well as a book geek?" Sage asked skeptically. But he dropped his hand from the screen, allowing her to turn the computer to face her.

"Not really. But I've hung around with Rocky enough to know he wouldn't be so dumb as to protect an important program with a password any member of the Vengatti could guess in less than two minutes," Alex answered. She began typing, starting with a four-letter password. Denied. That made sense, most passwords required six characters. She picked six. Denied. With a confident smile she added two numbers at the end. Access granted.

"How'd you do that?" Darian asked. He sounded impressed, but also annoyed.

Alex smiled at him. "You two really need to be more observant." She had no intention of explaining, but Sage ruined her fun by plucking the password from her head.

"That grungy t-shirt he wears twice a week?"

"It's a Santana jersey. I think he's a pitcher," she said. Darian still looked confused. "NYMets57," she said. "So what is this?"

Alex scanned the screen that came up. It seemed to be a map grid with a series of dots. Some squares on the grid had a single dot, others none at all, but there was one in the center with a concentration of them. As she rolled her finger over the touch pad moving the cursor over a few of the red dots, they lit up. Alex realized they were hyperlinks and clicked on one. A separate screen opened. She was skimming over what she thought looked like a report, when Markus came up behind her. He reached over her shoulder and closed the window.

"A new way of keeping records of our encounters with the Vengatti," he answered. He pulled the laptop over to where he had sidled up to the island and zoomed in on the map. As the street names became larger, Alex recognized a few of them. The neighborhood Markus landed on was on the east side of the city, on the edge of the old mill district, and no more than fifteen minutes from where she grew up.

"And tonight it served its main purpose." Markus pointed to a grid on the screen. He smiled widely at Darian, who nodded, obviously pleased. Markus turned to Alex and pulled her close to him. She could sense his pleasure, pride, and excitement. She looked up at him for an explanation.

"We think we found him."

Alex dug her nails into his arms. She tried to steady her suddenly soft knees.

"Levi? You found him? We can go get him?"

"Maybe," Sage cut in. "We were caught outside before we could confirm." He turned to Darian to elaborate. "Three of them ambushed us just outside the house, and after we injured one, two more arrived. It was a good thing we had Dalton and Donel as back up. No way there were that many of them there by coincidence."

"What does that mean?" Alex asked, not caring which male answered her.

"The Vengatti feed from humans as often as each other. They're not as dependent on each other, which means they're less likely to live in concentrated areas," Markus began. "If five of them are in one place, there's a reason."

"They're guarding him?" Alex suggested, understanding what Markus was implying.

"Probably, but it could just be where their Regan lives, Alex. That would also explain the large numbers," Sage said. She understood that he was trying to prepare her for disappointment, but she didn't care. She had a one-track mind.

"So we'll go tomorrow?" She knew it was too close to morning to act immediately, not that she didn't want to.

Darian leaned on the counter, his thumbs hooked in his belt loops. After a moment's pause, he turned to his warriors.

"They've got to know after tonight," Markus said. "We've been getting closer for a week." He pointed to the conglomerate of red dots.

"And *if* he's really there," Sage said, shooting Alex another look which she ignored, "they'll move him if they think we're coming back for him. It has to be immediate."

Alex was ecstatic. She'd be rescuing her brother in less than twenty-four hours. She looked up at Darian eagerly.

"Fine." He closed the computer and stood. "Let's go eat and work out the details upstairs. Sarah, could you just bring up plates, please? Alex, could you make sure Rocky's not forgotten?" Darian was already sweeping from the room as Alex replied.

"Sure, I'll be up in a minute." She was more than willing to have the opportunity to personally thank Rocky. He had created this program after she had convinced them that Levi was still alive and in the hands of the Vengatti. Rocky had undoubtedly developed it with her mission in mind. She was so overwhelmed with gratitude that she almost didn't register the others' emotions.

Darian had stopped. Markus and Sage exchanged glances. Alex was on alert instantly. If they thought they'd keep her home tomorrow, they were insane.

"I'm coming, Darian," she said before he could speak.

"No, you're not. It's dangerous and unnecessary."

"It'd be dangerous and reckless to send your coven members into a situation not knowing what you're facing," she replied, "especially when you have someone who can provide that information." She looked from Darian to steal a glance at Markus. She wondered how angry he would be at her for putting herself in danger. She was surprised to sense his conflicting emotions. He was thinking as a warrior and a lover. She was astounded and triumphant.

"You nearly fainted at the sight of Markus's injury tonight," Darian began. "You think you could control yourself during a real battle, Alex? You'd be a liability. Do you want to be responsible for someone getting hurt trying to protect you?"

"I was taken off guard tonight. I won't be tomorrow," she started, but she could see him shaking his head and knew her arguments weren't having any impact. She grudgingly admitted it might be because he had a point. "What if I helped with the head count and then waited in the car? I could be of use and be there as soon as Levi is released. But I'll be out of the way before any real action starts."

Darian sighed but still shook his head. Alex looked to Markus again. Surely this would be the best of both worlds. As leader of the warriors he could have the intel he needed, and as her lover he could be assured of her safety, which was what he desperately wanted. He seemed to understand her pleading look.

"It's not a bad compromise, Regan," he said. Alex was relieved; Darian looked shocked. "I want Briant on-scene anyway to deal with injuries. He can also protect Alex in the van. Knowing numbers ahead of time would allow us to call in back-up before we got into trouble."

Darian turned on Alex. "If you come, it's as a warrior, which means when Markus or I tell you to do something, you do it, instantly." Darian approached her. "Can I trust you to do that, no matter what?"

Alex could think of a dozen situations where doing what Darian was asking her to promise would be excruciating. But staying back would be worse. Not knowing would be worse.

Alex held her clenched fist over her heart. It was the same gesture Rocky had used when he swore to Markus to protect her. When she had later asked him what it meant, he explained it was a pledge of one's physical strength and one's essence, which in their world meant one's honor, integrity, and goodness.

"You have my word."

Having been up and dressed for over an hour, Alex sat cross-legged on the edge of Markus's bed watching him get ready. Despite

Darian's mandate sometime around noon that they all try to go to bed and get some rest, Alex was pretty sure she wasn't the only one who had lain awake most of the afternoon. Markus had stayed in his room for the first time in weeks after she had told him and Darian that she wanted to try to contact Levi one last time. She was hoping not only to prepare him, but also to get any last-minute information she could that would help her and his rescuers safely complete their mission. But just as every other time she had tried to initiate the communication, she had failed.

With this added anxiety, she sat twisting the black winter cap Markus had found on the bottom of her closet for her to wear despite the late July heat. He said he wanted her to blend in as best as possible. She didn't argue with him, though they both knew that covering her feminine haircut would do little to hide the fact she was female, human, and would be, by far, the smallest one near the battle.

Since she no longer wore the cuff bracelets on her right wrist, she repeatedly ran her fingers over the Patriots logo embroidered on the front of the hat as a form of nervous release. She watched as Markus dressed as he had advised her to, wearing sturdy jeans, a dark long-sleeve t-shirt, and boots. She studied her own sneakers. They wouldn't provide the protection the males' shoes did, but as she had no boots, and her main goal would be to get info and get out, they'd do.

She looked up again at the clattering sound of metal. Markus had opened the top drawer of his dresser. Instead of the expected array of boxers and socks, Alex saw an arrangement of knives, handguns, and ammunition that looked like it belonged on the cover of an NRA sponsored magazine, rather than laid out in the cherry dresser.

Her already quick heartbeat raced even faster as she watched him tuck a sheathed knife into each boot and both sides of his belt. Finally, after checking the chamber, he tucked a handgun into the back of his pants and pulled his shirt down.

"Gee, only one gun?" she asked squeezing the hat into a ball.

Markus was too focused to hear the sarcasm in her voice. "Guns are too dangerous. Vampires move too fast. You're as likely to hit an ally as an enemy," he said. "If we use anything other than our hands and our fangs, it's knives."

"And I suppose I don't get one of those?" Alex asked, though she already knew the answer.

Markus looked at her reflection behind him in the mirror and made an indistinguishable noise Alex guessed meant something between "heaven help us" and "hell, no." It was probably for the best. She didn't have a good track record with sharp objects. She rubbed at her bare wrist.

"Ready?" Markus asked.

Alex nodded. She had been ready for this since she realized Levi was alive, but that didn't stop her from fearing what she was about to witness and what they might find.

Halfway down the stairs Markus's cell vibrated in his pocket. He flipped it open and cursed.

"What's up?" Darian asked from the entrance to the kitchen.

"Liam's mate is having the baby. Now. He can't leave her."

"You mean won't."

"Darian," Sarah spoke up from behind him. Her opinion on the matter was quite clear from her tone.

"I know," he muttered. "But with the twins still recovering from the scuffle last night, and the skeleton crew needed to patrol the rest of the city, we're down to eight. I don't like it. If they had five last night, they'll have ten tonight, at least." Darian began to pace the foyer, his hands in his hair. "Is there anyone else who's had the experience whom we can call? I only want to use less-experienced volunteers if absolutely necessary."

Sage entered from the basement, tucking a weapon into his waistband. "I know one more who's trained and more than willing to fight."

Darian stopped walking and turned to him. Before he could ask, Sage finished.

"But he'll need to be fed."

Alex realized to whom Sage was referring just as Darian did. He shook his head, but Alex noticed his hand went into his pocket.

"What's the worst that happens, Darian?" Sage asked. "He helps, and you say he risked his life for the coven. He gets hurt, and Lucas and family get what they wanted."

"Sage!" This time it was Alex who shouted the reprimand. Though, sadly, she knew it was the truth. She also knew Rocky would rather be injured in a battle than sitting locked up and useless while his friends and coven members fought one male short.

Darian pulled his hand out of his pocket and handed Sage his keys. He also went to the porcelain dish by the door and grabbed a second set, tossing those, too, to the Knower.

"He has an hour to get geared, fed, and downtown where we're meeting the others."

Sage nodded before flashing back down the stairs.

A little before midnight their three vehicles pulled up on three separate sides of the building they suspected held Levi and members of the Vengatti. Alex was in the back of the windowless commercial van with Briant, who was to serve as an on-site medic if needed and as Alex's guardian once she had fulfilled her duty. Alex hoped sitting with her and waiting was all that would be required of the male across from her.

Markus opened the door and offered her a hand as she jumped down. He exchanged a quick nod with Briant, who quietly shut the door. Alex stood by Markus's side and looked around at the neighborhood they were parked in. At least half the duplexes had for sale or foreclosure signs in the lawns or nailed to the boards covering broken windows. The few houses with cars in the driveways were quiet. It took Alex a moment to realize what it was that sent a chill down her spine. In addition to the quiet, there wasn't one working streetlight or porch light in more than a block. She doubted this was a coincidence. The street was a mosaic of dark shadows.

"Hopefully one of us will bring you back here," Markus whispered as he led her through the side yard of one of the abandoned properties. "But if for whatever reason we can't, you make it back through this fence and go right to the van. Briant knows your scent. He'll let you in."

They had stopped on the outer side of a chain-link fence. Alex put on her hat and peered into Markus's eyes.

"I'll be safe, if you will."

His response was a hard, intense kiss.

He hopped the four-foot fence, using just one hand to vault him over, then turned to help Alex. She shook her head, pushed aside the far corner where the metal bands holding the chain to the post had been broken, and crawled under, hardly having to duck. Looking up, she saw before her the run-down house that likely held her brother.

Sage, Darian, and Rocky appeared silently by their sides. Half of Alex wanted to give Rocky a quick hug, but the wiser half guessed warriors didn't embrace before battles.

She knew from the morning's planning session that the six other warriors would be spaced out around the edges of the property, ready to go at Markus's command.

"Just close enough to get a count," Darian reminded her, as if Markus, who would be escorting her, would allow her a step farther.

Sage would stay with Darian and Rocky on the perimeter to report what Alex sensed. Their silent communication was a safe way to relay information while hopefully remaining undetected.

Markus put one hand on the knife at his right side and the other on Alex's arm as he led her closer to the grey two-story building. Alex noticed the windows were all covered with shades, and she guessed that, like at the farmhouse, they also had heavy curtains covering them from the inside. If there was light inside the house, none escaped into the darkened yard. She knew it helped their cover, but it also made her uneasy.

As they neared the building she attempted to block out her own emotions, which was a more difficult task than ever tonight. Reaching out with her sense, she tried to detect the Others who might be in the house. She realized there was a problem. She tapped Markus's right hand, the one holding her tightly. Without speaking she tried to get him to understand why she needed him to let go. Lately, contact intensified Alex's sense. After a moment of awkward miming, he seemed to comprehend. He removed his grasp, though it seemed to physically pain him.

Midway across the yard, Alex began to sense emotions of those with whom she was unfamiliar. She knew, not only from the direction they seemed to be coming from but also from the cadence of the emotions themselves, that these were not the six warriors from the Rectinatti. The males she sensed now were filled with enough unpleasant emotion to turn her already queasy stomach. Taking a steadying breath, she tried not to focus on their individual feelings. She just needed a number. Due to their unfamiliarity, she found the need to count on her fingers, as if assigning them each a digit would help her keep them straight. She stopped at ten. But not because that was all there were to count.

She held up ten fingers to Markus, then with shaking hands another six.

"Sixteen?" he mouthed. He grabbed her arm again and started to drag her away toward the fence where the others waited. After half a dozen steps Alex stopped, nearly falling over when Markus, still clutching her arm, continued without her.

A flurry of her own emotions overtook her as she sensed a seventeenth male. She sensed him stronger than any human, stronger than Sage, but he was not a vampire. Unfamiliar to her new sense, yet as familiar to her as her own essence, her own self.

Levi was here. Only the sense wasn't coming from the house. The sense was closer. She spun around peering into the shadows of the overgrown pines that lined one side of the yard.

Markus registered the movement before she did, yanking her behind him. As Levi came out of the dark and made his way across the yard, Sage also flashed to Alex's side, followed almost immediately by Darian and Rocky.

"Levi, you're free," Alex burst out, forgetting about their goal of remaining silent and undetected. Seeing him in person and speaking to him shook her with an eerie unease she hadn't anticipated.

"Little thanks to you, squirt."

Alex tried not to be upset by her brother's comment or his cold glare. She had prepared herself for this. She knew it was a possibility they would find him recently fed from. She knew it would take time for him to recover from years of this. What she hadn't known, couldn't have known, was how much it would hurt, how much she still wanted her older brother's love and approval.

"Son of a bitch," Sage said quietly beside her. All but Levi looked to him, confused. Levi turned up one corner of his mouth in a sneer as Sage explained the outburst. "He heard what happened last night and told them he knew we were coming back for him. Their preparation provided him the distraction he needed to escape."

"So? That was smart, wasn't it?" Alex said, still not understanding Sage's anger. "He's free. Let's just get out of here."

Sage turned to look at her, shaking his head. "He exaggerated our numbers, partly to panic them, but partly in the hopes we'd destroy each other. He was planning to stick around to watch. Well hidden, of course. You coward."

Levi actually laughed. A chilling cackle that caused Alex's whole body to shiver. She turned from Sage to Levi, but it was Darian's gaze she met first. He had turned from his protective stance in front of her to look back. Alex sensed his doubt, his flickers of betrayal, and guessed what he was thinking.

"I didn't tell him our numbers. I told you, I couldn't even contact him." Her voice shook. She was unable to process what caused her the most pain, her bother's betrayal or Darian's accusation of her own.

"Please, Alex, don't tell me you thought they'd trust you, accept you as one of them? It's not in their nature. You're just a pawn." Levi surveyed the males surrounding her with a look of disgust that matched the hatred that Alex knew coursed through him.

Still, she had to believe this wasn't really her brother. This wasn't Levi. She broke free of Markus's grasp and rushed forward before the others could stop her.

"Levi, you're wrong. The Vengatti are like that, but—"

"Don't talk to me about what those animals are and are not like. You know nothing about what they've done, what they do. Do you remember the dream I sent you, Alex?"

Levi closed his eyes and suddenly Alex was back in her recurring nightmare of the night her brothers disappeared. She had never awakened able to remember anything more than the fear and sadness. But as Levi dragged her mind through his memories, she recalled the horrors vividly. Levi shouted at her as she hit the grass. "You weren't holding him as he died!"

Alex cried out as pain seared her. Not physical pain—Levi was still feet from her, his hands at his side. But because of their connection as Seers, Alex sensed Levi stronger than she had ever sensed anyone. What she was feeling was emotional pain. Levi's pain.

Relief came before she realized why. When she looked up, Markus had her brother's arms pinned behind him with one hand. The other hand held a knife up to his throat. She started to scramble to her hands and knees, crying out for Markus to release him. But Rocky and Darian had each grabbed one of her arms and were dragging her away.

She watched in shock as Markus dropped the knife and hit the ground. Levi swiped it up. In a heartbeat their positions were reversed. Markus was writhing on the ground, even more intensely than Alex had been. She realized the reason for this as she watched Levi holding Markus's bare neck with his right hand, while pressing the blade to it with his left.

Sage lunged forward, but Levi stopped him with a slight flick of the knife. It was obvious he was threatening to press it further into Markus if Sage moved.

"Go ahead, touch me. He'll be dead, and you'll be next," Levi taunted. "It'll be even easier with a Knower; the added connection makes the pain more intense." He nodded to Markus who cried out again.

Sage whipped out the concealed handgun from his back. "I don't need to get close enough to touch you, you little bastard. I can blow your knee caps off from here."

"No, Sage." Alex struggled against Rocky and Darian's hold, kicking at them uselessly. "He's just projecting. Markus isn't really hurt." But even as she said the words, she wished she could take them back. The pain in her lover's eyes was more excruciating to witness than any physical injury would be. Still, there was a reason for Levi's cruelty.

Sage pulled back the safety. "Let him go," he ordered Levi. "Now."

"Look at his neck! Those wounds are fresh. They've just fed from him," she cried. "Levi, stop it. This isn't who you are. Let him go. I love him!"

Levi dropped his hold on Markus who crumbled on the ground gasping for breath, trying to recover. Her brother locked eyes with her. He looked at Alex with total disbelief.

"You love him? You love one of these monsters?" Levi staggered back like he had been dealt a blow. "Oh my God. You do love him. You love all of them. What the hell is wrong with you, Alex?"

It was obvious Levi had sensed her emotions. Because at that moment her love for her future mate and her protectors was all she knew for sure. Her brother's capacity for redemption was in doubt, a doubt that intensified the instant Levi spoke to her again.

"And to think I worried when I first learned they had you, felt a twinge of guilt even, for leading them all to you. It's almost sad to know your own lack of sense led to your destruction."

Alex's heart shattered when she realized there was no real sadness in Levi as he contemplated this, only a strange void where sympathy and compassion should be. And somewhere deep down she knew that's all there would ever be. Alex shook her head unwilling to accept this. Her brother mistook the meaning.

"Yes, Alexandra, because whether you are killed or captured, it'll be the end of you. Pray you go like Dave did and die quickly."

Levi had barely uttered the last word when he was flattened. Markus, having recovered, swept Levi's legs out from under him, knocking the knife from his hand. Sage had a boot on his throat and a gun at his head the moment he hit the ground.

Searching the cold blue eyes that peered up at her, Alex desperately tried one last time to find a scrap of the Levi she had loved and admired. Those blue eyes were almost the same as the ones she remembered on the boy who had told her to be honest, always, with those she loved.

She remembered the night her father, furious over the broken living room window, had her by the arm asking if she had been the one to throw the ball inside the house. She must have been at least eleven and old enough to fear the spanking she knew would come, but also old enough to know right from wrong. Yet the first words that had escaped her were, "Levi did it." She remembered the long look her father gave her. She wanted to fess up but was too afraid. When she had remained silent he shook his head and turned to his son. Levi was young also, but old enough to be protective and loving enough to forgive her. He saw the tears welling in Alex's eyes and falsely admitted to the infraction. Of course, what neither of them knew then was that their father, even with limited powers, likely could sense the dishonesty and guilt both his children felt. So Alex hadn't understood why they were both punished and sent to bed, but Levi did. And later that night when she crawled into the bottom bunk of his bed in the room he shared with Dave to apologize, he explained.

"Dad, didn't punish me or you for breaking the window, squirt," Levi had said, tugging her braid. "He punished us because we lied to him. Accidents happen, we make mistakes, but we need to be honest about it, especially with family. It's wrong, and Dad always knows when we're not being good. And we always know it, too." And back then, he did.

Unable to let her delusions put others in danger any longer, Alex let herself accept what she had worked hard to deny. Looking in those eyes now, with a pain that stole her breath and shook her frame, she knew it was time to fess up to the lie she had let herself belief: that Levi could be saved. Because he couldn't be, because he no longer knew what was right or good. Because there wasn't enough good left in him to anchor him to the person he was, the person she knew he would never be again. There was nothing left in Levi but pain and anger and corruption.

Alex finally understood why the Vengatti rarely killed their victims. Because turning to Darian and nodding to show her acceptance of what had to happen was the hardest choice she had ever had to make. Both he and Rocky released their hold so she could turn away. She closed her eyes and covered her face waiting for the shot, waiting to feel Levi's essence, polluted and weak, fade into nothing.

Chapter 18

With no one holding her and no energy left to control her sense, Alex was flooded with the emotions around her. And suddenly she realized they were all around her.

She opened her eyes and the blood drained from her face. Absorbed in the emotions of the events she had been immersed in, she had not sensed the dozen members of the Vengatti who had silently surrounded them from behind. As soon as she opened her eyes, they lurked out from behind bushes and around the corners of the house.

Either seeing the movement or hearing the horror in her head, Sage yelled out to warn Darian and the others.

"No, by all means, don't let us interrupt you. Go ahead; kill the little bastard. He's served his purpose, bringing us the girl."

Staggering back into Darian, Alex recognized the vampire speaking as the one from the dream, her brother's memory, which had tormented her sleep. It was Ty, her oldest brother's murderer and likely the main cause of Levi's ruined state. The greed and hatred Alex sensed from this large daunting male was powerful. His feeling of justification was disturbing. But his pleasure was indescribably sickening. She swallowed hard, trying to hold down her bile along with her fear and disgust. She wanted desperately to sense anyone but him. What she sensed instead shook her just as badly.

Even as the six other Rectinatti warriors entered the yard, responding no doubt to Sage's yell, Alex could sense the worry in her males' emotions. They were gravely outnumbered. Levi's interruption had kept them from calling back up. They'd need a miracle to keep this from becoming a deadly disaster.

A miracle, or a distraction of their own.

Alex stopped trying to block out the emotions sticking her like a hundred different pins in a pincushion. She allowed them in, let them fill her up.

Don't panic, she thought to Sage, the only one she could warn without alerting the Vengatti.

With one exhausting effort, Alex forced the emotions outward. She held them as long as possible before they rebounded back on her. Even knowing what to expect, they slammed into her like a wall of concrete. The last thing she remembered before blacking out was watching Ty stumble backwards. And feeling satisfaction. And hope.

Alex awoke in the arms of a male. Without even opening her eyes, she knew it wasn't the male she wanted.

"Take her to Briant. And don't come back. You shouldn't be here either, Regan." Markus was near. She wanted to reach out to him. Before she could find the strength to look at him and speak, she was being jostled by Darian's movement.

When she opened her eyes, she thought her projection had messed with her vision. The scene around her was a blur. But as the movement stopped, her vision cleared. She wished it hadn't. From over Darian's shoulder she saw skirmishes all over the small backyard. Most were blurs of movement she couldn't really decipher. But when a warrior stopped or slowed to change direction, they came into focus. These glimpses were enough for her to realize the Rectinatti were still outnumbered and struggling.

Darian dropped Alex's feet, but held her upright. The reason for their stopping became terrifyingly evident. Two attackers, Ty, dark and menacing, and a second pale, cold-looking male, had flanked Darian. The Regan held a knife in his free right hand, but was hindered holding Alex with his left.

"Down. Fight," Alex managed. She hoped Darian would understand. He looked at her with concern, but gently slid her down his right leg to the grass. Now armed in both hands, he remained protectively over her. When the flashes of movement began, Alex froze in her position hunched on the ground. Even sitting up, she feared, would get in the way as they fought over and around her.

Finally they came into focus. Darian let out grunt of pain. While slashing at Ty in front of him, the white-blonde vampire had come from behind. Lunging on the Regan's neck, he tore at Darian's flesh with his fangs. Darian flipped the grip of the knife in his left hand and stabbed it behind him. From the ground Alex watched as the blade tore the blonde from naval to sternum. The body fell next to where she lay. Finding some strength returned, she scrambled back, tearing into the dirt to pull herself away from the bloody corpse.

"Darian!" Markus's voice jolted her. Alex looked from the body at her feet to the mass of bodies above her, just as Darian crashed to the ground. Markus and Sage arrived a moment too late. Ty had taken the opportunity to strike provided when Darian had one hand behind him. The Regan now lay bleeding from a six-inch gash across his chest.

Alex tried to make her way through the tangle of fast-moving feet to get to him. It was obvious from how they fought that Sage and Markus were trying to keep her and Darian protected. Darian saw Alex's movement and shook his head.

"If you can go, go!" he said. She could tell he was struggling to get back up, to continue fighting.

"Stay still. I'll get Briant."

Though Alex was still finding breathing difficult, and her whole body was hot and clammy, she knew she had to make it back to Briant. It was her insistence that brought them here. It was her brother who saw to it they'd be outnumbered. She couldn't be responsible for the coven's fall. And somehow she knew that if Darian died, the rest would be inevitable.

Halfway through the chain-link fence, two massive hands yanked her back. Her palm tore on the rough metal link she tried to grab onto. Blood dripped down her fingers as Ty wrenched her other arm behind her back. Taking her bloody right hand in his own, he brought it to his face. He inhaled deeply. To Alex's revulsion he licked the blood from her wound.

"Mmm, someone's in transition," Ty purred. Alex struggled against his hold, but she had little room to move without dislocating her left shoulder. "Looks like we got you just in time to train you our way."

"I'd rather fucking die," Alex said, slamming her heel into his kneecap.

He grunted, but recovered, twisting her arm painfully. "Too bad, because family tradition dictates the oldest one dies. You just get to watch." Ty thrust Alex over his shoulder and moved at vampire speed back into the midst of the melee. Before she could react, he dumped her hard onto her stomach, knocking her already labored breath from her lungs. His left boot slammed onto her back, pinning her to the ground in a position eerily reminiscent of Levi's on the night Ty had killed Dave as he watched. With his right hand, Ty rolled over the body on the ground next to her. Alex gasped at Levi's bloodied face. Despite her earlier acceptance of what Levi had become, the gashes and swelling that marred the features she associated with the Levi of her youth still pained her.

Ty removed his boot from her back, so he could pull Levi up by his hair with one hand and put the knife to his throat with the other. For a fleeting moment Alex contemplated fighting for her brother. But for the second time that night she had to make a devastating decision. She knew Ty was right; she was maturing. The energy that left her with would hardly be enough for one more fight. If she could use it to save just one of them, she knew who it had to be.

"Any parting words for your little sis?" Ty said, yanking Levi's head back further.

Alex expected nothing, hoped for nothing. So she was stunned when he rasped one final word.

"Fight."

Ty laughed his cruel laugh. And Alex turned from them both. She would not watch as her brother's blood was spilled. She felt the wetness on the back of her neck and tried not to register what it was, what it meant. But she couldn't deny or control the wrath that boiled up from within. Now was the time to fight.

She grabbed the knife Ty had unknowingly tossed her onto. She knew, as she had felt it digging into her chest for the last minute, that it was the one of Markus's that had been lost during the first scuffle with Levi. Using both hands she slashed her mate's weapon across the back of Ty's left knee, hoping she dug it deep enough to render him immobile.

Ty's sick, smug grin turned to a shriek of agony as he crumbled. Alex tore across the yard, her adrenaline the only thing that kept her body from collapsing.

Trying desperately to remember where she had left Markus and Sage protecting Darian, Alex spun around, searching. Flashes were everywhere. But if Darian were still here and injured, he should have been visible. Alex tried to focus; wiping the sweat from her face, she closed her eyes just for a second. Markus and Sage were close. She turned in their direction. Opening her eyes, she knew the skirmish directly in front of her had to be where they fought.

"Where's Darian?" she called out, hoping one of them would answer, but only when it was safe.

Markus slammed a larger vampire to the ground with a sickening crunch.

"I thought he left with you. What are you still doing here, Alex? You promised." His pleading look lingered as long as he could maintain it before having to fend off a second attacker.

"Shit." Alex focused again, finding it harder to find the Regan's sense among the chaos. "They have him in the house," Alex yelled behind her as she began sprinting through the yard to a back door that was ajar.

"Alex, no!" Markus screamed. Her heart ached as she ran away from his plea, but she knew what had to be done. And he was too entrenched in his own fight to do it for her or even to pursue her.

Inside the house Alex heard voices and made her way to them, creeping along the wall of the hall.

"With you dead, I can finally have both covens that are rightfully mine."

"They'll never bow to you, Leonce."

Alex recognized Darian's voice. But she also heard the strain in it. She found the doorway it was coming from and peered around the frame.

"You sure of that, little cousin?" Alex didn't have time to contemplate Leonce's meaning. She sucked in her breath as he squeezed Darian's jaw. But he didn't seem to hurt Darian further as he stared intently at him. Darian was still bleeding heavily from his earlier wounds to the neck and chest, and his nose was broken. He was pinned by Leonce's knee on his shoulder, and Alex thought the way his right arm stuck out at an unnatural angle was an ominous sign.

"No. That's what I thought. You have doubts."

"Doubts you're trying to plant there. You can't fuck with my mind, Leonce. I understand how Knowers work."

Alex realized with surprise that the leader of the Vengatti, the tall, powerful male with brunette waves matching Darian's, was the Knower Levi had told her about. Alex would have to act immediately. It wouldn't be long before Leonce would hear her as clearly as Sage did.

"Fine. You can die with what little piece of mind you have left."

Alex was across the room before the knife in Leonce's hand began to descend. With as strong a force as she could muster, she threw her small body at the side of his large frame. The shock of it unstabilized him, sending them both crashing to the floor. Alex landed on top, feeling like she tackled a sack of bricks. She frantically searched for the knife she thought she heard hit the floor. But Leonce capitalized on her split second lack of focus. She suddenly found herself beneath him.

"I'd kill you, bitch, but I hear you'll be more useful than your brother. How about your first training session instead?" Leonce bared his fangs. Alex thrashed wildly. She knew the pain would come, but as his fangs tore into her neck, she shrieked. The pain of her soft flesh tearing was nothing compared to the anguish of having her blood, her essence, drained against her will. Nothing compared to the knowledge that her energy, her goodness, was strengthening an enemy who would use it against those she loved most.

Her agony doubled, then eased in a blur. Leonce had been torn from her neck by Darian. But it had expended every ounce of the Regan's remaining strength. Leonce whipped the fallen knife from the ground ready to finish off Darian who lay crumpled on the floor.

Alex knew what was coming, but didn't have the force to stop it. Her body was numb. Only her heart ached as she realized she was losing everything she had fought for, everything she had learned to love. Her anger flared as she looked at the leader of the group responsible for it.

Maybe she couldn't fight it, but she could make him feel it. She managed to roll over and clutch his ankle, hoping the physical contact would make it easier. She tried for the second time that night to project.

Leonce stopped inches from Darian's throat. His look of confusion matched what Alex was feeling. Something was happening. Something very different from the uncontrolled surges of emotion she had managed to project just twice before. Instead of an instant erratic push, Alex found she was sending a continuous stream of pain, anger, and fear. And she could feel Leonce's emotions change as she maintained contact. Realizing what she was doing, Alex tried to manipulate it further. She attempted to alter the emotions she projected, causing Leonce to feel two emotions she doubted he had ever felt before: remorse and self-loathing.

With a glassy stare Leonce straightened his torso so he no longer towered threateningly over Darian. The knife point dropped away from the Rectinatti Regan. Alex didn't stop. She couldn't stop. Leonce turned the knife tip toward himself. With a final surge of energy Alex intensified the feelings. Leonce thrust the blade into his own chest and collapsed. Alex felt a brief flash of the same disturbing pleasure that had disgusted her earlier in the evening. Only she was no longer holding Leonce's leg. She was no longer sensing anyone's emotions but her own.

Markus stood at the doorway with Sage beside him. Having finally killed or incapacitated the three Vengatti they had been fighting, they had flashed to the house. Markus easily followed Alex's familiar scent. When they arrived, he thought they were too late. Both Alex and Darian lay bleeding at the feet of the Vengatti's Regan, Leonce. Before Markus rushed forward, Sage stopped him. Leonce had turned the knife on himself, and with one jab, pushed the blade between his own ribs. Markus almost missed seeing Alex's hand on the vampire's ankle before he fell.

"Did she do that?" Markus looked to Sage, unsure how to feel.

Sage watched Alex for a moment before answering. She turned her head and vomited violently. "Yeah, and she's not handling it well. Markus, she's maturing."

"Now?" Markus rushed to Alex's side. For the last month and a half the thing they had worried most about was her being in perfect health when she matured. He examined the extent of her injuries, and his heart raced. Not wanting to panic her, he spoke softly to her as he tore off his shirt and pressed it to her neck.

"Alex, you're going to be fine. You saved Darian. Now you need to be strong and fight, okay?" Markus could see she was fading in and out of consciousness.

"Go. I'll help Darian. He's bad, but he'll pull through. But I can't move him fast with these injuries," Sage said.

"I'll help," Rocky said, appearing in the door. His left eye was swollen shut and he had a gash over his belt on one side. He was carrying a gasoline canister. "Cops were called. We gotta fly."

Markus didn't stick around to see him and Sage remove Darian before setting the blaze that would hide most of the evidence. He was at the van where Briant waited with the doors open to accept Alex's limp body. Sage climbed in the back with the Regan. Rocky had the van rolling before the doors were shut.

"Home or clinic?" he called into the back. Sage was already working on Darian's injuries. Briant had Markus maintain pressure on Alex's neck wound while he checked her vitals. Markus felt his breath catch in his throat when Briant looked up from his watch, removed the stethoscope, and answered.

"Clinic, Rocky, fast."

The beeping of the monitors attached to Alex was all that could be heard in the room. The six vampires surrounding her sat in silent vigil waiting for some change. Markus held Alex's small hand in his own, rubbing the soft, tanned flesh that felt cool in comparison to the heat that had emanated from her every pore just an hour ago.

As Briant, Sarah, and Sage had finished treating both her and Darian's physical wounds, Alex's fever had spiked. Her blood pressure became dangerously high and her heart raced. Her small body shook from the transition it was undergoing.

Markus had never let go of her hand. Even as Briant bustled about adjusting IVs and Sarah dabbed her limbs with ice-cold cloths, he held on. It was excruciating to just watch. But he held her and spoke words of comfort, words he realized were as much for himself as for her unconscious mind.

And now he waited. As soon as Darian had fed from Sarah to regain some of his strength, he insisted on sitting up in a chair by Alex's other side. Despite advice from Sarah and Briant to remain resting completely, he had also called the Elder Regan. Ardellus had advised there was little else they could do. If Alex made it through the fever and racing heartbeat, she would either wake with her powers fully matured, or she wouldn't wake at all.

Two months ago Markus couldn't have imagined caring for another female like he had loved his Alia. But as he watched Alex's chest rise and fall, he knew the pain of losing her would be even greater than with his first love. Alia, with her quiet thoughtfulness and eagerness to serve and please, had complemented him; they had been two wholes well matched to make a pair. Losing her had left a void next to Markus, where she had felt so right. But Alex fulfilled Markus, as he fulfilled her. They were interlocking puzzle pieces, fit together to reveal a more complete picture. Losing her would leave a gaping hole inside of him, one he wouldn't fill again.

One of the machines began to beep. Briant rushed to check the read out.

"What is it?" Markus asked, his own heartbeat racing to match the rhythm of the alarm.

"Her blood pressure's dropping."

"That's good, isn't it?"

"It was when it was high," Briant said. He looked at Markus with sympathy. "It's low now. Too low. Her heartbeat's weak." Markus didn't want his sympathy. He wanted action.

"Can't you do anything?"

"I don't know what else to do. Physically she should be healing by now." Briant touched Markus's shoulder momentarily after he reset the machine and then went back to where he had been standing.

Markus didn't want to grasp what Briant meant, but he did. Alex's recovery wasn't one her body had to make. Briant could shock her heart if it stopped. He could pump more chemicals into her blood. He could keep her body alive with machines and technology no Seer had ever had the luxury of before. But it wouldn't save her. Alex's essence and her sense were what needed jolting. And there were no machines for that.

Markus squeezed her hand and lifted it to kiss each knuckle. He looked up to see Sarah wiping away her tears.

"Wait. What if we don't need a machine," Sage said. No one in the room but Markus understood the context. And even he didn't understand the meaning behind it.

"We *can* shock her sense, Markus. You're right—her body's survived the maturation. It's her spirit, her essence, that's fighting to deal with her power." Sage had crossed the room and was speaking just to his friend. The others seemed as confused as Markus.

"How?"

"Let go of her."

"No." Markus's hand would have to be pried from Alex's in order for him to leave her side.

"Just for a minute, Markus. If it's going to shock her, it needs to be strong and sudden," Sage began. "Rocky, get over here." Sage also motioned for Sarah to come closer. Darian struggled to his feet not waiting for the invitation. Even Briant came to Alex's bedside to see what Sage was trying to do.

Markus still didn't comprehend until after Rocky did.

"What should we try to feel?" the young vampire asked. Suddenly Markus understood. He looked to Sage, who nodded, before he would let go of Alex's hand.

"If your feelings all match your thoughts, I think they'll more than suffice."

Markus watched as first Rocky, then Sage, Sarah and Darian, with his unbroken arm, and finally Briant held their hands out over Alex's battle-scarred arms. He reached his own hand out over her forehead and waited for Sage's nod.

Alex's world was blackness. Her body was numb, likely due to the anesthesia and painkillers that had been pumped into her. But her heart was numb, too. The reason for that was more complicated.

She should have been feeling grief for the loss of her brother. She should have been feeling anger at the coven that had tortured and literally sucked the goodness from him. She should have been feeling worry for the males who risked their lives for her and Levi, and guilt knowing that some of them had not made it home unscathed and others wouldn't make it home at all. She should have felt disgusted that she had used her power to kill another and afraid that she could do it again, probably with ease now that her body had undergone her maturity. But she couldn't feel all these emotions at once. So instead she felt nothing.

What her own focus and will had never been able to do before her maturity, when it should have been easier, her subconscious was doing for her now. But as some part of her fought to control her power by repressing her sense completely, another part of her realized she couldn't fight it this way forever. She could give in to her power and let her emotions and those of others engulf her. Or she could lose herself in this void until her body gave out.

This was a battle between her body and her gift. Alex was a fighter. But she had fought hard these last weeks. She had fought hard tonight. And now she was tired. She knew her power was putting up a fight. She didn't know if she had the strength to face it.

"It's not working."

"Give it a minute."

"Alex, please, don't fight it. Feel this."

Don't fight? It was the opposite of the advice Levi had given her before he died. It was even contrary to the advice Markus had given her as she lay injured in his arms. That advice had been right then. It had been what she wanted to hear.

But this advice was what she needed to hear now. And it was right. Because the voice saying it was right. He was always right for her. So she gave in.

Instead of being swallowed by the darkness and numbness she thought she sought, she was flooded with emotion. She couldn't control it. She couldn't separate herself from it. And then she realized she didn't want to. What she felt was encompassing but comforting, purifying.

"Alex?" Someone's flicker of worry mottled her sense. She knew whose it was and wanted to allay his concern. But she couldn't.

"Let go. We'll overwhelm her."

The intensity of her sense diminished. She sucked in a deep breath, found herself again in her own skin, and opened her eyes. Blinking as they adjusted to the bright industrial lighting of the room, Alex tried to make sense of what she was seeing. She looked from face to face watching as their expressions reflected what she already felt inside: relief, concern, and, as pure and nearly as intense as before, their love and compassion.

"Welcome back, Seer. How're you doing?" Sage asked with a grin, though Alex appreciated the concern it hid. "Crap. That answers that question." Sage was apparently still hearing the thoughts in her head, just as she still sensed him the clearest.

"Ditto," Alex said, her voice more of a croak. The others enjoyed the release laughing at the two of them provided.

Alex turned to Markus, wincing at the pain in her neck. He still had his hand outstretched to her, hovering mere inches above her head.

"Will you kiss me already?" she asked.

The fear fell from his face, replaced with joy and relief. He leaned over to gently kiss her, but when his lips touched hers, Alex's sense soared. She used her returning strength to reach up and hold him in place. Her emotions melting seamlessly with his, it was by far the best kiss she ever had.

When Markus finally broke away, his cheeks were pink. He avoided the others' amused expressions. For once, Alex didn't blush a bit. She turned to Sage unabashedly and answered his question.

"So far, so good."

Author Biography

Lauren Grimley lives in central Massachusetts where she grew up, but her heart is on the beaches of Cape Cod where she spends as much of her time as possible. After graduating from Boston University she became a middle school English teacher. She has her seventh graders to thank for starting her on this path; it was they who convinced a skeptical new teacher vampire stories were worth reading. She now spends her time writing them when she should be correcting papers.

Malachite Quills presents a dark adventure on the unforgiving seas:

There are vampires on the Titanic! Mina Harker, one the undead, returns to haunt the gas-lit alleys of Edwardian London. From a brooding house by the Thames she hunts and feeds. Beautiful, voluptuous, merciless, her overwhelming and irresistible sexual allure brings willing victims.

In the east-end the death toll rises and a trail of scarlet is left on the mean streets. As life in the great city goes on, millions are unaware of the unseen yet deadly war that rages on for the soul of the metropolis.

But there are those who know the old ways, those who have the knowledge to end her reign of terror. Hunted, the vampire looks across the Atlantic to the vigorous New World as a place of eternal safety. At Southampton, the Titanic, the mightiest ship in history, waits to sail...

(Adult Themes)

ABCDE

Made in the USA
Lexington, KY
08 September 2013